ruin me

SCARLETT FINN

Also by Scarlett Finn

GO NOVELS
GO WITH IT
GO IT ALONE
GO ALL OUT
GO ALL IN
GO FULL CIRCLE

EXILE
HIDE & SEEK
KISS CHASE

WRECK & RUIN
RUIN ME
RUIN HIM

THE BRANDED SERIES
BRANDED
SCARRED
MARKED

FORBIDDEN PREQUEL DUET
ALL. ONLY.
ONLY YOURS

THE FORBIDDEN NOVELS
FORBIDDEN DESIRE
FORBIDDEN WANT
FORBIDDEN WISH
FORBIDDEN NEED
FORBIDDEN BOND

BOMBSHELLS & BILLIONAIRES (ROXIVERSE)
NOTHING TO HIDE
NOTHING TO LOSE
NOTHING IN BETWEEN: ONE
NOTHING TO DECLARE
NOTHING TO US
NOTHING IN BETWEEN: TWO
NOTHING TO SAY
NOTHING TO GAIN
NOTHING IN BETWEEN: THREE
NOTHING TO YOU
NOTHING TO THIS PREQUEL: ONE WILD NIGHT
NOTHING TO THIS
NOTHING IN BETWEEN: FOUR
NOTHING TO DO
NOTHING TO NO ONE
NOTHING TO FEAR
NOTHING TO DENY
NOTHING TO BEAT
NOTHING TO THE WEDDING
NOTHING TO TELL
NOTHING TO IT
NOTHING TO SEE
NOTHING TO WIN
NOTHING TO OFFER
NOTHING TO PROVE

LOVE AGAINST THE ODDS STANDALONE COLLECTION
SWEET SEAS
HEIR'S AFFAIR
RESCUED
MAESTRO'S MUSE
GETTING TRICKY
THIRTEEN
REMEMBER WHEN...
RELUCTANT SUSPICION
XY FACTOR

KINDRED SERIES
RAVEN
SWALLOW
CUCKOO
SWIFT
FALCON
FINCH

MISTAKE DUET
MISTAKE ME NOT
SLEIGHT MISTAKE

LOST & FOUND
LOST
FOUND

THE EXPLICIT SERIES
EXPLICIT INSTRUCTION
EXPLICIT DETAIL
EXPLICIT MEMORY

TO DIE FOR...
TO DIE FOR TRUTH
TO DIE FOR HONOR
TO DIE FOR VIRTUE
TO DIE FOR DUTY
TO DIE FOR LOVE

RISQUÉ & HARROW INTERTWINED
TAKE A RISK
FIGHTING FATE
RISK IT ALL
FIGHTING BACK
GAME OF RISK

ONE

TULSI TERN'S MIND wandered. Despite its meandering, her thoughts kept returning to one question: why on earth had she agreed to this date?

Kieran Rigby had been asking her out for months. Every time she went into the gym where he worked, he'd find a pretext to start a conversation. In turn, he'd come up with some way to work his impressive physique into the discussion. Each time she was polite in her attempts to excuse herself.

Kieran wasn't the type of man who understood subtlety. Nor was he often rejected. Many of the women at the gym huddled and giggled whenever he was nearby. Other females wanted reasons to get closer to the man they dubbed "The Hunk." Tulsi was the opposite. "The Hunk" didn't do anything for her. No butterflies. No anticipation. In fact, her gut groaned whenever he appeared.

Over time, she'd learned the hard way that her gut knew more about men than her head. If she'd paid more attention to her instincts then she wouldn't have wasted so much of her life with Bradley. Thinking about her ex while sitting at dinner with another man probably went against a zillion first date rules.

Tulsi tried to focus. Kieran was talking. He did that a

lot. He talked about muscle groups and workouts, protein shakes and his latest diet. He told her about where he got his hair cut and what different colognes he wore on different occasions. She'd heard it all but absorbed none of it.

They'd gotten through the entrée and she was trying to figure out a plausible reason to refuse dessert. Her date liked to take care of himself; maybe she could come up with an excuse about calories or fat content.

His cellphone began to buzz next to his glass. It wasn't the first time the device had interrupted his rhythm. Hence how it had ended up on the table. He'd taken the animated handset from his pocket almost the moment they sat down. At regular intervals, it sprang to life, buzzing and skittering across the tablecloth.

Each time she told him to pick it up. He never did. Kieran just ignored it and kept on talking. She had no idea why he didn't divert the calls to voicemail. It suggested that he didn't want whoever was calling to know that he was ignoring their attempts to get in touch with him.

"You can answer it," she said again.

His head moved in a shake on his linked fingers that were arched under his chin. His elbows on the table supported its weight.

"No," he said, his eyes fixed on hers. His smile grew again. "It isn't important."

"Clearly it is," Tulsi said, adjusting her napkin in her lap. "Someone needs you. You should pick it up."

Again, he shook his head. "It's only my brother; it's really nothing. He was taking care of something for me tonight. He's probably just calling to say it's done."

"Or not," she said. "There could be a problem. Maybe he needs your help or something went wrong."

Throughout their conversation that night, he hadn't once mentioned a brother. He hadn't mentioned his family, but she hadn't asked. The date could only be described as dire. No way she'd repeat this fiasco.

"I waited six months for you to say yes to going out with me," he said. "I don't want to waste a second talking to Rowdy. I can do that any time."

"It doesn't make the best impression," she said. "That you're unreachable to people who care about you."

His expression loosened as he considered her words. "I'm reliable."

Tulsi eyed the facedown phone that was still moving across the table. "Prove it," she said. "I'll wait."

He picked up the device and answered it, making no secret of his irritation. "What?" he snapped.

Almost as soon as the word was out of his mouth, his face hardened. He stood up, showing her his forefinger to ask for a minute, and strode toward the exit.

Tulsi folded her arms and sank back in her chair. This was the story of her life. Going around in circles, hitting the same hopeless disappointments one after another. Nothing in her life clicked. Nothing had for a long time. She tried to be like other people. She tried her best.

Starting her own business was meant to be a triumph. As much as she enjoyed her boutique jewelry store, it didn't thrill her. Nothing thrilled her. In moments like the current one, the speed of the seconds of her life slipping away seemed to accelerate. Numbness crept through her. Tables around were occupied by couples and groups, laughing and talking, going about their lives. It all seemed so nothing. So pointless. So benign.

Tulsi didn't want what she had, but had no idea what she did want. Experience. Excitement. Anything but this. Anything but normality. Niceties. Pleasantries. Mediocrity. She paid her bills and her taxes. She smiled at customers and always did her chores. One day became the next until a week had passed. A month. A year. And, still, her life was middling.

One thing was clear as day, Kieran didn't give her a thrill. No man did. At least, none that she'd already met. She didn't think it was too much to ask to feel some iota of excitement. Arousal. Chemistry.

All she wanted was the magnetism that she'd been promised all her life. That women the world over were promised and never received. She wanted the zing. The bubbles. The butterflies. Tulsi didn't want to be polite. She wanted to be insane with lust. To act on impulse. To be with a man who would drive her so crazy that she wouldn't be able to contain herself around him. A man who would not only want her to take risks but encourage it. A man who'd always be there to protect her. To catch her. A man she could need and who'd need her in return.

Those thoughts were probably worse than the ones she'd had about Bradley. This was a date and she wasn't thinking of the man who'd brought her out or any she'd ever been with. Tulsi was conjuring a fantasy. One that had joined her many times through the years when she was alone picturing what life could be.

He didn't exist. Not really. She had to get over him.

For sure, Kieran wasn't going to live up to the fantasy.

Despite her overwhelming urge to flee, she stayed put. Her mother had always taught her the importance of manners. Kieran knew where to find her anyway. He'd showed up at her store more than once. No doubt he got her information from her membership paperwork at the gym. Raiding her file for his own personal gain was probably illegal. But did it matter?

He was pursuing her. Just as women were raised to believe Prince Charming was on the horizon, men were raised to believe they were supposed to pursue. To chase. To hunt down the object of their desire. Sure, it was creepy and made her uncomfortable. But he was fulfilling his societal role. It wasn't always easy to know where the lines were drawn. What was healthy romantic interest? What was criminal stalking?

Sometimes the only distinction was the female at the center of their interest. And if, like Kieran had shown, he couldn't read her disinterest, he probably believed this was all part of the "hard-to-get" chase.

The server was heading her way. Tulsi contemplated ordering more alcohol. At that, Kieran reappeared at her side, tugging his wallet from his pocket. He didn't sit down, just tossed a few bills on the table.

"You were right, something did happen," he said.

"Oh," Tulsi replied, not sorry that their evening was going to be cut short.

Except Kieran had other ideas.

He snatched her hand the moment she stood up. "I'll take you home. I just have to make a stop first."

"A stop?"

"Yes," he said, taking her purse from the table.

"I don't need an escort," she said. "I can make my own way home."

"I was raised better than that," he said, putting an arm around her to sweep her out of the restaurant and onto the street. He flashed a quick smile her way. "Besides, how can I kiss you goodnight if I don't make it to your doorstep?"

The question awakened her gut, but not in a positive way. To her, it was obvious they had no chemistry. She didn't understand how Kieran could see it any other way. He hailed a cab while she renewed her objections. They fell on deaf ears.

Less than a minute after leaving the table, she was in the back of a cab with Kieran's hand on her knee. Kieran chatted to the driver, which gave her some reprieve. At least until she noticed the bustling cosmopolitan center was thinning and becoming much more ghetto. Wherever they were going it was in a shady area of the city that she'd never visited. Even the cab driver's tone became wary when Kieran started to give directions.

Realizing that her knowledge of Kieran was limited to where he worked and what he looked like, Tulsi wondered what she'd let herself in for.

The cab stopped. Kieran paid the driver and bundled her out onto the sidewalk again. Above them were broken streetlights incapable of fulfilling their original function. A distant siren offered some comfort, proving that they hadn't walked off the end of the world. Yet, there was no one on the streets. The darkness was enhanced by grime and graffiti that made her question what this stop involved.

Kieran took her hand and led her to a building, shoving through a door that was loose on its top hinges. Ahead, two figures loomed in an unlit corridor. The curse of naïveté landed on her shoulders. She'd tried to refuse to join him. If she'd had any idea they were coming to this sort of place, she'd have been much more forceful in her objections.

Everything had happened so quickly that she hadn't had the chance to think it through.

"Who is she?" one of the featureless figures asked.

The pair were disguised by shadows. Other than their shapes being tall and broad, she couldn't decipher anything else about them.

"My date," Kieran said, slinging an arm around her shoulders.

"You brought a date?" Tulsi shook her head. Before she could say anything, the figure spoke again. "She looks terrified. Why would you bring a woman out here?"

"We were on a date," Kieran said, like that was explanation enough.

"You knew we were doing this. You picked tonight. Said it was urgent."

"I thought you could do it without me."

Tulsi shrugged his arm off her shoulders, which forced her closer to the two strangers who she noticed then were actually standing at the foot of some stairs. "What exactly is going on?"

"I like this one, she's spunky."

"You keep your hands off, Rowdy. This one is all mine."

"All yours?" she objected, twisting to look up at Kieran. "So far, this night has been miserable. I don't see it getting any better. Where are we?"

For a moment, it seemed that Kieran didn't know which way to turn. His behavior confirmed her suspicions: the idiot was ignorant to her disinterest. It was a mystery how he could be. The restaurant had been boring. Wherever they were now bordered on dangerous. It was one extreme to the other. Confidence had a lot to answer for.

The danger was made more palpable by the presence of the third man. The one who hadn't said a word. Being closer, with her eyes more adjusted to the dull illumination, Tulsi could see more of him. His hair was dark, his eyes too. They cut a more severe scowl than any she'd ever seen. Stubble on his jaw surrounded straight lips that displayed little expression.

Somehow, he seemed angry. But there was no tension in him. He was at ease. His demeanor should've quelled her apprehension. He didn't look like he was about to throw a punch or rush into war. There was no sweat on his brow. His arms were loose at his sides. He wore a leather jacket over a dark tee-shirt and jeans that had seen better days.

Something about him drew her focus. Allure terrified and intrigued her in equal measure. The sensation was the same she'd experienced when driving past a pile-up on the highway. Her stomach churned with fear, regret, heartache… Yet, there was also fascination. Curiosity forced her to keep looking even when she knew she should turn away.

Even though she was looking right at him, it took her at least half a minute to realize that he was looking back at her. As terrifying as his aura might be, there was also something comforting about it. About the confidence and capability his ease suggested.

The danger of this neighborhood would surely set anyone on edge. Not him. She got the feeling that even if ten armed men rushed through the door, he wouldn't do more than blink.

Their eyes locked. Tulsi had never been one to stare. It wasn't that she was easily intimidated. Her mother had just taught her it was rude. Usually she felt a compulsion to fill silence. Not this time.

She didn't know what he was doing to her, but it felt like something profound. He had no sense of expectation and yet, there was anticipation crackling in the air. That may have had something to do with wherever they were going. Whatever the men were planning to do was intense. Already she knew this quick stop was more than just a casual errand.

This area was nothing like anywhere she'd lived. Tulsi hadn't been raised with wealth or poverty. She'd been somewhere in the middle. A non-descript kid in a nondescript neighborhood with a nondescript family. Growing up, nothing about her was interesting or exciting. Nothing interesting or exciting ever happened to her.

She'd never known her father. But that hadn't mattered. She had never needed him. Her mother worked to provide everything. Sure, they didn't have fancy cars or the latest gadgets, but she was never made fun of for not owning decent sneakers or having holes in her clothes.

Her mother looked after her. When she came of age and her mother got sick, Tulsi had cared for her in return. Her mom didn't often come into her thoughts. Though that night was turning out to be an exception to the norm. She tried her best not to think about the woman who she'd lost more than half a decade ago.

Whoever the stranger was, he didn't make a sound. Didn't speak a word. He just stood there looking at her as she looked at him. Rowdy and Kieran had exchanged words, but she hadn't heard a single one. The chill that had touched her fingertips as she'd walked through the broken door, dreading what lay ahead, began to ebb.

If this man was on her side, she'd be safe. Without ever hearing him speak or seeing him move, she understood he was her best chance at getting through this.

"I'm sorry, miss," Rowdy said. The sound of his voice unlatched her gaze from the stranger's. "We're already late and the guy we're going to see doesn't like to be disrespected. Cabs come by once an hour in this neighborhood. We don't have time to track one down. This should only take a minute."

The stranger went first. He ascended the stairs, his long legs taking them two at a time like the one between didn't exist. Still, he didn't make a noise.

Tulsi was mesmerized again. He disappeared around the corner at the top of the first flight. Rowdy went after him. It wasn't until Kieran put his hand on her lower back to urge her forward that she started to move.

"That's Wreck," Kieran said, tilting to murmur in her ear as they followed farther behind the other two. "He doesn't say much. Never has. And he doesn't like to be touched. I don't know why, just a weird thing about him. Not sure there's anything normal about him though... He's just here for backup. To provide some muscle."

That didn't inspire confidence. If she wasn't already aware that something shady was going on, he'd just confirmed it. Only people who were going to do something dangerous needed muscle.

On the second floor, they congregated in a group. "What's the apartment number?" Rowdy asked.

"You called me and demanded I come down here because you needed the apartment number?" Kieran asked, trying again to put his arm around her shoulders.

Stepping away from the attempt brought her arm up against Wreck's. When Tulsi looked up, he was fixated on Kieran and didn't seem to notice that she was touching him. Maybe it was just skin to skin contact he didn't like. Or, it could be that she was so inconsequential he didn't even register her feeble self against his capable form.

Being so close to him, she caught the scent of something. His soap maybe? His deodorant? It wasn't potent enough to be cologne. Whatever the smell was, it sent a bolt to her belly like a punch that made her breath burst from her lungs.

Rowdy and Kieran looked at her. Tulsi didn't dare look up to see if Wreck was looking too. Fighting to find composure wasn't easy when clarity identified what she had just felt. The spark. The thrill. That's what she experienced standing next to this man who was a head and shoulders taller than her. He hadn't said a word. They'd barely shared air for more than a couple of minutes. Yet, she wanted to pick up his arm to wrap it around her body and nuzzle herself close to his chest.

Her imagination was getting carried away with itself; she couldn't control it.

"Tuls, you okay?" Kieran asked.

For the first time that night, she felt something positive toward her date. The question was genuine. Even so, she couldn't admit what had caused her to gasp in such a way.

"No shock that dating you made her sick," Rowdy said. "How long you guys been going out? Maybe she's just come to her senses."

Kieran shoved his brother. "Tonight is our first date."

Rowdy snorted a quiet laugh. "This is a helluva first impression. How do you follow a date like this?"

As was to be expected, Kieran wasn't discouraged. "I've got big plans for this girl. Big ideas."

"Ideas are all they'll ever be," Tulsi said causing Rowdy to jeer and shove his brother.

She hadn't really known that she was going to speak her thoughts out loud. Her mind was still reeling from the revelation that her gut had found what it had been looking for all her life.

"Let's get this done," Wreck said. The rumble of his voice was almost a growl. Impatient and unimpressed, he was certainly more fed up than scared. "The woman stays here."

"Tulsi," she said, garnering the courage to peek up at him. "My name is Tulsi Tern… And I can make my own way home."

Except she didn't want to. Her instincts screamed at her to stay close to the man at her side. The attraction was primal. Pure feral hormones drove her fascination. It was also ludicrous. Nothing could come from it. He'd be in her life for a matter of minutes. They'd part and never see each other again. It wasn't like she could hand him her number. If he didn't like to talk, he would never call anyway. Depending on the guy code rules, Kieran could claim to have seen her first and ask Wreck to keep his hands off.

So even though her immature hormones wanted to throw caution to the wind, reality, as always, brought her crashing disappointment.

"You're not getting any tonight, brother," Rowdy said.

"There's still time," Kieran said, though it did seem his mood had flattened.

"Apartment number," Rowdy said again.

"I can't believe you wrecked my night for this bullshit," Kieran responded. "The night was perfect until you called… asshole."

"Whose debt is this?" Rowdy asked.

Kieran sighed. "Mine."

"And who is paying this debt for you?"

"You," Kieran said, moving closer to dip down and whisper at her. "He never just does anyone a favor."

"Get over it," Rowdy said. "Like Wreck said, let's just get this done."

Kieran mumbled a response. "Last door on the right."

Wreck marched down the corridor. Rowdy went next. Instead of leaving her at the top of the stairs, as Wreck had suggested, Kieran put an arm around her to take her with him when he trailed along after his brother.

TWO

"WE WOULDN'T HAVE to do this if we could trust you with the money on your own," Rowdy said when Wreck stopped at the apartment door.

"Leave her," Wreck said.

Once again Tulsi found his glare glued to Kieran.

"When she's your girl, then you can make decisions for her. 'Til then, that's my job," Kieran said. The declaration was so shocking that she had to replay it in her mind. "I'm not leaving her standing out here alone when anyone could walk by and hurt her."

Rowdy knocked on the numberless door. The three men gathered around her in a gesture of protection, which only served to reignite her unease.

After a second round of knocking, the door was pulled open so suddenly that she once again bumped against Wreck, who didn't push her away or object. Tulsi guessed that her second assumption was correct; that she was just so unimportant, he didn't even notice her.

"What?" The broad black man who'd answered the door glared at them. He must have decided that she deserved his focus because he took a long time perusing her figure. Though it was Kieran he eventually settled on. "You've got balls showing up here. You brought muscle too. That mean you're not ready to pay up?"

"I've got his money, Delray," Kieran said, though she knew that wasn't entirely true if Rowdy was the one paying the debt. "Let us in."

"Empty your pockets," the guy said. At first, no one moved. "You don't turn 'em out, you don't get in."

Delray bent to pick up an empty shoe box from by the door and shook it at them. Kieran was the first one to exhale and do as he was told. Tossing his wallet, phone, and keys into the box, he gestured for Rowdy to do the same. Wreck turned out his jeans and his jacket pockets, showing nothing in either.

The guy must have been satisfied. He backed off and gestured inside leaving her no choice but to walk into the apartment with her party. The scent of cannabis hung in the air. It didn't take long to see why. They were ushered into a living room. Three couches were angled around a central television that stood on a wooden crate. Four men and two women lay around on the couches and on the floor. From the paraphernalia she noticed scattered round the room, cannabis wasn't the only drug on offer.

"You got my money, weasel?" the guy in the center of the furthest couch asked.

Tulsi was still nestled in the triangle of men around her. She hadn't known two of them for more than five minutes. With so many other strangers in the room, the ones around her were the least of her worries. Any intimidation she may have felt in the past was nothing compared to what she experienced in that moment.

She'd never bestowed trust on anyone so quickly. All she knew were the names of the three men surrounding her, but it was more than she knew about the others dotted around.

Rowdy handed a bundle of cash to Kieran, who tossed it across to the man who'd spoken.

The guy who'd answered the door loitered close, giving her the creeps.

The one on the couch flicked through the bills.

"You're a dead man," he said, something of a smirk on his face.

"No. No," Kieran said.

"You're not going to get away with fucking around," the guy said.

"Teal, man, I—"

"What happened to Merchant's shipment?" The guy on the couch slid to the edge of his seat and tossed the money over his shoulder like it was nothing. "You come here with a crappy ten grand when you know you walked out the door with Merchant's hundred Gs."

"A hu… hundred?" Kieran stuttered. "No, man! No, that wasn't me."

"That's not what Merchant says."

A bone-chilling scream interrupted their discussion. A doorway at the side of the room burst open and a naked woman was thrown into the living room. When Tulsi was grabbed from behind, impulse made her panic. She inhaled to scream, but glanced over her shoulder to see Wreck's hands were the ones on her upper arms. The sight of his fierce vehemence, his unerring focus, filled her with relief. Her panic dwindled to nothing and her breathing evened out. She couldn't explain it, but being in his grip gave her security.

The woman on the floor tried to scramble onto her knees. Her body was bruised and bloody. She cowered, focusing on the blackness of the shadowy room she'd been thrown from. Nothing inside was visible. There was no light inside. After half a beat, a broad figure emerged from the abyss wearing only a pair of jeans.

The pasty white guy had definition, but it was the gun held loose in his hand that woke Tulsi's panic again. She was still focused on the weapon when Wreck moved around from behind her to put himself between her and the danger. He blocked her body from whatever was about to happen with his own.

The guy with the gun kicked the crying woman, sending her onto her back on the floor. When she wailed again, he aimed his weapon at her head.

"Whoa now, wait a minute," Rowdy said, stepping

forward. "What's the—"

"Fuck you!" the guy shouted, raising the gun higher to put Rowdy in its sight.

Rowdy lifted his hands in surrender. "What's the problem? You can't shoot her. She's already a fucking mess, man. You did your job. You fucked her up. Well done."

The bully kicked the woman again and widened his own stance like maybe he was preparing to shoot.

Instinct made Tulsi's hand move. Her eyes were wide, focusing past Wreck's arm to the man threatening Rowdy. She wasn't really aware of where her hand was going until her fingers laced between Wreck's. He didn't flinch. Not his head, not his shoulders, no part of him she could see. Yet, his fingers curled to lock around hers. Maybe it was just instinct for him too. Maybe he wanted to offer her comfort.

"Rowdy," Kieran whispered. "Let it go."

The bully's gaze moved a fraction, just enough to land on her. The barrel of the gun descended a couple of inches when he leaned to the side. "You're a pretty thing. Come around here, Pretty Thing," he said to her.

"Leave her out of this," Kieran asserted.

The last thing Tulsi wanted him to do was play the hero. Especially when there was such obvious apprehension in his voice. He couldn't take on a shooter alone.

"Who does she belong to?" the bully asked. "One of you or all of you? We'll pay for the pleasure. Come on out, Pretty Thing." He smirked at her. "Come on, girl. I've got something to show you."

The woman on the floor wept, though she had to be feeling relief that the bully was losing interest in her. Seeing few options, Tulsi began to move, but she didn't get far. Wreck's grip on her hand became crushing. He twisted his arm to his back, forcing her to return to her previous place, shielded by him. She tried to let go, but he wouldn't release her.

"Don't fucking speak to her," Wreck said, his voice vibrating with a sinister edge.

"Yeah," Kieran asserted. "Leave Tulsi out of this."

"Tulsi?" the bully said. "Tulsi. Tulsi. I like it. You

don't have to hide from me, pretty, little Tulsi. I know how to play nice."

This man had to be more important than the one on the couch or maybe he was just scarier. Whatever the reason, no one else stood up to him. The woman on the floor kept sobbing. If the state of her was any accurate measure, this man didn't play nice. He played rough. The sadist played to win.

In this stalemate, she didn't know what to do. She didn't want to go to the bully, but they couldn't stay there all night. Tulsi tried to move again. Wreck still wouldn't let her go.

"Let me go," she murmured.

"Yeah, let her go," the bully said, adjusting his aim to land it on Wreck. "I'm not selfish, I know how to share. Let her go and I'll stretch out her ass for you… She looks like the type who needs it. Come show us that neat body of yours, Pretty Tulsi."

"What?" she asked, forgetting the pain in her hand where Wreck was holding her tight.

"Sure, we've got nine men in here, four women. Women work for the men around here."

"She's not a working girl," Rowdy said.

The bully tightened his grip on the gun. "She is whatever I damn well say she is. If I say she fucks every man in this room then she fucks every man in this room."

As a chill went through her, another wail came from the naked woman sprawled on the floor. Tulsi couldn't help herself. If this man got his way, that could be her future. The hapless woman may have started out just like her; dragged along against her will, oblivious to the danger and forced into her current position.

"I'm fair," the bully said. "I'll let her start with her boyfriend. I bet he knows how to fuck her good."

"No way," Kieran said.

"Either one of you three fuck her or I'll do it for you," the bully snarled.

Cowardice made her move closer to Wreck's back. She didn't want to see any more. Didn't want to hear it. Tulsi closed her eyes and rested her head against the cool, soft leather, wishing her imagination would save her from this moment.

"No one touches her," Wreck said without letting go of her hand.

"Are you getting in my way, boy?"

"Wreck," she said from behind him, tightening her hold on his knuckles.

Giving her to the bully may be the only way they'd get out of the apartment alive. Tulsi couldn't imagine such horror.

"Anyone who stands in Baines' way has a death wish," the guy from the couch said.

The bully, who she guessed was Baines, laughed. "I'll wipe the floor with you all—stop with the fucking noise! Jesus!"

Tulsi was still cowering when the blast of a gunshot made her jump. She tensed and grabbed for Wreck's other arm. Her shield didn't drop. She didn't see or hear anyone fall to the floor. It took her a minute to realize that the sobbing had stopped.

Controlling her breathing took effort. She had to concentrate to prevent herself from hyperventilating. She wanted to look and yet, she didn't want to know.

It was possible he'd shot the floor or the ceiling and missed his target completely. Except that didn't explain why the woman who hadn't shut up for a moment was suddenly mute.

"Round 'em up," the guy from the couch shouted.

"Wait, Teal," Kieran said.

From left to right, the men were on their feet and closing in around their group.

"Merchant's had a bounty out for you since the shipment went missing," Teal said. "I'll have to find out what he wants me to do with you. But no matter what, I'll be collecting."

"You can't take us all," Rowdy said.

"Baines can put a bullet in you, in your buddy and his girl, or all of you can go quietly."

That didn't give them much choice. Teal wanted the

bounty and wouldn't let Rowdy or Wreck or her go, probably fearing they'd bring reinforcements or try to rescue Kieran from whatever fate awaited him.

Everything slowed down as she tried to come to terms with what had happened. Her night had changed so suddenly; everything felt surreal. She was still trying to figure out how she'd ended up in this nightmare when her purse was snatched from her hand. There wasn't even time to argue or seek it out because they began to move. Surrounded by Teal's men, Tulsi had no choice except to go too.

As she moved from behind Wreck, she noticed the woman on the floor, prone with a circle of blood on her forehead. Her eyes were wide and unblinking though her still damp tears trickled toward the floor, pulled by gravity.

She immediately turned away, grabbing for Wreck's arm to bury her face against it. Their fingers were still locked together. He wasn't letting go and neither was she. They were taken from the living room, down a narrow hallway and bundled into a dark space. The door was closed behind them with shuddering finality. The sound of more than one key turning on the other side signaled their fate. They were prisoners.

THREE

SOMEONE FLICKED A SWITCH and the overhead light came on, which was at least something. Except the light didn't reveal anything good. The windows had been bricked up. The only thing in the room was a bed with a bare mattress and a couple of pillows on it. The handcuffs attached to the frame betrayed what this room was used for on a regular basis and it was nothing consensual.

The floorboards were exposed. There were no drawers or pictures or knickknacks. This was the closest thing anyone would find to a cell in a residential neighborhood.

"What the fuck?" Rowdy said, turning on Kieran. "A hundred thousand dollars? What the fuck is this shipment he's talking about?"

"I don't know! I don't know," Kieran said, driving his fingers through his hair. "I swear to you, I didn't know! I help with the shipment sometimes. With transporting, logistics. Merchant gives me a deal. I move what I can through the gym and—"

"A hundred thousand dollars? How can you miss a hundred thousand dollars?"

"It's not like that. I didn't miss anything. I didn't touch the last shipment… I don't know what happened! This is fucked up!"

"Fucked up?" Rowdy asked. "I'll say!" He spun to face Wreck. "What the fuck are we gonna do?"

Wreck didn't answer Rowdy. He walked away from the brothers by the door, leading her across the room. Putting her back to the side of the bed, he let go of her hand but stayed in front of her. He took off his jacket and swooped it around her shoulders. The warmth and comfort of it was short-lived.

When he tried to sit her down, Tulsi objected. "No," she said, shaking her head. Resisting the attempt meant moving closer to him. While her skin quivered at the proximity, he didn't show any sign that he even noticed. "I don't want to sit there." Tulsi blinked up at him. "Look at those handcuffs; you know what they're for."

"That's not your future," Kieran said. She heard him, but kept her focus locked on Wreck's. For the first time, she noticed curiosity behind his stern intensity. "Tulsi, babe, I am sorry about this."

Kieran came over to them and seemed to be trying to muscle Wreck aside. For a few seconds, she stayed put and wondered what would happen if Kieran got more physical.

Before that could happen, Wreck side-stepped and grabbed a pillow from the bed. He tossed it into the corner and thrust a finger toward it. "Sit there."

The command was issued like there was no doubt it would be followed, then he marched back to Rowdy at the door.

"Tulsi," Kieran said and tried to reach for her face.

She dipped back. "Don't touch me." Shaking her head, she held up both hands. "I really don't want you to touch me."

"I know that you're mad——"

"She's not the only one," Rowdy said. "Look at us." He opened his arms to the room. "Two fucking minutes, you said. Pay him the ten grand and split. You were worried about getting kneecapped and now we're gonna fucking die. Us, the guys, we'll get a quick bullet. She..." Rowdy thrust a finger toward her. "She will probably spend the next six months begging for death. She'll be fucked by every lowlife scumbag who has enough dough to pay for their sick pleasures." His attention shifted to her. "I'm sorry, Tulsi. I'm not trying to be a dick—"

"I'm not an idiot," she said. "Well, maybe I am…" Tipping her chin up, she scanned the bleak space. "How the hell else did I end up here? I should've split while you were on the phone at the restaurant. I thought about it." She inhaled and slipped her hand under her bangs to cup her forehead. "I should be careful what I wish for… Excitement and thrills…" Tulsi wasn't sure who she was talking to, the words just tumbled out. "So much for my big imagination."

Slinking away from Kieran, she went to the corner where Wreck had thrown the pillow and dropped to sit cross-legged on it, leaning against the cold concrete wall.

"We have to figure this out," Rowdy said. "Yeah, you're an asshole; fixating on that gets us nowhere." Marching over to his brother, he was determined. "Tell me what happened."

Kieran glanced her way.

Her attention was on the floorboards. Tulsi wasn't thinking; she was numb. Whatever he wanted to say, he was obviously worried about saying it in front of her. She couldn't decipher the specifics of his expression because he was only just encroaching in her peripheral vision. But it was too late for him to play coy.

Wreck began to move. She looked up just in time to see him grab a handful of Kieran's shirt to thrust him back against the wall. "Talk," he snarled.

"Okay. Okay," Kieran said in surrender. "I swear I didn't touch the shipment. I was supposed to. I waited at the pick-up point. I knew it was a big one. I didn't know how big. Styx was supposed to pick me up, he never showed. I figured something had changed. Maybe there was a delay or someone had fucked up. I didn't think that much about it. Things change all the time and I'm not exactly Merchant's first call, you know? I'm pretty low down on the food chain."

"Styx, what do you know about him?" Rowdy asked.

Kieran seemed to hesitate again. Wreck bent his arm to pull him forward and then slammed him back to the wall, locking his elbow to hold him in place.

"There's been stories about him… He's closer to Merchant than I am, but not close. No one's close. Baines maybe. I don't know why he's here… It's weird. Baines shouldn't be here…"

"Because Merchant is missing a hundred grand," Rowdy said. "Maybe that's why he's sent his lieutenant in."

Kieran should've figured that out on his own. Even Tulsi could draw that conclusion. Anyone who was missing a hundred thousand dollars would be doing all they could to figure out what had happened to it.

"What was it? Steroids? Coke? Meth?"

Kieran tensed and closed his eyes tight as he shook his head. "No, I don't know… maybe… I swear to God, I'm not one of those guys. I do what I do for extra cash… for street cred. Where do you think I got my car? I've got a lifestyle… that's all… I don't do it 'cause I want to be like these guys or even want to be close to them. Most of them are scum… You know what it's like…"

"Because I'm scum?" Rowdy asked. "That's what you mean. Because I've been inside."

"I don't think that," he said. "It was easy money."

"Always taking the easy route," Rowdy said. "That's always been your problem."

"And you love lecturing me about it," Kieran said. "What are we going to do?"

"We?" Rowdy asked. "I don't know… We're stuck here until Merchant decides what he wants."

"We can't just sit here!"

Rowdy laughed. "What do you want us to do? Break through brick walls? Smash our way through the door? Even if we could, then what? Everyone in this neighborhood knows Teal, knows what goes on around here, they're not gonna snitch. They're sure not gonna save us. Baines is out there. They have six guys, we have three."

"We can take six."

"Yeah?" Rowdy said. "So why didn't you?" Although he gave his brother time to answer, none came. "You know Wreck is good for it and I've always had your back… 'Cept you know Baines is armed… and he's a fucking psychopath. As soon as we walk out that door, one of us gets a bullet. Maybe two of us before we even get close to those guys… And if you're lucky enough that Merchant wants you alive to question you, Wreck and me will be the ones taken down… or Tulsi will take the heat for all of us. We're not taking that risk."

"So much for anything for family."

"You should've told us about this," Rowdy said. "We walked in here blind and with a fucking woman for God sakes! Do you know how much it pisses off Wreck to be blindsided? You fucking should."

"I know," Kieran said, switching his focus to the man who still had a hold of his shirt. "Sorry, man. I know you just came for effect."

"He's in it now. We all are. Whether we want to be or not. We just watched Baines kill that girl, whoever the hell she was. They're not going to just forget that we witnessed a murder. So now we're here on the hook for the hundred grand of gear you say you never saw. Even if by some miracle that pans out, how the hell do we make them believe that we're going to keep quiet about that girl losing her life?"

"Baines murders people all the time," Kieran said. "He probably doesn't give a shit. I'm sure they have cops on the take."

"You think it's reassuring to tell us the man is a serial murderer? Do you think it makes Tulsi feel better?" Rowdy asked, backing up enough to gesture at her behind Wreck. "You think it makes her feel better to know the sick fuck is a serial rapist too? Merchant has whorehouses in a dozen cities in North America. You know it and I know it." He marched around the bed to flick the handcuffs that were attached to the frame. "These aren't here because they go with the décor. The women Merchant uses don't work for him by choice. He buys them in shipments from dealers in other countries. He doesn't traffic them, but he sure as hell exploits them. That girl out there probably came to this country with a dream and look what the fuck she got."

"Tulsi's not like that," Kieran said. "She's different.

She's special."

"Yeah, and as soon as Merchant finds out you're dating her, he's gonna use her against you… We saw out there just how great you are at standing up for other people."

In his defense, Kieran had made a couple of attempts to stand up for her. But he hadn't been the one she'd hidden behind. Rowdy had been the one to step up for the woman who ended up dead. If what Kieran said about the shipment was true, the chances were Rowdy was right. Merchant would want to question him, which meant if he needed to be persuaded or Merchant wanted to make a point, Rowdy, Wreck, and she would be disposable.

"He took my purse," she said, her gaze returning to the floor. "These people know everything about me."

Her bank cards, her ID, all of it was in that purse. If she was lucky, they would throw it in the trash without going through it. Somehow, she doubted her luck was in. The more information Teal's goons and Baines gave Merchant, the happier he'd be. Despite never having met the man, Tulsi already had strong opinions about Merchant's character.

Merchant, whoever he was, was a drug dealer and a pimp. He commanded people who feared him, or at least those who relished being rewarded. If he could afford a hundred thousand dollars in drugs, his business was going well.

On top of that, there was the bounty Teal referenced. If she made it through this experience, she had a feeling that one day she would come face to face with this Merchant. Already Tulsi was dreading the moment she would have to look him in the eye.

"All we can do is wait," Rowdy said.

Wreck's head snapped in his direction, away from her. Tulsi had no idea what secrets were being revealed in his expression.

"Wait?" Kieran asked.

"What else can we do?" Rowdy asked Wreck.

There was something different about the way Rowdy spoke to Wreck, something she couldn't put her finger on. Yes, Rowdy was familiar with Kieran. He spoke to him like a brother. When he spoke to Wreck there was respect and deference, but not fear. Though somehow, she sensed there was a connection, maybe an intimacy between them.

She had no idea about Wreck's relationship with Kieran. He'd said so little. Maybe the three were related by blood. They didn't have the same look about them though.

With another shove, Wreck pushed away from the wall, letting Kieran go. He turned his back to walk toward the door. When he got there, he laid his hand against it and just stopped.

"We should get some rest," Rowdy said. "You get over here."

He was looking at his brother who was kowtowed enough to do as he was told. Kieran traipsed around to the opposite side of the bed. Rowdy got on and lay in the middle, folding his arms and fixating on the ceiling.

"I'm too wound up to rest," Kieran said.

"Sit your fucking ass down," Rowdy replied, nodding at the side of the bed. "If we get a chance to rush these guys, the more rested we are, the better. Besides, we could be here for a week before they open that door. Unless you have some other secrets to share, I'd say it would be best for all of us to just shut the fuck up and reflect on what a clusterfuck this is."

Wreck didn't want to talk. Tulsi couldn't say that she did either. Rowdy was right; there was nothing more to say. They couldn't plan an escape; they didn't know enough. They didn't have numbers or weapons.

From what she'd gathered, Rowdy and Wreck had been there to back Kieran up while he paid his debt. She wasn't sure what the debt was, whether it was for drugs he used or drugs he sold. But there was a hell of a difference between ten and a hundred thousand.

Kieran lay on his side, putting his back to his brother. Tulsi was glad that he was as far away from her as the bed would allow. She didn't want to look at him. All she wanted to do was sit and stare.

FOUR

KIERAN WAS SNORING. The man had faults enough; snoring was an insignificant one. At least the rhythm gave her something to focus on. Something soothing.

Rowdy was asleep too.

Tulsi didn't have her watch on and didn't have her purse. She had no idea how long they had been in the room or since anyone had spoken. Hours no doubt.

Wreck was sitting on the bottom corner of the bed. His boots were on the floor, his elbow rested on the bar at the foot of the bed. He was wearing a tee-shirt so she could see a heavy watch on his wrist. But if she was going to ask him to speak, she wanted to know more than just the time.

More than once since she'd gotten over the deepest of her reverie, she thought about opening her mouth and asking him something. Except, she couldn't work out what to say. Each time she talked herself out of speaking to him before returning to her reflection.

He wasn't asleep and neither was she. As far as Tulsi could tell, they were staring at roughly the same spot on the bare floor.

"Would you like your jacket back?" she asked, finally breaking the silence. "Are you cold?" The only response she got was a grunt. At least that was an acknowledgement he'd heard her. "It's crazy, isn't it? How quickly life can change." She'd had her arms wrapped around her knees for some time, hugging them close to her chest. Releasing one, she turned up the collar of the jacket. Burying her nose against it, she inhaled his scent. "They're going to kill us, aren't they?" His gaze shifted. Tulsi felt his eyes on her. Hers were still focused on the floor, so she didn't see his attention move. Yet, there was no doubting it; the sensation of his gaze locking onto her was undeniable. "I suppose I should be grateful. Life hasn't been so bad."

Just a massive disappointment. Tulsi was thinking about the highs and lows of her life when his voice rose to a mumble.

"You should sleep."

"Why?" she asked. "So I can spend my last hours on earth unconscious? I have a horrible habit of dreaming." She'd never considered it a curse before, but in this situation, she couldn't conceive what positives her subconscious would be able to conjure. "If I close my eyes now, all I'll see is that woman on the floor. Feel the way my heart was racing when Baines demanded I show him my body."

"You'll live," he said in a tone that wasn't reassuring or pessimistic. He stated it as fact.

"How can you be so sure?"

"Women are a commodity."

Because this guy Merchant knew how to exploit them. "I think I'd rather die," she said.

"You're strong. You'll endure it."

"Why would I want to?" she asked. "Strength is relative. A person needs something to fight for. To live for. If they want to survive a trial. I've been coasting for so long; I barely know what month it is until I look at a calendar. One day is the same as the next."

"Life is a shitshow."

Another fact. That one made her smile. "It sure is. You know what's crazy? For months, I've been rejecting Kieran's advances. I didn't want to go out with him. I just ran out of ways to say no. This is what I get for being polite. I thought one dinner and he'll realize there's no chemistry between us. I thought the decision was smart… My gym membership has another six months to run and I like the facilities." She smiled and pulled the collar of his jacket up to her nose again. "I sound like an idiot." He didn't respond. "I am an idiot. Look at where the hell I am, think that's proof enough."

"I'm here too," he said and their eyes met.

The darkness in his gaze was shaded by the line of his lowered brow. "You frown a lot."

He took his attention away. "You should get some sleep."

"I'll sleep when you sleep."

"Someone should stay awake."

"Why?" she asked. "If they're going to storm in here and put bullets in us, there's nothing we can do to stop them now… And if they come in to drag me out by my hair, I'll make enough noise to wake you… Not that you should put yourself in danger to help me."

It was amazing how quickly silence could fall. Kieran's snoring had lessened, but she was so fascinated by the man at the end of the bed that she almost forgot the other two were there.

Tulsi looked at the scuffed heavy black boots on his feet. She guessed they were functional, keeping his feet warm and allowing him to move fast when he had to. The denim of his worn jeans looked soft and bore the wrinkles of where it had creased when he walked or sat.

His narrow hips were circled by a distressed leather belt. It wasn't one of those designer numbers that people paid a fortune for to get the homeless look. It looked more like an old friend that he used because it had never let him down. The dark gray of his tee-shirt appeared new. Not new exactly, but newer than the jeans.

"Are you related?" she asked. "To Kieran and Rowdy?" He shook his head. "How do you know them?"

"You should sleep," he said, curt in his response in a not-so-subtle signal that he didn't want to talk.

Tulsi heard the signal, but chose to ignore it. "I

wouldn't be able to sleep even if I wanted to. I'm not a good sleeper when I'm anxious… You sleep." Standing up then bending down to flip over the pillow, she fluffed it. "It's not much, but…" Tulsi gestured to the floor and side-stepped out of the way. "Lie down and get some sleep. I'll wake you if I hear anything… There's no use in both of us staying awake. If anyone's going to be kicking ass and getting us out of this mess, it's more likely to be you than me."

"I'm no one's hero. The only ass I'm interested in saving is mine."

She smiled, which seemed to narrow his eyes. "Then you better conserve your energy." Taking his jacket from her shoulders, she went over to offer it to him. "Don't get cold."

It seemed silly to say that when he was wearing more than her. His jeans and tee-shirt were probably warmer than her silk dress and heels.

He took the jacket and stood up. Instead of putting it on, he swept it around her shoulders. Only this time, he didn't let go and finished the move by tugging the leather, forcing her to stumble against him. She flattened a hand on his torso to steady herself before peeking up at him through her bangs.

"You'll keep me warm," he said, his voice dropping an octave to hit deep in her gut.

Still with a hold of the open edges of his jacket, he turned to walk backwards, forcing her to walk with him until they reached the corner where she'd left the pillow.

"Down," he said.

Another command, like when he'd told her to sit. Their eyes remained locked, but her knees buckled. Tulsi lowered herself down onto her knees. Arousal was already thrumming at the apex of her thighs.

They weren't even touching anymore. She was on her knees with his jacket around her shoulders and he stood in front of her, tall and domineering. She didn't know what command he would give next, but knew she wouldn't refuse it. Licking her lips, she let them part, aware of how difficult it was to drag air into her lungs.

Staying high on her knees, her mouth was just a few inches from the buttons of his jeans. The heat of their bodies mixed and merged, charging the air around them. Tulsi was loathed to close her eyes in a blink. Wreck didn't seem to need to, he was so intent on her.

Just as she began to wonder if he expected her to take the next step, he lowered down to sit on the floor. He took the edges of her jacket again and pulled her to him, yanking her toward his hard body as he lay down. Crooking a leg, he curved it around her thigh and tugged her across the floor to put her between his thighs.

"Close your eyes and sleep," he said, pulling her down so her chest was on his stomach.

The contact made her aware of exactly the reaction his body was having to their proximity. He may have seemed unaffected, but she felt him, hard and proud, pressing into her belly.

"Wreck," she whispered, peeking up at him.

He put a hand on the back of her head, and turned it to lay her temple on his solid body. "Sleep."

Another command. Tulsi closed her eyes and complied.

FIVE

TULSI WENT FROM asleep to awake in a second. The sudden action of being shunted sideways snapped her from her slumber. She was still trying to figure out what was going on when her hands came into contact with the hard wooden floor. Swallowing a yawn, she couldn't order her thoughts. The air was cold, yet, she was warm. The smell around her wasn't familiar, but it was comforting.

Heavy boots next to her moved. When she looked up the line of the leg beside her, she saw Wreck standing above watching the door.

He began to move toward it. "Row," he barked, at a higher volume than any he'd used last night.

Her memory was still foggy, but Tulsi recalled where they were and how she'd ended up there.

Wreck got to the end of the bed as Rowdy vaulted onto his feet.

"What's going on?" Kieran mumbled, still on his back and, from the sounds of it, still half asleep.

"Get up," Rowdy snapped.

It was then she heard the click of something metallic. The door began to open. Someone was coming. Her mouth was dry and her senses still not at their peak. But Tulsi did her best to rise to her feet. Once she was up, she put her back against the wall.

Baines came in with four other men behind him. Every single one of them was armed.

"You're in luck, motherfuckas," Baines declared, far jollier than any of them felt. "Here's what's gonna happen. One at a time you get out for a piss, then we're all going on a road trip."

He started across the room toward her. Tulsi was the only person in that corner. Kieran was still sitting on the far side of the bed. Wreck and Rowdy were standing at the end of it. It must have been obvious to the duo who the murderer was heading for too. She didn't expect Wreck to side-step to block Baines' way. But he did.

Baines stopped to eye him. Wreck had a couple of inches of height on him, and they were definitely mismatched for muscle. If she had to put her money on either of them in a fair fight, Wreck would be her choice every time. He seemed more aware, smarter, quicker. But there wouldn't be a fair fight. Baines had a gun.

Even if Wreck could take the firearm from him, the men he'd come in with each had a weapon of their own and would finish Wreck maybe before he could get a shot off.

"Take him first," Baines said, keeping his eyes locked on Wreck.

The other guys came deeper into the room. One pointed a weapon at Rowdy. The other three approached Baines from behind.

"Don't be thinking about trying nothing," one of Baines' men said. "There ain't no window in there. No weapons or nothing. Just do your business, that's it."

With the other thugs backing their leader, Wreck had no choice except to stand still when Baines strolled around him.

"Don't worry, we have plans for you too, Pretty," Baines said, sauntering over to her. "I'm sorta hoping these motherfucks try some shit… 'cause I plan to take out all my frustrations on my pretty Tulsi… So, please, gimme an excuse."

He raised his gun to the center of her forehead. Tulsi

fought her urge to react even while the pace of her pulse kicked up. Her heart was beating so fast that she could hear it in her ears, but she stayed still. Memories of the woman from the previous night flashed across her mind's eye. The barrel of Baines gun was pressing into the same spot he'd shot to end his victim's life.

"Move," one of Baines men said to Wreck, waving his gun in the direction of the door, and getting out of his way.

Wreck could try running, but someone would get a bullet in him first. He went out with the other three around him.

Baines kept his focus on her. An image began to grow in her mind of her own body in the place of the murder victim's. Would she one day be prone on the floor, lifeless? Naked. Used. Spent. Another of Baines' discarded toys?

It didn't matter that Tulsi couldn't imagine a worse fate. The way Baines leered at her and let his gaze trail up and down her body, she knew he was painting his own mental picture of their future. She dreaded to think of what it looked like from his perspective.

"Who are you loyal to, Pretty Little Tulsi?" Baines asked.

"Leave her alone," Rowdy said.

Baines glanced back and exhaled a sort of snicker. "Guess she's used to being shared… Good. That will make her transition easier." He looked at her. "How many men can you take at once, Pretty Tulsi? What's your fantasy? Do you like servicing three? How about four… or six? I can make it happen for you, darlin', anything you want."

"Leave her alone," Kieran was the one to speak up this time.

"You said road trip," Rowdy said, obviously trying a different tact to protect both her and Kieran from Baines' attention. "Where are we going? To Merchant?"

"Don't worry about it," Baines said, his gun descending in a straight line from her forehead.

Using the barrel to push the neckline of her dress lower, he revealed more of her flesh. She kept her focus straight ahead. It was difficult not to react. If she squealed or objected, he'd get exactly what he wanted. She wouldn't give him the satisfaction.

"How about we go right now?" Baines asked, edging in closer. His gun only moved higher on the mound of her breast. "We can do it right here, in front of all three of your boyfriends. Let them see who your daddy is now."

"Leave her alone!" Kieran objected, climbing over the bed.

The moment Kieran got on his feet, Wreck reappeared in the doorway with the other three men at his back.

"Who's next?" Baines' man asked.

"I need to go," Tulsi said.

It wasn't exactly true, but she hoped going to the restroom would get her out from under Baines' scrutiny.

He stepped out of her way. "Then you go, sweetheart. Don't you forget I'm the one who can give you everything you need. You want me to take you? You want to have a little private time with me?"

"No, thank you," she said, garnering as much courage as she could to walk past him.

His arm shot out straight in front of her, blocking her way. Keeping it across her chest, he eased closer to push his hips against her, letting her feel just how much he liked being in control.

"Always been my experience women are as fickle as they are gorgeous. 'Specially when their guy's luck changes… I'm your ticket to ride, Pretty Tulsi. These fucks are finished. Any time you want it… Any time you're ready to switch to the winning side…"

"You didn't answer my question," Rowdy interrupted Baines. "Where is this road trip headed?"

"You're not in control, fuckwit," Baines said. "Shut the fuck up 'til I ask you a question."

When his arm dropped, Tulsi started walking again, creeping away while Baines was distracted by Rowdy. Only one of the thugs went with her to the bathroom. She did what she needed to fast and drank some water from the faucet knowing her next drink wasn't guaranteed.

By the time she got back into the bedroom, Wreck, Kieran, and Rowdy were in three separate corners facing the walls.

"What's going on?" she asked.

"Just keeping order," Baines said as two of the men took Rowdy out of the room. "You come stand over here by me, Pretty."

She didn't want to. Except he shook the weapon at his side reminding her that he was the one with the power. Not only that, but she was the leash Baines was using to control his trio of male captives.

After Tulsi trailed over, he put his arm around her to pull her close to his side. Being so close to him disgusted her, but at least he wasn't talking anymore.

Rowdy came back and Kieran went last.

A ruckus followed not long after.

Baines pulled her tight to his side. "That fucker better not be causing shit," he said, though he didn't sound concerned. "You know I won't punish him, I'll punish one of you." He touched the underside of her chin with his weapon to raise it up. "Do you like to be punished, Pretty Tulsi? I know how to make it hurt real good… Maybe you'd like to know what it's like to be fucked by a real man." Wreck began to turn their way. The weapon left her chin and without looking at him Baines swung the barrel in Wreck's direction. "Face the goddamn wall or someone's brains will decorate it."

Any one of them trying to rush the thugs would be pointless. Someone would lose their life and for what? They were under Baines' control.

Kieran came back wearing a streak of blood above his temple.

"Try to play the big man?" Baines asked, a snicker in his voice. "Never suited you, asshole… Wrap 'em up."

One of the guys put his weapon in the waistband of his jeans and produced a bundle of zip-ties from his pocket. He went to Wreck first. She heard them being fastened, but it wasn't until the guy moved aside that she saw what he'd done. Wreck had one tight around each wrist and a third looped through the others to create a set of makeshift handcuffs.

The guy did the same for Rowdy and then for Kieran. Tulsi expected to be next. But when the guy came back into view, the zip-ties were gone, and the gun was back in his hand.

"Take him," Baines said, nodding Wreck's way. "Unfortunately, sweetheart…" Baines once again used the barrel of his gun to raise her chin. Two of his guys grabbed Wreck to pull him away from the wall. He objected and shrugged them both off; one with such force that he hit the floor. The sound of him dropping startled everyone, including Baines. "Get up you fucktard, and don't forget who you're dealing with. Take Delray with you. I told you already, he's the one to watch… Why do you think they brought him? He's their muscle. Bet he'd kill at least two of you fucks before I put a bullet in his buddies."

Tulsi didn't know what Baines knew of Wreck or even much about Wreck herself. In spite of that ignorance, the air in the room reeked of relief when Wreck stalked toward the door, marching out without further incident. It seemed he wasn't going to cause any issues as long as Baines' men didn't put their hands on him.

"Sorry, sweetheart," Baines said. "What was I saying? Oh yeah, the boss. Merchant. He wants me to keep eyes on your little boyfriend. See as you probably guessed last night, he's chosen the wrong guy to fuck over. So, until this all gets straightened out, your boyfriend doesn't leave my sight, understand?"

She didn't understand. No one in the room was her boyfriend and she knew little about this Merchant everyone kept talking about.

Baines' attention shifted up and to the left, toward the corner where Kieran stood.

"How you want it done, boss?" asked the only thug left in the room.

"Keep the strongest and the weakest together," Baines said. "Common sense, dumbass."

"Sure, boss."

Another two guys came in, different from the ones who'd been in before. Tulsi wondered how many people were in the apartment. Already it was becoming clear that Merchant had a lot of pull.

Those two dragged Rowdy out, while another duo appeared to take Kieran.

Baines seemed happy, sauntering from the room with her under his arm. "Means we won't see much of each other on the trip, Pretty," Baines said, continuing their one-sided conversation. "See, I have to ride with that fucker. But I swear when we get where we're going, you'll have my undivided attention."

They moved through the apartment to the hallway and kept on going to the sidewalk where two cars were waiting. Two men sat in the front of the rear car; Wreck was in the backseat. Kieran and Rowdy were pulled toward the car in front and stuffed into the back.

"I'll see you soon," Baines said, walking up to the open back door of the rear car.

Another man stood there holding a weapon. Before she could figure out who was who, the cold metal of Baines' gun touched her chin again. He tipped it up, and instead of speaking, he bowed to press his mouth to hers. Tulsi had never felt so sick. It took every ounce of her will not to retch or vomit right there.

The moment he pulled back, he shoved her into the backseat. She climbed in and the door slammed behind her.

The man in the front passenger seat twisted to prop an elbow on the shoulder of his chair. With an impressed whistle, he checked her out. "You are gonna be a sweet ride." Another asshole. Tulsi sealed her lips. "That's Coombs," he said, pointing at the driver, then he closed his fist to jab his thumb toward himself. "Hillam. You don't fuck with us and we won't fuck with you. Stay back there and shut the fuck up."

She hadn't said a word and hadn't been intending to say much anyway. Tulsi adjusted her position to sit up straighter. Peeking around at Wreck, she found him glaring toward the front of the car, his eyes fixed and unmoving. It couldn't be comfortable to have his hands trapped behind his back, but she didn't think that was the reason for the glare.

Baines was outside talking to someone. They exchanged a few more words then Baines stalked to the front car to get in the passenger side. The thugs left the sidewalk to go back into the apartment building just as the front car started moving. Theirs was just a whisper behind.

Without his hands, Wreck couldn't put on his seatbelt. Tulsi didn't trust the men in the front; the strangers she didn't know. Kieran had told her that Wreck didn't like being touched. If he hadn't said it, she wouldn't have known it. For some reason, Wreck didn't mind making contact with her. He'd never commanded her to take her hands off him or recoiled from her touch.

Assuming, and hoping, it was only men he didn't like touching him, Tulsi took it upon herself to be responsible for his safety. Twisting around to press herself against him, she reached over his shoulder for his seatbelt.

When her head bumped his chin, she looked up. His eyes were still fixated straight ahead. Seeing him wound so tight was tough. It couldn't be good for his health and certainly didn't bode well for the men in the front.

With one hand on the seatbelt and the other on the seat supporting her weight, she leaned in to bump her nose against the stubble on his jaw. Maybe he didn't expect her to make contact. The first time was an accident, the second wasn't. The next time he closed his eyes in a blink, they opened again to land on hers.

Being out of control had to be frustrating him. A man of his physique wouldn't be used to it. They were, according to Baines, the strongest and the weakest, and could be stuck in the car for a long while. The trip would be easier on him if he could relax.

Tulsi smiled. She didn't know why; it wasn't like there was much to smile about. She wanted to reassure him and got something of a thrill when curiosity grew in his gaze again. Like it had last night.

Bumping her nose on his chin, in a more playful gesture, she caused his frown to deepen. She confused him; that much was clear. Though it wasn't much of a shock, sometimes she confused herself.

When his attention descended to her mouth, her amusement dwindled.

They'd known each other less than a day. It wasn't like she'd thought about kissing him… That was a lie; one she couldn't fool herself with for long. Tulsi had thought about it. Fantasized about what she'd assumed could never be a reality. It had never occurred to her that he would be open to it. But as she sat there pressed against him, watching the way he scrutinized her, her thoughts from the restaurant returned.

The thrill. The excitement. A man who would encourage her to take risks. A man she could be wild with. Free with.

Wreck didn't know her; didn't know about any of her insecurities or hang ups. He'd proved that he felt at least some form of attraction to her by the way he led their sleeping arrangements the previous night. Whether he wanted to or not, he desired her.

At any time, she could lose her life. It had never been more in danger. Life felt short and fragile. Just hours ago, Tulsi had watched someone die. Her own life was under threat. She'd spent a night imprisoned with strangers.

Life was precious. That was one of the last things her mother said to her. The memory of promising her mother she'd never be afraid of taking risks faded up like a scene in a movie. For years, Tulsi hadn't honored that promise. Since her mother's death, she'd let herself float along without much aim or ambition. Just getting by had been enough.

Tulsi could be freed tomorrow or Baines could kill her at any second. She couldn't be afraid. Fear wouldn't get her anywhere. The time to go with the flow was over. If she wanted something, she had to take it.

Wreck seemed to come to his senses and his eyes moved toward the front of the car again. She put on his seatbelt and sat at his side to fasten her own. She was still thinking about what she wanted and how she'd go after it when Hillam spoke in the front.

"We're going to the drive-thru 'cause we're hungry. Don't expect nothing fancy."

As much as Tulsi wasn't hungry, it made sense to eat. It would be harder for Wreck without his hands, but she didn't mind helping him out. In one regard, he was luckier than

Rowdy and Kieran. If they both still wore the plastic cuffs, they wouldn't be able to help each other out.

The strongest and the weakest, that's what Baines had said. It made sense not to put all of the strength together. Tulsi might be the shortest, the leanest, the least muscular of their group. Yet, next to Wreck, she felt an odd kind of empowerment that gave her strength.

She'd told him that people needed something to live for if they were to survive a trial. She didn't have much in the way of assets or friendships, but when Baines had started across the room toward her that morning, it had been Wreck's instinct to get in his way. To protect her as he'd done the previous night.

So as long as Wreck needed her help, even if it was just with French fries or egg muffins, she'd make sure he could rely on her. That gave her something to live for.

SIX

"WE'RE LOCKING THESE doors. So just stay fucking put," Hillam said, getting out of the car to join Coombs who was already walking around the hood.

As promised, the door locks clicked into place, trapping her and Wreck in the backseat alone. Tulsi dipped her head to watch the two men cross half a dozen parking spaces. Baines and Teal were waiting outside the vehicle that had transported Kieran and Rowdy.

"You see an opening, run."

Tulsi had become so used to Wreck being silent that she hadn't expected to hear his voice.

Taking her attention away from the men outside, she did a double take. "Excuse me?"

Wreck wasn't looking her way. Just like her, he'd been watching the thugs' progress through the side window. After she'd asked him to repeat himself, his head swung in her direction. There was no equivocation in his staring gaze, the severity of which, she was almost coming to expect.

"You see an opening, you run."

She felt her head shaking before words had formed in her mind. "No." Tulsi hadn't thought his expression could get any more brutal, but her response brought his brow down further, proving her wrong. "What would be the point?"

"You'll live."

"Will you?" she asked. "Will Kieran? Will Rowdy? I wouldn't even know where to go or what to do. This isn't the kind of life I'm used to. We've driven like two hundred miles today, maybe more… I don't even know where we are."

"You get to the nearest bus or train station," he said. "Get on the first pony out of here. Doesn't matter where it's going. You get on and you go. Run."

"With what?" she asked. "They took my purse, remember?"

His attention dropped to her chest, but she didn't get the impression he was about to suggest she prostitute herself.

"Inside pocket," he said.

Tulsi had been wearing his jacket since last night. Even if Wreck wanted to put it on, he couldn't while the zip-ties restricted his wrists. Her own expression morphed to a frown as she opened one side to check the lining.

"Where?"

"Under the arm," he said. "Behind the seam."

She slid her hand to the location and was shocked to find a slit in the lining—a secret pocket. Tulsi put her hand inside and felt a bunch of folded bills. Leaving them in place, she exhaled her incredulity and dropped her hand to her lap.

"I thought it was the way the leather folded."

He nodded. "No one's supposed to know."

Except for some reason, he was telling her.

"What about the girl?" she asked. "The one we saw Baines murder."

Wreck ignored the question. "Keep your head down. A low profile. You'll have to change your name and think quick. Work cash in hand—"

"My life is over," she said. "That's what you're telling me. I'll never be me again. No matter how this works out, I'm always going to be living with this hanging over me."

"Yes."

The answer was definitive. People said being honest was preferable over lying. Yet, there was something in between that involved subtlety and tact to soften the blow. It didn't seem that Wreck knew the meaning of those words.

"I can't just run away."

"You can."

"No, I can't."

"You don't owe anyone anything. They relax with you because you're not a threat. There will be an opening. When you see it, go."

"They've kept you and Rowdy and Kieran in line by threatening me. If I run, they'll take it out on you and Rowdy."

"We can handle it," he said.

"You might think you're Superman, but you can't stop a bullet."

His attention began to swing away from her. Keeping an eye on their captors was smart. Tulsi could see the thugs and they were still in the same position. Before Wreck's focus went too far, she put a hand on his cheek to bring it back around to her. Maybe most people wouldn't dare do such a thing. His scowl seemed fierce, like it was habit to lash out. Except when he set eyes on her, he gritted his teeth instead, in a show of restraint.

"I saw that woman die," she said. "I could go to the police."

"Doesn't work like that."

Tilting her head, she peered into him. "Who are you? Why did Baines say you were dangerous? Why does Rowdy speak to you like he knows you but Kieran doesn't understand you?"

"Kieran understands dick about the world."

From what she'd walked into, she could say the same about herself. "That doesn't tell me anything about you."

"You don't want to know anything about me."

"I do," she said, strengthening her hand on his cheek when he tried to turn away again. Moving her thumb across his stubble toward his lips, she scrutinized him, trying to see what was beyond his hard shell. "You said you weren't related to them. If you were hired muscle, Baines would've let you go or offered you a job." Remembering how Baines had questioned her loyalty, she wondered if he'd done the same with Wreck. "Did he offer you a job?"

"You ask too many questions."

"I have to ask questions because you don't offer anything. We're in this together. You might not like being stuck with me, but you are. I want to help. To do that, I need you to trust me."

"I don't trust anyone."

She smiled. "The lone wolf. I get it. Guess I've been like that myself these last few years. After my mother died, I was a mess. I lost myself. I didn't know much about who I was. I rushed into a relationship with a man who it took me five years to realize, I didn't know. Whatever is going on here, I don't want to be a part of it. But running away isn't the answer."

If she ran, like he'd suggested, she would be running forever. This had to come to a head. Either she negotiated a way to get out or the thugs would kill her. Tulsi didn't like her chances in a streetwise world, living off the grid.

She wouldn't know the first thing on how to go about it. How to find the right people or even how to get a cash-in-hand job as Wreck had advised.

"They'll rape you."

That much had been made clear to her. Every time it was suggested or implied, sickness churned in her belly.

"Everyone likes to keep telling me what they're going to do to me. What about you? What about Rowdy? What about Kieran? I'll be the first to admit I don't know him. Maybe he's full of shit. But if he is then he's the only one who can get Merchant's shipment back. If he's not, we need to find out what happened to it. Maybe if we can, Merchant will let us go."

"Look around, we can't do fuck all."

"What's the alternative? I run, they kill you. You run, they kill me. There has to be trust. We have to be able to rely on each other or else we're all dead already. You told me to run," she said, putting a hand on his thigh, twisting further around to face him. "You showed me your stash of cash. You gave me advice on how to break free and be safe. Let's say I followed those instructions. Either you cover for me or you tell Merchant, which makes it easy for him to track me down.

Whether you mean to or not, you're asking me to trust you too."

"I owe Merchant nothing."

"You owe *me* nothing. Why do you care if I run? If I'm safe?"

He looked away. Keeping her hand on his leg, she gave him time to process whatever was in his mind. The four men still stood half a dozen parking spots away talking to each other, probably making plans. There was enough distance that they had no hope of eavesdropping.

Sliding her hand higher on his thigh, she watched her pale fingers move on the dark denim. The fabric was soft, but the muscle beneath so hard. It wasn't the only thing, she realized when her fingertips came into contact with his groin.

Raising her chin, Tulsi found him looking at her again. "I feel safe when you look at me," she murmured.

It was an insane thing to say. The man was as trapped as her. More so since his hands were bound at his back. But safe was how she'd felt last night. It was the truth. If they were going to be stuck in this together, like she'd said, someone had to open up first.

"You don't know who I am."

"Maybe not," she said, moving her hand back toward his knee to ease in closer. "But I know you feel it too."

"Don't fuck with me," he said and looked away.

Her attraction was there whenever he was near. It intensified when he focused on her. There was a heat and an energy that throbbed within her. It was visceral. Somehow it made her aware of each inch of her body. All of her was enlivened by him.

Wreck was a powerful man and wouldn't be impressed by a woman who couldn't match his virility. Everything about him turned her on. His height, his eyes, his hair, his scent, the way his bicep curved and disappeared into the soft fabric of his dark tee-shirt.

Drawn closer like a moth mesmerized by the flame, her hands slid further up his thigh. Her tingling fingertips moved with the ridges of the denim. But it wasn't until she opened her mouth and her teeth came into contact with the tempting muscle of his arm that she realized what she was doing. Even then, she didn't stop.

Digging her teeth in deep, she formed suction and moved her tongue against him, taking her first taste of his flesh. The muscle bunched beneath her amour, hardening, she guessed, as he clenched. Tulsi didn't apologize. She pressed her teeth so deep, no doubt she'd leave a mark. It took effort, but she forced herself to release and move back a few inches to peek up.

Wreck was looking down at her. The frown was there, curiosity too. But the heat alight in his gaze told her that she hadn't made a mistake.

"Did you feel that?" she asked, letting her hand glide deeper between his thighs. "I'll find a way to get through to you. To show you that I'm real."

"Don't fuck with me," he said like he had before.

The ragged edge to his heavy tone was obvious. Digging her nails into his leg, she pushed up, bringing her mouth even closer to his. "If you had your hands, what would you be doing right now?" she purred, conjuring all sorts of fantasies in her minds-eye. "I have my hands. I don't want to keep them to myself. They are mine and they are yours."

One snuck under the hem of his tee-shirt to curl around the buckle of his belt.

"You're Kieran's girl," he said, which made her smile again.

"No. He's never had me. He never will. He wants me." Tulsi pushed higher. "I don't think he's the only one."

They were still examining each other when the snap of the locks alerted them to their jailors return. Tulsi may have said that she wouldn't run. But she couldn't count it out. If the situation became more dire, she would consider it. Especially now that Wreck had counselled her on how to be free.

Until the moment for decision came, she was going to aggravate the men who were in control as little as possible. As long as they were alive and unharmed, being compliant seemed the best course of action. If Tulsi screwed over Wreck, Rowdy, and Kieran, they'd have no reason to look out for her anymore.

Coombs and Hillam got in the car and then they were on the road again. It was already dark out. She'd hoped that they would stop to rest. Although their accommodations last night hadn't been the best in the world, she wasn't sure she could expect much more that night. All Tulsi knew for sure was every mile they covered was a mile closer to Merchant. She wasn't sure she was ready to meet the man face-to-face.

SEVEN

THEY DROVE FOR another couple of hours. Everyone was getting tired. The men in the front were starting to snark at each other. Tulsi could feel her eyes getting heavy, but falling asleep would make her vulnerable. The longer they went, the more difficult it was to stay awake. The monotony of the journey was starting to catch up with all of them.

Not a minute too soon, they pulled into a motel parking lot. Teal, Baines' driver, got out to go into the office. After, he came back to give Hillam a key before he returned to his own vehicle.

Hillam and Coombs got out first and weren't discreet about drawing their weapons. They came around to the side of the car as Tulsi unfastened both her and Wreck's seatbelts.

Hillam opened the door. "Out," he said to her, shaking the gun. "You get out first. Just you."

Tulsi glanced back at Wreck, who, as usual, gave very little away in his expression. She slid along the seat to climb out the passenger side. Hillam immediately spun her around and locked a forearm across her clavicle to pin her against his chest. There was no doubt of his control once he pressed his gun to her temple.

He reversed toward the walkway that ran along the

length of the motel building. Tulsi did her best to keep her footing, while contemplating what would happen if she screamed. The motel clerk would hear her, but she didn't want to put anyone else in danger.

Coombs bowed to say something into the back of the car and then Wreck was getting out. His hands were still bound, but that didn't put Coombs at ease. Their captor kept his weapon trained on their second prisoner, who otherwise walked without hindrance. The men were using threats of violence against her to keep Wreck in line. None of this was her doing, yet she felt guilty about limiting her capable cohort.

"Unlock the door," Hillam said, letting go of her body to stuff a key into her hand.

The gun stayed against her temple. The physical manifestation of their peril was enough to keep her quiet and compliant.

Her experience with guns was limited. She didn't appreciate that fate was making up for that with this horrendous situation. Hillam shoved her, forcing her to fall against one of the motel room doors. He was quick to crowd up against her, holding her against the solid wood he expected her to unlock. His shadow and weight were limiting her ability to move, so it was hard to see the lock. With shaking fingers and a little fumbling, she unlocked the door. Falling forward into the room with Hillam at her back, Tulsi was kept in his grip while he flicked on the light.

A couch stood to the left, and twin beds to the right. The door at the back of the room had to lead to a bathroom, at least, that was her guess.

"Home, sweet home," Hillam said as Wreck came in with Coombs who still had him at gunpoint.

Coombs closed the door and Hillam snatched the key from her to toss it across to his buddy who locked the door, leaving the key in the lock.

"We're all going to play nice," Hillam said, swinging the gun from her to Wreck and back again. "You two want food? You want to sleep. Hell, you want to take a dump, you need our permission. Both of you, all the time. You do nothing without our say so. You piss us off, we'll just say no.

Think about that before you do anything stupid."

Hillam wasn't quite as threatening as Baines. He probably watched the master and thought he was doing a good job mimicking him, but he wasn't.

"What did Baines say?" Coombs asked Hillam.

The question was unusual; it made her consider each of the men. Didn't seem like Baines would want them to discuss insider information in front of the prisoners. Tulsi didn't like the way Hillam leered when he turned her way.

"Whatever we have to do to keep her in line," Hillam said. A smile curled his lips as Coombs laughed. The sinister sound wasn't one of happiness. "Take 'em off."

Licking her lips, Tulsi sought an explanation from him and then from Coombs. The man who'd been laughing just a moment before was fixated on her body.

"I don't know what you're—"

"Your clothes," he said. "You want to be comfortable? Take off the jacket first."

Their jailors weren't demanding that Wreck get undressed or undressing themselves. Coombs didn't offer her a robe or a towel or anything to change into. He wasn't even suggesting she use the privacy of the bathroom. Standing there, two feet away from her, his air of expectation made her wary.

"Hurry up," Hillam said. "And the shoes."

"I like the shoes," Coombs said.

Hillam's expression became a semi-smirk. "You think you do 'til they're digging those pointy heels into your ass. You can fuck around with that later. Right now, we do this hard and fast."

Wreck stood opposite her, about ten feet away. He growled and started forward. But he didn't get far. Both captors raised their guns, training them on Wreck.

"No one asked you to do anything, asshole," Hillam barked. "We can do it nice. Take our time with the lady and maybe she'll enjoy herself too. Or you can piss us off…"

That sentence was left hanging. Tulsi recalled what Baines had said that morning. The look on Wreck's face didn't inspire confidence. She worried that he was still considering taking action in her defense. The two men must have thought the same thing because Coombs cocked his weapon.

"No," she said. "It's fine. It's good. Yes, it's okay."

Taking off the jacket, she tossed it toward the couch and kicked her shoes off in the same direction.

Hillam was still pointing his weapon at Wreck, but had switched his focus to her. "Everything," he said. "Now the dress."

Adrenaline began to surge; her pulse kicked up. She could feel the blunt thump of her racing heart in her chest. She'd had sex before. Been naked in front of men before. But never in front of three at a time and certainly never at gunpoint.

Tulsi took a deep breath and blew it out slowly. The only way to get through this was to focus on Wreck. Locking her eyes on his, she drew down the zip under her arm. Without relaxing a muscle, she slid each of the straps from her shoulders so the material fell to the floor. Looking at Wreck gave her focus. That anchor gave her courage. He was the only positive in this mess.

Safety.

In Wreck she found safety and security. Concentrating on him made her feel safe. It was for Wreck. She could get naked for Wreck without fear. The fantasies of him had played in her mind since she'd sunk her teeth into his muscle. Something had to happen between them, or would happen between them, or could at the very least.

"Keep going," Coombs snapped.

Setting her jaw tight, she tried to imagine that the words had come from Wreck instead of the letch beside her. It was possible Wreck remembered what she'd said in the car and that was why he kept his gaze pinned to hers.

That was all he could do to reassure her. Moistening her lips again, she fixated on his strength, and steadied her breathing. Reaching around behind her, Tulsi slid her thumbs under the clasp of her bra and unhooked it. She waited as long as she could before touching the straps on her shoulders.

Hillam's frustrated exhale forced her to ease them downward. Undressing herself was bad enough. To have the thug do it for her would be worse.

"That's more like it. Fuck me," Hillam said, apparently impressed by her figure.

Coombs snorted. "That's the idea, buddy boy."

Elation buzzed between the two men. They were like teenagers or frat boys who she knew would spur each other on.

"Panties too. All the way."

Conflict and disgust battled within her. Proximity to these men in her vulnerable state opposed her feelings of pride in Wreck who was holding himself calm and steady. Tulsi pushed the elastic of her panties down over her butt and let them drop to the floor.

Hillam whooped and Coombs cheered. Something about their reaction made Wreck snap. He took one long stride toward her and both men suddenly silenced.

"Hey, asshole! Don't move a fucking muscle!"

Wreck didn't listen, he kept coming. Without touching her, he spun around to put himself in front of her, blocking her body from the view of the other men.

"What did I just fucking say?" Hillam said.

"Maybe we put one in his eye," Coombs said, raising his weapon higher.

Tulsi grabbed Wreck's waist, eager to protect him, though she knew there was little she could do.

"Not in his eye," Hillam said. "I want him to watch. Put one in his leg… Hell, put it in his balls and then he'll never be able to enjoy her again."

"I say we just kill him," Coombs said. "Baines said he's trouble. Said he'll fuck with us. Said he can't be trusted."

"None of them can be trusted."

"Yeah, you're fucking right… We'll say he rushed us."

"No!" Tulsi called out, hurrying around Wreck before he could notice she was moving. "No, he'll behave. We'll behave." Her body distracted Hillam. Using that to her advantage, she edged closer, pushing aside her anxiety and reminding herself what she'd decided about compliance. "You just want a good time." She inched closer. "Don't you, baby?"

Hillam's gun arm began to loosen. Though it went against her every instinct, Tulsi forced herself to touch the obvious erection in his jeans.

Rubbing his member, she tilted her chin up to pout at him. "What would you like to do to me?"

Hillam looked from her to Coombs and grinned. "Let's tie him down and have a party with his bitch."

"Move," Coombs said. "Over there, asshole."

An old skinny radiator was attached to the wall beneath the window. Coombs swung the weapon from it to Wreck and back again.

"Here," Hillam said, taking a zip-tie from his pocket to hold it toward his colleague who lunged across to grab it. "Move, asshole."

Hillam put his gun arm around her waist. The weapon weighed heavy against her hip in more ways than one.

"Move or you get a gut shot," Coombs said to Wreck. "You're gonna sit and watch us party with your bitch. Does it fucking sting? She wants us, man. You're old news."

Forcing herself to smile, Tulsi nodded and attempted to laugh.

"Hurry it up," Hillam said.

With his teeth gritted and his jaw tense, Wreck marched across the room.

"Sit down," Coombs demanded. Try as he might, he'd never have the same authority that was effortless for Wreck.

Hillam pointed his gun at her head again. "Sit nice."

"Yeah, and don't think he won't shoot," Coombs said, tucking his gun into his pants. "That guy's so desperate, he'll fuck her dead or alive."

"Right?" Hillam said.

The men enjoyed the joke, snorting and laughing with each other.

Coombs reached behind Wreck, presumably to attach the new zip-tie to the fixed pipe. Her smile was gone when their eyes met again. He wasn't impressed. Tulsi hoped he understood her actions. The last thing she wanted was to be intimate with these men, either of them. But watching Wreck suffer would've broken her.

A shout from outside brought them all to attention. Coombs leaped to his feet.

"What was that?" Hillam asked.

"Baines," Coombs said, peeking out the curtains. "I think he wants us out there. Come on."

Coombs started toward the door. Hillam let her go, but pointed the gun at each of them. "We're locking this door and we're right outside. Don't fuck around. We still have your buddies out there."

Coombs took the key from the door and opened it. Both men went out and she heard the key turn in the other side of the lock.

EIGHT

THEY WERE ALONE. A sense of relief flooded through her. The men couldn't violate her if they were out there. But that didn't mean they wouldn't come back, possibly with others, to finish what they'd started.

"Get dressed," Wreck said, focusing her mind.

"I didn't have a choice," she said, drawn toward him. "I couldn't let them hurt you. I won't."

"So you'll fuck them…" His chin stayed down. "I'm not usually so wrong."

Tulsi dropped to her knees next to his outstretched legs. "Wrong about what?"

His fierce eyes leaped to hers. "It's only rape if you don't want it."

"Want it?" she asked, incredulous. "You think I want to be with men like them?" Her fingers opened as she laid her hand on his thigh. "I think you know what I want… Even if it makes no sense… Even if it's insane… You know exactly what I want… You've known it since we stood at the bottom of those stairs at Teal's place."

Rising on her knees, she slid a leg over his thighs to straddle him.

"What are you doing?" he asked.

Maybe it was crazy. She shouldn't be so forward, but her hands skimmed higher, up over his hips to his tee-shirt to stop on his chest. Pressing her fingers into him, Tulsi curled them, testing the resistance of his flesh beneath the fabric.

"Showing you what I want," she said and bowed to open her mouth on the bicep she hadn't bitten earlier.

Giving his arm its due, she marked him again, digging her teeth into him, tasting him.

"Tulsi," he warned. "Don't fuck around."

This was more than that. It seemed like much more than that. Insane as it was, Tulsi felt drugged the nearer she got to him. Her need only grew the more she surrendered herself to him. That they were alone in a bedroom and had been running on instinct for more than a day probably contributed to her desperate need to connect with him.

"Tulsi," Wreck said again when she released the suction of her mouth and trailed it up to his neck.

Her hands slid up his arms, under the sleeves of his tee-shirt, pushing it up to drag her nails on his muscular shoulders.

"I've thought about nothing but you all day," she breathed.

When he tried to lower his chin to block her mouth, she grabbed his hair in her fists and rose higher on her knees.

Pushing herself closer, Tulsi yanked his head back to trail her lips up his neck. "Tell me you don't want me," she murmured, kissing up to his chin and back down his throat. "Wreck."

The muscles of his jaw bunched under her lips. "Don't do this," he said, his voice hissed through gritted teeth.

"I'm alive, Wreck… We're alive…" Shifting forward, she lowered herself slowly, coming to rest with her knees behind his hips, her pussy nestled over the hard heat in his jeans. "You want me."

Rocking against him, she stimulated herself, undulating her hips, rubbing and arousing him.

Wreck hissed again. "You're Kieran's girl."

It didn't even feel like he was saying that to her. The statement was his last barrier. Something he needed to say as though he was reminding himself why hooking up with her was a bad idea. The excuse was flimsy. She wasn't with Kieran and had made that clear to Wreck.

Taking her lips from his stubble, she let her drowsy eyes meet his. "I choose you," she whispered. "You may be the last man I ever choose for myself." His lips curled back from his teeth to show they were clenched tight. "Be my last, Wreck. Ruin me for them."

Other men may force themselves on her. They may take something that she didn't want to offer. Wreck was the first man to fire the inferno of chemistry that she'd always craved to feel with a lover. Whichever way this turned out, their time together was limited. Having a chance to be alone was a gift, one Tulsi wanted to take advantage of.

"You don't want me," he growled, turning his face away when she tried to kiss his mouth.

Driving her fingers into his hair again, she forced his head back and fell against him to suck hard on the side of his neck. "I've never wanted anything more," she said, her breathing labored. "I need you, Wreck… I need to feel what it is to be owned by you…"

Kissing her way across his neck, she felt the shallow motion of his chest begin to move faster. Her hands slithered to his belt. Gripping it, she pulled him down while she wriggled higher.

"You don't know what I am," he panted.

"I know you're a man," she said, pressing her cheek to his, then riding higher to catch his earlobe in her teeth. "I know I want you."

With his hands attached at his back, he couldn't use them to push her off or stand up. Except, if he really wanted her to stop, he could use his body to shove her away. Slowing her hips, Tulsi pressed her pelvis down hard on his and licked her lips. Her eyes were closed as she edged her mouth to his jaw and down his cheek. Keeping it in contact with him, the warmth of his breath heated her skin as she moved closer to his mouth.

"Nympho," he grumbled.

Keeping her eyes closed and looping her arms around

his neck, she smiled. "For you… yes."

Parting her lips, she sought his. This time, he didn't resist. His powerful kiss fought for domination. Tulsi had started this, and it was a thrill to learn that her instincts about him hadn't been wrong. The heat of his slick tongue pushed into her mouth, taking control with a mixture of anger and lust.

Maybe he didn't want her. Maybe he was indifferent and was just taking advantage of the chance to get off before he ate a bullet. Whatever the truth, there wasn't exactly time to talk it out or play it coy. Even though they weren't in the best of situations to start anything sexual, this may be the last chance they had to be alone with anyone of the opposite sex. By choice anyway, Tulsi may soon dread being by herself with an amorous man.

Wreck's hips rose, forcing themselves deeper into her. A groan rumbled from the back of his throat, vibrating into her mouth. Releasing his kiss, Tulsi stroked both hands across the width of his shoulders and skimmed them up the back of his neck into his hair.

"Maybe I'll ruin you instead," she said, riding him and scratching her fingers through his scalp. "You want to be in control, don't you, my Ruin?" Her lips curled in a smile. Wreck wasn't impressed. She moved in to touch her lips to his again. "I'm in control… You're at my mercy."

"Revenge will be a bitch, Nympho."

Breathing in through her nose, she stole his mouth again and lost herself in his kiss. Though she'd been teasing, her hormones were already vibrating in anticipation of this man punishing her for being so brazen.

His strength prompted her to be bold. This powerful man wanted a woman who'd take what she wanted. Somehow, her instinct told her being brash was the right way to be with him.

Gripping his hair tighter, she forced his mouth one way while she tilted her head the other. Each inhale grew longer as both of them dragged more oxygen into their lungs, fueling the fire of their union.

When he yanked his head back, he proved his

physical strength. Just with his neck muscles, Wreck broke their mouths apart. "Pussy," he snarled. Tulsi shifted her hips and grabbed for his belt. He surprised her by bending his knees, boosting her forward so she collided with his body, trapping her hands between them. "Nympho doesn't get her prize until I taste mine."

The quaking words came out almost like a threat. Tulsi shivered. Her jaw moved, but she needed to breathe for a few seconds before she could talk.

"Shit," she whispered. "You are going to ruin me."

"Stand up."

A command. Always a command. She'd never known a man so good at imposing his will. All she wanted to do was comply. To be his plaything.

Garnering her courage, Tulsi found her feet and straightened her legs. "Be gentle with me, Ruin."

"Never," he said, stretching his neck to bury his face against her thigh. "Closer, baby. I want the full deal... Put your foot up."

Edging closer, she raised her foot to the top of the heater, exposing herself to him. A grumble of masculine satisfaction made her hold her breath. Each kiss he bestowed brought him closer to the prize he wanted. His tongue slid south, opening her body to him until it found her most sensitive spot.

She gasped for breath. "Oh, Wreck," Tulsi panted his name and drove her fingers into his hair again as he shifted onto his knees, pushing her leg further out of his way.

Rocking against the motion of his flickering tongue, she arched toward him, eager for his mouth to go deeper. "That's it, baby... Show me that clit... Use your hand..."

Letting one hand loosen from his hair, she did as he asked, sliding her fingers down to give him an unhindered view. She mewed in protest when he leaned back to check her out. The hand she still had in his hair tried to force him back, but he resisted.

"Please," she whined.

"You'll get it, Nymph... Stick your finger in your pussy, finger that beaut for me."

"Wreck," she said, touching her clit.

"You want cock, you do as you're told, Sextoy."

The man didn't like to talk… until he was turned on. Peeking down, she saw the searing heat of his gaze burning into the center of her body. If he looked so intent now, she couldn't wait to see what he would look like when she started to finger herself.

Tulsi wasn't disappointed. The moment she dipped her finger into herself, he licked his eager lips. A long exhale of his breath urged her to go deeper. Pushing her finger into herself, she eased her hips closer.

"Like this," she murmured in a sultry purr.

"Just like that," he said, surging forward to suck hard on her clit.

As her finger came out of her pussy, he licked the length of it and used his mouth to push her hand back in. Repeating the action, she picked up the pace. Wreck managed to tease her clit and taste her, taking her closer to the apex of pleasure. After he grabbed her hand in his teeth to pull it free, he drove his tongue into her forcing orgasm to slam into her.

"Wreck," she screamed out, pushing against his mouth and scrunching her fingers in his hair to hold him against her. "Oh, fuck."

Panting, she didn't even try to hold herself up on the descent of her climax. Her knees buckled. She collapsed onto the floor in front of him. As soon as she felt the carpet against her lower legs, she bolstered herself to grab for his belt again.

That was just the start. Tulsi wasn't done with him yet. Except Wreck seemed to have a different idea. Shifting off his knees, he stretched his legs out again, angling himself away from her.

"Go get my jacket."

"What?" she asked and exhaled a laugh. "Baby, I want—"

"They're on the porch, they could walk in any second."

Blinking at him, she focused her mind. He was right. There *were* voices outside, muffled and non-specific, but definitely masculine. Tulsi hadn't even noticed until Wreck pointed them out.

"Oh my God," she said and leaped up to rush across the room.

Grabbing up her dress from the floor, she lunged forward to get his jacket from the couch. Stepping into her dress, she pulled the straps onto her shoulders and didn't bother with the zipper before putting his jacket on again.

Spinning around, she swept her bra and panties from the floor and stuffed them into the pocket. She'd intended to go back to Wreck, but at the last moment, adjusted her trajectory and rushed over to the closet.

"You've got seconds, girl."

"I know…" Opening the closet, Tulsi grabbed out a pillow and a spare blanket. "I take care of you, you take care of me…"

Tulsi managed to say the words while rushing back to him and dropping to her knees to stuff the pillow upright behind him. It wasn't much, but it was better than subjecting his back to the hard metal.

Opening the blanket, she spread it over herself and sat next to him. She was about to lay her head on his thigh when he bent the knee closest to her, raising it from the floor.

"Go under."

Lying down, she slithered under his crooked leg to lay her head on the other. He rested his leg down on top of her, holding her in the clamp of his powerful thighs. She spread the blanket over them both as best she could and wriggled in close to him.

Brushing her hair from her face, she peeked up at him. "Wreck," she whispered, noting how his frown was fixed in the direction of the door. "Baby…"

Curling her fist around his belt, she kept her eyes on him until he glanced down. She wanted confirmation that they weren't over. That the orgasm he'd gifted wouldn't be the last he'd grant her. That she would experience more of him.

"Sleep," he said. "They think you're out they might leave you be. Sleep, Nymph, no matter what."

Closing her eyes, she followed his lead. Those thugs wouldn't care about waking her. But if Baines had given them something else to think about, they may have forgotten about her.

Wreck's instructions hadn't steered her wrong so far. Tulsi didn't know if being intimate would change their level of trust, but she sure felt better knowing he'd tasted her. If nothing else, she had taken control in a time when control could be wrested from her at any second.

With her fingers warm against his abdomen behind his belt, Tulsi closed her eyes and breathed him in. The danger wasn't over, it may never be over again. But she was in the safest place for her. Wreck was her cornerstone and her only hope of making it out of the situation alive.

NINE

"IF I KEEP EATING like this, I'll need to take up some new strenuous workout," Tulsi said, folding up the last of their food wrappers to put them in the paper sack.

Peeking up at Wreck who was next to her in the rear of the car with his hands zip-tied at his back, she expected some reaction to her innuendo. He didn't so much as make eye contact. His attention was trained on the front windshield. Sure, his scowl was normal, but that intent tinge to his hardened expression piqued her concern.

She laid a hand on his thigh. "Wreck?"

"Baines kept going," he muttered.

Their car was slowing down to turn into a huge parking lot. When she turned to look out front, she caught a glimpse of the other car continuing on the long straight road.

"Where are we going?" she asked.

That day had started much the same as the previous one. Only difference was, Wreck woke her up before the goons stirred. He'd instructed her to go to the bathroom, shower, do whatever she needed to do, quietly, behind the locked door. The orders were matter of fact, but she understood what they implied. She wasn't to give the goons any excuse to get her naked and alone. The reprieve the previous night had been lucky. They wouldn't necessarily be lucky again.

Coombs and Hillam had come back into the motel room just moments after she'd closed her eyes. They'd been engaged in some mumbled discussion and hadn't paid her any more attention.

"You're going inside with Coombs. You and your boyfriends are gonna need supplies," Hillam said. "I'm gonna stay out here with lover boy."

"No," she said, pushing herself back in the seat to link her arms around Wreck's. "I go where he goes. I won't go without Wreck."

Without Wreck, she was vulnerable. With him, she was vulnerable, though in a completely different way. Together, they at least had the illusion of support. Coombs pulled the car into a space and killed the engine to twist and lay a glare on them.

"You don't come voluntarily," he snapped. "Hillam will put one in your boyfriend's leg, and he won't be able to go anywhere."

Hillam held up a gun that he must have had nearby and pulled back the hammer.

Fear quaked through her, but she didn't blink. "You can't put a bullet in him," she said. "Someone will hear the gunshot."

"Maybe that's a risk we take," Hillam said, lowering the gun to aim at Wreck's leg.

"No," Tulsi said, letting Wreck go to clamber onto his lap. Covering as much of him as she could, she wrapped her arms backwards, curling them down his sides. "You shoot one of us, you shoot both of us... Then you'll have nothing to show your master. How will he like that?"

The guys in the front looked at each other like they really didn't know what to do. Triumph erased her fear. Taking a stand had put them in their place.

Wreck slid a little lower in his seat, brushing his lips against the back of her ear. "Here," he said. Turning her head, she knew he wanted to speak to her in what illusion of privacy they could muster. "Go."

The whispered word made her twist further. Hooking an arm at the back of his neck, she pulled herself around to meet his eye. He wasn't telling her to leave with Coombs to go into the big-box store across the other side of the parking lot—if that was indeed where Coombs wanted to go. Wreck was telling her to go... to run.

Shaking her head slowly, Tulsi didn't like this order. It was an order to abandon him. "No."

"Yes," Wreck said, a scowl fixed on his face.

"You do what you're fucking told," Coombs snapped. "I'll drag you out by your fucking hair if you don't—"

"She doesn't do what you tell her," Wreck snarled, glaring beyond her to the men in front. "But she will do what I tell her." On a blink, he snapped his focus to her. Tulsi's head still moved in a slight shake. "Nymph."

The slow command made her clench her jaw, pressing her lips together. His commands had never steered her wrong. But if he thought she was going to save herself and leave him to a grave fate, he would learn how it felt to be wrong.

On a single nod, he expected her to go. Instead, she boosted up to rub her cheek against his. They'd been at each other's sides since they met. They'd never been more than a room away from each other. Walking away felt wrong.

"Didn't think you were so sentimental, Wreck," Coombs said, slamming out of the car. He opened the side door and reached across the back seat to get hold of her. "Move your fucking ass."

Tulsi didn't want to be torn from Wreck's side, but he'd asked her to go quietly. Letting Coombs pull her out of the car, Tulsi kept her focus on the vehicle for as long as she could. Eventually, she lost sight of it. Coombs yanked her along, through the other cars toward the entrance of the store.

"You don't get a lot of dates, do you?" Tulsi asked.

Coombs thrust her toward the shopping carts. She pulled one out, but he grabbed it away from her.

"You do the shopping," he snapped. "Get what you and your boyfriends need. This is your only chance."

Apparel took up a huge section of the store. Without asking about budget, Tulsi grabbed clothes for herself and multiplied everything for the men by three. They weren't too difficult to buy for, jeans, tee-shirts, underwear, sweatpants and a couple of hoodies each. Picking socks from the rack, she speculated about their shoe sizes.

Thinking about whether or not they'd need new footwear shot a dart of fear into her. They'd only need new boots or sneakers if they were going to be with Merchant for a long time.

"Didn't get much for yourself," Coombs said, using the cart to force her back into the women's section… The lingerie section to be exact. "Get those ones."

The basques and garter belts did seem to be more his style than the plain cotton bras and panties she'd selected while there before. "I don't need any of those things."

While Tulsi had been putting tee-shirts and jeans in the cart for herself, Coombs had tossed in more than a few dresses and skirts. Seemed he preferred the short and low-cut varieties.

"I say you do," he said. "If you don't pick out your own sizes, we'll take a trip to the changing room and I'll check the fit of everything up close."

The last thing that she wanted to do was strut around in a private fashion show for the letch.

"You do remember Wreck is right outside," Tulsi said, doing as he'd said and selecting her size in the negligees he pointed out.

"Who fucking cares? He's at gunpoint, what's he gonna do?"

"He won't always be at gunpoint," she said. "If we're in here for hours, he'll know that something happened… I'll tell him everything you make me do… He does like to say that revenge is a bitch."

Okay, so he'd only said it once and in a different context, but the implication wasn't exactly a lie.

"Do you think I'm afraid of your thug?"

Her lips curled as she fingered the lace of another bra. "I think if it was a fair fight, you wouldn't stand a chance."

Wondering what kind of underwear might entice Wreck, she began to pick out some pieces for herself.

"How the fuck did you get mixed up with Wreck and his stooges?" Coombs asked, checking the sizes she'd picked out and hunting down more things he liked the look of to throw them into the cart. "I never heard of Wreck having a girl."

"Why do you care?" she asked, heading across the section to select some nylons.

Most of the dresses Coombs had picked out were daywear, but she'd rather be prepared with as much protection as possible, just in case.

"It's weird," he said. "Even Merchant said it. Everyone hears whispers that Rowdy and Wreck are tight. But tight enough to share a girl? Never heard of it. You paying a debt?"

"Maybe," she said, holding her head up as she wandered through the store to look for the toiletries section.

As she passed various stands, she selected some snacks and made a mental note to stop at the produce section too.

"Merchant will pay it off for you," he said. "Whatever you owe them, Merchant will clear it."

"In exchange for what," she asked, picking up shower gels, deodorants, and shampoos for all of them.

Tulsi knew there was no debt to pay. That didn't mean she wouldn't take advantage of this opportunity to glean some information.

"Loyalty," he said, moving in closer when she went to the dental section to drop more items into the cart. "Merchant can protect you."

"From what?" she asked, taking her attention from the floss to lay it on him. "I can't be loyal to a man I've never met."

"You have met Baines," he said. "Baines told you at Teal's… this is the winning side. You stick with your stooges, you're only gonna end up dead."

Walking sideways, she perused the aisle. "And that girl Baines murdered? Was she one of Merchant's?"

"Alexis was one of Keaton's," Coombs said, like that should mean something to her. "Baines tracked her down for information. Soon as there's a hiccup in operations, we guess Keaton's involved… Alexis said no… She would know. Alexis was one of Keaton's favorites."

After grabbing shaving gel and foam, Tulsi chose the most expensive razors she could find. "If he's questioning people that means he's not sure Kieran did it."

"Nah," Coombs said, staying back when she glided toward the tampons.

Since having the contraceptive implant put in her arm, Tulsi had stopped having periods. But she wasn't about to tell Coombs she didn't need the items that made him uncomfortable. For the first time since entering the store, she had space to breathe.

"Nah, he's not sure?"

"Nah, he's sure," Coombs said. "Him and Styx took the shipment from the courier… After that the trail goes dead. Something happened on their watch. That makes both of them responsible whether they took it and sold it themselves or not."

"You asked Styx?" she asked, touching the hair products, paying more attention to the conversation than what she was putting in the cart, even though she tried to make it appear she was intent on the merchandise.

"Me?" Coombs asked on a scoff. "I'm containment not investigation, sweetheart." Coming up behind her, he wrapped both arms around her, holding her tight to him. "It's my job to keep pretties like you in line… You sign on with Merchant, I can ask to have you special… for me… We could have some fun… Baines, he listens to me."

Keeping the disgust away from her stance was difficult. Thankfully, it was a reprieve to have him behind her because he couldn't see her face. He was grinding his erection into her ass, but it wasn't the first time she'd felt such an unwelcome intrusion.

"What does it involve?" she asked, tipping her chin toward her shoulder, trying to distract him before his slithering hands reached her breasts. "Giving Merchant my loyalty… Would he let me go?"

"Might," Coombs said. Releasing his embrace, he took her hand to lay their joined digits on the cart handle together. "Eventually… You'd have to prove you meant it first."

"How do I do that?"

Coombs shrugged and directed them down another aisle to head straight for the condoms. "Don't know exactly… You'd have to tell him what you know."

"About Kieran?"

Unfortunately, that didn't amount to more than Kieran had told them in their cell at Teal's.

"About whatever he asks," Coombs said and spun to hold up a box of condoms. "You like cherry?" Making herself smile, Tulsi nodded. Just the assumption that she might be open to being intimate with him seemed enough to buy his confidence. More than a few boxes of condoms went into the cart before he moved onto the pleasure gels and lubricants to throw in a bunch of those too. "Think all of these are edible… What's your favorite flavor?"

"I'll try anything once," she said. When he met her eye, she laughed. "Don't know until you try, right?"

"No," he said, his eyes a little brighter. "Guess you don't."

Her positive response only increased his glee and he selected even more products from the aisle. His mind was distracted, which worked out in her favor.

"The shipment went missing," she said. "Somewhere between the courier and Kieran." Seemed that Styx was the most likely culprit. If Kieran was telling the truth. "Does Merchant expect to get the drugs back or is it the money that he wants?"

Coombs was selecting other things, but she didn't pay much attention to what he was adding to her hoard. "Merchant doesn't give a damn about the money. Well, he does, but he has a thing about weakness… One guy steals from him, everyone thinks they can steal from him."

That meant it wasn't about getting what was his or even what was owed. "He wants payback."

"He's got to show everyone he's no limp-dick pussy... If his enemies took from him... if he has a mole in his ranks..."

So, if Kieran and Styx had stolen from him, Merchant wanted to punish them... maybe kill them. But if they were working for his enemy and had passed the shipment on to another boss, Merchant wanted their superior to know he wouldn't let it happen again.

"He needs to know who the mastermind is," she murmured.

"Gotta say, don't think it helped that Kieran showed up with his brother and Wreck... Set all kindsa minds turning."

What did that mean? "Because he showed up to Teal's with back-up? What does Merchant think that means? That Kieran is the mastermind?"

"Wreck is the guy you call when you're desperate. His loyalty is to whoever pays him the most or whoever he owes. Don't think anyone doubts he owes Rowdy, but Kieran is small time. So small time it should be crazy to see those two together. Kieran doesn't know shit. Thinks he's something, but he's nothing."

"If he's nothing, why do you want him?"

"Kieran is easy to squeeze, I guess," he said, scanning their wares. "Anything else you need, sweetheart?"

"Let's do one more lap."

Tulsi didn't want to push her luck by asking too much. The pieces Coombs had already given her were helping to build a clearer picture of what awaited them.

The next time they moved around the store, she paid more attention to what she was choosing. Covering all bases, Tulsi got everything any of the four of them would need and grabbed four large sports bags in different colors.

After going through the register, Coombs took her to the coffee bar, and gave her time to sort everything into the separate bags. Black for Wreck, indigo purple for her, dark gray for Rowdy, and blue for Kieran. That way everyone could make their escape as soon as possible.

Not that she put it that way for Coombs. Once her

work was done, she snatched up a bottle of water, and carried the bags, with Coombs help, back to the car.

Everything was dumped into the trunk. A tense air hung in the car when she climbed back in. But with a smile on her face and a laugh in her voice, Tulsi wasn't about to apologize to Wreck for coming back, even though it was obvious he hadn't wanted to see her return.

Coombs was lighter, joking with her, as he got them underway again. Ignoring Wreck's scowl, Tulsi tucked her arm around his and laid her head on his arm. She was in this, just like him, and he would have to get used to that, one way or the other.

TEN

SOMETHING ABOUT THE way the car jolted around a corner made Tulsi's eyes open. At some point, her head had slid from Wreck's arm onto his lap; she seemed to be drooling on his jeans.

Blinking her tired eyes, she sat up, wiping her mouth. "Where are we?" she croaked.

The car came to a stop. It wasn't easy to see where they were, there was so much darkness around them. Tall buildings stood on either side of the car. In the shadow of an alley, it was tough to make out, but she was sure there was another vehicle parked up ahead. A dumpster blocked her view of figuring out if it was one she should recognize.

Confirmation came when someone got out of the car to approach. As the figure got closer, she realized it was Baines.

"Keep him under control," Coombs said to Hillam and shifted to the door, opening it to put a foot on the asphalt. Before he got out, he surprised her by twisting to look her way. "You coming, sweetheart?"

"I…" she said, glancing at the scowling Wreck who was fixated on Coombs. "Yes."

Shuffling to the side door, Tulsi clambered out of the

car and stumbled toward Baines who was waiting against the opposite wall.

Wearing a proud smile, he held an open hand toward her. "Heard you might be interested in making the smart choice, Pretty Tulsi."

"Maybe," she said, fighting her urge to retch as she put her hand in his.

Baines tugged her hard, so she fell against him. "We'll have to report to Merchant, tell him if we can trust you."

"Depends if I can trust you," she said, raising her chin to look up at him.

"You're right to be suspicious," he said, still smiling. "He needs a new favorite… And so do I."

Bowing down, Baines kissed her. This was no brief encounter. Forcing herself to close her eyes because she knew Coombs was close, Tulsi did her best to respond. His tongue was hard and dry, not at all as sumptuous and in control as Wreck's. That his technique was so jerky and unnatural made it all the more difficult to remember she was supposed to be pretending to enjoy the moment.

Didn't seem to matter though. Baines couldn't have looked more pleased and aroused when he eased away from the kiss. Her meek smile didn't feel spontaneous, but it seemed to be enough to convince him.

"Unfortunately, we don't have time to finish this," he said, stroking her arm. "We've got orders from Merchant."

"What kind of orders?" she asked, lacing her fingers through his. "I thought we were going to see him."

"You'll meet him soon," Baines said, skimming his hand across her body to grope her breast. "Got a bit of business to take care of first."

Rather than grimace, she widened her smile, trying not to make it obvious that her jaw was so tight it was beginning to hurt.

"We had to make a detour," Coombs said, inching closer to her side. "We haven't been driving to Merchant… He gave us a job to do first."

"I thought we were the job," she said, playing the naïve innocent. "Getting Kieran to Merchant, I thought that's what he wanted."

"Sure," Coombs said. "'Cept another weasel took something from Merchant… Thought he could run and get away with it… We plan to show him that's not how it goes down. He's not in control. Merchant is always in control… and he never forgets. Fucker thinks he's safe." Coombs and Baines shared a snicker. "Thought he got away clean… But Merchant's got eyes and ears everywhere."

"Perfect opportunity to test out our new toys," Baines said. "Wreck is renowned for getting results. Merchant wants to know if that's true."

"You want him to work for you?"

"For Merchant," Baines said. "We're gonna find out how much he values his life… and yours."

She shook her head. "I don't think he gives a damn about me… not really."

"We're going to find out," Baines said. "Him and his buddy Rowdy are gonna deliver some payback or they'll find themselves on the receiving end."

"Want Hillam to take her and Kieran to the hotel?"

"Hotel?" she said. "We're staying in a hotel?"

Baines' fingertips edged under the fabric of her dress. Using all of her energy to restrain herself, Tulsi didn't react to the sickening violation.

"Nice one too," Baines said. "Your boy is gonna take down Putnam tonight…"

"Putnam?"

"The fuck who took what wasn't his… After, we gotta stick around to clean up the mess… shouldn't take more than a couple of days."

Tulsi didn't really know what that meant, but she kept her smile static. "Isn't it smarter to keep us all together?" she asked, noting the whisper of suspicion in Baines' expression. Sliding a hand up his body, she caressed his throat. "Merchant said you were the only one he trusted to keep an eye on Kieran."

"She's got a point," Coombs said. "Delray won't be here with the others until tomorrow."

Others. This was more than just a simple job.

"Grab Hillam and we'll talk strategy," Baines said to Coombs, picking her hand from his throat. He kissed her knuckles and began to guide her back toward the car. "You stay tucked up safe. You and me will finish this soon."

Baines opened the back door to push her inside while Coombs got Hillam out of the front. Once all the doors were closed and the men walked away from the vehicle, tension settled around her and the man at her side.

"You made yourself a deal," Wreck said. "Smart."

"They want you to hurt someone," she said, fixating on the center console between the front seats. "You and Rowdy. They're taking you somewhere to hurt someone who took something from Merchant... We were never going to him. Not yet. They want you to work for Merchant. You and Rowdy. This is the test."

"Who?" Wreck asked.

"Putnam," she murmured.

"Don't know him."

"That was the only name they mentioned. Said they're taking you and Rowdy to teach this guy a lesson... We'll be spending the next couple of days in a hotel while they clean up the mess... whatever that means. And they said Delray is arriving tomorrow with others."

"How many?"

She shrugged. "Don't know... What is it that you do?"

"Get results," he muttered as though his mind was elsewhere.

"I told them you didn't care about me," Tulsi said, keeping her volume low and her eyes on the stereo. "If you and Rowdy see a window to take them down or get out, you should do it."

"I should do it."

"I tried to tell Baines it was best to keep us all together, but he might take Kieran and I to the hotel first..."

"Nymph—"

"They need Kieran to fill in the blanks about the shipment... Either they already have Styx and he rolled on Kieran, or he's just as much in the shit. I don't know yet. But it's like you said, women are a commodity. They won't kill me. They won't kill Kieran. You and Rowdy are the strongest two, that's why they've kept you apart until now. Together, you'll make it out. You should go before the reinforcements arrive… Maybe this Putnam guy they want you to hurt will help you… maybe he'll have guys. This might be the only chance you have."

"You're right."

Trying to moisten her dry lips, she curled them into her mouth. For the first time, Tulsi was facing the truth that she was alone. To get out of this, she would have to be smart. Sharing herself with Baines, with Coombs, definitely with Merchant, she might gain enough favor to one day be set free. If not, she'd have to bolt and live on the run. Except, Baines had just told her that Merchant never forgot.

"Shit," she exhaled, swiping away a tear before it could leave her lashes.

"If Baines tells Merchant that you can be trusted, he won't put you to work, not right away."

"Not until he's bored with me," she said. "I know… Any other advice?"

"You don't need advice," he said. "You've already got it down… You know to listen. To use your assets to your advantage… You know how to smile when you want to scream."

Something she hadn't known about herself until meeting Baines. "This is not the kind of thrill I wanted," she whispered to herself and closed her eyes.

Giving in to emotion, letting herself cry, wouldn't achieve anything. Inhaling, Tulsi pushed her shoulders back and raised her chin. Whatever she had to face, she'd do it head on.

"You've gotta play both sides of this, Nymph. It's smart. Do what you have to do. Whatever you have to do. Forget morals and boundaries. Just stay alive."

"I know," she said with a nod and then glanced over her shoulder at him. "It's just… I'm going to miss having you around."

Turning and shifting onto her knees, she rose to press

her cheek to his. They'd only have another few seconds alone. The last seconds they'd ever exist like this. All that could've been deserved a moment of mourning. He'd never had a chance to ruin her, and now they'd never know if he would've.

The last thing she expected was for him to turn his head to capture her mouth. Tulsi wasn't sorry that his kiss would erase Baines', though she did regret it would be her last with the man who'd reached the deepest, most baser part of her desire.

"Wreck," she begged in a whisper. "Please… Don't make me want you more than I already do."

He didn't listen. Stealing her lips again, he plunged his tongue into her mouth, pressing hard like he wanted to pin her down. Yet, she pushed back, forcing him to kiss her harder. Wreck didn't even have his hands, yet she was owned by him. The man was in charge even when he was captive.

"Closer," he growled, ripping his mouth from hers to throw his head to the side.

Bringing it back, he caught her lip in his teeth.

Clambering on to straddle him as he slid down in the seat, she ran her hands down his body to cling to his belt. "I want it," she panted, dragging her teeth through his stubble down to his jaw. "Let me have it before you leave me forever."

As much as she wanted it, there was no way there would be time for them to consummate their attraction.

"Up," he barked, tossing his head back. "Get the fuck up."

Rising high on her knees, she yelped when he sank his teeth into her breast. "Oh," she gasped, driving her fingers into his hair. "My Ruin…"

Using his teeth, he pulled the edge of her dress away from her flesh and sucked her nipple into his mouth. Even believing that she may have switched sides, he still wanted her, and didn't hesitate to bury his face into her cleavage.

Dropping down, she stole her chest away from him. It wasn't that she didn't enjoy having him there. Tulsi wanted more. Wanted to have all of him. Yanking his belt loose, she tried to work on his fly.

"Baby, you'll get us both killed for sex."

"It's worth it," she said, sinking her hand into his underwear to grab hold of his cock. Relaxing her weight onto him, she rested her lips on his. "Tell me it wouldn't be worth it to feel yourself inside me."

"You're out to ruin me, Nympho," he said on a groan when she squeezed him tight.

Tulsi kissed him one way and then the other. "Tell me I can," she whispered, sliding her fist up and down his impressive length, testing the density of his girth that made her mouth open on instinct. "Please... Ruin me..."

Angling his head, he looked past her. "They're coming back, baby."

Much as she didn't want to, Tulsi worked quickly to fasten his pants. On a sigh, she tucked her breasts away.

Her eyes drifted up to his. "Guess this is goodbye, Ruin."

Wreck didn't respond. The determination in him could be suspicion; she'd understand that. He did think she was working both sides. Maybe she was, even Tulsi couldn't be sure what she was doing anymore.

Sense and attraction didn't go hand in hand, not when it came to Wreck. Baines was probably a smarter option, though he was more volatile. Not that it mattered; Tulsi couldn't rely on anyone except herself.

The door beyond her opened and someone was thrown in at her side. It was only when the door closed again that she registered who it was.

"Kieran?"

"Tuls," he said, shifting to look at her. His hands were zip-tied at his back, just like Wreck's, and she guessed Rowdy's too. "What happened? How are you doing? Have they hurt you?"

"This isn't a good sign," she said, and whipped around to seek Wreck. "They're separating us."

Wreck looked past her to Kieran. "Look after her."

The door behind him opened. "You, fucking move," Coombs said and grabbed Wreck's shoulder.

That proved to be a bad decision because at the same time as Wreck got out, he also shoulder barged the guy, sending him down to the asphalt.

Wincing, she ducked to look outside at Coombs. "Wreck doesn't like to be touched, honey."

It might seem that she was trying to help him out. But she was laughing at him on the inside. Coombs had been floored by Wreck who didn't even have his hands available.

Moving to the side, Wreck blocked her view of Coombs. That gave her the chance to slide closer and lick his fingertip. Kieran probably couldn't see what she was doing, but Wreck sure knew. Opening his curled fingers, he raised them to seek her out. Tulsi was happy to oblige and tilted her face to rub her cheek against him.

This was their goodbye, and the first real whisper of a caress.

"You're a fucking asshole," Coombs barked.

"Get up and give me my hands," Wreck growled. "I'll show you what a real asshole I can be."

He made her smile. Closing her eyes, she dipped her chin to kiss his fingertips. His words were vicious, filled with the promise of violence and terror. Yet, his hand moved with such slow deliberation, she was sure he was taking the time to memorize her texture.

Coombs did climb to his feet. Instead of doing as Wreck asked, he shoved him back. Somehow Wreck managed to cradle her and stay put, which probably only increased Coombs aggravation.

"You fucking touch me and I'll take your friends apart."

"My friends apart?" Wreck said, still blocking the open car door, his fingers moving on her face. "'Cause you can't face me man-to-man."

"I fucking could if I wanted to," Coombs said and got closer. "But I gotta save my energy for that beauty behind you."

The mocking satisfaction of Coombs voice was enough to contort her lip, both with disgust and anger. Wreck responded too. Curling his fingers away from her face, both of his hands tightened into fists.

Cupping them in her palms, she kissed each of his

knuckles. Her lips moved against them in a silent plea for him to be calm. This was not the opportune moment to flee. Obviously, they'd put Kieran in the car because they planned to take Wreck and Rowdy to Putnam in the head vehicle.

Wreck exhaled a sneer of ridiculing disbelief. "Even with all your energy, you couldn't keep up with that one… Why do you think it took three of us?" No doubt Coombs had no idea how to interpret that. Wearing a smile, she sucked Wreck's index finger into her mouth and closed her teeth around it, biting into him. "And she has a thing for sinking her teeth in."

Her smile grew. Tulsi dug her teeth in deeper before sliding her mouth back and then advancing again, mimicking a more intimate act.

Coombs laughed. "Yeah, you couldn't satisfy her, but I will. Get moving or your boy Rowdy gets a bullet between the eyes… Move."

Wreck had little choice except to listen when Hillam approached, gun in hand. "What's the problem?"

"No problem," Coombs said. "Just putting this fuck in his place." He side-nodded. "Move!"

Wreck was slow to edge away from the door. Coombs was the one to slam it. As he did, Wreck looked back at her. Lowering his brow in a way that almost felt intimate, Wreck's attention provoked her to smile in a similar hue. This would be their last moment existing together. She wanted him to remember her wearing a smile.

Coombs poked him in the back. Wreck lunged his way to startle him and seemed satisfied when Coombs recoiled. He sauntered around the hood and past Hillam to head toward the other car. If it wasn't for the zip-ties, no one would know that he was walking under duress.

"Did he treat you fair?" Kieran asked, his voice deeper, somehow more curious. "Wreck can be a real asshole."

"No," she said, watching the trio fade into the shadows further down the alley. "Not with me."

"You got close?"

"Two days practically strapped to each other. You

could say we got familiar."

"No one gets familiar with Wreck," Kieran said. "How about Coombs? Did anyone touch you?"

Coombs and Wreck disappeared into the car. Hillam headed back their way.

"Hillam's coming back," she said, sinking down in the seat. "We have to be quiet."

"Rowdy is beyond pissed," Kieran said, which actually gave her hope. "Don't be surprised if they fuck us over."

"If they don't…" she said just before Hillam reached the driver's door. "I'll be disappointed. I hope I never see Wreck or your brother ever again."

While she might miss Wreck and wonder what it might have been like to be with him, Tulsi would take his freedom over satisfying her curiosity. She'd always wanted to meet a man who'd thrill and excite her, and she had. Shame their paths had crossed for such a brief time. It was over. He was gone.

ELEVEN

TEAL TRAILED ALONG in Hillam's wake to take over the driving duties. Coombs was going with Baines. Their new driver talked a lot more than the previous one. He seemed to take particular delight in taunting Kieran. Tulsi felt for him. The guy might be a fool, but no one deserved to be bullied and ridiculed.

The fact that Kieran didn't say much suggested he'd lost his fight. If he'd been putting up with the same thing for days, he'd probably lost the will to argue.

Getting to the hotel was a reprieve. Baines had said it was a nice place. While they were in a city and that seemed to be true, the hotel wasn't top of the line five star. Teal took her with him to check in, after issuing the usual threats about the others safety.

Tulsi was taken from the vehicle first and treated to some alone time with Teal. Kieran stayed in the car with Hillam. No doubt her zip-tied associate was relieved to have a reprieve from the mocking.

Having already known that Teal wasn't the nicest of people, Tulsi figured that her opinion of the guy couldn't get any lower. Turned out, she was wrong about that too. The idiot was even more handsy than Baines.

She understood why he took her arm to lead her through the lobby. It made sense to keep her close in case she tried to bolt. The proximity also allowed him to whisper threats against Kieran, Rowdy, and Wreck. But there was no need for him to stick his hand up her skirt to fondle her ass at the front desk.

Even the clerk seemed uncomfortable when Teal began to make leery remarks about what they'd get up to in their hotel room.

Ignoring his immaturity, she tried to pick up on as many details as possible. The reservation had already been made under Baines' name. It was for two rooms, adjoining, each a triple. The clerk explained that each room had two full-size beds and a couch that pulled out into a third bed.

Just the idea that there could be a real bed waiting for her spurred her excitement. As soon as it occurred to Tulsi that one of the goons may expect to share it with her, she went cold.

Wreck wasn't coming back. After he and Rowdy escaped, Baines would be mad. He might not kill her, but he could take out his frustrations on her. Teal would be angry too, probably embarrassed. That pride of his would be dented. Coombs had already promised to take advantage of her, and she knew Hillam wouldn't be left out.

That realization made her phase out. Teal dragged her to the elevator and groped at her breasts while slobbering on her neck as they ascended. Tulsi didn't feel any of it. Losing Wreck, the prospect of him, was difficult. The repercussions of it were even more terrifying.

There was some solace in knowing that Wreck and Rowdy would be freed from what was never their fight in the first place. It wasn't her fight either. But at least with them gone, there were fewer people to threaten.

Teal used a keycard to let them into a room. He pushed her inside, past the bathroom and into the body of the room. Large as it was, it accommodated little more than the furniture. The hotel might be semi-classy, but they were in a budget room.

He locked the door and pulled a cellphone from his

pocket. Tulsi listened to him instructing Hillam to join them and bring the bags from the trunk. She sat down on the bed, looking toward the broad window that stretched the width of the room. Outside was darkness only broken by the twinkling lights of the city. The twentieth floor, they were on the twentieth floor, room twenty twenty-one. High up there, it was doubtful that the window even opened. There was no escaping. Not unless she could walk out the door.

Grabbing a pillow from beneath the comforter, Tulsi hugged it to her body. Some subconscious corner of her mind was screaming at her to protect as much of herself as she could, while she still could.

If Wreck was free, if he and Rowdy had made their escape, she imagined Teal would've got a call from Baines or Coombs. Unless, of course, her cohorts had taken out Baines or the goon was trying to pursue them. Tulsi hoped she'd find out how they made their escape. If the goons discussed it, she'd hear the tale, though she didn't imagine they'd be honest.

Teal hung up the phone and turned away from the window to look at her. "We're not gonna have much time alone," he said, like she should be disappointed by that. In truth, that was the best news she'd had since this started. "We should make the most of it."

Tulsi chastised herself for relaxing too soon. She should've understood that just because news sounded good, didn't mean it would end that way.

Holding the pillow tighter, she used her limited time to decide how she should handle him. Already Teal was sauntering around the other bed, tossing what he probably thought were his bedroom eyes her way.

If she fought him off, she would make him mad. Except she'd led Baines to believe that she might be open to coming across to their side. Being vicious with his man wouldn't encourage Baines to trust her.

"I don't know that we should," she said when Teal sat beside her. "I don't know the rules."

"Rules?" he asked, sliding closer. "What rules? Right now, I make the rules."

"I know… I know you're in charge… It's just… Baines said he wanted to be with me," she said, wriggling her fingers between his to take them off her leg. "But what if Merchant wants me? I don't want to upset him by being with all his men before I'm with him."

"Merchant is cool. He's shared women before."

"Maybe," she said, playing it coy. "But Baines said I might be a favorite… I want to go by Merchant's rules… Doesn't that show more respect?"

Curling himself around her, Teal touched her opposite leg. His fingers ascended and he wrapped their joined hands around his back. Already she could feel that he was pressuring her, maneuvering her into a vulnerable position.

"Merchant likes to know what a woman is into," Teal said, leaning in. "If I can tell him how to treat you, he'll be two steps ahead."

"I can tell him myself," she said, annoyed that all she could do was lean back. The pillow was still between them, she kept it clamped against her body. But his hand was getting higher beneath her skirt. "What if he wants me to himself?"

An abrupt knock on the door interrupted them. Tulsi had never been so relieved. Muttering to himself, Teal got up. Tulsi wasn't far behind. Still hugging the pillow, she leaped to her feet and got as far from the bed as she could.

"Thanks for leaving us with all the crap," Hillam said, complaining for no reason as far as she could see.

If anyone should be grouchy, it was Kieran. He was in front of Hillam, carrying the majority of the luggage. During their date, Tulsi hadn't been impressed by his talk of cardio and weight training. Now she saw how useful it could be because he hadn't broken a sweat.

All of the bags were dumped on the bed that she'd been on just a second before. As soon as his arms were free, Kieran came toward her.

"Baines said to keep them locked up until he got back," Hillam said, reminding Teal who was also coming her way.

Leaping out of Teal's way meant jumping into Kieran,

but she'd rather be in proximity to him than the goon. Hillam barged through them and opened the door to the adjoining room.

"Put him in the bathroom," Teal said, lunging past her to grab Kieran, who didn't budge.

Hillam got hold of him too and both of the thugs worked to pull him away from her.

"I'm not leaving Tulsi alone with you fuckers," Kieran argued, trying to wrestle free.

"Please," she said, unsure what Kieran knew about her playing both sides. "Just go with them… I don't want anyone to get hurt."

"That's right," Teal said. "Do what you're fucking told like a good little lapdog."

Kieran was less of a lapdog than Teal who seemed to delight in pleasing Merchant and Baines. But he was obviously used to running his own racket too. She got the impression he saw himself as a bigger dog than he actually was.

Her sorrow probably showed to Kieran when he made eye contact. They were helpless. Both of them. If he pushed back, the men would hurt her.

A new kind of anger bled from him when his attention switched to Teal. "You're a sick fuck. All of you are sick fucks," Kieran barked. "Who the hell forces a woman to—"

Hillam's slap was so unexpected that it silenced the room. Tulsi had been hit by a man before. It wasn't something that she often thought about. The moment Hillam's hand made contact with her face, she was taken back to her last experience with a violent male.

The impact sent a sting flashing through her head and heat burst behind her eye. Pain throbbed in her mind, giving her an instant headache.

"You fuck," Kieran said, leaping forward to swing at Hillam. Teal got a hold of him and hauled him back before he could make contact.

Hillam's arm rose.

Seeing his fingers curl into a fist brought her out of her daze and back to reality. "Wait, no," she said, stumbling back. "No… Kieran will behave, he'll behave." She said the words and followed them up with a beseeching look. "Please…" Though he still wore an expression of anger, Kieran did soften from his stance. "We're going to be good."

They had to be good. If they weren't, their jailors would be riled before they learned that the other half of their prisoners had freed themselves.

Trying to muster some sense of poise in spite of the pain in her head and the blurred spots in her vision, Tulsi side-staggered toward the bed to fumble for Kieran's bag. Without moving, she raised it up in his direction. Teal was the one to stomp forward to collect it.

"Yeah, that's your shit," Teal said, throwing the bag at Kieran.

"My shit?"

"Get the fuck out of here," Teal said, shoving Kieran into the second bedroom.

"I…" she said, hooking her arm through the handles of her bag and Wreck's to pick them up. "I'm going to take a shower."

She didn't know why she took Wreck's bag. It made no sense. The guy wasn't coming back. He didn't need any of the things she'd picked out for him. All she could attribute her confusion to was the slap. Until she reached the bathroom door, Tulsi didn't even realize that she still had the pillow tucked under one arm.

With a stupor still over her, she wandered into the bathroom and locked the door. Breathing out, she relaxed and let everything fall to the floor. Just a few seconds later, she followed by slumping into a crouch. Hugging her knees to her chest, she rocked to comfort herself.

Wreck was gone. Kieran was volatile. And what she'd been through was nothing to the horror that would no doubt follow.

TWELVE

EVEN THOUGH IT TOOK an age to dry her hair with the blow-dryer in the hotel bathroom, it was only as Tulsi stood there, trying to imagine some semblance of normality that she started to get over her disorientation.

The shower had felt good, washing her hair, even shaving her legs, gave her back some sense of self. Drying her hair had been the cherry on the cake. It was odd to feel such a sense of safety in such a confined space, but being alone was better than being in the room with the men.

After plucking and preening, there was nothing left to do. She pulled on a tank top and shorts pajama set and grabbed the toweling robe from the back of the door. Bringing the pillow in, even though it had been an accident, turned out to work in her favor.

Although the tile floor was all she had to lie on, at least she had somewhere soft to rest her head. Reaching up to pull the cord to switch off the light, she lay on her side, covering herself with the robe. Somewhere, out in the world, Wreck was gaining his freedom. That thought meant she closed her eyes with a smile on her face.

Sometime later, a loud bang scared her eyes open. Sitting up, Tulsi looked around in the darkness, trying to remember where she was and what was going on. The bang came again, this time, it was three short, sharp sounds. A door. Someone was knocking on a door.

"Open the damn door," someone snapped and a handle rattled.

The lingering humidity and smell of conditioner reminded her where she was. The bathroom. Stretching over her head, she searched for the light cord and used it to drag herself onto her knees. Shuffling to the door, Tulsi was turning the lock before wondering if it wouldn't have been a better idea to make them bust through it.

The moment it clicked, the door began to open. Tulsi fell back onto her butt and scrambled backwards, trying to get away from it.

"Get washed up," a male snarled.

The voice came from outside the room while another person was thrust forward into it like they'd been pushed. On her back, propped on her elbows between the tub and the toilet, Tulsi tossed her hair away from her face. As her chin rose, she set eyes on the last person she expected to see.

"Wreck," she whispered.

The door behind him slammed. Wreck reversed to turn the lock, trapping them inside.

Flipping onto her hands and knees, she crawled to him. "What did they do to you? Why the hell are you here?"

Crawling around him, Tulsi rose on her knees to cradle his hands. Shocked to find that they were once again zip-tied together, her heart hurt when she saw the swelling in his knuckles.

"Oh, baby," she murmured, rubbing her lips against him. Placing kisses across each of his knuckles she rested the cushion of her cheek against him. "What did they make you do?"

Although she'd asked the question, the answer was obvious. They'd uncuffed him just long enough for him to do their dirty work for them.

"Let me help," she said, shuffling on her knees over to the vanity to turn on the cold water.

Ice would be better to prevent swelling, but she had

to do with what she had. Grabbing a washcloth, she drenched it in cold water and wrung it out. As the water ran through her fingers, Wreck's boot touched her calf, betraying that he was behind her.

Twisting to peek up at him, she read his expression. It told her that water was the last thing on his mind. He'd come back. Tulsi didn't know why. Rowdy probably refused to go or maybe they had tried to escape and been unsuccessful. Whatever it was, they were together. They were alone. Together.

Forgetting about the water, Tulsi moved around until she faced him. Wetting her lips with a slow lick of her tongue, she began to unbuckle his belt. It didn't even matter that he hadn't said a word. It didn't matter that she had no idea what he'd done. All she wanted to do was take advantage of the gift they'd been given.

"My Ruin," she whispered, pushing his jeans and underwear down his legs.

Opening her mouth, she watched him watching her as she took his cock in both hands and guided him onto her tongue. Sucking him hard, she pushed forward and pulled back, warming and arousing him at an excruciating pace.

"Mmm," she purred, ducking forward, skimming her hands up, down and around his thighs.

Slipping both between, she played with him, picking up the pace, slowing it, cupping him, rubbing him, enticing him in every way she knew how. On her next powerful suck, his lips curled back from his teeth in a hiss. The reaction made her smile, but it seemed to make him angry.

"Fuck it," he growled from behind tight lips.

His hands moved higher, away from his back, as far as he was able to lift them in their bound position. Unsure what to expect, she was surprised when he brought them down hard against his body, using his form as a wedge to snap the plastic from his wrists.

"Wreck," she said, stunned and surprised. "You…" Shaking the plastic away, he wasted no time in bending down to get hold of her to haul her onto her feet. "This whole time you were able to…"

"Never makes sense to let the assholes know what you can do," he muttered, sweeping her hair away from her shoulder.

"But you just…"

"Yeah," he said, grabbing her hips to spin her around.

Bowing, he closed his mouth around her trapezius, the muscle that ran from her neck to her shoulder. Sucking and nibbling on her, he crouched to push her shorts down and only stepped back to draw her top off over her head.

"You get one shot," he said, running the tip of his tongue to her spine.

The quiver of need that tremored through her was hampered by the disappointment of the suggestion this was going to be a one-time thing.

"What if I need you more?" she asked, attempting to keep her vibrating voice steady while groping behind her to get hold of his cock.

He stopped with his tongue and stood so his face appeared above her head in the mirror. "One shot to say no," he said. "Once you're in, I have you any time I want you… Any time, Nymph. Until you say no… After that, I will never touch you again… Never."

The intensity of his voice gave gravity to his words. Wreck was giving her an out. Telling her she could refuse him. This wasn't a one-shot deal. He was suggesting more. "Any time" suggested a lot more. He'd keep on having her, at his whim, until she put a stop to it. Like a switch, she had the power to turn it on and then off again. Except, it seemed, she only got to use each option once.

Tulsi was already in whatever this was and couldn't envision a time when she'd want to say the word no to him.

Her lips began to curl though her heavy head sank back to rest on his body. "What about any time I want you?"

"Under me, you'll always be satisfied."

She didn't doubt that and may have considered the statement a joke if his hands weren't busying themselves with her breasts, driving her crazy.

"I won't ever say no to you," she whispered, inspired by his presence. "Command me, Ruin."

Instead of issuing orders, he bent down and hooked an arm under each of her legs. She whooped as he picked her up and put her on the vanity on her knees. Pushing them far apart, he spread her body wide open.

In this vulnerable position, all she could do was hold herself steady. With both hands flat on the mirror, she caught glimpses of him stripping out of his clothes behind her. Tulsi didn't get a full view of him, and may have been disappointed about that if it wasn't for the thrill of anticipation buzzing through her.

Her stomach jumped and flopped. Butterflies multiplied until they seemed to be fluttering through every inch of her bloodstream.

"Wreck," she breathed when he moved in closer behind her.

Bracing a hand on the mirror above her, he lifted his head to make eye contact with her reflection. "I will ruin you, Tulsi Tern. I swear you will regret ever giving yourself to me."

With creeping satisfaction, her smile grew. "I only regret that it took me this long to find you."

His eyes closed in a blink and he surged forward, impaling her with the length of the cock she'd had in her throat only moments before. An involuntary yelp sprang from her lips. His hand came around to clamp over her mouth.

Not that her sound of shocked pain slowed him down, he pulled out and slammed back into her, forcing her body to accommodate his need. He kept one hand over her mouth and the other on her lower back, pushing her down so she would stay in the submissive position, open to him, unable to close her legs or move or object in any way.

It took time for her body to yield to his. Tulsi was no virgin, she'd experienced men, though never in this kind of position. It could be the pose he'd put her in, but she could feel every part of him as he pushed up into her, hissing and grunting like he was offended her body wasn't immediately sure it appreciated his invasion.

"Fucking take it," he growled, sliding back and driving into her again, their bodies coming together hard.

The force of his hand slid closer to his own body,

pushing lower on her spine. He moved his hand from her mouth to grab her hip which he pulled up, tilting her pelvis to take him deeper and harder.

"Fuck… Yeah," he hissed, watching himself slam in and out of her. "That's fucking it."

"Wreck," she panted, moving her hips in opposition to his advance. Rocking in time and against him, working with the pressure of his hands and the motion of his skill, Tulsi found her rhythm. "Oh my… Oh my God!"

Tulsi didn't expect to come so hard or so fast. The call was involuntary. It came from her desperate desire and the sensual satisfaction of them finally consummating the want that had plagued her since laying eyes on him.

"Shut the fuck up," he snarled. "No fucking way I'm pulling out or letting them in before I'm done."

He didn't even stop fucking her to chastise her. On a smile, she heard herself laugh and then clenched her teeth to hiss out.

"Don't stop," Tulsi begged, reaching back to plant a hand over his on her hip, squeezing him tight. "Please… oh, fuck, my Ruin… Don't stop."

There was almost a whine in her voice. Keeping her volume low was difficult. Squeezing her eyes tight shut, she panted, hissing and wheezing with each new thrust.

"You want it. You love it… You want it?"

"Yes," she said, her voice coming from somewhere in her chest though her desperation came from her gut. "Yes, please, I want it. Yes…"

The next wave of orgasm was difficult to contain. Her head fell, loose on her shoulders. Wreck shoved hard into her, shunting her forward so fast that the back of her head hit the mirror. The cushion of her hair probably saved it from breaking. Another hit would crack the glass.

She didn't care. Tulsi didn't care. She lived for feeling like this. Her whole life had been about being occupied by the man driving into her.

Settled in the fervor of their rhythm, Wreck reached around her body to press a fingertip to her clit. "Right here," he growled, bowing over her to drag his teeth against her back.

"I own you. I control you."

"Yes," she whimpered, tears of climax dropping from her eyes as he rubbed her clit, torturing the pinnacle with another orgasm. "Oh, God, Wreck. Mercy… please, mercy…."

Though she pleaded for respite, some compassion in her relief, Tulsi didn't want him to stop. She didn't want his body to leave hers. Never again.

"This is what you want. You want me right here," he said, shoving his cock hard into her. "My little nympho wants it. Dreams of it. Craves it… You crave cock, don't you, baby? Tell me the truth, girl."

"I crave your cock, Wreck," she ground out the words. "Shit, baby… Oh my… Ah."

Tulsi turned her mouth against her arm, digging her teeth into herself to suppress the exclamation of climax. It hit her so hard that her head began to hurt again. Heat suffused every part of her, and imploded in an impact that clenched her pussy so tight around him it seemed to be claiming him.

Neither he nor his cock denied her. The growl of hot breath that vibrated across her back signaled his release. The imprint of his bite on her shoulder ached, yet joy curled her lips.

"Wreck."

"Stay," he said.

Smacking her ass, he withdrew, leaving her alone on the vanity. Tulsi's limbs were exhausted. They would probably be sore tomorrow, but she didn't care. Taking a few seconds to center herself, she was thinking about tossing her hair from her face when the shower sputtered to life.

She heard a zipper and some moving around. Dragging her knees further under her, she held the evidence of their joining to herself and kept on trying to breathe. She wasn't sure she would ever feel the same way about sex again. That in itself proved that Wreck had already ruined her for other men.

Tulsi was still contemplating that when she was suddenly scooped up off the vanity. On a gasp that she remembered to keep quiet, her arms fell around his neck.

Wreck's neck. Without even looking at her, he pulled back the shower curtain and bent to set her down in the tub. He stepped in with her, leaving her seated on the bottom of the tub while he went about showering.

There, in that position, she got the full experience of Wreck's form. The man was more than fit. The muscles of his thighs, his ass, his abs, all of him was pure in its peak definition. She didn't know why he needed to be so fit. She guessed that in his line of work, it helped to be capable of anything at any time.

"Wreck," she said, taking the handles at each side of the tub to pull herself onto her knees.

"Not yet," he said, rinsing the shampoo from his hair and shaking out the excess water.

Tulsi didn't know what they were waiting for. Despite what waited for them outside the bathroom, this moment was about as perfect as any she could've imagined. Hidden behind the closed shower curtain, there was an intimacy to the dimness around them.

One day. In another life. They could be a couple learning each other. Two people in the throes of early passion. Happy… Enraptured…

Shifting from her knees, she lay down to admire him. First, she trailed her toes up and down his lower legs. It didn't seem to bother him. Didn't seem to make him happy or angry. Tulsi just enjoyed the entitlement of being this near to him. Naked and vulnerable, both of them were exposed. Yet, there was no awkwardness. Nothing to be self-conscious about. Nothing to hold them back.

Raising her heels to either side of the tub, she opened her body to him, and waited for him to notice. It didn't take him long.

Once the soap was gone and he turned to reach for a razor, he spied her laid out beneath him wearing a saucy smirk.

"I gotta shave," he said, plain as day.

Tulsi wasn't going to have that. Closing her legs, she rose on her knees again. "No, you don't," she whispered. "Not before I've said thank you."

She'd lost count of how many orgasms he'd given her

on the vanity. He'd made her come in the motel the previous night too. It was unbelievable to think that had only been a night ago.

"Nympho," he said, but the stern tone didn't warn her off.

Slithering herself up his legs, she pressed her breasts into him and let her hands play between his thighs. "Yes," she purred, accepting the accusation. "I am. You've turned me into an addict... I'm addicted to you." Licking the length of his dick, she relished the sensation of it hardening beneath her caress. "I am addicted to your cock... I want to thank you for the delight... to thank him."

"You will," he said, touching her hair. "After I shave... Get the hell out."

If she wasn't mistaken, he was more amused than angry. That didn't mean he cracked a smile or revealed any humor. Kissing him again, she took him into her mouth and began to suck. After a half dozen advances, she switched to her hand and tilted her head to show his balls the same attention.

"Want me, baby," she murmured, kissing his head and sucking him into her again. "Want me as bad as I want you... Want me until it hurts..."

The movement of his jaw clenching filled her with hope. When he grabbed a handful of her hair, there was a moment of tension. Either he was going to throw her off or throw himself into it.

"Fuck you, Nympho," he said, grinding his teeth together, tightening his grip on her hair. "You want it? You prove it." Holding her so tight that he was almost pulling her away, he kept his dick just on her lips. "Work for it, Nymph... You prove how much you love my cock..."

Fighting the tug of his hand, her scalp screamed, but she fought to keep sucking his head, trying her best to pull more of him into her. When he let her go, she sprang forward, taking him so deep so fast that her body responded by trying to expel him. Tulsi breathed in through her nose on the withdraw, trying to recover as her eyes watered.

Wreck got hold of her hair again, and held himself

just on the threshold of her tongue. "Breathe," he commanded and gave her just a few seconds to recover. "Ready?"

"My Ruin."

He bounced in her mouth when she spoke.

"Regret it?" Her lips sealed around him in a smile. She shook her head, letting his fingers matt her hair. "Show me."

His fingers stayed in her hair, but loosened enough that she had control over how she pleasured him. Wreck didn't object to anything she did and within a couple of minutes, he was tightening his hold on her hair and spilling himself into her throat.

He watched her swallow and then drew her onto her feet. So many things had to be said. There were so many questions. This, them experiencing each other, was the most natural thing in the world. Tulsi had been waiting for Wreck her whole life. She'd found him, but it wouldn't be long until she lost him again.

THIRTEEN

WRECK EVENTUALLY GOT his chance to shave. Tulsi was busy blow-drying her hair for the second time that night. It wasn't all the way dry when the shower went off, but she was happy to watch him towel the water from his skin while she finished up.

He wasn't a patient man. She hadn't given it much consideration until Wreck took her wrist to pull her away from the blow-dryer before she'd hung it back up. He did like things his way.

The toweling robe was still on the floor; he shoved her toward it.

"Lay down."

"My pajamas are—"

"Not yet," he said, blocking her way when she tried to go toward the vanity.

Lowering to her knees, Tulsi took her time about sinking onto her side. "Not yet? What are we waiting for, Ruin?"

"Until I'm ready to cover you up," he said, picking up his bag to put it on the vanity. He raked around inside and pulled out a pair of sweatpants.

"Hey now, wait a minute," she said and laughed,

propping her head on her fist. "You keep me naked and cover yourself up. How is that fair?"

"Don't ever expect fair from me."

Closing his bag, he crossed to her. Dropping down on top of her, he distracted her with a kiss and then flopped onto his back, putting his head on the tile rather than the pillow.

"There is space for both of us," she said, sliding her head back to the edge of the pillow to leave most of it for him. She stroked the empty section. "I'd love for you to join me, but I can't promise not to bite." Putting a hand behind his head, Wreck turned his focus to her, and considered her for a moment. "What?" She exhaled a laugh. "I'm kidding. If you don't want me to bite anymore, I—"

He swooped toward her and grabbed her shoulder in his teeth, digging them in just deep enough to leave a mark. In a hiss of pleasured pain, Tulsi reached for him. Instead of letting her make contact, he released his mouth and pushed her onto her back with his body.

"You do what feels good," he said, stroking her stomach with his fingertips. "Do you like to bite, Nymph?"

"Never did it before you," she said, enjoying how he scrutinized his fingers trekking across her skin. "It's weird, but it just felt... natural with you... I wanted to mark you... It made me proud... You make me proud."

Looming over her, Wreck kept her trapped on her back between him and the wall. "If it feels good, it's allowed," he said, trailing his hands over her breasts, squeezing and pressing the sensitive flesh. "If it doesn't... use the word no."

"What if something I do to you doesn't feel good?" she asked, bending her elbow to rest her knuckles on his chest. "Will you tell me no?"

"I'm bigger than you, babe," he said, drawing his fingers down the center of her belly. "You do something I don't like, you'll be put in your place quick."

She laughed and tipped her chin higher to nip his arm with her teeth. "I might like that."

"You like force?"

"With trust," she said. "With you... I like that you're

bigger and stronger… I told you, it makes me feel safe. You make me feel safe."

"You know this ain't real," he said, his fingers just resting above her pussy. "Nothing in this clusterfuck is real. We do whatever is necessary to stay alive."

Something about the way he said those words revealed that this wasn't the first time he'd been in peril. Tulsi had guessed that, but the grimness of his words revealed the weight of his heavy conscience.

"I know," she said, disliking that she had to face the truth that there were no certainties.

"I told you to play both sides. It's the smart thing to do."

Advising her to play both sides was just a synonymous way to say he didn't trust her. Why should he? She'd been kissing Baines earlier that night. While he'd been away beating up people, she could've been up to allsorts with Hillam and Teal. Spilling his secrets, ingratiating herself, selling him out.

Just because they'd had sex didn't mean they meant more to each other or had more trust. Tulsi should hold herself back and be reserved. But Wreck was too powerful. The force of him sucked her into his orbit. Where her emotions and hormones were concerned, it seemed like his gravitational pull was inescapable.

"Why did you come back?" she asked, wondering if he was tempering her expectations or trying to convince himself. "Tonight. I thought you and Rowdy would—"

"I don't take orders from you."

"No, but you said you would—"

"I didn't," he said, sliding a finger south, over her clit. Rolling closer, he breathed against her mouth. "How does that feel, Nympho?"

Shimmers of tense pleasure sank into her. "You're using sex to distract me."

He kissed her. "Any time I can, I will."

"My Ruin… Tell me why you stayed…"

Licking the seam of her lips, he kept his tongue just out of her mouth. "I told you to leave and you stayed… If you can see this through, I can too."

Pushing his finger into her, he opened his mouth to inhale her exhale of pleasure. "Me? You stayed for me," she whispered, undulating her hips. Sliding her hands up his body, she looped her arms around his neck. "You stayed because I stayed."

"I stayed," he said. "Does it matter why?"

"The why is all that matters."

Wreck slid his tongue into her mouth and kissed her while his hand kept playing between her thighs. Only after he'd brought her to climax did either of them relax. His hand stayed on her, caressing her lower abdomen, right where the clench of pleasure was rooted.

"I love your hands," she said, picking his hand off her stomach to kiss his fingertips that tasted of her. "I love your mouth and your cock, sure, but I promise, I will never take your hands for granted. I can't believe I never thought about it before. They're so important."

"My hands?"

She laughed and cuddled his hand between her breasts. "Yes! They've been kept from me. Having them on me, having you feel me and hold me and touch me… Wreck, I—"

"I won't protect you," he said, his scowl deepening.

"I…" The warmth of contentment began to ebb. "I can't protect you either."

"I told you the only ass I'm interested in saving is mine. I don't make promises I can't keep… You're a good lay. A distraction. Something to do while there's nothing else going on. That's it. That's as far as this goes."

"I know. We're out for ourselves."

Except if that was true, the goons' threats of hurting others wouldn't work. Wreck didn't want to be responsible for her, she could understand that. If anything happened to her, he wouldn't want to live with the guilt of not fulfilling a promise.

"Rowdy is responsible for his brother," Wreck said. "Always has been."

"Coombs said you were tight. Where did you meet?"

"It was a long time ago," he said and sat up.

Stretching across the floor, he grabbed her pajamas.

"Done with me?" she asked when he dropped them on her chest.

"We're about to have company," he said, springing to his feet just a fraction before someone pounded on the door.

"You damage Merchant's merch, you pay for it, asshole!" Coombs called through the door. "You've been in there too long. What's going on?"

They were twenty floors up and there wasn't a window in sight. If the goon thought they were making a break for it, he'd overestimated their abilities.

"You have some weird kind of super hearing," she whispered.

"No," he said, crooking a brow. "You have a bad habit of being oblivious."

Under him, that was probably true. This lifestyle was new to her. Though she didn't know much about Wreck, it was obvious, he was no rookie.

She was quick to put her pajamas back on. Leaping up, she hung the robe on the door and grabbed up the pillow. Wreck started to scoop her things from the vanity back into her bag.

Suddenly, he paused. "What's that?"

She couldn't see what he was looking at and was busy tying her hair on her head. "What's what?" He picked something up to show her. "Tweezers."

"They're sharp," he said, noting the plastic cap over the end.

"They're pointed."

"Put on the robe," he said with urgency.

Coombs was pounding and calling to them, distracting her from what Wreck was getting at. "I… what?" she asked.

"Put on the fucking robe," Wreck said, snatching it off the back of the door to thrust it at her.

Dropping the pillow, she did as he commanded. "Okay, Jesus," she said, sticking her arms into the sleeves. "Happy?"

Wreck stuffed the tweezers into the pocket of the robe. "Do not go anywhere without those," he commanded.

The next bang made her jump. "Open the fucking door!"

"Wreck, I don't—"

Taking her hand, he pressed her fingers to the side of his neck. "Last resort. You feel threatened, pop the cap off those babies and drive them in here." He pushed her fingers deeper into the side of his neck. "Stab and drag." She glanced toward the door, but Wreck put a hand on her face to bring her focus back to him. "Tuls, tell me you hear me."

"I hear you."

"I could make a weapon out of the razor, but they'll notice if I take them apart... Those will kill as they are."

"Kill?" she said, taken aback. "I don't want to—"

"If it's kill or be killed..."

Hillam had hit her, she could take a hit. But if it came down to rape, she might be less inclined to accept the violation.

She nodded. "Okay."

"Forget morals and boundaries."

"Forget morals and boundaries," she repeated.

Wreck blocked her from the door when he unlocked it to let it swing open. Coombs was immediately ready to let loose... Until he saw that Wreck's hands were free.

Paling, Coombs staggered back a step. "How the hell did you—"

"Pretty is good with those nails," Wreck said, holding up his hands to show both were unfettered.

Coombs attention went to the side, in the direction of the body of the room. "Get over here."

Hillam rushed over. As soon as he noticed Wreck's hands were free and she was trapped behind him, he didn't seem to know what to do.

"What the... How do we..."

Could they rush now? Maybe. Wreck could take down both of these guys, definitely. But as soon as Baines and Teal heard the commotion, they could put bullets in Rowdy and Kieran.

"You try anything and your woman will pay."

"Again," she said on a sigh. "Guessed you had a taste for it. Wasn't the first time you hit a woman, was it?"

Wreck's head snapped around; he fixated on her. "He hit you?"

She nodded. Although she could tell he was tense, Tulsi had no idea what the admission would lead to. In a stride, Wreck tossed Coombs aside and pulled back his arm to punch Hillam in the face. The guy hit the wall and slithered down, blood spurting from him and pouring over his lips and chin.

Coombs hollered. Hillam screamed. But Wreck wasn't done. Bending down, he got the guy by the throat and dragged him upward, ignoring the blood that was gushing from his nose.

"I love a fight," Wreck snarled, pushing Hillam higher. "Nothing like a good fight or a good fuck to get the blood hot... I've got a new taste for both tonight."

Shocked, Tulsi couldn't take her wide eyes from the sight of the quaking man pinned by the one radiating with rage. Though there was movement in her peripheral vision, she couldn't check what was going on. Wreck was in charge, which meant Hillam, and his buddy, were in serious trouble.

FOURTEEN

SOMEONE GRABBED HER ARM. Tulsi was yanked out of the bathroom doorway and pinned back against someone's chest. Hard, warm metal met her temple.

"Put him the fuck down," Baines barked.

The vibration of his curt words on her spine revealed who had grabbed her.

"Wreck," Rowdy said, which suggested everyone was a witness to the chaos now. Even hearing his friend didn't divert Wreck's focus. "You gotta fucking yield, man… Let it go… Holy fucking hell, Wreck… Si!"

The exclamation made no sense to Tulsi. She doubted it made sense to anyone… except Wreck. On a hissing inhale, he stepped back and let Hillam crumple into a heap on the floor. Putting his hands together behind him, Wreck turned his back on the room, presenting himself to be restrained again.

"Get the ties," Baines said, releasing his hold on her as Coombs scurried away.

Tulsi was still trying to figure out what had just happened when Coombs came back. There was obvious hesitation when he had to step over his bleeding friend to approach the man who had caused the injuries. With nervous fingers, Coombs attached zip-ties to Wreck, looping one through the two on his wrists. Wreck was good and didn't cause any more damage.

"Turn around, fucker," Baines commanded, pushing her around to stand behind him. "You! Hillam, up."

"I think he broke my nose," Hillam said, not doing a great job of finding his feet.

Baines got in close to Wreck. "You try that shit again and we'll be delivering your corpse to Merchant... You and your buddy's. You're my fucking weapon now. 'Til Merchant says otherwise, you do what I tell you... No one else."

Wreck didn't react or respond, he just looked straight ahead. Baines stepped back and grabbed Hillam to force him away from the wall.

"Boss, I—"

"Pay it back," Baines said, giving Hillam a shake. "Hit for hit."

If that was the rule, Tulsi was due to hit Hillam. Though, she definitely preferred the way Wreck had done it. Before witnessing his ability or how quickly his mood could turn, she'd known that he was capable. Still, seeing it with her own eyes was... spectacular.

She shouldn't be turned on... Well, okay, so she knew that Wreck could turn her on. But he'd done that, injured Hillam, for her. Wreck could literally have taken the man apart with his bare hands. Facing the truth that Wreck had the ability to kill quickly, without a weapon, put a new slant on his admission that he got results.

Doing his best to widen his stance, Hillam pulled his fist back and punched Wreck's jaw. Tulsi winced more than her lover did. Wreck absorbed the blow on a slow blink like nothing more than a child had side-swiped him.

"Right, that's it," Baines said and cleared his throat. "Done."

He probably didn't want to acknowledge how pathetic his drone's hit had been. Baines turned and she got out of his way, flattening herself against the wall. Except, he paused to check her out. With a curious eye, he peered at her.

The tension rose. "Something wrong?" she asked.

"No," he said, distraction in his tone. Without taking his eyes from her, he waved over his shoulder. "Get to bed, all you bastards."

Baines grabbed her arm to pull her back into the bathroom as everyone else went past them to return to where they were supposed to be. When he closed the door, she tensed, fearing that Baines was about to erase the happy memories she'd just made with Wreck.

"You were wrong," he said. "Or you lied to me."

"I—"

"All three of them care about you," Baines said. "I don't know which way you're gonna come out of this. Either you're with us and you watch them go down, or you're with them, and Merchant orders me to kill you." No beating around the bush. "You've got a window to prove yourself, a small one."

"What do you want me to do?"

"Stay close to Wreck, to all of them. You hear about any plans, you tell me."

"What kind of plans?"

"Anything useful. What happened to Merchant's shipment," Baines said. "If they plan an assault on my guys."

Shaking her head, she worked to exude innocence. "I didn't know Wreck was going to—"

"I don't care about bullshit like that pissing match," Baines said, a frown seizing his features. "You stay close to them. Earn their trust. When the time is right, you'll prove to me, and to Merchant that you're smart."

"Did something happen tonight that—"

"No," he said. Angry suspicion narrowed his eyes. "Why? What do you know?"

Widening her eyes, Tulsi parted her lips in an innocent pout. "Nothing, I... I just wondered why you were asking now."

"We brought a guy back," Baines said. "Got him locked up tight next door. We're waiting for him to be... helpful ... The fucker is dividing my resources."

"Putnam?" she asked. "The one who stole from Merchant."

"That's right," he said, curling his fingers around a loose tendril of her hair. "Merchant wants his property back… You do this right and there will be a reward… Just keep 'em happy. Stay on the inside and report back. Nothing difficult. Nothing dangerous."

Sealing her lips, Tulsi took a slow breath while forcing herself to nod. Wreck was telling her to work both sides. Baines was giving her permission to do the same. Tulsi was smack bang in the middle of this. Earning trust when she didn't know how the situation was going to play out was tough.

"I will."

Baines smiled and gave her breast a squeeze inside her robe. "You are pretty, Little Tulsi."

Bending down, he captured her mouth. This time she didn't have to worry about closing her eyes, there was no one there to watch. It tortured her that Baines was stealing from her in this happy place.

Yet, kissing him kept the status quo. Tulsi couldn't pull away or refuse his advance even though all she could think about was how soon she could get to Wreck to replace one man's kiss with another.

When Baines pulled back, she showed him her smile. "Damn, I wish I could fuck you right here." She didn't say anything, just kept on smiling and laid a hand on his chest. "Gotta go back and be boss though, baby."

Of course he did. Because he was *so* important. Whatever. Tulsi was counting the seconds, waiting for his leering to end. Eventually, on an exhale, he opened the door and guided her out. He kept his hand on her back all the way to the bedroom.

Hillam was sitting on the edge of the bed closest to the door, Coombs was seated on the middle one. Wreck had been put in the pull out on the other side of the room, parallel to the window.

"Right, you fuckers, no more fucking drama," Baines said. "There are alarms on the doors, so don't even fucking think about pretending to be smart." That was said both to Wreck and toward the open adjoining room. "Try any more shit and your accommodations won't be so nice tomorrow… Pretty decides where she sleeps in here… Lady's choice 'til I say otherwise."

Sliding his hand up her back, Baines bent to press a kiss to her cheek, which she turned up toward him.

"Goodnight, honey," Tulsi said, wishing he'd leave the room.

"You be good," he said and smacked her ass.

It impressed even her that she managed a flirtatious laugh. Baines winked her way as he disappeared through to the other bedroom. Concealing her relief when he closed the door was difficult. She'd worried that the door would stay open, which would give him leave to come back through at any time. Though, it made sense. He wouldn't want Wreck, Rowdy, and Kieran to have any kind of access to each other.

After a breath of silence, Hillam spoke. "I've gotta wash this blood off."

Coombs got up to go after him. "Do you need ice?"

Tulsi's focus drifted to Wreck, who was already scrutinizing her through a scowl. Creeping toward him, she didn't hesitate to drop to her knees between his feet. Running her splayed fingers up the front of his thighs, she sighed out a moan of approval.

"My Ruin," she purred.

"Violence turns you on," he said, stating his observation.

"You turn me on," she said, curling her fingers around his waistband. Rising higher, she tried to seek his mouth with hers. "Punish me for wanting you, baby… Please."

"I'm not busting out of these for you again tonight," he said, nodding his head to the side. "Get in bed."

Without a smidge of hesitation, she climbed up onto the bed on her hands and knees and crawled toward the window. Pulling down the sheet that was laid over the bed, she plumped his pillow and combed her fingers through his hair when he lay on his side, facing her way.

"Don't do that lovey shit," he said, tugging away from her hand.

Reaching for the sheet, she laid it over him and made sure her robe was wide open before wriggling down beside him and tucking the sheet around them both.

"I wish you could put your arms around me," she said in a whisper, slipping her hand down the front of his sweats to stroke him. "You punched Hillam for me."

His glower stayed in place even after he closed his eyes. "I punched him because I wanted to punch him."

Clinging to his cock, she pushed closer and higher, brushing her lips over his jaw. "Did he hurt you, Ruin?"

He just breathed out a sound of disbelief. "You think a worm like that can hurt me?" Squeezing his dick hard, she worked one hand faster while the other deepened her caress. "Quit it." His hips retreated. "Don't wanna lie in my own spunk all night."

"I'd lie in it," she murmured, nipping his chin with her teeth. One of his eyes opened to peek down at her; his intrigue made her grin. "There are places you are welcome to put it too."

"Like?"

Circling her thumb around the head of his cock, she licked her lips before kissing him. "In my mouth," she whispered. "Or…" Taking one of her hands from his sweats, she peeled down the cups of her tank to press her breasts against him. "Here."

"You know where I prefer those."

Peeking over him, she ensured they were still alone before letting him go to wriggle upwards, aligning her chest with his mouth. Straight away, he kissed each of her breasts and her nipples, working back and forth between them both, spending plenty of time deep in her cleavage.

"Or you can stick with the classic option," she said, running her hands up and through his hair. Sliding her leg over his hip, she curled it around his ribs, tucking it under his restrained arm behind him. "My pussy won't say no."

"That implant you got still good?" he asked, his teeth closing on her nipple.

Her hands stalled. "How did you know I—"

"The scar on your arm isn't old."

"I got it done a few months ago," she said, slithering down to meet his eye.

"Before Kieran."

"Not *for* Kieran," she said, kissing him. "I told you who I choose. As long as I have a say, you will be the only man allowed to use my body for your pleasure."

"I told you to use your assets."

"You're giving me permission to be promiscuous… and to manipulate you with sex."

"Any time you can, you should," he said. "Don't give yourself to me so easy. You have a lot of power here, baby. No one's done anything to earn your loyalty… Make us earn it… Earn you."

"Would you want to?" she asked, combing her fingers through his hair. "Earn me? You said you couldn't protect me, so how would you earn—"

"I won't," he said, averting his eyes and pulling his head back from her fingers. "I said stop with the lovey shit."

"You said if it felt good, it was allowed," she said. "It feels good to touch you."

"Yeah, and I said if I didn't like it, you'd know," he snapped in a whisper. "Close your eyes and go to fucking sleep."

"You don't want to have sex while—"

"If I wanted to have sex with you, I'd be having sex with you." Something about his new brisk attitude intrigued her more than it discouraged her. Whatever was bugging him, she wanted to know more. "That's the way this fucking works, Nympho."

"Okay," she said, tucking herself closer to him. "I'll remember that, Ruin. You want me this way or would you prefer my ass on your cock."

Without explanation, he forced one of his legs under both of hers. Locking his thighs around her, he squeezed her. "You sleep right there."

"Okay," she said, hoping he wouldn't wake up with a dead leg. "So I can't get away or so no one can steal me?"

"Both," he grumbled. "Take your hair down… It's better loose."

Her lips curled. She turned her face up to his throat to kiss him as she did what he asked. Even though he'd claimed he wouldn't protect her, his actions suggested he wasn't quite ready to throw her to the wolves.

Of all the men in the room and the adjoining one, only one had matched violence with violence against someone who'd wronged her. Only one had advised her on how to be free and save herself. Only one had pleasured her to climax more times than she could count. And only one had returned to her despite having the perfect opportunity to flee.

"My Ruin," she whispered, spreading her fingers on his chest.

"What?"

"Dream of me," Tulsi breathed, fingering the definition of his torso. "Dream of my body… of being inside me… of what you want to do to me…"

For a second, he said nothing, and she thought he might have fallen asleep. Just as she'd almost given up hope of hearing his voice again that night, he exhaled a single word.

"Nympho."

FIFTEEN

IN THE MORNING, Tulsi awoke with an appetite only one man could satisfy. Her dreams were always vivid. A blessing and a curse all her life, never had her dreams conjured themselves into reality. But when she opened her eyes to find she was still against the hot, virile man who'd plagued her dream world all night, she wasn't sorry.

Rocking against his hard body, she was gratified to find his dick engorged. Only, she was clamped between his heavy legs and couldn't free herself to do with him as she pleased. Kissing his chest, she pushed up to try licking his throat and biting his chin.

He grumbled, probably preferring to stay in slumber. Tulsi was too awake to give up on her dream.

"Let me go, baby," she whispered, hoping the others in the room—if they were still there—were asleep. "Let me…"

Pushing on his thighs, she tried to pry them apart, but that only led to him clinging tighter. Squeezing her hands between them, she managed to get her hands inside his sweats. His legs relaxed when she began to stroke him.

His next groan was far more encouraging. Tulsi stifled her proud giggle against his chest. The last thing she wanted to do was wake the others in the room.

"Oh, you feel good, baby," she whispered, kissing his body. "So good… If only you were inside me… if only you were deep in my pussy."

His arms were still tied at his back, which presented a problem. Even on top, Tulsi could hurt him if she got too carried away. His legs relaxed a little more when she worked her fist faster around him. His body was yielding to hers even though it seemed like he was still asleep.

"That's it, my Ruin," she said, finagling her legs out from between his. "That's it."

Quickly pushing one leg of her shorts off, she stayed tucked as close to him as she could and hooked a leg around his hips to haul herself higher. She wouldn't get everything she wanted, but something was better than nothing.

Keeping her leg wound around him, she guided him into her pussy, pushing forward as best she could. Though with the way their legs were tangled, she got less than half of him into her. Still, he felt good filling her up, stretching her opening, whetting her appetite for him.

"Yes," she murmured, rocking her hips, tilting them so she could rub her clit and cup his balls at the same time. The gentle motion of her pelvis, taking what she could of him into her and easing back, then sliding forward again, felt almost tantric. Or at least what she imagined tantric would feel like. "Oh, shit."

The pulse of her pussy around him was quickening. Already her inner muscles were beginning to react to his invasion. She didn't doubt her hand meant for him was neglecting its duty, but the other was speeding over her clit. In her attempt to control her need to make noise, Tulsi dug her teeth into him.

"Put your arms around my neck."

His voice startled her. She'd been so caught up in what she was doing that she had almost forgotten anyone else was there.

"I was—"

"Put your arms around my neck, Nympho," he said, his voice gruff and deeper than normal as it hadn't yet woken.

"Hold on tight to me."

"Let me finish," she said, wriggling herself against him, trying to take more of him into her. "You feel amazing."

"You need to shower before these fuckers wake up."

Taking her by surprise again, he rolled onto his back. Somehow, he managed to coil his legs in hers to take her with him.

"I'll hurt you," she said, aware of how his hands clamped at his lower back were forcing his body to an awkward angle.

"Not if you put your arms around me."

In the new position, she was no longer pleasuring either of them, so she did as he said. Holding on tight meant he could move again. This time, he sat up on the edge of the bed, putting his feet on the floor.

Satisfied and relieved that he wasn't throwing her away, Tulsi let go of his neck for just long enough to direct his cock into her.

"You've gotta be fucking quiet, Nymph," he said as she began to move.

"I'll try," she whispered, occupying her mouth with his.

With her back to the room, she wouldn't be able to see if either Hillam or Coombs woke up. There was light coming from between the heavy drapes, but they were thick enough to block most of it out. From the dull illumination, she guessed the sun couldn't be all the way up. Although Tulsi didn't know exactly what time it was, it felt early.

Probably too quickly, she forgot all about the others in the room and began to move faster.

"Babe," Wreck said.

"Please," she murmured, squeezing her eyes closed. "I'm so close."

"Yeah, and I know what you're like when you come," he said and grabbed her lip in his teeth.

She yelped and kept on moving, but opened her eyes to find his concern was rising. He let go of her lip.

"Am I hurting you?" she asked, slowing down.

"Go into the bathroom."

"Ruin," she whined, rubbing her mouth on his stubble when he turned his lips away from hers. "Please, let me—"

"Do as you're told, Nymph."

Huffing, she climbed from his lap, grabbing for the loose leg of her shorts as they drifted down. Tulsi pulled them up and shrugged the robe back onto her shoulders as she trudged off, consumed by her petulance.

She could finish herself in the shower, but she didn't want to finish alone. Going into the bathroom, she turned on the water and shrugged out of her robe. Their bags were still in there and appeared untouched, though there was no way to know that for sure.

Stripping off her clothes, she pulled back the shower curtain to test the temperature of the water and grabbed a hair-tie from her bag to knot her hair on her head in a messy bun.

The sound of the door opening made her turn on a gasp. The shock of being intruded on was erased by seeing Wreck with his arms, still in zip-ties, but now in front of him.

"How did you…"

Her question trailed off when he closed the door and locked it. Hooking his thumbs into his sweats, he pushed them down and stepped out of them to come to her. Raising his arms high, it didn't take much effort for him to loop them over her head or to scoop his locked hands under her ass, between her legs, to pick her up.

"This is better," he said, carrying her to the vanity.

Throwing her head back in a laugh, Tulsi coiled her legs around him. "This is definitely better… Can I be loud?"

"Not if you want to go more than once."

True. If they woke the others, then they'd be interrupted. Wrapping her arms around his neck, she used his strength to pull herself higher and licked his lip.

"I definitely want to go more than once," she whispered, dipping her tongue into his mouth only to steal it back the moment his tongue tried to find hers.

"You forgot what I said about revenge, Nymph?"

Pulling the tie from her hair, Tulsi let her long locks loosen. "Definitely not," she said, boosting up again, this time to snag his lip in her teeth. As it slid lose, she began to rock, rubbing herself against him. "Do you want me, Ruin? Do you want me as bad as I want you?"

"My cock's been hard all damn night lying next to you, what the fuck do you think?"

That just made her grin grow. Clinging tighter to him, Tulsi tipped her head further back. "Do you want me so bad it hurts?"

"Want me to show you how bad I can hurt you, babe?" he asked, gritting his teeth. "Turn around."

"I want to ride you," she whimpered in a mock pout.

"You can do what the fuck you like after I take the edge off," he said, moving his bound hands to one side of her to push her around. "Flip over. Get on your knees like last night."

"You almost killed me doing me like this yesterday," she said, climbing around to get on her knees.

"Doing you without my fucking hands could kill me," he said, slipping a hand between her legs to dip his fingers into her pussy. "Damn, you're wet."

"I want you," she said over her shoulder, pushing her butt back. "Do you need me to—"

Somehow, he managed to get hold of himself enough to aim for the right spot. When he plunged into her, the instant spear of awareness darted through her eager body. On a hiss, Tulsi arched. The loop of his arms immediately tightened around her hips.

"Keep that ass up for me, baby," he snarled. "The deeper the fucking better."

The possession of his anticipation made it sound almost like he was salivating. That was just fine with Tulsi. His animal side could be heavy-handed, but fear didn't come into her mind when she was with Wreck. Brute or not, the only pain they caused each other was pleasure.

"Tell me I feel good," she purred, undulating her hips. "Please, Ruin… Tell me."

"You're hot, wet paradise, baby," he said, bending over her, slithering his hand up to fondle each of her breasts in turn. "And you're gonna take all the medicine my cock wants to feed into that sweet pussy and your hungry little mouth… Today, tomorrow, any damn time I want to feed you."

Sealing his lips against the back of her shoulder, he took his time about sucking her flesh, bruising her body with his need. Groaning in sheer delight, she pushed her butt higher and squeezed him within her.

"Yes," she panted. "Oh, fuck me, Wreck… Please, baby."

Straightening, he did his best to hold her body while thrusting into her. "Like this," he snarled. "This what you want, Nymph?"

"Yes," she said, pushing back every time he surged forward. "Yes… Yes!"

He slammed into her and halted. "What did I tell you? Keep it fucking quiet… Do I need to muzzle that mouth?" Raising her chin, she found his reflection, showing just how arousing that notion sounded. "Damn, baby… Draw me a fucking line."

But she didn't want to, not with Wreck.

Slipping a hand downward, she linked her fingers through his to direct it back to her clit. "If it feels good, it's allowed," she murmured. "Forget morals and boundaries… Make me come, Ruin… Make me come hard."

Tulsi gave the direction knowing that he wouldn't fail to deliver. Already they were in tune, seemed like they had been since the moment they met. It was difficult to fathom that he was the same man she'd met at the bottom of the stairs in Teal's building.

The man there had seemed so unattainable while the man thrusting into her seemed like an extension of her being. Tulsi had waited a lifetime for him and planned to make the most of him while they had the time to be together.

SIXTEEN

NO ONE HAD INTERRUPTED them while they screwed on the vanity. They showered together, with Tulsi helping Wreck who kept his tied hands linked over the shower curtain rod while she washed both of their bodies.

If he hadn't expected her to blow him before they got out, he didn't complain. Neither did he object when she crouched in front of him at the vanity to put herself in the loop of his arms again. Instead of sex, Tulsi hopped onto the vanity, seating herself there in his embrace to do whatever else was necessary.

He brushed his teeth with her nestled against his chest. She helped with the toothbrush and paste, and with the floss too. She asked him not to shave again and he didn't argue. He did grumble when she started to moisturize him, but he didn't fight her off. He stopped complaining when she applied her own, still in the circle of his arms.

She plucked a couple of his stray eyebrow hairs and sprayed deodorant for both of them. Wreck didn't even take himself away when she dried her hair. He seemed content enough to frown at her, his arms around her while she leaned back to dry her hair as straight as possible.

After she hung the blow-dryer up and ran a comb through her locks, Tulsi sprayed hairspray and tossed the comb aside to run her fingers into his hair.

"I prefer yours like this," she said, thinking a comb would be too much for his brutish, masculine style.

Wreck set his hands on the vanity behind her ass to loom over her. "This ain't real," he said, looking her in the eye, so close his nose almost bumped hers.

"I know," she said, laying both hands on his chest to slide them up and around to the back of his neck. "Do you want to go back to bed? You know so long as it's this lady's choice that your bed is my bed… Means you can't complain and I get to sexually harass you any time I want."

"When do you not?"

"So… bed?"

"They're out there," he said, admiring her face and then her breasts. "I prefer you naked."

"I prefer you naked too," she said, taking hold of his cock with complete entitlement. "But I prefer to be naked for you, not for every asshole with eyes."

He looked at her again. "This ain't real."

His insistence made her smile because she wasn't sure who he was trying to convince. Tulsi wasn't dumb enough not to recognize that she was falling for the man who couldn't stop holding her. But she had no expectation of him. Wreck was the kind of man a woman only met once. A man who swept into their life, rocked their world, and then disappeared, never to be seen again.

"You know what is real?" she asked, resting his cock in one palm while stroking it with the other. "How good this feels inside me."

"Everyone else will be waking up soon," he said. "We don't have time to shower again and I don't want you going out there smelling like sex… Puts ideas in a man's head."

Opening her fingers, she pushed them up into the hair behind his ear. "Wish I knew how to put ideas in your head."

"You do, Nympho," he said. "Don't fuck around."

He began to lift his arms and turn as she noticed something in his hair behind his ear. "What is that?" she asked, tightening her hold on his hair to pull him back.

"Shit," he said. "What the fuck?"

Rising higher to clamber onto her knees, Tulsi didn't hesitate to search his hair. "Is that a tattoo?" Using her fingertips, she parted his hair to find there was a black tattoo, almost indecipherable in his dark brown hair, unless someone got close enough to search. "What does it say?"

"Leave it the fuck alone," he said, yanking away from her just as she read it.

"S-I," she spelled it aloud. "Si… That's what Rowdy said to you last night." Taking his arms up and over her head, he walked away toward the tub. "What does it mean… Why did he say that?"

"Leave it alone," he growled, more like the stranger from the bottom of Teal's stairs than the lover who'd been inside her.

"Ruin—"

"I said leave it alone," he snapped in a growl so vicious that Tulsi sealed her lips in instant silence.

Wreck hadn't hurt her. He had enticed her and aroused her, but really… she didn't know him.

Sliding down off the vanity, she reached for the robe that was hanging on the back of the door again. Putting her arms in the baggy sleeves, she folded her arms, using the fabric to cover herself.

Wreck clenched his jaw, keeping his chin turned down and away. She could feel the annoyance reverberating off him. After a breath, he stomped over to snatch his bag up from the floor. Dumping it on the vanity, he searched inside, pulling out underwear and jeans. It probably wouldn't be so easy for him to put either on in his mood, especially with his hands still linked.

After him being so good about not busting out of the cuffs again, she couldn't let her question or his subsequent attitude undo that good work.

Going over, Tulsi took the underwear from him. "Your business is your business," she said, crouching to help him dress. "I shouldn't have asked. I apologize."

The man had said more than once that whatever was happening between them wasn't real. Tulsi had accepted the truth that she'd never have Wreck in the way she wanted him. It wasn't fair to punish him like a withholding boyfriend when he'd never even made her friends with benefits promises.

"I used to go out with this guy. Bradley Hershel," she said, reaching up to the vanity to snag the jeans while he adjusted himself in the underwear. "His father owns like twenty different companies across the world."

"The five years guy," he grumbled.

That he responded and that he'd been listening surprised her. Glancing up, it gave her some hope to discover he was looking down at her.

"Yes, the five years guy…" Exhaling, she went back to helping with his jeans. "I knew everything about him. I knew all the entry codes for his properties. I had access to his cars, had all the numbers for his assistants… I knew everything about how he grieved his mother. Everything about his inferiority complex regarding his father. I knew every illness he'd ever had, every habit, every mannerism. I knew what made him laugh, every part of his history, knew how to make him smile… how to please him in bed… I knew what he liked me to wear, when he preferred me to call, how a deal was going by the tone of his emails. I knew what got him hard, what got him off, how to tempt him, and how to put him off if I wasn't in the mood."

"Your point?" he said, still in a sour mood.

Pulling up his jeans, she did the top button then stopped to look up at him. "I didn't know he preferred blondes to brunettes."

Tulsi picked up the end of her dark chestnut hair. Wreck obviously knew her hair color and that it was natural. Letting her locks flutter back down, she'd made her point.

"Want me to cut his dick off?" Wreck asked.

His expression was so flat, his delivery so deadpan, that she had no idea how serious he was or wasn't. Something about his lack of finesse broke through the lingering tension of the previous moment. Her lips quirked before she laughed.

Putting both hands on his chest, Tulsi nestled herself close to him. "Oh, my Ruin," she said, sighing out her laughter. "He didn't hurt me. He freed me… But you are so sweet to offer."

"Sweet?"

Staying against him, she twisted to look up at him. "In your own way, my wonderful Wreck," she said. "You look at the world in terms of insult and revenge... I get it. I mean, I don't know why, I don't know how you ended up this way, but I'm not sorry. I love your sense of balance. I guess you're like karma come to life... It's sort of incredible... I'm so grateful to be in your life. I knew everything there was to know about Bradley and the relationship ended as a farce... I don't need to know everything about you. I just need to trust you."

And her trust in him was growing every second. He'd warned her about their situation, but until he did something to show her that he'd sacrifice her for his own sake, she wouldn't assume that he would.

"This ain't real."

"The mess we're in is," she said, tucking her forearms between them. "Baines said you brought Putnam back here last night. What do they want from him?"

"Is that what your secret talk was about?"

"No," she said, shaking her head. "Well, yes, that's when he told me Putnam was next door, but that wasn't why he wanted to talk to me alone."

"I bet it wasn't," he said. "Do me a favor, one of those guys spunks in your throat, bleach it before you kiss me again."

Though he sneered in a way that proved his disgust, she laughed. "One of those guys puts his dick anywhere near my mouth and I'll drown in their blood before I swallow their spunk."

He became more serious and stepped back to give himself enough room to raise his arms. She ducked forward beneath them and waited while he rested them on her back. Being in his embrace again was reassuring. It was a physical sign that they were on the right track.

"You could have to," he said. "I told you to—"

"Work both sides," she said, almost rolling her eyes. "I know. Geez, do you and Baines subscribe to the same newsletters? Last night he told me to gain your trust... He says you, Rowdy, and Kieran care about me." Repeating the words didn't help them make sense. She didn't know either of the brothers well enough to be important to them. Wreck, maybe, but he'd been clear about his lack of intention toward her. "It doesn't matter, he wants me to report back."

"So, you want me to give you the skinny? To fill you in on our secrets?"

"No," she said, ignoring his scowl. "I am being honest."

"And then you're going back to him to be honest?"

"I didn't tell him that I thought you were going to leave with Rowdy last night. I flat denied I knew anything," she said, sort of regretting that she was trapped against him. "You know, you can't tell me to work both sides and then get mad when the other side shows me trust."

"I can," he snapped.

"It isn't fair, Wreck."

"I told you, never expect fair from me," he said, tightening his hold when she tried to push his arm up. "It's smart for you to work both sides. Doesn't mean I like watching you walk away with him."

"You said this ain't real," she said, dragging her nails down toward his abdomen. "You can't say that and—"

"I can," he said, hauling her even closer until she was on the tips of her toes, clinging to his shoulders. "Fuck you, Nympho... I fucking can."

"Stop saying fuck me," she said, recognizing that he was ramping up, so she tried keeping cool. "If you want me to be yours, all you have to say is 'Tulsi, you're wonderful and incredible and amazing and I would be the happiest man alive if you'd belong to me forever and always.'" He just crooked a brow. She laughed. "Okay, how about..." She cleared her throat before doing her best Wreck impression. "Babe, your pussy is now private property. Trespassers will be—"

"Executed?"

Slightly taken aback, Tulsi took a second to regain her composure. "Uh... I was going to say persecuted. But, you know, if you're going to be landlord, I guess you decide on the punishment."

For a moment, she wondered if he was considering making a claim.

The illusion was shattered when he lifted his arms away from her and stepped aside. "Get dressed."

"Do I have to?"

"You said Delray was coming today," he said, nudging her toward her bag. "We don't know when he'll get here. Could be soon. Put clothes on, pack our shit, and we'll go back to bed."

"In our clothes?" Though he couldn't put anything on his top half while his hands were bound. "Just in case?"

"Yes," he said. "Protect yourself, every way you can… And put the robe on over your clothes."

The robe with the tweezers in it. Tulsi knew he was reminding her to look after herself without being explicit.

"Can I ask you something?" she asked, retrieving clothes.

"What?"

He probably expected the question to be about defending herself, about Baines, or about what could go down.

It was about none of those things. She finished hooking her bra before meeting his eye in the mirror.

"What's your real name?"

Approaching her side, he gave nothing away as to whether or not he planned to tell her. Putting a finger to her chin, he turned her face up to his. "Axton Wrecker."

He told her. Without making her fight, without blowing her off. Just showing trust made her smile. Even if it was public knowledge to others, it hadn't been to her. Now it was.

"Nice to meet you, Axton Wrecker," she said. "My Ruin."

"You got that right."

Bowing to join their mouths, he put to bed their conflict and reminded her that there was something more to life than terror and intimidation. Wreck was the only good thing she had to hold onto. Whatever it took, Tulsi was going to stick as close to him as possible. Giving him up wasn't going to be easy.

SEVENTEEN

A WHOLE WEEK went by and Tulsi only saw the outside world through the windows of the hotel room. Putnam, it turned out, wasn't as easy to break as Baines wanted him to be.

From what she'd gleaned, from eavesdropping on conversation, and the tidbits Baines had given her in the sickening moments he stole alone with her, Putnam was being left to stew. The point was to break him. Whatever they'd done in the first couple of days hadn't worked, so they'd moved onto ignoring him.

Rowdy and Kieran still had to use the bathroom Putnam was locked up in, as did the other guys in that room, but their prisoner was just ignored.

Baines was about to lose the plot. His irritation level was rising so high that Tulsi knew it wouldn't take much for him to snap. The man wasn't exactly the most stable to begin with. Putnam's sudden decision to be mute wasn't improving his sanity.

When she could forget that they were technically prisoners, Tulsi actually wasn't having an awful time. Delray and half a dozen other guys had shown up and taken up residence in surrounding rooms. Having the extra bodies meant the prisoners, excluding Putnam, were allowed to use the hotel gym… One at a time and with a posse of minders to keep them in line. They only went there in the dead of night when the gym was deserted.

It also meant that there were always goons loitering in the hallways, monitoring the rooms, ensuring that their "guests" didn't get any ideas about going anywhere.

Other than the gym, they were stuck in the bedroom. Well, not only the bedroom. Tulsi and Wreck spent as much time in the bathroom as they could get away with. Every night and every morning, they locked themselves in there for as long as possible.

The sex was only getting better and better, though she resented their limited space and keeping her volume down. No one had asked her if she and Wreck were having sex. Either it was too obvious to ask or Hillam and Coombs were oblivious idiots.

Tulsi didn't care which. Not so long as she got to fall asleep in the clamp of Wreck's legs, and to wake to him carrying her through to the bathroom each day.

Since the first morning in the hotel, when they'd come out of the bathroom and their guards had noticed Wreck's arms in front of him, no one had tried to put them behind him again. It seemed to be something they just accepted. Fighting with him made no sense. It was a compromise. Wreck got his arms in front of him, so he could do more for himself. And as long as no one argued the point with him, he was behaving and not busting out of his cuffs.

Again, more than once, she'd wanted him to, but understood it wouldn't make their situation any better to aggravate anyone more than they were already aggravated.

The sun had sunk in the sky. They'd eaten their room service dinner. Wreck was seated on the edge of the bed they'd been sharing while she kneeled behind him massaging his shoulders. Trouble with having his wrists locked together all the time was that he didn't get full range of motion. To stop him from growing stiff or cramping, Tulsi massaged his shoulders, his arms, and his back each day, often more than once, whenever he asked her to.

Wreck still teased her about her boundless appetite for sex, but she wasn't ignorant to how much he enjoyed having her attention. Often he'd command her to massage him when they hadn't touched for a while. Sometimes it was as short as a half hour. Tulsi never complained because she wasn't fond of being separated from him either.

Working the knots from his shoulders, she glanced up when Baines came through the adjoining room door. Both Hillam and Coombs jumped up from their beds. Coombs grabbed for the remote to mute the TV, meaning he was a few steps behind Hillam who rushed over to their boss.

"Outta luck, Baines?" Wreck asked, rolling his shoulders.

The three men probably hadn't expected him to speak. She hadn't expected him to. Wreck was a man of few words. Most of the time, unless they were alone or having sex, he would say as little as possible, sticking to only what was absolutely necessary.

"What the fuck are you talking about?" Baines snapped. "What the fuck do you know?"

"Babe," Wreck said, tilting his chin her way. "What do I do?"

"Get results," she said, pushing hard on his shoulder. "How does that feel?"

"Amazing, baby," he said, though there was little change in his tone as he turned back to Baines. "You want this fucker to talk. Use your assets."

"You think I'm gonna trust you with him?"

Wreck shrugged. "Why not?" he asked, rising, moving away from her massage. "I'm not the asshole embarrassing himself… How long did Merchant give you for this job? How long you gonna keep a bunch of his men holed up while you fail to get results? It's embarrassing, Baines. You're an embarrassment… Whatever this fucker stole, I'll find what it is and where it is within twenty-four hours… Just give me carte blanche."

"We need the fucker alive," Baines said, moving away from Coombs and Hillam.

Wreck lowered his head in a slow nod. "I can do

that."

"I won't give you a weapon."

"Don't need one."

Baines considered him for another moment. "What the hell… Got nothing to lose, right?" Wreck moved as if to go around him, but Baines stepped in his way. "You know my guys will be right outside the door. You twitch wrong and they'll fill you both with bullets… You and your buddy." Wreck didn't respond, but the threat hung in the air for a good minute before Baines spoke again. "Gimme a second to set it up."

When he side-nodded at Coombs, both he and Hillam went with their boss into the adjoining room. The door stayed open. They'd been told plenty of times that there were men outside in the hallway, so it wasn't like they could make a break for it. Kieran and Rowdy were still next door too. The threat of hurting others as punishment for their crimes was renewed daily.

Pouncing off the bed, Tulsi rushed across to Wreck. When she tried to get in front of him, he turned away.

"Don't," he said.

"Don't what?" she asked, still attempting to get his attention. Clutching for his torso, she did her best to turn him toward her. "Baby?" His sudden detachment confused her. "Ruin?"

"Don't," he snapped, whipping around in her direction. "Why the fuck do you push?"

Sensing that he wanted a fight, or at least distance from her, Tulsi considered being offended for a few seconds. But, suddenly, it hit her. The last thing Wreck needed going into an interrogation—if that's what he was going to do—was to be preoccupied. Other than his cryptic response about what he did, she didn't know specifics.

But she didn't really need it spelled out.

People had mentioned danger. They'd spoken about him being a force. About him being unrelenting. Wreck was powerful, she knew that first hand. What they'd been living this last week and a half wasn't his reality. He needed to be the him who was able to get results; not the him who spent his days and nights lazing in bed with her, stealing illicit moments any minute they could grab time alone.

"Me? Push?" she asked, thrusting both hands onto his torso to shove him backwards a step at the end of each sentence. "You fuck. You're the one who pushes. I'm here. I'm not fucking going anywhere. Where the fuck am I going to go? Push me. Ignore me. Do whatever the fuck you need to, but don't dare tell me I don't put up with all your bullshit without complaint."

In the darkness of the narrow corridor next to the bathroom, Wreck's scrutiny intensified. "What the fuck? Why start a fucking fight—"

"Because whatever it is you fucking do, you're out of practice," she said, smacking his chest. "You've been chilled, screwing and being lazy, doing whatever the fuck feels good. That's not where I need your mind right now."

Hitting his arm, she tried to push him again, but he grabbed both of her wrists to slam her back against the wall. "I warned you not to fuck with me," he hissed, getting down into her face. "I don't know what the fuck you think—"

"Nothing like a good fight or a good fuck to get the blood hot," she whispered, repeating his words to him. "Be aware, baby. Switch on whatever it is you need to switch on. Be as bad and as dangerous as you have to be… I'm not going anywhere."

The way he searched her eyes spoke volumes. Tulsi was no fool. This. Whatever he was about to do. It was what Wreck had tried to warn her about. She didn't know what he was, or what he was capable of, not all the way. Though she had a damn good idea.

Tulsi didn't want to be on his mind, in his mind, possibly making him hesitate. She had to know that he knew she accepted all of him.

Yanking her away from the wall, Wreck kicked the bathroom door out of the way and threw her inside. The door almost ricocheted back on him. He slammed a hand onto it, throwing it out of his way and then back into the frame.

A new kind of dark feral aura oppressed the air around him as he stalked to her. Grabbing for her chin, he hauled her onto the tips of her toes, stretching the muscles of her neck. Fumbling for the vanity behind her, Tulsi tried to get some stability, but he shook her, proving he had no intention of making this easy for her.

"Playing with the wolf will leave you with scars," he growled into her face. "You want me to be bad?"

Matching his glare as best she could, Tulsi wouldn't blink. "I am not afraid of you... I will never be afraid of you."

Spinning around, he threw her back against the door. She hit so hard that the air rushed from her lungs; she had to gasp and cough to get her breath. Still trying to recover, she wasn't even aware of him stalking to her until he grabbed the waistband of her shorts and shoved it down her legs.

"Wreck," she said, barely managing to say the word before he had her off her feet. "Baby—"

He plunged into her so hard that the word blocked her throat. Scrambling to grab for him, she was still clinging to his shoulders, her legs climbing his body as he thrust into her. Her mouth opened when their eyes met. He was there. In there. Somewhere. He was using her to prepare himself for whatever he had to do, to get to that place where he could get results.

He finished on a roar in a fraction of the time he usually lasted. Tulsi didn't even get her climax.

Wreck stepped away, leaving her to collapse to the floor at his feet. "You're irrelevant," he said.

Catching her breath, she was still panting when she straightened her arms to hold herself up enough to look at him. "Yes," Tulsi said. "Because this ain't real."

He grabbed the door and pulled it open, forcing her to scramble toward the vanity. Tulsi hadn't orgasmed and he'd been almost cruel with his words. Yet, when she heard the purpose in his gait, she smiled. Wreck could do what needed to be done and he'd come back to her... eventually.

EIGHTEEN

IT DIDN'T TAKE HIM a whole twenty-four hours. Took him less than twelve actually.

At somewhere around four a.m., Hillam and Coombs were sleeping. The door between the adjoined rooms wasn't closed; it wasn't open all the way either. The lights were off in both rooms though they were lit by the illumination of their televisions. The loud volume of the one next door, she guessed, was being used to muffle whatever was going on with Putnam.

The TV in her room was on too. She'd turned it around to face the window so that she could sit on the end of her and Wreck's bed to see it. The sound was off; some twenty-four hour news channel flickered constant images on the screen. She wasn't really watching.

Tulsi couldn't relax enough to sleep. She felt antsy. Either because she and Wreck hadn't spent their usual evening in the bathroom or because she had gotten used to sleeping with him. It didn't feel right that she couldn't see him. She didn't know where he was or if he was okay.

Until Wreck came back to her, she wouldn't be able to rest or concentrate. Her blood was hot. Her atoms vibrating. She didn't know if she wanted him to succeed or fail. For his ego, and his reputation, of course, she wanted him to do well. But, at the same time, she had no idea what would happen after they left this hotel.

There was still talk among the men that Merchant would be their next stop. Tulsi wasn't so sure that she wanted to meet the big boss man. It had to happen some time, but if Kieran couldn't give him the answers that he wanted, she had a feeling things weren't going to work out so great for them.

While still pondering what life would be when they packed up to get back on the road, the door from the adjoining room swung open. Leaping to the edge of the bed when she saw Wreck striding through, Tulsi expected him to acknowledge her.

Instead, he strode straight to the bathroom without sparing her a glance. Jumping to her feet, she rushed after him, thinking that maybe he'd want them to be alone. Except, as soon as he went inside, he slammed the door. The snick of the lock that followed was unmistakable.

Left alone at the mouth of the hallway, Tulsi wasn't quite sure what to do. Should she follow him and knock? If he wanted to be alone, she shouldn't aggravate him.

"Don't take it personally."

Turning around, she was surprised to see Rowdy leaning against the end of the dresser by the door to the adjoining room. Arms folded, ankles crossed, he was looking past her at the bathroom door Wreck had just used.

Hillam and Coombs were still asleep. She could only hear the TV coming from the next room.

"You shouldn't be in here," she said, taking two steps toward him.

"Baines is across in Delray's room," he said. "They took Kieran over there soon as Wreck came into our room… Teal is asleep, he's the laziest minder in the world." Pushing off the dresser, he stood up straight. "Wreck is a hard guy to get to know."

Breathing in, Tulsi calmed her agitated anxiety. "Did he get it? Did he break Putnam?"

Rowdy nodded. "Course. He always gets it. Everyone breaks under Wreck."

That was something. His ego and reputation would remain intact. "What does that mean?" she asked, glancing over her shoulder to the bathroom door. "Shouldn't he be happy?"

"Happy? Wreck?" he said on a snort. "Wreck doesn't do happy... You haven't figured that out yet?"

"Like you said, he's a hard guy to get to know."

"He's been the same since we were kids," Rowdy said. "All his life it's been drummed into him that his fists are the only part of him worth anything... He's got a little more finessed over the years... sometimes... But it all comes down to the same thing."

"What's that?"

"He's broken," Rowdy said on a shrug. "I thought I was fucked up... I mean, I am, but... I didn't have to see it."

"It?"

"The death of the only woman either of us ever loved."

That truth stunned her into silence. Tulsi didn't know how to process. The sentence didn't make sense. It did, but she couldn't figure it out.

"You loved the same woman?"

"Yeah. Still do," he said, turning to the side and sweeping his arm toward the bed she'd shared with Wreck. "Wanna sit?"

Rowdy may or may not have known that she'd been sleeping there with his friend. As it was the only unoccupied space at that moment, sitting there made sense.

It was as she passed him that she realized his hands weren't tied. Either Teal trusted him or he'd been helping Wreck. Both could be true.

"You still love her?" she asked, sitting on the edge of the bed. Rowdy sat next to her. "Wreck still loves her?"

"Yeah," he said, leaning back to rest his weight on his hands. "Don't know if Wreck has told you much about where we met and how we... you know." She shook her head. "Figures. He doesn't usually talk much."

Tulsi didn't want to push and shouldn't pry, but as she fingered the edge of the sheet they were sitting on, the words just spilled out. "Do you want to tell me?"

"That we were raised in the same children's home?" he asked. "Sure, well, Wreck was there long before I showed up... Kieran was fostered out, we both were, but, uh... Guess I wasn't really foster material. They didn't keep me long... He stayed with a family who treated him good, I ended up being tossed into the group home. Wasn't too shabby... Not for us... That's where I met Sienna."

"Sienna?"

"Most beautiful girl I ever saw in my life... A year younger than me and Wreck, she was light and air, in a place that was dark and claustrophobic, you know? She was twelve when we met... By the time she was fourteen, we were sleeping together... Nuts, I know, but the system isn't designed to protect kids. Sure wasn't back then..."

"You and Wreck fought over her?"

His eyes widened and he sucked in a breath as his chin swung down to the side. "Oh yeah. Fuck yeah... All the damn time... Sometimes we still do..."

"She chose you."

That the men could go from fighting over the same girl to lifelong buddies seemed incomprehensible.

He laughed. "Are you kidding me? She chose Wreck all the time. Any time I got into it with him, she wouldn't talk to me for weeks... Sure, we had plans to get married and have a life together, but all that meant shit if I fucked with her brother..."

Tulsi's head came up. "Her brother?"

Wearing a small smile that revealed he'd known she thought the love was romantic, Rowdy nodded and took her hand to his knee. "Sienna was his little sister. He'd have done anything for her... He got into plenty of scrapes defending her from scum... In the end, he couldn't protect her, and he's never forgiven himself."

"Defend her from what?"

The smile was long gone from his face. A distant memory. On a swallow, Rowdy's attention went down, as did his volume. "The three of us used to run away from the home all the time. We had friends on the street, places to sleep, we knew what we were doing… Usually, it was Si who was planning our escape. Wreck and me never knew why, didn't think to ask… He found out why on the night she died."

"Why?"

"He walked in on three of the male staff members pinning her down…"

Pain and sorrow welled up. In some feeble attempt to hide it, Tulsi covered her mouth. "They were abusing her?"

Another nod, this one slower than the last. "He went crazy, as any brother would. He tried to take them down… But he was alone, they tied him down and made him watch as they raped her… And that wasn't all… To cover their own asses, they hung her, in her own room. Made it look like suicide… No one listened to her messed up, waste-of-space brother… When he tried to push it with the authorities, the home threatened to have him investigated for her death."

"Oh my God," she breathed, tears pricking her eyes. "Why didn't you see it too?"

"Last time we were out, I'd been picked up for knocking over a convenience store… Me and Wreck both pulled the job. I was the only one caught. I was in juvie when it happened."

That made the situation all the more heart-breaking. Wreck must have felt responsible for his sister. To witness men in a position of authority abusing her would've been difficult enough, but to see them kill her and then have no one believe him…

"How did he live through something like that?"

"He said telling me was the worst… After actually having to see what he saw… telling me that he hadn't saved her… Can't say I did much to help. I probably did blame him. Both of us were angry… We didn't talk for a couple of years after that. By the time I saw him again, he was much darker… So much more… out of reach."

She swallowed. "He's not a lost cause."

"Maybe not," Rowdy said, linking his fingers with hers. "He's never said it, but I've watched him… He's worked hard to never be in a position where he's responsible for a woman…"

And as their eyes met, the pieces slid into place. "That's why you're telling me this… You don't want him to feel responsible for me."

"I don't think it would be a terrible thing for him to care about someone outside of me and Si… Given that half of us are long dead… But I don't know you, Tulsi… If you're going to screw us over… If Baines is—"

"You know Baines is talking to me… that he's shown trust," she said, pulling her hand out of his. "Shit, it's 'make a deal', 'play both sides', 'tell us what's going on', 'do whatever you have to.' What is it about men that they think they have to constantly tell women what to do?"

"This isn't your world, Tulsi," Rowdy said, his brow creasing. "That was obvious from the minute we met in Teal's stairwell. You're not used to this kinda shit… You're going to see what you think is the easy way out and—"

"What?" she asked. "I'm going to end up in over my head? I'll let you in on a little secret, it was your brother who dragged me into this. I didn't ask for any part of it."

"I know."

Tulsi stood up. "A quick stop is what he said. I told him I was capable of getting myself home. Would he listen? No!"

Rowdy looked past her, but it wasn't his voice she heard next. "She has a habit of getting loud." Spinning around, she found Wreck standing at the end of Hillam's bed, drying his hands on one of the bathroom towels. "What you two talking about?"

"Nothing," Rowdy said, standing up beside her. "Nothing important. What's the play?"

"We tell Baines where she is," Wreck said, throwing the towel at the dresser.

She? The word attracted Tulsi's attention.

"Or we don't," Rowdy offered and glanced at her.

Wreck exhaled. "I can't keep going in there pretending I'm working the guy for information he's already spilled."

"End him and we'll be the only ones with the information," Rowdy said, scanning Hillam and Coombs, probably checking that they were still out.

Hillam was drooling and Coombs was snoring, no chance they were playing covert ops.

"You want to use it," Tulsi said, folding her arms. "To save Kieran."

"To save all of us," Rowdy said.

She smiled, not quite believing the man who'd been semi-threatening her just a moment before. "You, your buddy, and your brother…" Her head shook. "I can't trust any of you, can I?"

"Tulsi," Rowdy started, but when he reached for her, she put her hands up and stepped away. He frowned. "We got you into this, we'll get you out of it."

"Why would you?" she asked. "The three of you walk out whole. What does it matter if I'm left behind?"

"Kieran wouldn't let that happen," Rowdy said. "Don't you know how worried he's been? How guilty he feels?"

"Guy's a pussy," Wreck muttered.

There was a chance Rowdy was telling the truth. Kieran could be struggling with guilt. Her and Kieran hadn't spent much time together over the last week. They'd caught the odd glimpse or two between the rooms, but hadn't exchanged words.

"He shouldn't feel guilty," Tulsi said and exhaled. "I am a grown up. I didn't *have* to go up Teal's stairs… Hiding the truth from Baines would be stupid and dangerous. He'll report back to Merchant that you're withholding. That will make him madder…"

In terms of their own safety and winning favor with the people who were holding them against their will, it made sense to be forthcoming. Yet, Wreck's personification of the information made things difficult. Tulsi had assumed Putnam was hiding an object, not a person.

"They're mad anyway," Rowdy said. "We have to take back some power."

They did know the situation better than she did.

Until Tulsi knew who they were selling out, she couldn't commit to one plan or another. "Who is the she?"

"Merchant's ex," Wreck said. "The last favorite… Putnam got her out. Merchant wants her back."

"He's been hiding her?"

Wreck shrugged. "Knows where to find her anyway… From what I heard, she's capable."

"This isn't…" Rowdy trailed off when Wreck nodded. "Shit… The things I heard she could do to a guy."

"Yeah," Wreck said. "But you know Merchant…"

Rowdy bobbed his head. "True. Possible he broke her… If he did… fuck knows what's left."

"Wait, who is she?"

"Svana Nilsson." That answer hadn't come from inside the room. Baines wandered through from the adjoining room, trailing his awareness over them all. "You should listen to Pretty. If you withhold, you'll regret it."

"We were just talking," Rowdy said. "Considering our options… Seems Wreck did you a favor, you should do one for him."

"How 'bout I let him come with us when we pick up Svana?" Baines said. The way he raised his brows and turned his focus betrayed his confidence. "You want to play in the big pond, asshole?"

"Row watches my back," Wreck said and waited until Baines nodded in acquiesce. "Tomorrow. We watch, and when she's alone…"

"We pick her up," Baines said, going over to him. He attempted to slap a hand on Wreck's arm, but Wreck moved out of the way. "Right… No touching… Guess we better get our rest. Big day tomorrow." Baines pointed at Rowdy. "You, with me."

Rowdy glanced at her, though his gaze shifted to linger on Wreck as he departed in Baines wake. The door was closed behind them.

Tulsi was on information overload. She didn't know what to do or what to say. Rowdy's story was intense enough on its own. But there was more than just that to absorb. Now they were going to be responsible for this Svana's life.

"Will Merchant kill her?" she asked, her focus on the carpet.

"I don't know," Wreck said. "Putnam said she wanted out… he got her out."

But Merchant wanted her back. Although she'd never met him, he didn't seem like the type of man who'd just want a chance to say sorry.

Yet, before Tulsi could think to question whether or not they should protect Svana, she recalled Rowdy's statement about Wreck going out of his way to avoid being responsible for others. Kieran apparently knew about Merchant's shipment. Wreck now knew about Merchant's ex-girlfriend or favorite or whoever this Svana was. Their position was precarious. Standing up for a woman they'd never met, who could be evil herself for all Tulsi knew, wouldn't be smart.

"This is so confusing," she exhaled and sank onto the bed, running her hands over her hair to scoop it back from her face. "How is it possible to decide what's right?"

"What's right is easy," he said and she glanced up. "Get over here."

"How is it easy?" she asked.

"You keep your focus… I knew what I was doing when I walked out of this room."

Tulsi stood up. "You knew Putnam was hiding a woman? That we'd jeopardize another life to save ours?"

"I didn't give a damn what he was hiding… You gotta have one goal, Nympho… I knew mine and it hasn't changed… Yours is usually one track…" His moving aside left the hallway to the bathroom wide open. "Ready to say no?"

The way he asked the question almost dared her to tell him that she was flicking their fling switch to off.

Tulsi just tilted her head. "I sent you out there to do what needed to be done," she said, strutting toward him. "If you're saying this is what has to be done…" She stopped in front of him. "I'm with you." Without touching him, she kept on going and opened the bathroom door. Putting on the light, she paused to look back. "You've done your job for them…" She took her time about licking her lips. "Time to do one for me… My Ruin."

Entering the bathroom, she had little doubt that he

would follow. The worries about Svana wouldn't vanish overnight. But Wreck was her touchstone. If she wanted his trust, she'd have to surrender some of her trepidation.

Rowdy had helped her understand more of the man. Tulsi couldn't ever make him feel responsible for her. Only now she felt more responsible for him than ever. No one had ever looked out for him. He'd held himself away from others to protect himself. Tulsi might never break through his defenses, but she'd sure never question them.

NINETEEN

TULSI HAD BEEN LEFT alone with Hillam.

Kieran was across the hall with Delray and whoever else was over there. She had never been hosted by them, and couldn't say she was sorry about that. Coombs and Teal had gone with Baines, Rowdy, and Wreck to pick up the unsuspecting Svana.

All day Tulsi swung back and forth between accepting that they needed to sacrifice Svana to have any hope of getting out alive, and back to feeling guilt over being selfish. Wreck showed no doubt, not an ounce. Not until Baines had opened the adjoining room door to order him out with them.

There had been no time to say any kind of goodbye, which probably worked out for the best. Baines stood there waiting for him, so all Wreck could do was meet her eye. She'd nodded once and offered him a smile. In a flash, his gaze had darkened as determination overtook him. He'd turned and strode out.

That purpose, that's what she needed him to have. If he was switched on, he'd come back to her. That was all she wanted. For him to come back to her.

Tulsi had been thinking a lot about that in the hours since the men had left.

While they'd been alone, Hillam hadn't said much. He'd ordered room service and raided the minibar. He'd called down for more alcohol about two hours ago. The loud violence of the movies he'd been watching had been replaced by the distinctive sounds of porn just a half hour ago.

Didn't matter to her. Tulsi couldn't see the TV because of the way he'd angled it. She was happy to just lie in the bed she'd shared with Wreck and contemplate the flexibility of her conscience.

Forget morals and boundaries. That was what Wreck had said to her. The previous night when he'd told her that he had one goal and it hadn't changed, she hadn't pressed him on what that goal was. Figuring he'd had a tough enough night, she didn't want to put more pressure on him.

They'd actually ended up falling asleep on the bathroom floor together, a folded towel substituted a pillow. Wreck having his arms free was such a novelty that even when she'd woken up stiff and sore, Tulsi hadn't wanted to move or wake him. She'd ended up falling asleep again.

Instead of lying side to side, Tulsi had slept on top of him, between his thighs, using his body as her pillow. Just like the first night they'd spent together. Her heart hurt for him. In the moments she'd been awake while he slept, she'd stroked him and wept. It wasn't like her to be teary. Of their own accord, the tears just slipped from her eyes as she thought about the torture his teenage self had gone through.

After falling asleep again, she'd woken up to him sliding into her. He'd pulled her sleeping body up his and parted her legs to move inside her as she slept. Tulsi couldn't imagine a more incredible way to wake.

That joining had been slower, lazier than most of their frantic encounters. Both of them were free. Both were tired and sore. But they relished the chance to enjoy each other. For that short interlude, they managed to pretend like everything was normal.

Wreck wasn't often patient with her slower pace any time she was on top. That morning, he'd let her take her time to enjoy him… Tulsi didn't know why or what was different. No doubt he just didn't want to leave the bathroom. That would mean facing their captors and the truth that nothing was normal.

Sure enough, when they had eventually left the bathroom, Coombs had been there to zip-tie Wreck's wrists again.

He'd left the room with them cuffed too. Knowing that he could bust out of them gave her some solace. If she thought Wreck was going into a situation rife with the potential for danger at a disadvantage, she'd have been frantic with worry. But she trusted that if he felt in danger, he would break the cuffs as he had for her in the bathroom.

Her mind wandered back to his purpose. What was the goal Wreck had been referring to last night? Freedom? Was that it? Except, if it was, why hadn't he taken the opportunity to escape when he'd had it?

"Yo!"

Hillam's call made her turn her head in his direction. He rolled off the bed, collapsing onto the floor only to surge back up to his feet and slump on the edge of the bed.

"You're drunk," she said, returning her eyes to the ceiling.

"Come on over here…" he said, gesturing with a loose arm. "Come over and suck my dick."

Her lips quirked. "Yeah, right," she murmured.

"You know you want it," Hillam said, grabbing his drink from the nightstand to gulp it down.

Tulsi heard the glass hitting the nightstand hard and noted the movement of him standing up. She tried her best to ignore him in hopes he'd pass out or forget about his request. A few seconds later, the sound of fabric made her peek around. The asshole was taking his clothes off.

"Baines said lady's choice," she said, trying to sound confident. "That means you're outta luck."

"You suck off that asshole you're sleeping with every night," he said, stumbling around Coombs' bed wearing only his underwear.

"I do a lot more than that for him," she said, getting her answer on whether or not the thugs knew about her and Wreck. "Unfortunately for you, he ruined me for every other guy."

"I don't give a shit," Hillam said, lunging down to grab her arm.

"Let me go," she said, hitting at his arm as he dragged her to the edge of the bed. "Let me fucking go!"

Tulsi hit the floor. Blocked in by beds on both sides, her only avenue for escape was to clamber over Coombs' bed. As soon as she got to her knees, Hillam snatched a handful of her hair and pulled her onto her feet.

"You do as you're fucking told, bitch," Hillam said, smacking her in the face with a closed fist.

Falling onto the pull out bed, dazed and trying to figure out what had happened, Tulsi couldn't fight when Hillam wrenched her arms from the robe and pulled down her shorts. On her face under him, she only had the window in front of her. There was nowhere to go. No avenue of escape.

The scent of Wreck in their sheets fueled her into action. He wouldn't just give up. He wouldn't give in.

"No!" she screamed on a surge of adrenaline and flipped over to fold her legs against her torso.

Planting her feet on Hillam's chest, she thrust him away with all of her strength, sending him sailing onto his back on Coombs' bed.

Instantly, Tulsi leaped to her feet and sprinted for the door. She didn't get even close to her goal. Hillam lunged off the bottom corner of Coombs' bed to grab her leg, pulling it from under her.

As she fell, Tulsi tried to get hold of something, anything, on the dresser, but only succeeded in pulling everything from the surface. Bottles, plates, food, even the television ended up crashing to the floor while she face-planted in the carpet.

"You fucking bitch," Hillam said, scrambling off the bed without letting go of her and flattening himself on top of her. "You're a fucking whore."

"I'm not *your* whore," she growled and spat in his face when he tried to kiss her.

Cursing, he rose to his knees. Pinning her arms at her sides with his legs, he slapped her once and then again. "You fuck," he snapped. "You bitch! Slut!"

Opening her mouth wide, Tulsi screamed. Arching and bucking, she writhed every which way trying anything she could to get away from him. The mess from the dresser was squashed beneath her. The plates were beginning to crack, the bottles were pushed aside or bruising her muscles, but she'd take it. Tulsi refused to give in. Refused to let him violate her.

"Get off me!" she hollered.

His fist hit her temple so hard that she was sure she blacked out for a second. The next thing Tulsi knew, the sound of a zip-tie being tightened razed the air. It took another second for her to realize that the plastic was cutting into her wrist. A drawer from the dresser was out above her head, the runner digging into her scalp through her hair.

"Now you're gonna get it fucking whore," he said, reaching over her to slam the drawer.

The stench of alcohol and unwashed man assaulted her, but the daze was slowing her reactions. Her actions felt clumsy even as she tried to fight. He stretched her arms over her head. Pushing her hand under the dresser, he thrust it against the foot of the furniture's short leg. The quick click of a zip-tie being tightened warned her what was coming. He intended to trap her hands around the leg of the dresser. If she didn't have her hands, she'd be helpless.

"No," she said. The sudden jerk of her arm was enough to pull it out from the second zip-tie just before it tightened.

"You bitch!" Hillam barked and slapped her again. This time a trail of his drool followed. The man was so out of it, he couldn't control himself. "Fucking stop fighting! You're gonna take it! Take it hard you whore! Slut!"

"No," she said, thrashing left and right. "No! No! No! No!"

She wouldn't give in. Wouldn't stop fighting. "You're my little whore now, Pretty," Hillam said, using all of his weight to flatten her on the floor.

He got hold of her wrists and used his legs to open hers. That was when she felt the smooth skin of his dick against her thigh. The fucker was naked. There was nothing between them.

"I won't!" she screamed, tossing her head back to keep it away from his slobbering mouth. "No! No!"

"Give me that fucking pussy, whore," Hillam demanded, clamping her wrists in one of his hands, using the almost fastened zip-tie to give him extra control. "You're my fucking slut now, Pretty. You're my whore!"

Squeezing her eyes closed, she fought and tried to block him out at the same time. "No! No! No!"

Something behind her banged. Tulsi opened her eyes and thrust her head back. From that angle, the person she saw was upside down, coming through the adjoining room door. Tulsi had barely registered who it was before the figure closed in. He took a final step and grabbed Hillam by the head. With a quick twist, Wreck broke her attacker's neck. The crack was so vicious in its finality that there was no doubt it was fatal, even before Hillam's lifeless body flopped over her.

"Wreck, what…"

Rowdy's voice trailed off. Tulsi blinked over and over again, trying to clear the blur of her vision to focus on Wreck who was standing above her and Rowdy who came into view at his side.

"Oh my fucking God," Rowdy said. "What the fuck did you do?"

Pushing Hillam's shoulders, she tried to move him, but the man's dead weight was suffocating. Wreck had killed him… snapped his neck if she wasn't wrong… He'd saved her. Yet…

Rowdy grabbed Wreck's arm and tried to turn him, but his buddy snarled and thrust him away. "They're gonna be here any second," Rowdy said, holding up his hands to remind his friend he was no threat. "Baines was pissed you stalked off. They're bringing Svana and if they see you killed this asshole. This is Merchant's guy——"

"Out," Tulsi croaked, fighting harder to roll Hillam out of the way.

"What?" Rowdy asked, looking down at her.

She tried to stand, but couldn't quite get over the adrenaline and crumpled again. Just managing to support herself on all fours, she ignored the wobble of her limbs to persist.

"Out," she said, shoving at Wreck's legs and then Rowdy's. "Get the fuck out of here! Both of you."

"Tuls," Rowdy said, pushing his friend toward the adjoining door.

"You didn't see a damn thing," she said, shoving at them again. "Neither of you were here. Get out!"

Rowdy pushed Wreck through the door. The moment they were on the other side, Tulsi stretched across to grab the adjoining door. Throwing it into the doorframe, she barely heard the sound of it slam over the ringing in her ears.

Flipping around, she crawled across the floor, and over the top of Hillam. Her goal was the robe that was hanging half on and off the pull out bed. Blinking what was either tears or concussion from her blurred eyes, she tugged it down to search the pocket while dragging it along beside her.

Once the tweezers were in her hand, Tulsi drooped back down onto the floor. Hillam was on his side, propped up by the dresser. Though her body revolted by retching, she pulled him down, not all the way on top of her, but enough.

With her zip-tied hand over her head, the second zip-tie hanging loose from it, she closed her eyes. Taking a deep breath, she held it for a second, giving herself a moment to come to terms with what she was about to do.

Her mouth opened in a long, pained scream as she brought the tweezers down, plunging them into the side of his neck. Pulling them out, she stabbed them into him again.

The rage of what he'd tried to do to her obviously hadn't subsided because although her eyes were closed, she hit him again, and again. Wreck had broken his neck. He'd come into their room to find her being attacked. She could only imagine that the sight brought back memories of what he'd seen his sister endure. It was instinct... trauma... impulse that had made him act in such a final way.

Tears flowed from her eyes as blood pooled and splattered around her. Whoever she was, it wasn't the person she'd always believed herself to be. Tulsi wasn't sorry that Hillam was dead. She didn't feel guilt or compassion. The man was an asshole, tangled up with monsters who exploited women for financial gain. She wouldn't mourn him.

"Whoa! What the fuck!"

The shout made her arm loosen, it grew limp and fell to the carpet. Her heart pumped hard. The adrenaline of anger and fear surged through her veins making her pant for breath. Whatever they did to her, she'd take it. Tulsi would endure whatever the punishment was because if she'd been able to take Hillam down without Wreck's help, she'd have done it.

Someone hooked their arms under hers to haul her onto her feet.

"What the fuck did you do?" Baines asked. What had happened was obvious to anyone. Exhaustion made it impossible for her to answer or even care about the people surrounding her. "Get her the fuck out of here. We have to clean up this mess."

"She killed him," Coombs hollered. "Why the fuck did she—"

"Because he deserved it," Rowdy said. "Guy was a prick… Damn obvious what he was doing… Just look at her."

Someone dragged her across the room. Tulsi picked out voices, but couldn't see faces. Everything was stunted. Disjointed.

"Yeah," Baines said, not as aggravated as before. "Get those two fucks out of here… The rest of us have to deal with this mess. Then I gotta call the boss."

Those two fucks, she guessed were Rowdy and Wreck. Merchant was the boss. Tulsi was tossed into the bathroom and given an order to clean up. She sank onto the floor and lay there staring at the door. She'd get with it, she'd clean up… In just a minute.

TWENTY

THE SHOCK DIDN'T TAKE long to wear off. That was what Tulsi told herself, though in truth, she had no idea how long she lay on the bathroom floor watching the shadows of movement under the door. Listening to the muffled discussions and activity going on beyond the room, she stayed in a daze.

At some point, she stripped and climbed into the shower. Washing herself from hair to feet, she scrubbed every inch, erasing any hint of Hillam's body from hers.

The door did open while she was in there. The sound made her freeze, unsure if Wreck might be coming to join her or if one of Baines minions wanted a shot at succeeding where Hillam failed. Instead, the door closed a few seconds later. Holding her breath, she peeked around the curtain to see who might have entered.

The room was empty. Whoever had come in had gone… with her top. Not that she'd planned to put it on again. Tulsi hadn't thought beyond washing herself. The shorts and robe were still out in the bedroom. At least, that's where she'd left them.

Her top had been covered in blood. There was still some smeared on the tile floor. Leaving the shower, she climbed out and used one of the hotel hand towels to clean it up as best she could. She tossed the towel into the tub, ignoring how it absorbed the water as she washed herself again.

Only after her fingers had gone wrinkly did she climb out and wrap herself in one of the bath towels. Sitting on the toilet lid, in the silence of the bathroom, she began to piece through what had happened. This room had once been a happy space. A safe place for her and Wreck to play together. Now, she didn't know what it was.

It felt like a cell.

Awaiting her fate, Tulsi was alone while others ran around to conceal her crime. Baines had said that he would call Merchant after the mess was cleaned up. She assumed that meant there was a protocol. There would have to be. After all, Rowdy had said Baines was a serial murderer.

Alexis was the name of the woman Baines had murdered in Teal's apartment. Tulsi hadn't seen the woman's body again. Someone must have cleaned up Baines' mess or he cleaned it up himself. Delray, Coombs, Teal, they had all been there in that apartment where Alexis died. They were part of the crew who'd dealt with Alexis. Now they were dealing with Hillam.

The difference was, Hillam was one of their own. Alexis had been a favorite squeeze of Keaton, who, Tulsi assumed, was one of Merchant's competitors. Baines had tried to get information from the doomed woman. When he'd used Alexis for all he could, he'd killed her.

Tulsi could be next.

She had no idea how Merchant felt about Hillam, or anyone taking the life of one of his men. Tulsi's minutes on Earth could be limited. Glancing around, she managed to find a smile. If she was going to lose her life anywhere, she was glad it was in a place that carried so many positive memories. The only negative was being unable to see him one last time.

Requesting to see him, or trying to sneak out to see him, was out of the question. It wouldn't serve either of them to be too close after this. Tulsi didn't want anyone to assume that she cared for Wreck so much that she might ever consider covering for him. While she was taking the wrap for a murder she hadn't technically committed, Tulsi wasn't innocent of the crime. Wreck had done what she'd been unable to, simple as that.

She'd wished the man dead as he attempted to violate her. Like her desperation had summoned a savior, Wreck had delivered for her. For that, she would be forever grateful.

Not that she assumed forever would last long.

Tulsi was still thinking about Wreck, hoping his conscience wouldn't be burdened by saving her, when the bathroom door opened. Surging to her feet, she was prepared to face her punishment head on.

The last thing she expected was for Baines to thrust a cellphone her way. "Boss wants to talk to you."

Boss… Merchant? Did he believe in delivering news of the sentence himself?

On a blink, Tulsi steeled herself and reached out to take the phone from him. "Hello?" she compelled herself to say the word.

It sounded more uncertain than meek, which was better than coming across as scared. Tulsi wouldn't fear them. Wouldn't give them any satisfaction.

"Pretty," the word was long, dragged out on an exhale that sounded anything but mad. "That's what they call you, isn't it?"

She waited a second before responding. "Yes."

"Do you know who I am?"

"I do."

At least, she assumed he was the esteemed Merchant that everyone had mentioned so many times.

"My men underestimated you… I underestimated you," he said, the note of intrigue obvious in his words. "Tell me something, Pretty… Would you die to defend yourself? To defend what you love?"

Although she let the words linger, Tulsi already knew what her answer would be. "Yes," she said, straightening up and meeting Baines' eye, proving her resolve. "I would rather die than endure that asshole forcing himself on me. So if that's what has to happen—"

"Oh no, Pretty," Merchant said. "That's the last thing I want… You have new power now."

Confused, she tried to maintain her confidence, but didn't really understand what he was saying. "What new power?"

"Baines has orders," Merchant said and became more optimistic. "You are something special, Pretty. I look forward to meeting you."

"You do?"

"Yes," he murmured. "I needed to hear your voice, to hear if it was true."

"If what was true?"

"That a woman I've never laid eyes on could be the love of my life." All the confusion of the conversation dwindled to pure shock. Love? She'd killed a man. One of Merchant's men. And he was talking of love? "Sweet dreams, Pretty. We'll see each other soon."

The line died just a second later. Her arm went limp. As she tried to figure out what alternative universe she'd slipped into, Baines grabbed the phone.

"We're rolling out tonight," he said. "We're almost done with the clean-up. You can wait in here 'til we're done. Someone will come get you and take you down to a car. Your stuff will be in it."

Baines began to turn as if to leave.

Tulsi leaped forward a step. "He said I had new powers."

Glancing back over his shoulder, the curl of his mouth seemed sinister. "Oh, you have way more than that, Pretty."

Without explaining what that meant, Baines turned away to leave. Except he didn't close the door all the way. Tulsi was about to reach for it, wondering if he'd been careless or intended for her to follow even though he'd just told her to wait in the bathroom.

Just before she made contact with the wood, she heard a scuffle outside and a feminine yelp. "Ba—"

The woman didn't get the word out. The door flew open. Tulsi jumped backwards. Then, a blonde was tossed onto the tile at her feet.

Tulsi was still blinking at her when Baines leaned in to grab the edge of the door. "Enjoy getting to know each other," he said. "You're going to have a lot in common."

Yanking the door closed, he left Tulsi alone with the stranger. Except the small woman could only be one person.

Crouching down, Tulsi was careful about easing the curtain of the woman's hair away from her face to get a better look. "Svana?" she said, noting the woman's bruised eye and smeared make-up. "I'm Tulsi."

The woman didn't speak. She scrambled away to pin herself against the door that had just been closed.

Tulsi held up both hands in a calming gesture. "It's okay," Tulsi said, keeping her tone even. "No one will hurt you. It's just us in here. You're safe."

"You..." Svana whispered. "You're the one who killed him..."

Closing her mouth, Tulsi sank back onto her ass. "Hillam was... He wasn't being a gentleman."

She knew nothing about Svana other than she'd been Merchant's favorite and had escaped with Putnam.

"You're supposed to let them do what they want," Svana said, wrapping her arms around her legs to hold them tight to her chest. "That's what you're supposed to do."

"Is that what you did with Merchant?" Tulsi asked, seeing a chance to get to know the woman. "Why did you run away?"

"Merch wasn't... he wasn't..."

The blonde's attention drifted toward the shower. While they sat there in silence, Tulsi checked her out. With a generous chest and a small waist, it wasn't difficult to see why Merchant had been attracted to Svana. Her slender limbs were long though she had a round face and a small pouty mouth. There was such elegance and grace in her, despite her hunched position.

Her tousled baby blonde hair hung straight from root to end. Although there was something worldly about her air, there was no denying the youth of her complexion. After living with Merchant for goodness knew how long, it was no surprise that the youngster had experience beyond her years. "How old are you?"

"Twenty-two," the blonde said in a response that was almost Pavlovian in its compliance. Like every question had to be answered within a certain time frame, the woman didn't hesitate to reply. "Why did they take me?"

"Merchant wants you back," Tulsi said, noting how Svana tried, and failed, to conceal her dread. "Were you with him for long?"

"Almost two years," Svana said, loosening her grip on her legs enough to coil her fingers together. "Where's Putnam?"

"I don't know," Tulsi said, shaking her head. "There are men across the hall, in other rooms, he may be with them."

It was possible, but she didn't know for sure. People told her what was done with Kieran because she'd been captured with him. No one had offered her information on Putnam that day.

"Did you kill him?"

"No!" Tulsi said, boosting herself up to sit on the toilet lid again, folding her towel over her thighs. "I hurt Hillam because he tried to force himself on me. I'm not an indiscriminate killer."

"Merch knows people like that," Svana said, letting her knees descend to the floor, so her legs were curled in front of her. "He knows all kinds of people." Tulsi didn't doubt it. "You should put ice on your face."

"On my..." Tulsi hadn't bothered to look at herself properly in the mirror. Only with Svana's suggestion, did she turn to the glass. What she saw shocked her onto her feet. "Oh my God."

Her eye was swollen, which explained why it kept blurring. Her temple and down the side of her face were inflamed and there was redness around her opposite jaw.

Tulsi was still gaping at her reflection, touching the affected areas and registering how tender they were when Svana appeared at her side to turn on the faucet. "Without ice, we can use cold water."

She ran the water long and hard while retrieving

washcloths from the vanity cabinet. Tulsi felt along the bone around her eye socket and across the bridge of her nose, trying to decipher if anything was broken.

Svana soaked the cloths and kept running the water as she touched the icy fabric to Tulsi's cheek. At first, she flinched away, but remembering that she wanted to make a friend, Tulsi turned toward Svana to let her help.

"You should keep the cold on it for about fifteen minutes," Svana said. "It will be difficult when we're on the road, but any time you can, apply ice or cold like this."

"For fifteen minutes?"

Svana nodded. "It's best if you can do it every hour or two… In a couple of days, move on to warm compresses."

"You know a lot about this," Tulsi said, wondering what the woman had endured.

There was no acknowledgement. "You should keep your head elevated, even when you sleep, helps to reduce the swelling… Merch doesn't mind bruises, but the swelling can get in the way of our beauty… that's what he says… Did he get you anywhere else?" Svana actually took Tulsi's hand to move it onto the cold compress, so she could turn her around. "Your arms are bruised and there's some marks on your shoulders… Bathing in cold water can help… Just for ten, fifteen minutes…" Her chin dropped a fraction. "It helps between your legs too, and anywhere else he put it."

Touching two fingertips to the underside of Svana's chin, Tulsi raised her attention. "Merchant raped you?"

The head shaking started slow, but it sped up. "No. No, of course not. I love Merchant." Moving away, the panic became more tangible as Svana retreated. "Please don't tell him that I—"

"Svana," Tulsi said, bounding forward to snag her hand. "You are safe with me. I will never tell him anything you say to me."

Like she didn't know whether or not that was true, Svana peeked at her. "He likes women that start out strong," she murmured, almost out of her own body. "I can't remember where I ever got that strength."

"Listen to me," Tulsi said, inching closer. "I know

that it seems unlikely now, but you can get out of this. You can get away."

Again, Svana was shaking her head. "I believed Putnam when he said that too. You don't know Merch… None of you do… Not like I know him. He's… he's single-minded, he's… Once he gets an idea in his head, nothing will change his mind."

"He's not the only man like that," Tulsi said, tossing the washcloth back to the vanity so she could rub Svana's upper arms in what was supposed to be a show of comfort.

"I know that," Svana said, shifting in a way that betrayed her discomfort. If Tulsi's assumptions were right, this woman had been touched against her will enough for one lifetime. In deference to that, she dropped her hands to her sides. "Merch won't give me up, he's proven that… I should've known. I should never have listened to Putnam."

"Putnam got you out once," Tulsi said. "Maybe with more help—"

"Who?" Svana snapped, seeming to reach the end of her patience. "I've seen what Merch does to women he's finished with… Baines has already told me I'll be turned out. That means I'm free pussy to them…" She thrust a straight arm out to her side. "Every man that's out there. Every one of them who came to grab me… Every one of them will take me any way they want to and I will just have to accept it… I will have to put up with their hands all over me, their mouths, their—"

"No, you don't," Tulsi said, almost reaching for Svana again. At the last moment, she recalled her reaction and stepped back to give her more space. "Baines had instructions to get you, yes. But not all of the men who were there tonight are Merchant's men. Not all of them are evil. Some of them are prisoners, just like you."

From the confused curiosity on her face, it was clear that Svana didn't understand. "Prisoner? They didn't seem like prisoners."

Taking an instinctive breath, Tulsi prepared to reveal the truth of how she, Wreck, and the brothers ended up in their current predicament. Something made her pause. Maybe it was common sense or what little savvy she'd garnered since going out with Kieran, switching itself on. But she remembered Wreck's words, *"You don't know what I am."* Who he was had worked out in her favor. Who Svana was may not.

The woman was tired, exhausted even. Her fear of Merchant was palpable. If she'd once been strong, there was little trace of that left. Tulsi didn't doubt that the woman was smart, switched on to the workings of Merchant's words. But her courage seemed thin and she'd needed Putnam to get her this far. Though, that hadn't worked out in her favor.

If Merchant got hold of Svana and used the sway he exploited, Svana could repeat anything Tulsi told her.

"Let's get a compress on your eye," Tulsi said, turning to the side to gesture to the sink. "We'll nurse our bruises and think about filling that tub with cold water while you fill me in on how you met Merchant."

"It's not a nice story," Svana said, joining her at the sink. "My mom was tempted to this country when I was fifteen. By eighteen, I was doing porn with her and stripping… I was twenty when Merch saved me from all of that…" The blonde became preoccupied with folding the washcloth. "I thought he saved me."

Being young and impressionable, Svana must have learned a lot about the negative side of relationships. Through those same ages when Svana had been exploited for her body, Tulsi had been nursing her sick mother. She thought of all those times when she was exhausted and strained to the point of resenting life. What she'd endured was nothing to what this woman had gone through.

In the end, Tulsi had ended up resenting every one of those seconds she'd wished for a different life. At twenty-one, losing her mother had left her lost and alone. She'd have given anything to care for her mother for another minute, another year. Anything just to have her again instead of feeling such loss.

Meeting Bradley on her twenty-second birthday had given her cause for hope and a feeling of purpose. It was incredible how one person, one man could have such an impact on someone's life. Svana had met Merchant and believed he was her future. Tulsi had thought the same of Bradley… They'd both been wrong.

"How did you meet him?"

"In a club," Svana said. By now, each of them were tending the other's injuries. "I was stripping and picking up what I could after hours… Baines saw me arguing with a customer who was trying to take without paying, you know? He asked me to come and see his boss's place… The rest I guess is history."

"You fell for him?" Tulsi asked.

On a laugh, Svana went to the tub. She pulled back the shower curtain and hung the damp end over the rod above. Tulsi winced, waiting for her reaction to the sodden towel that was still tinged red. Svana didn't even blink. Bending over, she picked it up to begin wringing out the water.

"I went to a club… Turned out it wasn't even Merchant's club. It was just one of his favorite hang-outs… He did end up buying it. For me, he said, not that I needed a strip club. I sure wasn't allowed a job…"

Once the towel was wrung enough that it was no longer dripping, Svana went to the bathroom door and knocked before opening it. It hadn't even occurred to Tulsi that there would be anyone outside. Yet, Delray was there, his back to the door, guarding them or keeping them in, one or the other.

"Miss Nilsson," Delray said.

Svana held up the towel. "Baines will want to burn this… And we need ice."

Delray took the towel and Svana closed the door again. Returning to the tub, the efficient woman rinsed the pink splashes and pulled the lever to seal the drain to begin filling the tub with cold water.

"You're good at this."

Breathing out, Svana turned to face her. "So long as you're pulling on their oar, it's easy to fit in… It's only when you push back that things get tough… That's why it's better, you know, to just… do what you're told."

"Pull on the oar," Tulsi said and folded her arms.

"I'm not so good at that."

Svana's smile was almost sympathetic. "Neither was I." She came over to lay a hand on Tulsi's arm. "Merchant likes spirited… He likes spunky… He wants a woman he can break… He wants a woman who will fight him right up until the moment that she doesn't."

"Then what?"

"At first, it's comments," Svana said, stepping aside to check herself in the mirror, running her fingers into her hair. "You have sex and then he starts talking about how it used to be… About how he has to be firm or we'll lose respect… What he really means is he has to be violent or there's a chance we'll disrespect him."

"He was violent with you? How often?"

"It starts with taunting and teasing. It turns him on to see you fight back. He wants a woman who'll curse at him and deny him… He lets you too, he lets you say no… for a while. I don't know what changes. Just one day he decides he wants you and then… he has you… Any way he wants you. Every way you can imagine." Svana's fingers moved through her hair in an almost comforting way while her mind meandered. "He's into everything, has everything. He'll collar you… He'll bind you… Demand you ask permission for everything… Absolutely everything. From eating, to sleeping, to peeing… He keeps his favorite on a short, tight leash…

"Sometimes he likes to let his men watch… Sometimes he likes to watch them with his favorite… Anything he wants, any moment he wants it, he gets it… He likes all kinds of sex, with all kinds of people. Women, men, older, younger, rich or poor, it doesn't matter. He doesn't think twice about it… I suppose he's so used to getting anything that he wants that finding a woman who resists is like sport to him."

Tulsi felt sick. She'd known that Merchant was going to be a formidable man, but the notion of being "broken" wasn't appealing.

"Least I know why you don't want to go back there," Tulsi said.

Svana turned away from the mirror. "The sex I could

live with. Shit, I've been doing porn since before I was legal, I know how to switch my mind off from my body…"

"Then why did you leave?"

"I have never been free," she said. "My mother dragged me over here, I lived the life she wanted me to. We worked together to put food on the table. Worked for every man who made her promises and never delivered. Just once I wanted to make a choice for myself… Merchant wasn't going to put up with me forever… I couldn't take the beatings anymore. The taunting. The ridicule…" Her shoulders sank. "He broke me. I was powerless. Helpless… Despair is lonely."

Svana returned to her inspection in the mirror. Tulsi sank down to sit on the edge of the tub. That life could be her future if she didn't get out of the mess. Merchant had said he was looking forward to meeting her. Maybe Svana just assumed that Tulsi was going to be Merchant's next victim or maybe Baines had said something. Either way, she didn't paint a rosy picture.

Once they left this hotel, they'd be moving closer to Merchant every second. Tulsi had wished for death in this happy place. Maybe Hillam had been the lucky one. If Merchant got his way, neither she nor Svana would have any happiness again. She didn't want to be broken and resolved to never let him win.

But some part of her niggled at the thought. Didn't every strong person believe they could never be overwhelmed?

TWENTY-ONE

THE ICE HAD BEEN delivered by Delray. Tulsi had bathed herself in freezing water while Svana iced her face again. The early intervention should stop a lot of the swelling, but there would be bruising, that was inevitable.

Once the women were both cleaned up and the bathroom was spotless, they only had to wait a few minutes for their release. Baines had appeared with a halter-neck dress for her. At first, she hadn't understood why it was necessary for her to be in a dress or one that tied behind her neck.

The reason became clear as soon as she finished tying. Baines told her to turn around and fastened the loose zip-tie around her wrist, locking both of her hands at her lower back in makeshift cuffs… Exactly what Wreck, Rowdy, and Kieran had endured from Teal's apartment onward.

A sweater, that wasn't hers because it was too big and male, was hooked over her shoulders to conceal her cuffed hands. After that they were taken down in the elevator and bundled into the back of the car waiting for them in a loading bay.

She didn't see any other vehicles and wondered where Wreck had ended up. It could be that only she and Svana were being taken to Merchant. The others could've been taken on other jobs or to other places. Wreck had proved himself, Rowdy had too, through his friend. The answers Baines couldn't get from Putnam had been extracted by Wreck. He needed Rowdy to watch his back, so both had gone with Baines' crew to retrieve Svana and been successful.

Most of the journey was just tense and uncomfortable. Not only because she had her hands at her back, keeping her from relaxing, but because Coombs was driving. The man she'd "killed" had been his buddy. Once in a while, she caught sight of him glaring at her in the mirror. Baines might follow orders, Merchant might issue her with undisclosed powers, but she would have to endure some kind of payback from the man in the driver's seat.

Little was said throughout the journey. Tulsi and Svana sat at opposite ends of the back seat while Coombs and Delray rode up front. They drove for the rest of the night and all through the day. Although Coombs pulled into the drive-thru, Tulsi wasn't offered food. Svana snuck her a couple of fries, but even that wasn't easy without her hands.

Without her seatbelt, she felt unsafe. She didn't ask Svana to do it for her, though she could have. After the food, Svana had poured the ice from her drink into a napkin and used it for Tulsi's face. The woman was sweet... even in spite of the horrors that she had endured.

Blocking out Coombs' bullshit and her concern for Wreck, Tulsi tried to sleep. She must have dozed off at some point because Svana shook her to wake her up.

"We stopped," Svana hissed across the backseat.

Still bleary-eyed, Tulsi pushed upward to sit straighter. Looking around, she discovered they were at a massive truck-stop. It wasn't that busy; she could see the majority of the parking lot. There was a gas station, with a diner behind it and to the other side was a motel. Other fast-food places and stores lined the lot behind them. There was a tire place too, but everything behind them was closed.

Lights from the gas station and diner were almost blinding in contrast to the darkness of the parking lot around them.

"What's happening?" Tulsi asked, dipping her chin to

try scratching her jaw on her shoulder, only to be reminded of her bruises.

"I don't know," Svana whispered. "I think there are others already here. Coombs got out and took a bunch of stuff from the trunk. He took it to that room over there."

Tulsi followed the direction of Svana's nod to see there were four men standing outside a central motel room that was directly across the lot from the diner.

"Do you recognize anyone?"

Svana shook her head. "Not yet. Coombs said the car was locked, if we set off the alarm…"

"They'll know we're making a run for it," Tulsi said, recalling how many times Wreck and the brothers had been threatened. "They still have Putnam… If you run, they could hurt him."

They sat for another few minutes, just watching the men mull around, shooting the shit on the walkway of the motel. Seeing others gave her hope that maybe Wreck had been brought here too. But there were no guarantees.

When the motel room door opened, she sat up straight, trying to see who emerged. Coombs came out first with Delray, Teal, and Baines right behind. Tulsi smiled. There was no sign of Wreck, but Baines had been told to stick with Kieran, she was sure that at least he had to be there. If he was, he might know where his brother and Wreck were.

"You're smiling," Svana said, taken aback, almost accusatory in the way she retreated to a meeker state. "What is there to smile about?"

Nothing. Not really. Their situation was desperate. Tulsi had told herself not to appear too close to Wreck. Keeping distance protected them both, though she was more worried about him than herself.

Baines spoke to the men on the walkway. Two stalked down the deck and appeared to go around the back of the building. The other two stayed outside the front door.

Baines and Delray came in the direction of the car while Coombs and Teal went to the diner. As soon as Baines got to the side of the car, he unlocked it and opened her door. With a hand on the roof, he bowed to speak to them.

"Ladies," he said. "We got you a room and you're gonna stay put in it. I have men out front and back. Armed men." That last statement was for her; Tulsi wasn't sure her wide innocent eyes worked to appease him. "Me and my guys are going to be in that diner. Just a spit away."

So, don't try anything. That's what they were being told. Baines grabbed her arm and hauled her out. He caught the sweater, but instead of putting it over her shoulders, he hung it over her cuffed hands. Delray went around to get Svana out of the other side. He began to haul her toward the guarded motel room.

Baines walked Tulsi toward it too, though he hung back, keeping her in his grip and close to his chest. "I'd invite you to eat with us, Pretty, 'cept we need your ears in that room," he murmured above her ear. "Boss is real intrigued by you… Don't let him down."

Tulsi glanced up. They made eye contact for a few seconds before he forced her up the wooden stairs. His insistence kept her going on past the guards on the walkway. One opened the motel room door, giving Baines the chance to shove her inside. She stumbled forward, which caused her hair to tumble over her face, and came up hard against someone inside.

"Play nice," Baines declared to the room and then a door slammed.

Tulsi didn't have to look up to know who she'd crashed into. The scent of the man she'd slept with for more than a week was familiar to her. Stepping back, she peeked up to the harsh glare on his face. As she scanned the room, she didn't find much warmth aimed her way.

Rowdy was seated on the end of one of the two beds with his brother at his side. Both were fixated on her. The stranger sitting on the second bed was peering at her with curiosity. His face was bruised, probably worse than hers would be, and he had cuts on his brow, nose, and chin.

"You're the murderess," the stranger said, struggling to speak in a way that suggested swelling in his mouth.

"Tulsi isn't all bad." Turning around, she found Svana next to the door, looking at the stranger. "You sold me out,

Putnam."

The stranger, Putnam, leaped to his feet. He wobbled, but rushed to the blonde by the door. As he offered his apologies and tried to make physical contact, Tulsi brought her attention back around, making note that the only one in the room wearing cuffs, was her.

Just as she garnered the courage to lift her chin to make eye contact with Wreck, Svana yelped. "Don't touch me."

Whipping around, Tulsi's feet were moving before she thought about what she planned to do. Putting herself between Putnam and Svana, she knew without her hands that she had little chance at fighting, but that didn't put her off making a stand.

"Step back," Tulsi said without flinching when Putnam opened his mouth. "Stay away from her. Anything you have to say can be said from over there."

She nodded toward the bed he'd been on when they entered.

"Who the fuck are you to tell me what to do?" Putnam demanded. "You know nothing about us."

"Ditto, Snitch," Tulsi said. "I'm asking nicely. Step back."

"What the fuck are you gonna do? You don't even have your hands."

"Says who?" That male voice startled even her. Switching her focus in its direction, Tulsi was shocked to see Rowdy rising from the bed. "Do as the lady asks or we'll be her hands for her. You need a reminder what my friend can do?"

Putnam glanced from him to Wreck. Kieran stood up too. She wasn't sure how or why they were stepping up like this, but she appreciated it.

"You know this is bullshit," Putnam said, reversing and opening his arms in a show of surrender. "They've put all of us in this room together for a reason… They want us to turn on each other."

Svana grabbed her arm. "We need to ice your face, Tuls."

She almost lost her footing, but caught herself enough to catch up with Svana who paused to grab a full ice-bucket from a table just before pulling her into the bathroom.

Another bathroom, another motel. This one was a lot crappier than the hotel bathroom. It smelled of mildew and the tiles were cracked. Svana didn't seem to notice and dropped the ice-bucket to the vanity as she grabbed a towel to fill it with ice.

"This is bad," Svana said. "It can't be good... Merch does nothing without a reason. Putting us in this room... with these guys..." She put ice to her face. "You think Merch wants them to kill Putnam?"

Tulsi was shocked. Svana obviously didn't know about her affiliation with the guys, which was fine. Merchant and Baines may have set up the situation to facilitate Putnam's murder, except that didn't really seem like him.

"Let's find out," she said, moving away from Svana and her ice to go to the closed door.

Tulsi got new respect for what Wreck had endured when she had to turn and rise onto her tiptoes to search for the door handle. Just getting the door open was a fight.

Once she swung it back, she sidelined her triumph to put on her determined expression. There was a closet opposite the bathroom, but Tulsi ignored that to turn and go the few feet into the body of the room. The bedroom stretched left and right from the end of the hallway with the main door opposite.

All of the men looked her way, but it was Rowdy she nodded at. "Can I..." Moving her head more to the side, it took him a second to get up and start her way.

"S'up?" he asked, doing little to be discreet.

Tulsi tried to figure out a way she could pull him down, but with her hands cuffed, she had little choice.

Eventually, she just sighed out a groan. "I want to whisper, and you're tall, can you..." Bowing down, he tipped his ear her way. Tulsi didn't miss his expression of amusement, though she chose to ignore it. "You got orders to kill Putnam?"

That erased his amusement fast. On a frown, he tilted

his head her way. "Where did you... No."

Sliding her eyes in Wreck's direction, she didn't actually look at him, but conveyed her meaning to Rowdy. "What about?"

"What the hell do you think we're about, lady?" he asked. "No is the fucking answer."

"Okay," she said, opening her hands, though that meant little given no one could see them. "Don't get bent outta shape, just a question."

Backing away from him, she retreated into the bathroom and used her body to close the door again.

"Where did you go?" Svana asked, taking the ice away from her own bruises.

"Putnam is safe," Tulsi said, crossing to the vanity. "You know, it's maybe not a good idea to distance yourself from him."

Svana frowned. "What do you mean?"

"It's not a good time to be making enemies," Tulsi said. "If something happens, you might need him on side. You trusted him to get you out... And I was there Svana, he didn't break fast. He held out to protect you."

The woman softened. "It's difficult to know who to trust."

"You're right about that," Tulsi said, considering how she had felt isolated when she didn't know who was on her side. "But you have to trust yourself. Trust your gut. If it tells you to trust someone, you have to put your faith in them. Trust them all the way... You have to trust someone. You can't make it through this alone."

Taking a deep breath, Svana nodded. "We might need him... What do I do?"

Tulsi glanced around and settled on the bucket beside them. "Take him some ice... peace offering. Make friends. Build bridges."

"Ice," Svana said, taking a moment to catch on. "Oh, for his face."

Wearing a smile, Svana got another washcloth and filled it with ice. Holding it up to show Tulsi, she seemed proud of herself as she slunk out of the bathroom to return to

Putnam.

TWENTY-TWO

ALONE IN ANOTHER bathroom, Tulsi checked herself in the mirror. Her bruises were darkening, but the swelling wasn't as bad as it might have been without Svana's quick actions.

The ice was disintegrating. Frozen lumps floated in the slush of the smaller cubes that had already begun to melt.

Having been deprived of food and water that day, Tulsi considered how she might take a drink. With her hands at her back, she had few options. Pondering how likely it was she'd snag one on her tongue, she was about to try when another face appeared above hers in the mirror.

The sudden sight made her gasp.

"You were wrong," he said in a deep growl, leaning forward to rest his hands on the vanity on either side of her.

"About?"

He lowered his mouth into her hair, keeping his eyes on her reflection. "You're afraid of me."

How he came to that conclusion, she had no idea.

Relaxing her shoulders, Tulsi breathed out a smile. "I only regret that it took me this long to find you."

Surprise flashed on his face. She'd never seen him surprised before. Resting on him, she brought her elbows out at her sides to raise her hands so she could reach for his groin to massage him through his jeans.

"Nymph, you're…" Taking her arms, he turned her around to face him. "Bend forward, slide your hands over your ass."

"Why?" she asked, doing as he said.

Wreck picked her up by her hips to slip her onto the vanity. Bending her knees, he pushed them up to her chest while guiding her arms down. Despite the stretch of her shoulders, when he let her go, she was overjoyed to realize he'd brought her arms around her feet to put them in front of her.

"Better?"

"Much," she said, holding her arms up.

Wreck ducked to let her loop them around his neck. When he straightened, her ass was lifted from the vanity, which forced her body against his. But this wasn't an unusual position for them. Her legs actually began to curl around his of their own accord.

"Why?"

He didn't need to say more. She understood the question. "Baines wants a reason to take you down. Coombs too. They're threatened by you. You know it. You must see it in guys all the time." He didn't respond. Either he didn't or he did and didn't care. Tulsi bet on the second. "I wasn't strong enough. You did what I failed to do. I let you down and you didn't deserve to—"

"Nymph," he said, putting a hand on each of her cheeks to turn her face upward. "I heard you scream."

Was it a scream that reminded him of his sister? A scream that spoke to him? If she hadn't screamed would he have come to her as fast?

Using her hold on his neck as an anchor, Tulsi kicked off her shoes and climbed onto her knees. The weight of grief was beginning to dull her senses. She unhooked her arms from his neck, which made him frown, but she folded them against his torso, nestling close.

"I was so scared," she whispered, touching her nose to his chest and closing her eyes. "I blacked out and I… I used your strength. My Ruin—"

Her voice cracked, so she stopped talking.

"You fought," he said, burying his hands in her hair. "You didn't have to take the rap for—"

"What?" she asked, laying her hands on his chest and tipping her head back. "I would've done it if he hadn't taken the robe when he did. I wanted him dead."

"You don't protect me," he growled.

"And you said you wouldn't protect me," she said. "So, I guess we're even."

"Don't pick a fight," he warned. "Don't fuck around. You could've been killed."

"So could you," she said. "I wasn't going to take that risk."

"That was my risk!"

Tulsi put her fingers to his lips. "It's done, Ruin," she whispered, trying to soothe him. The last thing they needed was him on a rampage. "It's finished."

His chin hitched an inch, forcing her fingers from his mouth. "Why whisper with Rowdy?"

"That's why you assumed I was afraid?" she asked on a snorted laugh. "Fat chance, baby. I told you I could never fear you."

"Maybe you should," he muttered. "I didn't kill that guy by accident."

That much was obvious just from how fast he took care of business. "You could never hurt me, Ruin," she said, curling her fingers around his jaw, feeling nothing but gratitude and adoration. "Wreck, you would die before you'd ever consider hurting me in anger." His brow descended. "I don't care if you know it. I know it… I whispered with Rowdy 'cause I figured it would be smart if no one suspected us of being close. I don't want any doubt about *my* crime."

"What did you want to know?"

"If we were here to end Putnam." Rowdy's voice made both her and Wreck look to the doorway. "This doesn't look good."

"What?" she asked, noting how Wreck tried to be discreet about stepping away. "I was upset about the Hillam stuff. Wreck was comforting me."

Rowdy snorted and closed the door. "Wreck doesn't do comfort. Even when I was shot, he still told me to carry my own bag."

"You don't have tits," she said, pushing hers forward with pride. "Mine are something special."

Rowdy set eyes on his buddy. "Never made a lick of difference to him before… When were you thinking of giving Ki a clue?" Sauntering closer, he slipped his hands into his pockets. "You know he's still into this girl… Talked about her all damn day."

"I know," Wreck grumbled, turning his head down and away from her.

If Tulsi wasn't mistaken, there was more anger than guilt in that acknowledgment.

"Ki doesn't take losing well," Rowdy said. "He can be a vindictive cunt, you know that. He holds a grudge… This could blow up in your face, man… I've never seen you move in on another guy's girl."

Although there was no obvious judgment in Rowdy's tone, she didn't like it.

"Don't talk to him like that," she snapped. "I literally attacked him while he was chained to the wall. Wreck had no choice."

That made Rowdy raise his brows at his friend. "Attacked, huh? She's what? Buck ten soaking wet? Maybe five three?"

"Almost," she said, knowing she was just a fraction shy of that height. Sliding down onto her feet, she put herself in front of Wreck. "Your problem isn't with him. It's with me. So look at me."

"Chica, who my brothers fuck is their own goddamn business," he said. "Kieran is my blood. I love the little bastard. I'd die for the asshole if he asked me to… Check where we are, I might have to. Wreck is the brother I chose. He wouldn't have to ask."

"You don't trust me."

"I didn't," he said. "'Til I watched how fast you made the decision to take the fall… Now I don't know what to think… I have never, in my life, seen anyone make that choice so fast. And I've been in prison where people have their lives threatened if they don't own up to shit they didn't do to cover someone else's ass."

"There was no decision to be made," she said, resolved in her choice. "Baines wants a reason to challenge Wreck. I will not be that reason."

"Merchant could've given the order to kill you," he said. "He'd have been justified. Blood for blood is how Merchant usually operates… You took a massive risk."

It frustrated her that neither man saw the situation from her point of view. It almost stupefied her. "Not as big a risk as letting Wreck take the fall," she said. "Does Kieran know?"

"No," Rowdy said, suddenly treating the situation with more solemnity. "Shit, no. Anyone who knows the squirt wouldn't ever trust him with their confidence."

"And you think I should *date* him? You want me to date a guy I can't trust?"

"I don't give a fuck who you date," he said. "But putting yourself in the middle of these two could cause a problem… We already have enough of those. If Kieran decides to make this a thing…"

The way he glanced at Wreck over her head brought what he was saying into focus.

"You think he'd be insane enough to challenge Wreck? He must know that—"

"Wreck would own him? Physically, yeah," Rowdy said. "He would never be dumb enough to start a fight, but he won't take this easy. Baines isn't the only dude around here threatened by the asshole you're screwing… You have been fucking, right?"

The answer to that question was none of his business as far as Tulsi was concerned. That men like these could so easily put up with drama pissed her off.

"I wasn't Kieran's wife. We went on one crappy date where he talked about himself the whole time. Trust me, Wreck didn't rip me from his arms. I already knew I wouldn't be going out with him again."

"Yeah?" Rowdy asked, widening his stance. "That's harsh. You always label guys that fast? How soon after we were locked up at Teal's did you decide you wanted to ride this fucker?"

Given cause to smile, Tulsi exploited the chance to be honest. "I knew I wanted to ride this fucker at the bottom of the stairs in Teal's building before we ever went into that damn apartment."

Tulsi liked surprising Rowdy who took a few seconds to close his mouth. "You think the same about me?"

"Oh, God no," she said, sagging back, knowing Wreck was there to hold her up. She let her head fall against him. "You're far too wholesome for me."

There may have been a whisper of a laugh in Wreck's response. So slight, it was only perceptible because she was leaning on him.

"Wholesome," he muttered.

She raised her chin. "My Ruin—"

"You're right, baby," Wreck said, wrapping both arms around her shoulders, holding her from behind around her neck. "He'd never be able to handle your kinda filth."

The statement seemed to offend the man in front of them. "I am not fucking wholesome," Rowdy said. "I like filth."

Tulsi kept her smile sweet and patronizing. "Course you do, honey."

Licking her lips, she turned in Wreck's arms to dig her teeth into his arm. It had been too long since she'd put her mark on him. One of his hands moved to the back of her head to stroke her hair.

"What do you need, Row?" Wreck asked, without acknowledging how hard she dug her teeth into him. "You didn't come in here to bust us."

"No," Rowdy said, while she relaxed her jaw and curled her fingers into Wreck's waistband. "I sold Kieran a line about watching the people we don't know. I came back here to find out why Tulsi stepped up..."

Kissing Wreck's reddened arm, she spun around, sinking into his half-embrace. "Curiosity satisfied?"

His gaze became more discerning. "No," he said. "I can't figure you out. Wreck's not usually wrong about people."

"He told me that."

"If we trust you and you screw us over…"

"You said that before," she said. "I respect you as Wreck's friend, but I only need to work on gaining his trust. I don't need yours."

"If he vouches for you, I'll trust him," Rowdy said. "But I've gotta protect me and mine too. If I think you're bad for him…"

"Another speech? More stories?" she asked. "I'll listen. But if you've really got a problem with me, tell Wreck to stay away from me. You have influence with him. You have none with me."

"Stories?" the man behind her asked, sending a tremor of foreboding through her.

To his credit, Rowdy didn't hesitate. "I told her about Si."

Wreck's arm fell from around her. "Why?"

Again, without holding back Rowdy maintained admirable resolve. "Because I'm not ashamed of your sister, Wreck," he said. "Because talking about her keeps her alive."

"Don't start this shit," Wreck grumbled. "Si is not a cautionary tale."

"That wasn't why I told her," Rowdy said. "I knew you'd been forced together and I didn't want her to fuck you over."

"So you trusted her with our biggest secret?"

"Si shouldn't be a secret."

"Look," Tulsi said, moving away from Wreck to turn, so she could look at both men. "It's in the past."

"Fuck, we can't just forget about—"

"You telling me," she said, cutting Rowdy off with a glare. "Our conversation is in the past." Softening her expression, she set it on Wreck. "Look at it this way, I know, and you didn't have to be the one to tell me." Anything that saved him from baring his soul was probably a plus to him. "Knowing about Si helped me understand why you reacted to Hillam the way you did."

The irritation on his face faded to a deeper frown. "You think I killed him 'cause of Si?"

"Of course," she said, raising her hand to touch his chin. That her other one had to just hang there connected was frustrating. After a smile, she moved to look at Rowdy again. "I appreciate you being honest with me, Rowdy. I hope you'll learn to trust me. But I won't lose any sleep over it if I don't."

"Just tell me straight," he said, becoming serious. "Why risk your life for something you didn't do? Why take the fall?"

Wearing a smile, her eyes ascended to the ceiling as she gave a shake of her head. "God, men are such idiots," she whispered and looked straight at Rowdy. "Because I'm in love with him." Shock made Rowdy blink and recoil. "Because even just the thought that he could be hurt tears me up inside… I did what I did because it was right and because there's nothing I wouldn't do to keep him safe." The way Rowdy blinked up at his friend who was behind her again made her laugh. "Don't worry. I'm not a crazy stalker person. Wreck has been more than clear about what this is to him. It's not real. I'm a distraction. I'm okay with that… I know we're on a clock. In a few days, few weeks, we'll go our separate ways and I don't plan to make a scene about it."

"Tulsi, I—"

"Let me guess, you still don't trust me," she said. "It's not a big deal. Can we focus on what to do next rather than what's already happened?" Turning to Wreck, she ignored his scowl and carried on. "Baines left me in here to be his ears… He hasn't asked me to report anything yet, but he might… I think Merchant is starting to trust you… Baines isn't… He's worried about his position."

"Tulsi," Rowdy said, moving in closer.

His expression of sympathy was enough to betray he hadn't moved on from the last topic of conversation.

"Rowdy," she said, as matter of fact as she could muster. "When we get to Merchant's we might not get another chance to talk… I need to know if there's anything you guys need from me."

The bathroom door opened. All of their focus swung

that way. Kieran was the person coming inside. "What's going on?"

TWENTY-THREE

"NOTHING," Rowdy said, trying to dismiss his brother. "Go wait in the other room."

"No," Kieran said, stomping across to join them. "Whatever this is, I'm in it too."

"We're in it because of you," Rowdy reminded him.

"I need to talk to Tuls." She didn't expect that. Neither did the guys. "We're not gonna get another chance like this. I need to talk to her."

"Okay," she said, curious about what Kieran had to say.

"Tulsi," Rowdy said, something of a warning in his tone.

She nodded. "It's fine. Just give us a few minutes."

Offering a smile, she waited for Rowdy to relent. Once he did and gave Wreck a nod, the two of them began to retreat. Wreck didn't look at her, or wouldn't. Maybe it hadn't been such a good idea to be so honest. But she didn't regret it. If one thing had become clear to her, it was the urgency of life. It could flip on a dime, or be stolen at any moment.

After the duo were out of the room and the door was closed, she leveled her attention on Kieran.

"Tulsi," he said, reaching for her.

She stepped out of the way of his hands. "Say what you have to say, Kieran," she said. "I don't want you to touch me."

"I understand," he said on a nod. "I get it. After what Hillam did to you—"

"I don't want to talk about that," she said, turning around to go over to the vanity again. "What did you want to talk about?"

"We haven't been alone, not properly alone since our date, and… I just want you to know that I will make this up to you… I will fix this."

That he could even believe that possible was absurd. "How do you fix abduction? Imprisonment? Physical attack? Sexual assault? There are no amount of dinners or flowers that can make up for something like this."

"Whatever you need me to do, I'll do it," he said, ignoring her request and taking her shoulder to force her around. "Please, Tulsi, I'll do whatever it takes to be with you…" Shocked, she was stunned into silence. "I know why you did what you did to Hillam… I didn't know you were capable, but… Man, was I proud of you."

For taking another's life? That didn't compute. Though, Tulsi couldn't judge him for having positive feelings about Hillam's demise when she'd felt the same way.

His fingers on her face made her shiver. It wasn't easy to keep her hands to herself. Though, her compulsion was to shove him away, not welcome his touch.

"Kieran…" she said, searching for the words to let the man down gently. "We can't—"

"Rowdy and Wreck are suspicious. I know this is a tough enough situation without people like them doubting you." He smiled. "I don't doubt you… I'm going to talk to Merchant as soon as I can. I'm going to get you out of this."

"I don't think it would be a good idea to mention me to Merchant."

Kieran frowned. "You're my girl," he said. "I'll make him see you had nothing to do with this."

Pushing his hand away from her face, she leaned away. "Getting Rowdy and Wreck out of this is more important… He's going to use them to pay your debt. Who knows what they'll be asked to do?"

Without showing any worry or remorse, he shrugged. "At worst, it will be enforcing. They've done that before. It's not a big deal to them."

"It's a big deal to me," she said, realizing what he hadn't said. "Wait a minute… you didn't say it wasn't your debt… Is it… Is it your debt?"

His smile took its time about dropping, but it definitely vanished. "It's complicated," he said. "There's politics involved."

"Politics," she said, her creeping sense of suspicion increasing. "Kieran, what—"

A shout from beyond the bathroom silenced her. Pushing Kieran out of the way, she rushed past him. The door was easier to negotiate with her hands in front of her.

In the bedroom, Rowdy and Wreck blocked the end of the hall. Peeking between them to find out what was going on, Tulsi was horrified to see Coombs and Delray had a hold of Svana.

"Svana," she said and tried to squeeze between the men in her way. Wreck twisted to block her, managing to pen her in against the wall. "Wreck."

Although she pushed at his back, he ignored her.

"Rigby, you're with us," Delray said, snapping his fingers.

Kieran appeared from the hallway, Wreck didn't get in his way.

"What's going on?" Kieran asked, walking into the bedroom.

"You're coming to party with us."

It was then Tulsi realized that she hadn't seen Putnam. He could be around the corner, but she wasn't sure.

"Maybe if you're a good boy, we'll let you have a little fun yourself."

"Don't take her," Tulsi called out, though there was no way to get around Wreck. "Svana stays here."

"Sorry, Pretty," Delray said.

"Yeah, you've got a pass," Coombs said. "Least for

now."

The door slammed and silence hung in the air.

The next time Tulsi gathered herself to shove at Wreck's back, he moved out of the way with ease.

"I can't believe you just did that," she said, shoving at him again.

"I didn't do a damn thing," he said, strolling over to the table where the ice-bucket had been. On it were a bunch of bottles and a stack of sandwiches.

"Exactly! You just let them take Svana out of here! You know what a party means with men like that."

Wreck opened his beer and tossed the cap aside. "Yeah," he said. "She's in for some night."

"They'll rape her," she said, storming past Rowdy to face up to Wreck. "Every one of those sick sonofabitches will—"

"Fuck her," he said, tipping his beer past his lips. "Yep."

"Wreck!" she called and jabbed his torso with the heels of her hands. "How could you do nothing? How could you—"

"One goal," he said, putting a finger up in front of her face. "You remember that?"

"You didn't tell me what it was. But yes."

"It doesn't involve risking me and mine for a stranger," he said. "They can have her. I don't give a damn about her."

"She's innocent," Tulsi said, trying a different approach. "She doesn't deserve to be violated. They'll torture her... She's so young—"

"Toughen up," Wreck said.

When he tried to go past her, she blocked his route. "What if it had been me?"

Lowering to get closer, he growled in her face. "If I'd stepped in, it could've been. Long as you're off their radar. They get to do what they like."

Again, he tried to move around her, but she put her hands to his torso to stop him. "Ruin," she murmured, showing him her pain and torment. "I know what it's like to be held down and terrified."

He laid his hand on the side of her neck. "Won't happen again on my watch."

Though his watch was finite. Wreck had told her that he couldn't protect her, so there was no reason to believe he'd step up for someone else. Someone who was a stranger to him. He put the bottle in her hands and went around to talk to Rowdy.

She started with a sip. The taste reminded her of her thirst, so she ended up downing most of the bottle and quickly going for another. Tulsi stuffed one sandwich in her mouth and punctuated the next with mouthfuls of beer.

"Man, look at her go," Rowdy said.

Glancing over her shoulder, she saw both of them studying her. Forcing the lumps of sandwich down her throat, she swallowed a bunch of times and then took another swig of beer. "Coombs put me on hunger strike," she said.

Wreck frowned. "He won't let you eat?"

"Don't worry about it," Rowdy said. "We'll be at Merchant's in a couple of days."

"Yeah," Tulsi said. "Stupid of me to be worried about being starved or dehydrated."

Wreck went into the bathroom without saying anything else.

Rowdy sighed at the beds. "Guess I should be glad there's two of them."

"Beds?" she asked. "Wreck doesn't snore… Not bad anyway."

"I've slept with Wreck before," Rowdy said, then frowned at himself. "In the same room as him… Never heard him fuck before though… not up close."

That made her feel saucy. "You're missing out."

Rowdy cringed as Wreck came back to join them, carrying a glass and the ice-bucket.

Her lover thrust the glass at her. "Drink."

Taking the glass, she gulped the liquid. Once it was done, he took it from her and stuck it into the ice-bucket to fill it again.

"More?" Wreck wasn't the kind of guy to take no for

an answer. "I'll be up all night peeing."

"You'll be up all night," Wreck said while she drained the glass.

Watching him over the opposite rim, she recognized the darkness that descended in his gaze.

Returning the glass to the ice-bucket, she smiled. "Rowdy doesn't want to listen."

"No, he doesn't. So no screwing tonight," Rowdy said, coming over to take the ice-bucket from Wreck to put it on the table. "I'll let the lady pick her bed."

It was late. They should be thinking about getting some sleep while they were in a safe environment... Though "safe" was relative.

Wreck didn't give her the chance to reply. He just pushed her toward the bed furthest from the door. "Lay down."

"Such a gent," she said, crawling onto the bed to pull down the covers. "Let me guess, you want me in the corner?" A single nod was the only response. "So no one can steal me and I can't run away."

Rowdy went across the room to turn off the light as she wriggled down beneath the covers. The artificial light from the businesses opposite seeped around the closed curtains, so they weren't exactly plunged into darkness.

Wreck was doing something at the end of the bed. When he stood up, he dumped his bag to the floor between their beds.

On her back, Tulsi was trying to get comfortable when a pair of boxer-briefs landed on her chest.

She held them up while he bent down to unlace his boots.

"You've never told me to put underwear *on* before," she said, tucking them under the covers as she raised her feet.

Wreck lay down to snatch them from her before she could slip her feet into them. He rolled over and stuffed them under her pillow.

"If they come back, put those on," he said and grabbed his shirt at the back of his neck to tug it off. Once he'd discarded it, he got under the covers.

Rowdy came sauntering over to the bed by theirs, taking off his tee-shirt as Wreck stuck a leg underneath her to tug her between his thighs. Seemed to be his preferred way to sleep, with her on top of him. Settling her cheek on his solar plexus, Tulsi watched Rowdy let go of his tee-shirt and peel back the bedcovers.

"Wow, Rowdy's ripped," she said, laying one hand on top of the other to squeeze them between her cheekbone and Wreck's body.

Rowdy paused to glance over his shoulder at her. After making eye contact, he laughed. "Yeah, this is what wholesome looks like."

Wreck untied the dress at the back of her neck and she rose just an inch or two to let him push it down to uncover her breasts. When she relaxed again, her chest squashed against him, which was probably exactly what he was going for.

"Rowdy, do you have a girlfriend?"

"Do I—no," he said. "But I think you've got all the cock you need over there."

"Damn right," she said, wriggling lower to kiss Wreck's stomach. "Svana is young, only twenty-two."

During her explanation of how she'd met Merchant, Svana had said they'd been together for almost two years. The woman had endured the bastard for almost half of her whole adult life. Her official adult life anyway. With what she'd been through in her earlier teenage years, Svana would've grown up fast.

"So? You trying to set me up? We not got enough problems with you two and my brother? You want me screwing Merchant's girl too?"

"I'm lying here wondering what she's going through right now," Tulsi murmured. "I'm safe… and happy… She's being tortured and violated."

"Why you telling me?" Rowdy asked.

"Because once Wreck says no, there's no changing his mind."

Rowdy shifted in his bed to face her, his head half-obscured by his pillow. "So you're appealing to the wholesome one?"

Tulsi didn't know Rowdy well enough to assume she'd be able to manipulate him into taking action. "No, I'm just busting my Ruin's balls by proxy."

"Find something else to do with that mouth, Nymph," Wreck grumbled.

She surged up to dig her teeth into his pec. "Come on, you've been without me for a whole day and night. I know you've missed me… Some teeny, tiny little corner of you wanted to see me again."

He raised his head just enough to glare down at her. "Mouth. Cock. Now."

With a smirk trying to contain the thrill of her laugh, she boosted higher to press his lips to hers. "Yes, my Ruin."

He was kind enough to lift the covers up high so she could wriggle lower and comply. Wreck had accused her of fearing him. That couldn't be further from the truth. They'd only known each other for a couple of weeks. Already she didn't want to imagine what her life would be without him.

TWENTY-FOUR

TULSI BECAME AWARE of her position before anything else. Without opening her eyes, her curiosity zeroed in on why she was on her back. She was quickly distracted from the thought of not having Wreck's legs around her by the sensation of his tongue sliding over her clit.

"Mmm, there you are," she purred, snaking her hands beneath the covers to tangle them in his hair. Her hips rose toward his intimate kiss. She curled her leg around his head, stroking his back with her calf. "My Ruin."

The moment the words seeped from her lips, he began to rise. Her still-joined wrists caught at the back of his neck, so she was holding him when his mouth met hers. Their tongues only played for a few seconds before his teeth were dragging their way down her chin to her throat.

Glancing to the second bed, she expected to see Rowdy sleeping through her half-open eyes. Instead, she noticed an empty bed and a lot of light coming in around the curtains, suggesting the day had come.

"Rowdy," she mumbled. Wreck stopped enjoying her breasts and rose to meet her eye, a scowl creased his expression. Realizing that she'd just said his best friend's name in bed, she laughed and hooked her arms around his neck again. "He's gone."

"Shower," Wreck grumbled.

Only after he said it did she register the distant sound of water coming from the bathroom. "Nice of him." She grinned. "We've never done it in a bed before." They had sure done other things in their bed at the hotel, but they'd never gone all the way. "Fuck me, Ruin. Make me scream."

"We'll hit Merchant's today or tomorrow."

That wasn't exactly what she'd expected to come next. Part of her was desperate to take advantage of this rare opportunity. Another part understood they had limited time to share information. Whispers were one thing. In that moment, they had privacy. Actual, real privacy.

She nodded. "I figured. I think we're going back the way we came… Wherever he is, it's not too far from where we started." His scowl had changed hue. Wreck wasn't angry, but there was something keeping him tense. That he was so intent on her piqued her anxiety. "What? What is it, Wreck?" His lack of a response only encouraged her concern. "Stop staring… You're scaring me."

Sleeping in his arms left her feeling content. Her dreams were happy and her body settled. Anything could have happened; there was a distinct possibility she'd have slept right through any drama. It could've been Svana or Kieran. Maybe one of them had returned hurt or worse, maybe someone had lost their life.

"When we get there…"

The murmur of his words conveyed more than just their meaning. He wasn't apprehensive; he was telling her that things were about to change.

"You'll have to work for him," she said. "To pay off Kieran's debt." Stretching and bending her fingers, she enjoyed the feel of his hair between them. "Last night, when he wanted to talk to me in the bathroom… He said something, rather, he didn't say something."

"Nymph?"

"I mentioned his debt and what you would be asked to do to settle it. He said the worst it would be was enforcing, which you've done before."

His eyes narrowed in warning. "Nymph."

"No, I'm not asking about that. I'm saying that he didn't deny it was his debt. I mentioned the debt and he didn't say it wasn't his. I asked and he said it was complicated, that there were politics involved."

"Fucking weasel," he grumbled.

Tulsi had always gotten the impression that Kieran wasn't his favorite person in the world. She pushed aside ridiculous notions that Wreck might want to know Kieran had referred to her as his girl. Wreck didn't care who claimed her; she was a distraction for him. The more her feelings grew, the more she had to remind herself of that.

"You think we'll be separated," she said and his attention came back to her. "That's what you were trying to say… That's why you were staring… You'll be put into the employ of Baines or another goon, someone who'll watch you until they trust you." Taking a few seconds to seal her lips, Tulsi gathered her courage before speaking again. "And I'll be handed off to Merchant."

"I don't know that."

"I do," she said. "He said I'm special… that I could be the love of his life."

A different kind of frown settled on his face. "You talked to him?"

She nodded. "On the phone. After they put me in the bathroom… after Hillam. Merchant said he was looking forward to meeting me. That he'd underestimated me… He wants me. Svana gave me an idea of his process, so at least I'm a little prepared."

She couldn't quite bring herself to smile. Dread vibrated through her breathing. Tulsi could front it out if she had to. Except Hillam had given her a taste of what helpless could be. Fighting Merchant off would lead to her death, no doubt about it. He had men, dozens of them at his disposal. The horror of what could await her was almost unimaginable.

"Do what you have to do, Nymph," Wreck said, just like he'd told her before. "Forget morals and boundaries. Stay alive."

"It's easy to say that," she said, focusing on the curve

of his shoulder. "I know I should… I know I'll have to… I… It's odd to be traumatized by the prospect of something. It hasn't even happened yet and I… Svana said she used to be strong. I haven't been through half of what she's endured." Closing her eyes, she opened them again on his. "She's terrified of him, Wreck. Terrified."

"Four walked in. Four'll walk out," he said. "We'll do whatever we have to do to get out of there."

While shaking her head, she licked her dry lips. "He won't give me up that easily… If I go in meek and pathetic, he won't be interested and he'll ship me off somewhere straight away. If I show strength, he'll want to keep me until he breaks me."

Wreck ducked down, grabbing her arm to pull himself out of her embrace. He got out of the bed and snagged his jeans from the floor to pull them on.

"I'll take the heat," he said. "I open the door, you bolt to the gas station."

"The gas station?" she asked, sitting up.

"Yeah, one of the truckers will give you a ride," he said, lunging down to grab her arm to haul her up to her knees. "Turn around."

"What are you…"

Tulsi had no time to follow his command before he was flipping her around and grabbing the ends of her dress from where it had fallen around her knees. Pulling them up, he tied the halter ends at the back of her neck, paying no attention to how her hair was caught with the fabric.

"You'll be faster without your shit so leave it."

"Wreck—"

"Put on the underwear."

"Stop it," she said as he hauled her off the bed onto her feet. "I'm not going anywhere."

"Yes, you fucking are."

"If you open that door, every one of Baines' goons will come running. There are half a dozen of them, not counting Baines, Coombs, Teal, and Delray. That's ten! Ten against you alone. Even Rowdy is in the goddamn shower. You'd be alone. Why in the world do you think I'd leave you to them? Did you not hear what I said to Rowdy in the bathroom last night?"

He tossed her from his grip. "You didn't mean that bullshit."

"Okay, fine, I didn't," she said, knowing it would be pointless to argue with him. "But you stayed. I stayed and you stayed. You said if I could see it through then you could too. If you can see this through, so can I."

Baring his teeth, he bent to get in her face. "They're not going to ruin me," he snarled.

"Me either," she said, opening a hand on his stubble. "You've already done that for every other man who follows. I told you you'd be the last man I chose for myself. I don't regret it. I don't regret the date with Kieran. I don't regret walking into Teal's place. I don't regret meeting you, Wreck."

"You should."

"Yeah, I probably should," she said, smiling as she moved in closer. He straightened up and backed off, putting distance between them. "I was wrong. This *is* the thrill I was looking for... Not them. Not Kieran's mess or Merchant's perversion. You were the thrill I was looking for."

"I told you this ain't real."

"For you, it isn't. Doesn't mean I don't feel what I feel. There's no rule that says you have to feel the same. I'm happy I could give you what you needed, even if that was just a distraction."

"Stop with the lovey shit," he snapped. "I fucking told you."

"Okay, fine," she said, raising her joined wrists. "Then you stop trying to save my ass. That's my responsibility. Yours is to save yours. I'll do what I have to do, when I have to do it. You concentrate on getting yourself out of this mess."

"Take the damn out."

"No," she said, shaking her head once. "You open that door if you want. I'm staying here."

"Why?" he asked, narrowing one eye like he just didn't understand.

"Because they'll kill you, Wreck. Don't you remember Coombs conversation with Hillam that first night? They wanted to take you down. This will give Coombs and the rest of them the opportunity they want. To hurt you. They'll have witnesses that you started the fight too. I don't want that on my conscience. Shit, hasn't that been Baines' strategy since the beginning? To use the four of us against each other? You have no chance against ten armed men. If Rowdy comes out and sees you in trouble, they'll kill him for jumping in too."

He sneered at her. "Merchant will break you."

"Maybe. Don't write me off yet... I have a few ideas on how I can play him."

Wreck scrutinized her for a few seconds before setting his shoulders back. "We're done."

"I'm surprised it took you this long," she said without blinking. "You want this over that's your prerogative... I haven't said no. You said that until I did you would have me any time you want me... You don't want me..." She sauntered closer, getting as near to him as she could. "Don't have me."

Their gazes locked. Tulsi didn't know if it was just his stubbornness that was keeping him from blinking or looking away. She hoped his vehemence was a sign of his conflict; that maybe he did still want her. Nothing had changed in the few minutes since he'd been eating her pussy. Nothing except their argument.

The bathroom door opened and Rowdy came into her peripheral vision. She and Wreck just continued to stare.

"Whoa, is it chilly in here?" he asked. "I was worried you'd have steamed the windows. Guess I was wrong."

Before either of them could consider replying, the door opened. Both she and Wreck gave up their stare to check out who was coming in.

Putnam, Svana, and Kieran came into the room. Delray leaned in only to grab the handle and close the door again.

"Oh my God, what happened?" Tulsi asked, rushing across to the exhausted Svana. Even in the few hours since she'd been gone, the woman seemed more broken. She tried to move forward, but almost fell on Tulsi when their trajectories met. "You need to lie down."

Guiding her over to the bed, Tulsi helped Svana to sit and began to search her face and arms for more injuries.

"They took her into another room," Putnam said. "Those assholes, they…"

"Took turns," Rowdy said, finishing the statement. "I'm sorry, Svana."

Least he was good enough to apologize. Wreck didn't utter a word.

"They weren't the only ones," Kieran muttered.

The shame of his contrite tone made her head turn his way. He was rubbing the back of his neck, focusing on the carpet.

"Oh my God," Tulsi exhaled.

"Ki… you didn't," Rowdy said. "You fucking raped her?"

"No!" Kieran and Putnam said at the same time.

"No," Svana said, seeming to gather her strength. "I gave them permission. All of them permission. I give all of you permission… Every one of you will have to be with me eventually."

Trying to hold onto her outrage, Tulsi stood up. "I am going to draw a bath for Svana."

TWENTY-FIVE

SVANA HAD EXPLAINED the importance of an ice bath for intimate injuries. After enduring a night of being passed around, Tulsi dreaded to imagine what her new friend had been through. Still, there was an element of deception in her urgency to leave the others.

So many things were going through Tulsi's mind as she went into the bathroom to begin filling the tub with cold water. The permission Svana had given to Kieran and the other men wasn't genuine, it was coerced. During their conversation in the hotel bathroom, Svana had told her it was best to just do as she was told. That was what she'd done, taken the path of least resistance and fallen back on Merchant's rules.

If her future was going to be the same as Svana's, Tulsi would have to undergo one helluva transformation to give twelve men rights to do whatever they wanted with her body. Counting Rowdy and Wreck, the number would be higher at fourteen. She just couldn't imagine it.

"I'm sorry, Tulsi."

Kieran's voice made her spin around. He was standing just inside the door exuding an air of sorrow and guilt.

"Apologize to Svana."

"I did. I have," he said, approaching her. "I didn't want to do it. I resisted. It wasn't like I was aroused by her. I only thought of you and I—"

"Please don't, Kieran."

He stopped. "Don't hate me. Please. They threatened your life. Said if I didn't do it, they'd drag you over there and hurt you."

"No," Tulsi said, shaking her head. "Do not put this on me."

"She touched me. It was biology. Not passion. They told her to touch me and I… My body just reacted to what she was doing."

Svana had mentioned being in porn and working in strip clubs. She'd also implied doing more than just taking off her clothes for clients. No doubt the young woman had several coping mechanisms for getting through an experience like she'd suffered the previous night.

"What you do with your body is your business," Tulsi said.

"When you left, I… I knew it must have hit you hard to hear I was with another woman. I promise, it will never happen again."

"You can't make that promise," she said. "Apparently all Baines has to do is order you and you'll do whatever he says. Were you at least smart enough to wear a condom?"

"I… the—"

"My God, you are an idiot."

He frowned. "I know you're unhappy. That you're jealous and—"

"I am not jealous."

"Tulsi."

Rowdy was in the doorway with Svana in his arms.

"Bring her here," Tulsi said, turning off the water even though it was less than a foot deep. "Put her in the tub."

"She's exhausted," Rowdy said, crossing the room.

Tulsi grabbed a wash cloth and towel from the vanity and went to the tub to support Svana's head as Rowdy lowered her into the water, still clothed.

"We need ice," Tulsi said, smiling in a feeble attempt at comfort when Svana's head rolled her way. "And she needs to eat."

"All we have are the sandwiches and warm beer from last night."

"Something is better than nothing," Tulsi said. "Go onto the porch, ask the stooges for ice. The worst they can say is no."

"Okay," Rowdy said. "You need anything?"

"Food and clothes. There should be something Svana can wear in my bag," she said. "And get him out of here."

Tulsi wouldn't even look at Kieran. She dipped the washcloth into the water to soak it. Wringing it out, she used it to wipe Svana's face.

"Tulsi, don't—"

"I don't give a damn, Kieran," she snapped. "This is not about you!"

"Come on," Rowdy said, grabbing his brother's shoulder to shove him toward the bathroom door.

Once the two men were out of the room, Tulsi smiled at Svana again. "Are you sore?"

Svana nodded slowly and tried to wet her lips. "I've gone through worse."

The sorrow she felt for this woman was impossible to keep from her expression. "If you are Merchant's favorite, why would he let his men hurt you?"

"Punishment for leaving him," she said, her voice cracking just as Rowdy came back in. The door was on the other side of the room behind her, but he was kind enough to be heavy-footed, so they heard him coming. "Sometimes he likes to share. Other times he'll murder a man for looking at me."

Rowdy put a tray down on the floor beside her. There were stale sandwiches and a few beers.

"Not much of a breakfast," he said, dumping the clothes he had draped over his arm.

"We appreciate it," Tulsi said, tearing a corner from a sandwich to offer it to Svana's lips. "We'll be as quick as we can. Make sure everything is packed up out there."

"Yes, ma'am."

Fearing she may have offended him, Tulsi looked up, but he smiled and winked. Rowdy had claimed not to trust her. Maybe he didn't. The gesture of reassurance was the most promising one she'd received so far.

He went out of the room and this time, closed the door behind him.

With the new privacy, Tulsi helped Svana out of her dress and kept washing her body. It was difficult with her hands connected. Along the way, she gave Svana a beer and more to eat.

The woman gave her a commentary of what had happened. Knowing that listening was the most she could do, Tulsi pushed down her own horror at the tale.

"Merchant will want every detail," Svana said, finishing another sandwich.

The bread was crispy on the outside and soggy in the middle. Tulsi had hazarded a few bites herself. Svana didn't complain and neither did she. The food might not be appetizing, but at least it was food.

"From you or his men?"

"Probably both," Svana said, wringing out her hair after Tulsi finished rinsing the conditioner with the showerhead she'd brought down from above. "He likes to watch people squirm." That much, Tulsi had figured out on her own. "Let me help you."

Svana drained the tub and took the shower from her. While Tulsi steadied her friend, she stood and hooked the showerhead back into its slot. Tulsi was desperate to wash, though she hadn't expected anyone except Wreck to join her in the shower.

Still, she didn't object when Svana untied the halter, untangling Tulsi's hair as she went. The women held onto each other as Tulsi got into the shower. Many men would probably make a big deal of two naked women in a shower together. There wasn't anything sexual about it.

Svana probably despised even the thought of anything sex related. Tulsi was just pleased to have someone to help her out. If she was going to be cuffed for the foreseeable future, and Wreck was serious about ending their association, Tulsi was going to need all the help she could get from elsewhere.

They had just finished rinsing her hair when the bathroom door opened. The transparent glass screen didn't hide either of them from Wreck who was standing in the doorway. With both of their injuries still healing, they'd kept the temperature of the shower low, so there wasn't even steam to conceal that they were in there together.

"We took too long," Svana said, thinking nothing of being on show to him. "Can you help me?"

Svana wasn't reaching for her, she took the few steps down the tub holding onto the screen and reached out toward Wreck. He came striding across the room and didn't hesitate to put an arm around Svana's waist to lift her over the edge of the tub.

"We're done," Svana said. "Long as you don't mind us drying our hair, you can use the shower. Leave it on for him, Tuls."

So, Wreck was just going to strip off and shower while she and Svana dried their hair? Needs must. They were on a clock and under scrutiny, they didn't have the luxury of choosing modesty. Tulsi told herself it was just about efficient use of resources. They needed the blow-dryer which was attached to the vanity and Wreck needed to shower. Baines and his henchmen could order all of them out at any second. They couldn't afford to be modest.

Doing as Svana said, she left the shower on and moved to get out of the tub. Wreck didn't back off, but he didn't help her either. Tulsi held the edge of the shower screen in her joined hands to steady herself as she climbed out.

Wreck had seen her naked dozens of times. There were marks on her body that he'd put there. His tongue had been inside her just that morning. Except as she glanced up at him, she didn't see any indication of arousal. The blow-dryer went on, reminding her that they weren't alone.

She tried not to hear Wreck's jeans hitting the floor. Tried not to see the admiring expression on Svana's face as she walked away from Wreck to approach her friend. For the first time that morning, Svana smiled.

Svana turned off the blow-dryer to run her fingers through her hair. Her attention was obviously on the man in the shower. The sound of the water hitting the walls and base of the tub told Tulsi that he was washing.

"He's not bad to look at," Svana said, a saucy tone of interest flavoring her words. "I don't even think hot covers it... I love that dark brooding thing, don't you? So powerful."

Seemed shocking that Svana could be thinking about sex or attraction after being violated all night long. Tulsi knew that Wreck was impressive. He worked hard to keep himself in shape. At any other time, if Svana was zeroed in on his cock there would be valid reason to salivate. Any straight woman would be intrigued and stimulated by the sight.

"Maybe we should give him his privacy," Tulsi said.

"He doesn't mind. Men never do," Svana said, putting the blow-dryer on again to continue drying her hair.

The woman who had come into the room that morning had been shattered and spent. Even in the tub, that she'd had to be carried to, there was something drained and used about Svana's broken body that had awoken Tulsi's deepest sympathies.

But as she stood there, proud of her naked body, Svana didn't seem depleted anymore. She didn't seem traumatized and distressed. She appeared to be a woman on the prowl.

Wreck might be interested in another distraction. Messing with Merchant's favorite could get him into trouble. Although Tulsi hadn't considered that when she was taking advantage of him.

"Do you want a towel?" Tulsi called out.

Svana dismissed her with a wave. It didn't take long to dry off the woman's poker straight hair. She turned off the blow-dryer at the same time Wreck got out of the shower. It didn't bode well that he left the water running. That could mean others were going to follow him. Tulsi glanced over her shoulder to see him snag the towel she'd left on the floor by the tub to dry himself off.

"Wreck," Svana said. "That's what they call you,

right?"

The beauty stepped around her and moved toward Wreck who stood up straight, holding the towel in one hand against his lower abdomen, so it covered his groin.

"Yeah," Wreck said, running a hand into his hair to shake off the water.

"I…" Svana's voice became meeker. Except when Tulsi glanced in the mirror to see her stop in front of Wreck, she didn't have the stance of a weak woman. "I want to tell you that it's okay."

"What?" Wreck grumbled.

"When they tell you to take your turn… You have my permission."

Wreck's gaze flicked to hers in the mirror. Tulsi quickly busied herself by picking up the blow-dryer to examine its switches.

"I'm no rapist."

"That's what I'm saying," Svana purred. "It won't be rape… I want it."

Tulsi's mouth fell open. Was that what Merchant demanded she say to every man or was Svana hitting on Wreck? Closing her eyes, she thanked the stars that his towel was over his dick because if she had to witness him getting hard for another woman, she'd probably combust.

"I don't," Wreck said. Tulsi's eyes opened at the same time Svana reached for his chest. The quick reflex of his hand leaping up to snatch hers before it could make contact made both of the women gasp. The darkness in his focus grew as it narrowed on the small woman before him. "I don't like to be touched."

Svana seemed aroused by his growl; her breathing was shallower than it had been. She certainly wasn't afraid.

"For me, you'll want to make the exception," Svana pouted. "I can make your wildest fantasies come to life."

Wreck bowed to get closer. From the way Svana's chin rose, Tulsi wondered if she was anticipating a kiss. He did look like an intent man, but that wasn't his expression of lust.

"I can make what Merchant did to you seem like

child's play," he snarled. "Touch me again and I'll start mailing you back to him, one digit at a fucking time." He stooped to grab the clothes from the floor and flung them against Svana. "Get the fuck out of here."

Taken aback, Svana glanced around at her. Tulsi didn't know what to say to the stunned expression that met hers. Quickly Svana shrugged off that surprise and replaced it with affronted outrage. Holding the clothes against her body, she stalked out of the bathroom, slamming the door behind her.

Tulsi didn't know what to do or what to say. Already, she felt more at ease that Wreck was the only other person present. Or maybe that she was the only person present with a naked Wreck. Her focus was still on the door when movement in the mirror heralded Wreck coming toward her.

Putting down the blow-dryer, she poked around in the arrangement of complimentary items left out by the motel. Ignoring him coming up behind her wasn't easy.

"If I want to fuck her, I'll fuck her," he grunted.

"I didn't say anything," Tulsi said, paying more attention to the writing on the tiny pack of soap than she needed to.

"No way she's traumatized."

She raised her attention to meet his in the mirror. "Different people have different responses to abuse," she said, sidelining her own misgivings. Svana's transformation from tortured victim to tempting seductress did seem rather abrupt. "Maybe she likes the illusion of control."

"Don't trust her," he snapped, still frowning.

Being hit on couldn't have been that offensive. Though, there was one element of what had just transpired that intrigued her. Tulsi was so busy scrutinizing his expression that she didn't realize she hadn't responded.

"Do not trust her," Wreck said again.

"Okay, geez," she said and turned around. "I won't trust her."

She didn't meet his eye. Instead, she kept her attention on his chest as she raised her pointed middle finger to trace the tip down his pec. While her finger moved south, her focus ascended to his.

"What are you doing?"

"Testing a theory," she said, tipping her mouth closer to brush it against his chest.

"We're done."

"You said that earlier," she said. "Except you also said this wasn't real. You can't end a relationship we never started." Pressing a kiss to his sternum, she trailed her tongue across his body, keeping her eyes on his. "We're nothing. We do what feels good…" Twisting her wrist, she let the back of her fingers trace a path downward. "You're bigger than me. Isn't that what you said? If you don't like it, put me in my place."

The towel was gone. At some point, he must have dropped it. She had a clear route to wrap her fingers around his cock, which was already hot and full and ready.

As was so often the case, she hadn't really thought about what she was going to do. All she'd wanted to know was if he'd toss her away like he had Svana. Kieran had said Wreck didn't like to be touched. That hadn't been her experience. Tulsi had assumed it was a gender thing. Except Svana was female and she hadn't been afforded the same courtesy Tulsi took for granted.

Her eyes drifted shut. "My Ruin," she whispered, deepening her kiss on his hard body.

She intended to lower to her knees to see how far he'd let her take this encounter. Wreck didn't let her progress. Stepping back, he snatched her wrist and tugged it up. Tulsi thought she was about to be rejected when he took her by surprise and ducked to loop her arms around his neck.

"You never fucking learn," he snarled, scooping her off the floor and turning to slam her back against the wall between the vanity and the shower.

The beat of the water gave them some cover for her surprised inhale when he plunged into her. This was dangerous. So dangerous. Anyone could walk in on them. Svana had slammed the door, but neither of them had gone over to lock it.

Rowdy knew about them, but he had also used the

shower already. If Kieran came in to witness Wreck driving his cock into her hard and fast while she clung to him, writhing and panting in her haste to keep up, he'd go ballistic. Putnam, she knew even less about. If he wanted to save himself, he could use the knowledge to rile Kieran or reveal them to Merchant.

Svana had just been rejected by the man who was fucking Tulsi like his life depended on bringing her to climax. Wreck had told her not to trust Merchant's favorite. After her behavior that morning, Tulsi didn't know what to think.

"Ruin," she gasped. "Oh my—"

He forced his mouth over hers, pulling her higher and loosening their connection to silence her. "Keep it fucking quiet," he hissed against her. Hooking his arms under her knees, he opened her wider and forced himself deep into her. "You want me right here. Want my cock right here?"

"Always," she said. The humidity of her breath rebounded from his skin. "I am safe when you're inside me. We're safe. I want your cock in me every minute of every day… I choose you, Wreck. You and only you, my Ruin."

The way he gritted his teeth suggested anger. She feared she'd said too much. Crossed a line that he wouldn't let her retreat back over. That he refused to believe what she'd told Rowdy betrayed how important it was to him that she mean nothing to him.

She thought about what Rowdy had said. About how Wreck had made it a point to never be responsible for a woman. Protecting her was beyond his means, beyond anyone's means. When they got to Merchant's she'd be whatever he wanted her to be. It was possible she and Wreck would never even see each other again.

When he pulled himself all the way out of her, she held her breath, fearing that he was about to withdraw from her completely. He released her legs, letting her feet fall to the floor as he dropped to his knees. Picking up her leg closest to the vanity, he put her foot on the counter and leaned in to rub his mouth against her clit.

The kiss reminded her of their first intimate encounter when he'd demanded to taste her. Back then, they'd been so limited in what they could do. Her bound hands found his hair. As he licked and tormented her, she arched toward him, feeling the burn of pleasure rise as climax approached.

This could be their last time. Their last moment alone. Tulsi didn't want to come under his mouth, she needed something else from him. Pushing him back, she bent her knees and climbed into his lap, managing to guide him into her pussy again.

Wreck grabbed her ass, steadying her movements, speeding them with his tightening grip. "Fuck," he hissed when she looped her arms around his neck and buried her face against his shoulder to sink her teeth in.

Using the strength of her bite to stifle her climax, Tulsi didn't even think about how much she might be hurting him, not until he flipped her onto her back and surged into her hard. The tension of his gritted teeth and lowered brow revealed how hard he worked to keep himself quiet during his own orgasm.

Just the pressure of his groin on her clit pushed her into a second, shorter burst of release. Tulsi dug her teeth into her lip, though Wreck was quick to steal it away from her. Plunging his tongue into her mouth, he punctuated the end of their joining with an overwhelming kiss that left her with more questions than answers.

Before she could make sense of it, he pounced to his feet. Tulsi was still lying on the floor, staring at the ceiling, listening to the shower when a pair of boxer-briefs landed on her face.

"Put 'em on," he commanded. She didn't really think about what she was doing and just followed his instructions. Tulsi had just pulled them on when her dress landed on her. "That too."

Putting the dress over her feet, she stood up only to have the material wrenched away from her. On that occasion, she was quick to toss her hair forward to ensure he didn't tie it into the knot again. When it was pulled tight, he grabbed her upper arms to spin her around.

The first thing she saw was the deep angry red welt

on his shoulder exactly where she'd bitten him.

"Shit," Tulsi whispered, reaching up to touch it. "I'm sorry."

"Get outta here."

"Wreck—"

"We've been alone too long. Out."

He didn't seem to care about the wound she'd inflicted on him. Tulsi never intended to hurt him, that wasn't what she wanted at all.

"I—"

"Jesus," he barked and grabbed the zip-ties that bound her wrists.

Dragging her across the room, he opened the bathroom door and brought his arm around in a wide arc to toss her out.

The door slammed in her face and she was left there alone. Staring at the wood that barricaded her from him. There were so many barriers between them and that kiss... She just couldn't figure out what he was trying to tell her.

TWENTY-SIX

TULSI COULDN'T STAND staring at the bathroom door all day. Every day brought new challenges. Until that morning, she had always taken solace in Wreck's proximity. Some part of her wanted to believe that he found security in her too. That somehow they weren't alone as long as they had each other.

She had underestimated his need to maintain distance. His physical self might desire her. His emotional and mental self didn't. A woman meant complications. Meant taking responsibility for someone other than himself. Rowdy could look after himself; Wreck saw his best friend as an equal. He saw her as a liability.

In truth, she *was* a burden on him. Tulsi could take risks with her own safety. That was her choice. Whether she took the right risks was something of a crapshoot because she was a rookie.

Wreck was more capable and savvier than her. Anything anyone could threaten to inflict on him, he could combat. Wreck could match hit with hit. Injury with injury… in a fair fight.

After enduring what he had with Sienna, he'd consciously held himself away from developing any kind of bond with a woman. Tulsi hadn't known it when they started being intimate, but she never had a chance at getting close to him.

Wandering down the hallway from the bathroom to the bedroom, she was still thinking about the man she'd left when she noticed Svana kneeling by a large purple bag, her purple bag, raking through what was inside.

"You have some great stuff," Svana said, picking out lingerie Coombs had selected.

"Help yourself."

"Tulsi," Kieran said and stood up from the bed to approach her.

Rowdy was quick to get in his brother's way. "You need to wash up. Putnam, you gotta use the bathroom? Now's it. We're running out of time."

Tulsi appreciated him stepping in because she couldn't handle a confrontation, especially not in front of an audience. With a heavy pat on the back of his shoulder, Rowdy sent Kieran off to the bathroom. Putnam went after him.

"I thought you were drying your hair," Svana said, looking up at her.

"Wasn't as easy with this"—Tulsi raised her hands in an open butterfly to show her cuffs—"as I thought."

"I can help," Svana said, boosting onto her knees.

"No, it's okay. The guys need their turn in the bathroom. It dries fine on its own."

Not that it was as straight as Svana's. Tulsi crouched by the bag to see what else she could pass off to Svana.

"I'm gonna talk to Ki," Rowdy said, heading into the bathroom with the others.

After the door was closed on the men, Svana grabbed for her hand. "How well do you know Wreck?"

"What do you mean?"

"Putnam said he was the guy who beat him," Svana said. "Last night Baines was taunting Putnam, he said Merch was going to hurt him for stealing me… I think Wreck might be working for him."

"For Merchant?"

Svana nodded. "He'll do anything, go to any lengths to get what he wants. I don't know what Wreck told you about how he was captured—"

"He's not working for Merchant," Tulsi said. "He was captured at the same time I was."

The bathroom door opened. Wreck strolled out, shirtless as he had been before. He didn't look at either of them as he grabbed his bag and dumped it on the end of the bed to retrieve a shirt.

They were still in silence when the door opened. Baines and Delray appeared, but didn't come inside.

"Time to move," Baines said. "Grab your shit."

Tulsi zipped her bag with Svana's help and Wreck put on his tee-shirt.

"Where are the other three?" Delray asked.

"Bathroom," Svana said, getting to her feet.

Tulsi stood up too, holding the strap of her bag.

Baines looked to Delray. "Grab a couple of guys and go get them."

Delray nodded once and disappeared down the walkway.

Coombs was quick to take his place. "Your turn tonight, Pretty," he said, checking her out. "Boss is gonna work you good."

"What the boss does with her is his business," Baines said. A couple of other guys came past Coombs to enter the room. "Wreck, you're first up."

"For what?" Tulsi asked.

Wreck didn't show the same concern. He sauntered forward, grabbing her bag as he passed. He went outside, with the two bags and the two guys, into the glare reflecting off the asphalt. Tulsi couldn't see exactly where they went.

"Got a new mode of transport, ladies," Baines said, gesturing them out.

Svana linked their arms and drew her across the room and out onto the walkway. Tulsi didn't like feeling led. Despite that, there was no alternative to following Baines' orders. None that would leave them all uninjured anyway.

Backed up, a few feet from the sidewalk were two vans. The two back doors were open, though it was difficult to see much in the shadows.

"In you go," Coombs said, grabbing Svana first to toss her into the back of the van on the left. "Sit on his other side. Passenger side."

There was someone already in there. Wreck maybe. Tulsi assumed she'd be thrown into the other van. But Baines pushed her toward the same one.

"Get in, Pretty," he said and Coombs stepped aside.

Climbing into the back of the van, she gave her eyes a moment to adjust to the darkness. A bench was attached to each side wall. They ran parallel from the back of the seats up front to the back door. Wreck sat in the middle position on one side with Svana seated next to him nearest the front.

"You sit on this side," Coombs said, getting in behind her.

He pushed her to the seat on Wreck's other side and then turned to catch a bag that someone from the outside threw his way. He put it in a covered compartment near the front, where she guessed Wreck must have put their bags too.

Tulsi took her seat and Coombs jumped out the back again. "Our guys will be getting in to keep an eye on you just as soon as we get your buddies settled in. Don't get ideas."

He slammed the back doors and she heard the handle jiggle like he was checking it had locked.

"Why are we changing vehicle?" Tulsi asked.

"Makes us harder to track," Svana answered.

"Who's tracking us?"

"Could be cops," Svana said. "Or someone who wants to help you?"

"Me?" Tulsi asked. "I don't think so."

"Maybe Kieran or Rowdy," Svana said. "None of Putnam's contacts are crazy enough to take on Baines." Silence reigned for a few moments. "Wreck? Anyone out there who'd come to your rescue?"

"Maybe," Wreck said.

"That's it then," Svana said. "They have obviously figured it out."

"He only said maybe," Tulsi said, pinning herself back against the cold metal panel at her back when Wreck leaned across her. It took a second to realize he was pulling a seatbelt across her lap. "Thank you."

"Quit talking," he said, not looking at either of them in particular.

The back door clunked. "Was I being oblivious again?" Tulsi asked.

Wreck didn't look at her, though she did note his closest brow descended. His focus was intent on the back door, probably anticipating who might join them. Tulsi didn't want to know. She didn't want the doors to open. There were still moments that the reality of her situation just floored her. Her life was supposed to be boring and uneventful.

The doors did open. Three guys got inside; the men Delray had brought with him. The last one closed the doors. The three of them sat down on the opposite bench. At first, Tulsi kept her attention away from them. Looking anywhere to escape having to register their faces.

The surprise of hearing Wreck's voice brought her attention around.

"You got a problem?" he drawled.

The depth of his menacing intonation was enough to make even her shiver. Except, he wasn't looking at her. His focus was on the men opposite them.

"None of your fucking business," the one in the middle said.

Tulsi wasn't sure why Wreck had chosen to talk when he usually stayed quiet. He'd been the one to tell her and Svana to stop talking just a few seconds before.

"We've got a lot of hours to kill back here," the one opposite her said and that was when she noticed, all three of them were focused on her. "Maybe we find out what Pretty has the boss might like."

Shit. Tulsi could almost feel the walls closing in. Squeezing her thighs together, she was relieved Wreck had given her the underwear. Though it wouldn't slow these guys down for long if they decided they wanted a piece of her.

"I don't give you permission," she said, recalling what Svana had said about Merchant's rules and the necessity of showing strength.

"Remember what she did to Hillam," the third one

said.

Though he was staring, he was smart enough to appear somewhat wary.

"No weapons in here, man," the one opposite her said, becoming more intent. "Someone's gotta take the first taste."

"It won't be you," she said, drawing on bravado. "Come near me and I'll make sure there's nothing left for your precious boss to put back together."

The guy snickered and began to slide forward in his seat. "Aww, baby, you don't wanna hurt me," he said, lowering to a crouch, reaching out for her leg.

Wreck didn't let him make contact. In a swift move, he twisted and brought his foot up to slam his boot heel against the guy's temple sending him flying sideways. The thug's head bounced off the back door with a thunderous boom. As he slithered to the floor, a daze in his eyes, the other two jumped.

"I do," Wreck snarled at the stunned man strewn across the van floor.

The back doors opened and the semi-conscious guy almost fell out, except his buddies leaped up to pull him back in.

"What the fuck is going on back here?" Baines asked.

The two uninjured men were doing their best to prop the third back in his seat.

"Your men try to touch me without permission again and they'll get a lot worse than that," Tulsi said, shirking her own shock to exude confidence. "Are we going to get on the road or what?"

Baines turned his annoyance on his men. "Sit your asses down and don't say a fucking word."

He slammed the door again and silence settled over the van. Tulsi didn't have to worry about the guys anymore, none of the three of them would dare look her way.

"Was that for her or for Merchant?" Svana asked.

The woman, who'd been dubbed Merchant's favorite, had just seen Wreck step in for her. Tulsi hadn't expected him to do anything, though she couldn't claim he'd never protected her before. From Teal's apartment all the way through to this moment, he'd always intercepted danger before it could hurt her. Hillam being the most potent example of that.

Wreck was saved from answering when Coombs and Delray got in the front. "Right, motherfuckers, not a damn word. Let's get this shit over with."

Over with. Coombs might want to get where they were going. Tulsi wasn't looking forward to reaching their destination. Not one little bit.

TWENTY-SEVEN

THE VAN'S STEREO BLARED music for most of the trip. Tulsi figured it was a way for Coombs to keep the chatter to a minimum, which was fine by her. The three men on the opposite side of the van were so wary of Wreck that they barely looked her way. Any time she caught them stealing a peek, they'd immediately avert their attention elsewhere.

Later on in the day, Coombs had gone to a drive-thru and ordered a bunch of food. Once again, he didn't provide anything for her. But with Wreck at her side, Tulsi had no choice except to eat. Her arms were still in front of her, so it wasn't like he had to feed anything into her mouth. He just dumped half his food onto her lap in the wax paper that had been around his burger. Once he was done with the soda, he handed it off to her. All without uttering a word.

Tulsi couldn't deny that travelling with him again was better than without him. But with her thigh pressed to the side of his and his heat scalding her skin, her mind kept returning to their last kiss in the motel bathroom.

Something about it felt like goodbye. Yet, it had made her feel valued and special. At the same time, it felt hateful in a passionate sort of way. Kind of like Wreck was desperate to consume her but hated her for making him feel that way.

The sun had gone down. The rain had started and the night outside felt foreboding. At least, that was what she remembered from before her eyes had closed. Tulsi hadn't meant to close them. The rocking of the van and boredom of the trip gave her a good excuse to slip into slumber.

All of the dread of the road trip dwindled in her dreams. Her mind was playing with a happier image. One of light and bliss in her bed. Her actual bed in her apartment above the store. Wreck had his mouth between her thighs, much as he had that morning. Stimulating her to the apex of pleasure, he used his hands to pin hers down to the mattress when he reared up over her.

No one was bound. The only danger came from the man looming above her, gazing down at her through drowsy eyes that provoked her arousal almost as much as his mouth.

"Mmm," Tulsi exhaled, arching to push up. Except that made him squeeze her tighter. "Ruin…"

Suddenly, she was jolted. Her eyes opened, but she couldn't focus for a good thirty seconds. The van. Yes, she remembered the van, but… Her head was on Wreck's shoulder, her whole body twisted toward his so both her hands could rest in the vee of his thighs. If that wasn't bad enough, her legs had coiled their way around his shin. Tulsi had literally wrapped herself around her safety, which might make sense if the guy hadn't made such an issue of disliking being touched in front of Svana.

Guessing that he'd been the one to jolt her, she couldn't argue against him not wanting to be sleazed on. He had dumped her that morning… twice. Though he'd quickly followed the second dumping with sex, so she didn't know where they were at.

Wherever it was, it didn't include letting anyone else in on their association. Hillam had known about them, so it stood to reason Coombs did too. He'd also shared a room with them while they'd shared a bed. Still, she didn't want to be responsible for denting Wreck's street cred by drooling on his tee-shirt.

"We're here."

Tulsi had been so focused on her ridiculous position

and pulling herself out of sleep that she hadn't even noticed how they'd slowed down. Looking to the front, out of the windshield, she realized they were in an alley. The van turned to descend a slope into an underground parking area.

"Boss likes his privacy," one of the men said and all of a sudden she had a hood pulled over her head.

Although she tried to jerk away, she didn't get far. There was nowhere to go. No avenue of escape. A drawstring was closed around her neck. Not too tight, but tight enough to keep the hood in place. The sudden darkness made her grab for Wreck's thigh again. He was nice enough to lay a heavy hand over hers, probably just letting her know that he was still there.

The van stopped and a few breaths later, the back door opened. Tulsi heard movement outside and assumed there were others there to greet them. The men inside the van jumped onto the asphalt. The van moved, something metallic clanged. It sounded like the compartment Coombs had opened. Another metal crash followed, which she assumed was it being closed. Her concentration was on trying to pick up sounds that she almost missed someone undoing her seatbelt.

"Move! Come on."

She recognized Coombs' voice. It was so close that he had to be the one who grabbed her zip-tied wrists and yanked her off the seat. In a stoop, she staggered forward, aware that she'd probably fall on her face hard because she had no idea where the van ended.

Except before she could fall, someone grabbed her hips and yanked her backwards. Pain shot through her shoulders. Coombs was pulling her forwards, while someone else, someone whose touch she recognized, was pulling her backwards.

"Slow down," Wreck said behind her.

"Fuck off," Coombs snapped and yanked her wrists.

Except that just prompted Wreck to coil an arm around her hips to pick her clear off the floor. She was dangling there, bent over, unsure what the hell was going on when the sound of his heavy boots hitting concrete prefaced her own feet being planted on the ground.

Under Coombs lead, she was jerked forward. It wasn't easy to fumble her way in the darkness, especially knowing she couldn't trust the man who'd have been happy to spill her blood. All she could rely on was the occasional nudge from behind, which she supposed was Wreck making sure she didn't walk into anything or anyone.

There were doors and then stairs Coombs commanded her to ascend. It felt like they were going upstairs for a while, though there were only about ten in a flight before they turned to go up another set. They went up maybe four or five floors and then through another door to be marched down a corridor.

"Don't let 'em out for nothing," Coombs said as a lock was turned. "Stay on this door all the time. I don't care who is bleeding or if there's a fire. They stay in here."

Whoever he was talking to must have signaled their understanding somehow, but she didn't hear any words. Suddenly whipped around, Tulsi was shocked to feel the plastic loosening from her wrists. There was no time to really register her freedom before she was shoved backwards so hard that she stumbled and dropped onto her ass.

"Stay."

Coombs final word came seconds before the slamming of the door. Silence, except for the huff of her own breaths, hung around her. Tulsi didn't know if she was alone, or what was going on. She must have sat there on the carpet for half a minute before daring to lift her hands to the drawstring around her neck.

Loosening it slowly, she braced for someone to shout or hit out. Neither came, so she pulled the hood off and blinked up at the door a couple of feet away. Brown wood, it was like any apartment door she'd seen. The walls were a muted beige kind of color. Next to the door was her purple bag, and Wreck's black one.

"Two bedrooms. Windows don't open."

Whipping around at the sound of his voice, she was horrified and overjoyed to see Wreck striding through a door in the far corner.

Scrambling to her feet, Tulsi glanced around. It wasn't a huge room, but wasn't small either. The couch and coffee table faced a wall-mounted television that was between two windows. Well, what she guessed were windows. The curtains were closed over them.

To the left and right in each corner was a door, which she supposed led to bedrooms. Beside the door on the left was a dining table without any chairs around it. She didn't care about chairs, but did care about the food laid out on it and the plastic bottles of water. Wherever they were, they were being provided for.

"Where are the others?" she asked when Wreck went past her to grab their bags from the floor.

"They took the woman upstairs."

"Svana," Tulsi said, watching him carry their things to the coffee table to dump them down. "That's her name."

He shot a glare her way. "What did I say to you?"

"Not to trust her," she said. "Doesn't mean I forgot her name."

He pointed a finger at the ceiling and circled it. "Don't trust these walls either."

"What does that mean?" she asked, hurrying toward him as he raked through her bag. "You think they're listening to us?"

"They could be," he said. Shoving a pair of jeans and a sweater her way, he kept searching in her bag. "Put those on."

Examining the clothes, she tried to figure out what was going on in his head. "Why? He told us to stay here. Doesn't that suggest we'll be here a while?"

He straightened and she wasn't surprised to see he was still glaring. "So?"

"So it's nighttime," she said, dropping the clothes onto the table. "I'm tired. Let's just go to bed and worry about this in the morning."

"Chances are Merchant is upstairs."

She still didn't get it and shrugged. "And?"

"The woman went up there. Coombs will be up there too. Baines won't be far behind."

"Anything they know about us, Merchant learned as we travelled. Baines has been in contact with him."

"He's looking forward to meeting you," Wreck said. "Isn't that what you told me?"

"Merchant? Yes," she said, glancing down at the clothes. "If you think a pair of jeans will protect me from him, you're not as smart as I gave you credit for."

"Jeans will slow him down," Wreck growled.

Sensing his tension, she looked up to notice he wasn't just glaring, he was angry. "Why are you mad?" she asked, reaching for his face.

Ducking back out of the way, he gritted his teeth. "Fucking stop it."

"Stop what? I asked a question."

"Touching me! You're always fucking—"

"You don't like to be touched," she said. "Yeah, Kieran told me. I just…" Steeling herself, she prepared to be humiliated. "I didn't think it applied to me."

"If it had, we wouldn't be in this damn mess."

Tulsi was at a loss. The way his jaw clenched and his shoulders rose suggested he was carrying more than just a casual tension. Except they were safer than they'd been all day in this private room alone together.

"I got into this mess because I went out with Kieran," she said. "Neither of us are here now because you let me touch you."

"That's not what I fucking meant," he said, turning his back on her.

Giving him a moment to breathe, Tulsi understood his concerns about their location, if it really was Merchant's headquarters. But, as far as she knew, they'd spent the last couple of weeks in a precarious position under the threat of violence. This day wasn't much different from the others they'd experienced together.

"Ruin," she murmured. Edging forward to snake her fingers under his tee-shirt, she curled them around his belt. "I am not your responsibility." Tulsi kept on going until her mouth was resting on his back. "Whatever happens to me, it won't be your fault. There's nothing you can do to stop it."

He spun so fast that she had to think fast to yank her fingers free of his belt.

"I should never have let this happen."

"You had no choice," she said. Still close to him, she tucked her fingers into his waistband, holding it in a light grip. "The second we stepped into Teal's apartment, our fate was inevitable. This was always where we were going to end up."

"I'm not talking about Kieran's fucking mess," he growled and tightened his jaw again.

Tulsi smiled and picked up his hand to put it on her face. "I know. Neither am I… Did you think I was ever going to let you go? Do you remember what happened the first night I got naked for you?"

He jerked his hand away from her face. "That wasn't for me," he said, the strain of his words was stretched by the memory of who'd demanded she strip.

"It was for you," she said, taking his hand again. Pressing her palm against the back of his hand, she held it on her cheek. "Why do you think I didn't take my eyes off you the whole time? The only way I got through that was imagining I was doing it for you. You've got me through all of this. Everything. I wouldn't have made it this far without you."

"Don't say that shit."

"Why? Because you don't want me to be grateful? You don't want me to see your strength? Wreck, you're my inspiration. I fought Hillam because of you. I believed in me because I wanted to be good enough for you."

"Stop it," he demanded, being more forceful about wrenching his hand away.

Once it was free, he tugged her hand from his waistband and turned to walk away again.

Tulsi wasn't discouraged. "If it helps, keep telling yourself that this ain't real."

Frustration was building inside her. She was desperate to scream at him to be honest about what was going on rather than putting up these brooding barriers. Except she understood why it was necessary. Wreck wasn't pushing her away because he didn't want to care about her. He was pushing her away because he knew there was nothing he could do to save her from Merchant. His sister's demise still weighed on his conscience. He was reliving the agony of it with every second closer she got to being Merchant's mistress.

"Do you want me to tell you that I want it?" Tulsi asked. He whipped around to lay another scowl on her. "I can tell you that I'm excited by the idea of being his moll, if that's what you want to hear."

"That's a lie."

"Yes," she said, raising her brows. "It is. But I don't know how else to help you. I don't want you to feel any guilt. This is not your fault. You said from the start that you wouldn't be able to protect me and I accepted that."

"That was before."

"Before we got here, when it was easier to deal with the prospect of him. Now that we're here, you know at any second that door could open and we could be separated for good."

"You say it like it's nothing."

When she smiled, he recoiled in disgust. "No," she said. "I say it knowing that no matter what happens to me, you'll get out of here. You're right. This is easier for me. It's easier to be the one in pain than the one watching it happen." Approaching him at a cautious pace, she relished the opportunity to be honest. "I'd beg for torture every minute of every day if it meant saving you from enduring one second of pain."

His hand rose to her face without her direction. He ran the pad of his thumb down her temple. As it descended his other fingers curled around her chin. Something in the way he examined her spoke to the turmoil he was going through. For the first time, she felt like he was really letting himself feel for her. That maybe there was a chance he'd embrace what they meant to each other rather than spurning it.

Before either of them could say or do anything else, the sound of the lock on the door broke the air. As she'd just said, she could be taken out of the room at any time. Wreck's services could be called on too. She didn't place any authority on the idea that Merchant would give a shit about Wreck's safety. He could be called out on a job and never come back.

Merchant wouldn't lose a minute of sleep over Wreck losing his life or his liberty.

Tulsi's pulse kicked up as anxiety for both of them began to course through her bloodstream. Wreck got hold of her and pulled her backwards to put himself in front of her. He had to know that it was a hollow gesture. If Merchant wanted her, Wreck couldn't fight every man sent to retrieve her, especially if they were sent all at once.

She was reminded of being in Teal's apartment. Back then, she'd cowered behind him too. What she felt now was more than protected. The weight of him shielding her from the world was increased by the sheer will pulsing from him. He wanted to keep her safe, even though he would never be able to.

"My Ruin," she whispered, curling her fingers around his waistband and closing her eyes as she settled her face against his spine.

Whatever was going to happen, was going to happen. She wouldn't let him be hurt. She just wouldn't. But she wanted these seconds, wanted to remember his warmth and his scent and the beat of his heart.

"I got ya, Nymph."

Tulsi hadn't expected any kind of response. His murmured words were probably supposed to be a comfort. They had the opposite effect. His tone betrayed the truth. He'd fight. Even if it was futile. He'd keep himself between her and danger for as long as possible.

All of a sudden, her concern became panic. Tulsi had wanted him to face how he felt for her. It may not have been a series of grand gestures, but each of the little ones told her the truth. Her safety meant something to him. Whether it was residual guilt over Sienna's death or genuine love for her, she didn't know.

Tulsi was sure of her own feelings for him. Forcing him into any admission was immature and dangerous. If anything, she should be encouraging him not to feel for her. Not when it could get him killed.

Her fingers loosened from his belt and she began to retreat as the door opened. Tulsi heard it, but couldn't see around him.

"Fucking asshole!"

That voice was Kieran's.

Leaping aside, she watched as Teal slammed the door behind Kieran and Rowdy, who'd been dumped inside much as she and Wreck had. As the door locked again, the four of them considered each other.

"Come here often?" Rowdy asked in a shot at wry humor, kicking aside the bags that had been thrown in next to them. "Got a lay of the place?"

"Two bedrooms," Wreck said. "Windows don't open. Figure it's ballistic glass."

"Which might matter if we had guns," Rowdy said, crossing to hook an arm around the curtain, probably to inspect the window, though he didn't actually look around it. "Where's the woman?"

"Took her upstairs."

Rowdy nodded and pushed the curtain aside to look out.

Tulsi moved further away from Wreck. "I'm a woman too, you know," she said, going over to the dining table to check out the food.

"You're Tulsi," Rowdy said. "She doesn't get a name." Before Tulsi could respond, he switched his focus to Wreck. "Walls have ears?"

Wreck nodded.

Whether he knew that for sure or was just erring on the side of caution, Tulsi wasn't sure and Rowdy didn't question him.

"Tulsi," Kieran said and began to come her way.

She tossed aside the piece of chicken she'd been snacking on and backed away. "Don't talk to me… Don't come over here. Don't touch me."

"You have to let me explain."

"What are we explaining today?" she asked. "Did you steal any more drugs today? Rape any more women?"

"That's not fair," he argued. "None of this is my fault."

"Look, we'll get nowhere fighting among ourselves,"

Rowdy said.

Tulsi pointed upward. "We can hardly talk progress when we don't know who's listening or watching."

"You think they're watching us too?" Kieran asked, turning a suspicious and dubious eye upward.

"This guy is your friend," she said. "You tell us."

Tulsi didn't expect support from Rowdy or Wreck, so she was surprised when their expectation was as heavy as hers on Kieran.

"What do you know?" Rowdy asked.

"I've only heard about this place. I've never been here… I wasn't sure it was real. I mean, I don't even really know where we are," Kieran said.

Rowdy got closer to his brother. "But you think you know," he said. "Talk."

Wreck cracked his knuckles, startling both her and Kieran, though the latter was certainly more shaken by the sound. "All I know is he owns the whole building. It's an apartment block. Got the idea from Keaton who owns a place on the other side of town… I think Merchant lives on the top floor. Has space on the lowest floors for his guys to hang out. A bunch of them stay in apartments too."

"So there is always someone on premises ready to take down prisoners," Rowdy said. "Who he obviously keeps here too."

Rowdy turned to look at Wreck.

Tulsi was more intent on sorting her own thoughts. "I don't think you have to worry about being considered a prisoner," she said, fixating on the carpet. "Merchant is fair."

"Why do you think that?" Rowdy asked.

"Blood for blood is what you said," she replied. "Hit for hit was how Baines put it. Merchant lost this shipment that Kieran and Styx were supposed to retrieve from the courier."

"Hey, but I didn't steal—"

"Whatever happened," she said, ignoring Kieran's outburst. "Merchant thinks Kieran is somehow responsible. Either he wants that shipment back or he wants you and Wreck to work off the debt."

"A hundred thousand?" Rowdy said. "You know

how long that will take? Most guys are lucky to get a couple of hundred for a job."

"You've already started paying it back," she said. "Putnam. He was your audition. Merchant knows you are capable. He knows he can get his money back from you two… Kieran is useless to him; he has no menace. He couldn't intimidate a bug… That said, if Kieran does know something…"

Again, when she set her sights on him, both Rowdy and Wreck did too.

"She's right," Rowdy said. "You have to be honest, man. If you know something—"

"I don't know anything."

Tulsi wasn't sure that she believed him. But if Wreck was right about them being surveilled then she couldn't push the issue.

"That's a shame," she said. "Information would've given you a decent bargaining chip."

"You think that he'll let us go if we lead him to the shipment or work off the debt?" Rowdy asked. All she could do was shrug because she'd never even met the man. "What about you? Are you going to work off the debt too?"

"I don't know about me," she said. "Maybe or maybe I'll be used as bait. If I'm here, he may assume none of you will abandon me."

"We won't," Kieran said, moving her way again. "Tulsi, we're not going to leave you here."

"I don't know how this will play out," she said, feeling the weight of the day catch up with her. "You three have more experience with this than I do. I am just repeating what I've heard and assumed… I'm going to take a shower… Is there a shower?"

Wreck pointed to the bedroom she'd first seen him coming out of. The one farthest from the dining table.

Making a choice to walk around the front of the couch, past Rowdy rather than Kieran, Tulsi picked up her bag from the floor and slung it over her shoulder.

They'd made it to their final destination. Tulsi had no idea what was going to happen next. All she could do was wash and rest and hope that she had the strength to make it through to the other side of the ordeal.

TWENTY-EIGHT

AFTER HER SHOWER, Tulsi climbed into bed. Sleep didn't come quickly, though at some point she must have drifted off. Sleep was an excellent way to process thoughts and pass time.

Unfortunately for her, it didn't last. Something dark encroached on her slumber. The sensation of metal around her wrists and the metallic snap of a key turning cut through the shadow of her dream. The heat of someone's breath warmed her cheek. Somehow, she knew straight away it wasn't Wreck. Her body tensed until it ached. Nausea hit hard and began to quake in her belly when the impression of someone's fingertips ascended her forearm.

Tulsi wanted to scream, she wanted to fight. But she couldn't move. She was paralyzed. Fear kept her still. She was too afraid to twitch.

"Nymph."

The whisper of his voice speared her with an eruption of panic. He was in need. Not with her. Far away. They were lost. Apart. Separated.

Waking fast, Tulsi sat up on a desperate inhale. The night around her added to her confusion. She was alone, in a strange bed. Looking all around, it took her a few seconds to remember why Wreck wasn't with her.

They were at Merchant's. This strange room wasn't safe. It was the beginning of their end.

Her hair stuck to her forehead, betraying the sweat that moistened her. With the image of that haunting dream still lingering, she climbed out of bed and grabbed the blanket from the end to wrap it around her shoulders.

Tulsi was yawning when she opened the door to find Wreck and Rowdy at either end of the couch facing each other. Her interruption drew both of their attentions around.

"Why are you still up?" she asked, scooping her hair away from her face to push it down her back. "What time is it?"

"After three, according to the TV," Rowdy said.

It was off now, but she wasn't surprised to find out they'd checked what was available. She headed their way. "Anything good?"

"Just sports and movies," Rowdy said. "Why are you up? Couldn't sleep?"

"Bad dream," she said, putting a foot on the couch to climb onto the middle seat with her knees pulled up to her chest.

"Figures," he said. "Don't think any of us will sleep right in this place."

"You two should rest," she said, wondering if there was a movie on that might lull her to sleep. "God only knows when you'll be pulled out to do something important. Where's Kieran?"

"In the other room," Rowdy said, nodding at the only door she hadn't used. "We figured you wouldn't want company."

"Maybe if I'd had company, I wouldn't have had the bad dream," she said, looking Wreck's way. "You know I sleep better on you. Freaked me out to wake up alone."

"Yeah, but he can't," Rowdy said. "There's a queen-size in each room and this couch pulls out. Kieran suggested sharing with you, I thought Wreck was gonna put him through a wall… You're lucky I'm here to control them both."

Yeah, she probably was, but Tulsi wasn't ashamed of their association. "There are three beds, four people."

"And this isn't the best time to, you know…"

When Rowdy didn't finish, she scrutinized him. Remembering what Wreck had said about the possibility of being listened to, Tulsi exhaled.

"Reveal all," she said, meaning telling Kieran about them. "It's fine anyway. There's nothing to tell."

"Nothing?" Rowdy said and frowned. "You through?"

"Yeah, we are."

"But you just said—"

"I can share a bed with a man without it meaning anything. I could share a bed with you if I had to. Doesn't mean I'd have sex with you."

"So I should've let Kieran—"

"Kieran? No," she said. "Definitely not. I don't trust him."

Rowdy's swagger increased. "That mean you trust me?"

"More than Kieran, yes," she said. "The bed is free now, so if either of you want to use it. Go ahead. You can't stay awake forever."

Rowdy looked past her to Wreck. She didn't know what signal he was expecting, but he must have received it because he pushed off the couch to stand up.

"I should close my eyes for a while," Rowdy said. "Just in case."

"You're more useful refreshed," she said, watching him progress toward the bedroom door.

He pushed open the door, but paused to point at them. "Take it easy, okay?"

Which was probably his way of telling them not to get up to anything loud or explicit that may attract Kieran's attention. The guy could wake up at any time. If he came out into the living room to find them going at it, there wouldn't be any more secret.

Wreck waved him away and Rowdy went into the bedroom, closing the door. Being aware that anyone could be watching or listening left her with a creepy feeling. The hair on the back of her neck stayed on end. Tulsi wasn't even sure what to say or if they should say anything.

The lingering atmosphere of her dream probably wasn't helping to put her at ease.

"What was the dream about?" Wreck asked, boosting himself off the couch.

"You don't want to know," she said, pushing her hair away from her face again to frown at him as he picked up the coffee table. "What are you doing?"

He didn't answer her question. Instead, he took the coffee table over to put it on the floor in front of Kieran's bedroom door.

"I wouldn't have asked if I didn't want to know," he said.

"If we were anywhere else, I would tell you."

Revealing what had freaked her out when Merchant could be listening wasn't appealing.

"You're getting smarter, Nymph," he said, approaching her.

Without explanation, he bent to grab her upper arm. Hauling her off the couch, he pushed her toward the coffee table. He tossed the cushions off the couch and grabbed the frame to pull out the bed. Once it was out, he threw the cushions back onto it. They were bulky cushions meant to make up the backrest, so they weren't typical bed pillows, but that didn't stop Wreck from getting onto the bed and laying his head on them. He lifted just long enough to pull off his tee-shirt and toss it aside.

"Ruin," she said, adjusting the blanket on her shoulders.

"C'mere," he said, extending an arm her way.

Crawling onto the bed, she unfolded the blanket to lay it over both of them and smiled when he curled his legs around her. "I'm sorry about the van, falling asleep on you like I did." He said nothing. "I know you don't like to be touched. You told Svana that, then I went and—"

"Close your eyes, Nymph."

Her eyes were actually already closed. It was the best way to relish having her cheek resting against his torso absorbing the security of his aura. She understood that he was telling her to stop talking and sleep.

There was just one more thing that Tulsi had to get clear before anything else happened. To be honest with him, she needed to open her eyes and focus on her determination. Losing herself in him would distract her from making her point.

"If Merchant makes you an offer… if he gives you an out… I want you to take it."

"What's that mean?"

Shifting position, she propped her chin on him so they could look at each other. "This isn't your debt. None of it. I understand that Merchant will probably want you to use your skills for him, but I think you should plead your case."

"My case?"

"You didn't touch his shipment. The only reason you're here is because Kieran was too chicken to go to Teal's himself."

That and he apparently didn't have the money he owed Teal, but she didn't think it was to anyone's advantage to make a big deal of that to Merchant.

"So I should skip out on you and Row?"

"We'll be okay," she said. "Rowdy is tough and you never know, maybe Merchant will take one look at me and send me away."

"If he sends you away, you'll be in more danger."

"I can't make him be attracted to me."

"He will be," he said. "You just gotta know how to take care of yourself."

Tulsi couldn't claim to be the most street-smart person at the best of times, but she had learned a lot in the last couple of weeks.

"You know, you haven't said the words," she said, splaying her fingers on his ribs to stroke his torso.

"What words?"

"Declaring what's your private property."

"I never will."

"I figured," she said, watching her fingertips glide across his skin. "You knew even before I did."

"Knew what?"

"How this would play out."

"I have experience," he said, pressing his hand to her temple to flatten the other side of her face against his torso again. "I've seen a lot of guys taken down by their woman."

"That won't happen to you," she said.

"'Cause I never had one," he said. "Connections are used against you."

"Yeah. Without them, you wouldn't be here. This can't be the first time you and Rowdy have been in this kind of position."

"First time. Rowdy and me are smarter than this."

His fingers moved into her hair. Using just the tips, he kept the bulk of his hand off her head and just combed the digits down a few inches, losing them only to the first knuckle. Raising them from her locks, he repeated the action over and over. It was soothing, like a clumsy massage. Though a professional would be more finessed, there was something reassuring about the strength in those fingers.

"Usually," she said, finishing the sentence for him. "Guess this is what happens when amateurs get involved." He didn't respond. Wreck preferred to be silent over stating the obvious. "Do you think, after all of this is over, after you're free from here… that I'll ever see any of you again?"

"No," he said, without pausing to give it thought. "I'll make sure of it."

That hadn't really been the answer she wanted. Her dream from the van played in the back of her mind. Having Wreck in her bed for real was unlikely. As he'd said, they weren't real. What they had was an illusion. One that could be shattered at any second.

TWENTY-NINE

WRECK WAS UP before her in the morning. Tulsi only knew that because upon waking to the sound of someone closing a door, she was in bed alone. In fact, the only person in the room with her was Kieran.

Because he tried to talk to her again, she excused herself to the bathroom, only to find Wreck was already in the shower.

Although Tulsi made an attempt to join him, he got out as soon as she stepped in. By the time she departed the shower, he was gone.

Rowdy was just waking up as she went through the bedroom. After he entered the bathroom, Tulsi slid into the bed he'd vacated. It wasn't so much that she was tired, simply that she wanted to avoid Kieran.

He didn't leave her alone for long. He came into the bedroom with Rowdy who wanted to let her know that last night's food had been switched out for breakfast. Tulsi didn't ask who'd done the switch or if they said anything. She got a whiff of the scent of coffee and leaped up to satisfy her caffeine craving.

The rest of the day was spent doing little. The TV was put on and frequently switched between different channels. No one really commented on anything. The few times Kieran tried, he got no reaction, so he gave up.

No one came to clean up the breakfast stuff or to give them lunch. Though there was enough food for them to graze if they were hungry.

The sense of expectation hung in the air. Everyone was expecting something to happen, to change, any second. Any time there were footsteps outside the door, or movement, or sound of any kind, they all braced, waiting for their seclusion to be shattered.

The clock they could bring up on the TV signaled that it was six thirty-six in the evening.

Tulsi hadn't been paying much attention to the action flick playing on the screen. Her stomach was beginning to consider dinner when the sound of the door lock made Rowdy grab for the remote.

He turned off the TV and all of them rose to their feet to watch the door. Someone was unlocking it. There was a chance that whoever was out there was bringing dinner. But there was also a chance one of their group was going to be taken away or issued instructions.

It seemed to take an age for the door to open, though it was likely only a couple of seconds. It swung back and then Delray was there with a garment bag slung over his shoulder.

"Pretty," he said and whipped the garment bag around to hold it toward her. "You've got a date for dinner."

"I have a… What?"

"She goes nowhere without us," Rowdy said.

Delray just smiled and two other men stepped around the door to guard his shoulders.

"You've got no choice. Someone will bring food for you three in a while." His focus bounced back to her. "You got five minutes to change… Boss isn't patient."

Tulsi was confused. Much as she'd known this moment would come, she wasn't prepared for it. If Rowdy or Wreck tried to withhold her, blood would be shed and she'd end up having to eat with Merchant anyway.

"Okay," she said, going around the couch to take the bag from Delray.

"Tulsi," Rowdy said as she turned to head for the

bedroom.

"It's okay," she said, offering a smile and doing her best not to look at Wreck. "I'll be fine. It's just dinner."

"Boss says you don't need underwear," Delray said, the sinister amusement in his voice didn't put her at ease.

Tulsi paused for a breath before reaching for the door. Having heard his words, there was no need to give him the satisfaction of a response. No doubt Wreck would be doing that for her. He'd tried to put her in jeans to offer some sort of shield, Delray just announced that she'd have none.

In the bedroom, she laid the garment bag on the bed and unzipped it with a sense of trepidation. Being sent an outfit before dinner was so reminiscent of Bradley that it creeped her out. At least with her ex, she knew there would be something decent within the garment bag. With Merchant, she had no idea what to expect.

The first thing she noticed was the glint of metallic fabric. Opening out the garment bag, she stepped back and covered her mouth. The barely there dress was a backless silver cowl that would hang so low, she'd have to arrange it around her breasts if she wanted to keep her nipples concealed.

It was so short that it almost looked like a top. In any other circumstances, she'd probably wear pants underneath it. But that wasn't what Merchant wanted. He wouldn't have given the order about underwear if she was allowed to wear pants.

Covering up was an option. Tulsi could put on the dress, but don jeans and a sweater too. Except she didn't want to aggravate their host, not until she had a measure of how far the boundaries could be pushed. If the guy was a total psychopath, he might put a bullet in her just for fun. She didn't want to die for the sake of covering a little skin.

"Hurry it up!"

The call from beyond the bedroom prompted her to take the dress from the bag. It was worse than she thought. After shirking her clothes and figuring out how to get into the dress, Tulsi discovered a slit up each side. They rode so high on her hip that the side view of her ass would be on show.

There was no time to panic. Any sign of reluctance could have an effect on Wreck and she didn't want him getting into a fight on her behalf.

Sealing her lips, she took a deep breath through her nose. Whatever it took, she would keep Wreck safe. This was a chance to collect intel. To find out what had happened to Svana and to Putnam. Tulsi wasn't afraid; she wouldn't let herself be afraid.

It was a date. Just like the dozens she'd been on in the past. All she had to do was forget that the man seated with her was capable of murder. If Baines could do it, Merchant could do it. But she was smart, she'd keep her eyes open and do her best to conceal her anxiety.

The next big step was just leaving the bedroom. Tulsi didn't care about Delray or Rowdy or Kieran seeing her in such a revealing outfit. She'd been able to strip naked in front of Coombs and Hillam. Learning how to detach her mind from her body had been a necessity.

Wreck was the one she was worried about. He'd made it clear that he would never claim her. But he knew, probably better than she did, what she could face upstairs with Merchant. He hadn't done anything when Svana was led out to a night of rape and torture. Though, she hadn't been summoned in such a civilized way.

Stepping out of the bedroom, she ignored the trio of men around the coffee table and kept her focus on the leering Delray. Tulsi couldn't blame him for taking a look. He had maybe known what was in the garment bag. Maybe not. Either way, he was enjoying the view.

"Tulsi," Rowdy said just before she reached Delray. "Take care."

If she could, she would. Her trio of cohorts couldn't offer her much in the way of support. Leaving them behind meant stepping into the unknown alone. But there wasn't any other choice.

Abandoning her only allies, Tulsi did her best to stay calm. Panicking wasn't going to change the fact that she was on her way to eat with the man responsible for their captivity. If only she could say that the prospect of him was intriguing.

Trepidation outweighed her curiosity.

Nothing that her imagination could conjure ended with a positive vision of their keeper. How could any man who ordered people shackled be good? Their own ordeal was nothing to what Svana had endured. The prospect of suffering a future that mirrored Svana's past filled Tulsi with dread.

Every second brought them closer to the moment Wreck would be freed, but that was little consolation. She wanted his liberation to bring her relief. Wanted to hold onto his happiness as a goal; it was the future she wanted for him.

Except a selfish part of her got comfort and strength from knowing he was nearby. It didn't matter that he couldn't come to her aide or swoop in to save her. Tulsi needed the prospect of him to keep herself going.

She'd once told him, not long after they first met, that people needed something to live for if they were going to fight for themselves. The only thing she had to live for was him. Yet, every step along the hallway took her further from her lover and any chance of convincing him they could have a future.

Delray and one of his buddies led her to the stairwell, which she guessed would lead down to the garage they'd parked in. Only this time, they didn't go down, they went up.

There were only two more floors. The ascent seemed the quickest in history. Before she had time to steel herself, they reached a square hall, larger than the one on her floor. The men steered her to the central door, which could only be opened by a security code.

Delray entered the code, blocking everyone from watching with his body. For a split second, Tulsi considered bolting. With both men in front of her, she would definitely be able to reach the stairs. Except she wasn't sure there was a chance of getting much further. There would be more goons on lower floors, who could quickly be mobilized to block her route.

She also wanted to get a measure of Merchant before thinking about attempting escape. Leaving the guys behind wasn't an appealing prospect, but she could always call the cops and hope they'd be liberated in a raid that could take

Merchant down for good.

Baines had referred to her coming across to their side, which was how she'd ended up in the middle of the mess. Until Tulsi knew if Merchant believed there was a genuine possibility of that, she didn't want to risk undoing any good work by showing her true intent in an escape attempt.

If Merchant believed she could trust him, or sympathize with his cause, she might be able to manipulate him. At the very least, she may learn something that could be useful to Wreck.

Holding her breath as the door opened, Tulsi repeated the word *confidence* over and over in her mind. If she could just fake strength, maybe it would be enough to convince Merchant that she wasn't afraid of him.

Delray went through the door first. The other man who'd accompanied them stepped aside to let her follow. Instead of joining them, the man closed the door, leaving her and Delray in a hallway that was much shorter than the one on her floor. There were doors to the left and the right, and grander double doors at the head of the hall.

Her escort guided her to the second door on the right and put in another code before opening it. This time, he didn't go inside; he held the door and gestured for her to enter.

For whatever came next, Tulsi was on her own.

THIRTY

THE WHOLE APARTMENT she'd shared with the trio of guys the night before was smaller than the room Tulsi entered. It seemed that the whole top floor had been renovated. Presumably for use by the boss. Obviously, that room was supposed to be a statement on his stature.

There was no one in the room at that moment, giving it an eerie air. Faint piano music played and smells from the food on the table, which was under silver, drifted her way.

As she crept forward, the door behind her swung shut, startling her. Alone, she kept her guard high. The lights were low and candles were lit in various corners as well as on the table. Someone was trying to set the scene for romance. Tulsi didn't feel seduced; she was too on edge to relax.

A door in the far corner opened; she waited to see who would reveal themselves. The man who came in wore a smile that took her aback. Tulsi had expected him to be more menacing, more intent on intimidating her. Instead he came in, closed the door and took a few seconds to appreciate her.

Wearing black pants and a white shirt that wasn't buttoned all the way to his throat, there was something roguish about his tousled black hair and the glint in his eye. If he was Merchant, he didn't carry the immediate appearance of a person descended from the devil.

"Pretty," he said, his deep voice immediately reminding her of the person she'd spoken to on the phone. "Hardly does you justice." He opened an arm toward the table. "Please, join me."

He wasn't seated at the table, yet he offered her space as though his presence was enough to relax her.

"What am I doing here?" Tulsi asked, without moving an inch.

"This is a chance for us to get to know each other," he said. "I'm sorry I couldn't meet with you last night. I had to take care of a few urgent matters. I needed to ensure we wouldn't be interrupted. I've looked forward to this. To meeting you."

Taking her time about licking her lips, Tulsi began to feel the itch of curiosity that she'd expected and hadn't experienced before. "I don't know what to make of you," she said, choosing to go with honesty. "You're not what I expected."

"What did you expect?" he asked, still wearing his smile as he sauntered closer to the table. "Horns and a tail?"

Something about the ease of his joke made her relax enough to offer a breath of a laugh. "Maybe."

"You're tense," he said, picking up a bottle of wine from the middle of the table. "You're smart to be cautious."

"I don't know what you want from me... or my friends."

"Your friends owe me something," he said, pouring the wine into the two glasses already on the table. "Baines knows better than to make decisions without my input. He was sent to track down Styx and Rigby." Which was Kieran's last name. "He got word that Rigby was going to pay a debt to Teal. We expected him to show up there. We didn't expect you or his brother. Getting Wreck was a real coup."

Such honesty was so unexpected that Tulsi didn't know how to respond. This could be the bait meant to lure his prey, but it was difficult not to be seduced by his openness. Not in a sexual way, but her wariness certainly began to fade.

"If he didn't expect Wreck and Rowdy, why did

Baines lock them up?"

"As I said, he wouldn't make decisions without my input. Baines kept all of you until he got instructions from me," he said and opened his hand to the seat next to him. "Please, Miss Tern, sit down."

"You know my name," she said, crossing to the table where he helped her into the seat.

After she was seated, he took his place next to her. "I know a lot of things about you… We've had some time to track down your information."

Because her purse had been taken at Teal's. Tulsi had been worried that one of Merchant's people would investigate her. Not because there was anything sinister to find, just because it felt like a violation to have someone look into her history.

"Why would you do that?"

"When Baines told us Rigby had brought a woman, we had to know who you were."

"And?"

"Nothing was turned up that you should be concerned about," he said, raising his glass. "A toast to new friends?"

Svana had told her that this man enjoyed taunting and torturing women. While it was obvious that he had a capable physique beneath his crisp shirt, she couldn't quite visualize him attacking a woman for his pleasure. Still, she hadn't thought that of Kieran and it hadn't taken much for him to be talked into enjoying Svana.

Wreck's words from the motel bathroom came back to her. He'd said that Svana didn't act like a traumatized woman. After witnessing the blonde hitting on Wreck, Tulsi had her own misgivings about that. Now she was beginning to wonder if she'd misjudged the woman completely.

After they both drank, Merchant removed the silver cloches from their food to reveal a steak and vegetable dinner.

"You're not a vegetarian," he said, like he knew the statement was accurate. It was, though she didn't know if he wanted an answer, so shook her head just in case. "Please, enjoy."

Tulsi took her time about cutting the meat to ensure that Merchant took a bite first. She let a few seconds go by before hazarding a question.

"Where is Svana?"

Merchant's fork paused in its descent. For a moment, he said nothing. In those tense seconds, she feared her question had awoken his inner monster.

Eventually, his fork continued to his plate and he cut another piece of meat. "She is close by," he said. "My swan and I have a complex relationship… You don't have to be worried about her."

"I'd feel better if I could see her. Talk to her," she said. "To make sure she's okay. She's been through so much."

"She has," he said, nodding his head in a show of apparent empathy.

Tulsi got more of a sense of condescension than real concern. "Your men weren't kind to her."

"As I said, we have a complex relationship," he said, picking up his wine. "I didn't invite you to dinner to talk about Svana. I invited you here because I want to get to know you."

"You already know so much about me. I know so little about you."

"That will come," he said, putting down his glass. He reached over to take her hand from her knife. The contact pricked her caution again. Tulsi hadn't anticipated him making physical contact so soon. "You're so different to any woman I've ever known." The way he tried to look into her gave her a sense that he wanted something. "We learned about your history. You have a business. Live a good life. We knew Rigby had an association with you… We had no idea you were capable of…"

It wasn't just that he wanted something. He was aroused by her… in more than just a physical way. Need and intrigue bled into his words.

"Hillam," she said, knowing that event had shaped his opinion of her.

"Yes," he said. "Tell me, how did it feel killing your first man? It's been so long for me, I can hardly remember."

That wasn't encouraging. It didn't inspire confidence

that she and her friends would get out of this situation unscathed.

"I didn't set out to kill him. It wasn't my intention. I was protecting myself."

"I understand," he said, lacing their fingers together. "That instinct is fascinating. It's so primal, it's so… So few women understand the kill or be killed mentality. You might find it hard to believe, but more women freeze than fight."

"I couldn't do that," she said, her mouth drying. "I couldn't let him take from me."

"And I am pleased that you didn't. When Baines told me what you'd done…" His smile widened until a joyous and proud laugh joined it. "I was speechless. In the most incredible way… There are dozens of women in my past, maybe hundreds. Women became so generic that they were almost interchangeable. When Baines told me how you'd defended yourself and claimed responsibility with such vehemence and without apology… I knew you were different. In that minute, I realized your kind of different is exactly what I've been looking for. I don't want a meek woman without any fight to bow down to me. I want a partner, someone who can match me. Challenge me… Stimulate me."

Svana had talked of Merchant's love of a strong woman and the pleasure he took in breaking that spirit. It could be that he planned to do the same with her and thought she'd be more of a challenge than others.

If not, then what he was really suggesting was that she abandon life as she'd always known it and adopt his morals as hers. Wreck had told her to forget her morals and boundaries. It wasn't the drug dealing or the violence that deterred Tulsi, it was the man.

"Mr. Merchant, I—"

"Ilias," he said. "Call me Ilias."

She hadn't known for sure that Merchant was his last name. She still wasn't sure. It could be a nickname or alias. Granting her the right to use his real first name didn't relax her. There was no sensation of intimacy. His permission only made her feel that she was much deeper in the lion's den than she'd appreciated.

Extricating herself from his web was not going to be easy if he continued to tangle and tie her. "Ilias, you don't know me. Not really, and I—"

"Bradley Hershel knows you," he said, surprising her again. "He was very helpful in educating us about your likes and dislikes."

"Bradley?" she asked, stunned. "How did you…"

"For a man of such means, he is surprisingly unguarded," he said. "He offered information about you quite freely."

It didn't take her long to figure out how they'd made the connection between her and Bradley. Her ID would have given them details such as her address and social security number. Her phone contained numbers as well as texts and emails. Her past with Bradley was right there for them to discover.

"We've been broken up for a long time."

"I know," he said, releasing her hand to eat some more. "He is no threat to what we have. If he becomes one, it won't take much effort to get rid of him."

That statement was the first real hint of insanity. The words weren't even a threat, they were just delivered as fact. Like if Bradley became a nuisance, Merchant would just erase him. Making the statement to her with such ease assumed she would be okay with that fact; that she would support such insanity.

"Bradley doesn't know where I am. He doesn't know about what's happened in the last few weeks."

"No, because he's far too self-involved to really care about you." He took her hand again. "That is why we can be different. You can be yourself here. Be yourself with me. I can give you everything."

"You want us to have a relationship."

"We are having a relationship," he said. "As of this night I promise to take care of you and give you everything you need."

Everything she needed included the freedom of herself and the people she'd been captured with. Somehow, Tulsi knew it would be a bad move to even suggest that.

"In exchange for?" she asked.

"Loyalty. Companionship."

"Sex."

He paused to meet her eye, confusion in his gaze. "Eventually. Yes… Tulsi, I am offering you everything you have ever wanted. You will have a place closer to me than anyone else has ever had. It is a privilege."

And a curse, but she couldn't say that either. Instead, she smiled. "Let's just take it slow, okay?"

"Slow," he said and nodded. "Yes. We can get to know each other completely. I want us to trust each other with every secret. To share everything. You will be my primary counsel. The most trusted and respected woman on my team."

"And Svana?"

"Pretty," he said, picking up her hand to kiss it. "You don't have to be jealous of her or any other woman. You are going to be my queen. None of them will measure up to you. You have power over all of them."

All of them. So she had to give him her loyalty, but he didn't intend to be faithful. Tulsi didn't care about that, though she couldn't miss the double standard.

"Power?"

"Here," he said, taking his napkin from his lap to put it on the table as he stood up. "Let me show you."

They hadn't finished eating, but she didn't really have any choice about joining him when he held a hand out to her. Tulsi tried to be subtle about inhaling a deep breath as she slid a hand into his. Just by accepting his hand, it seemed she was accepting his proposal.

Drawing her to her feet, he guided her toward the door he'd entered by. Tulsi had no idea what was on the other side and wasn't sure that she wanted to know. There was no going back. All she could do was go forward. Merchant glanced her way and opened the door.

As they went into the adjoining room, she was almost tempted to close her eyes. That wasn't exactly a long-term plan though, so she made herself look. To her surprise, she found herself in a bedroom. Decorated in pale and pastel shades, it was the most feminine space she'd seen in the building so far.

There were no doors on the wall that would double as the hallway. To the right, there were long drapes pulled closed over what, she hoped, were windows. On the furthest wall were three doors. She could only guess about where they would lead.

Merchant let go of her hand as he went to stand at the end of the bed, opening his arms to the room. "This is your suite," he said. "From here you will be able to call for anything you need." He pointed to a phone that was on the nightstand. "That is a direct line to your concierge."

"My… my what?"

Her surprise amused him. "Anything you want, you get," he said, moving toward her. Sweeping an arm backwards, he gestured at the door closest to a window. "You have a bathroom. The central door is your closet. Take your time looking through what's in there. If anything's missing, call the concierge."

He stopped in front of her and rested his hands on her upper arms. Tulsi was suspicious enough that her instinct demanded she pull away. Fighting that urge, she stayed put. Rejecting him while they were alone could have grave consequences. Still, accepting a man's kindness could be problematic if she had no intention of seeing a relationship through to the end.

"What if I'm not what you think I am or if you're not what I need?"

"I will be," he said without an ounce of doubt. "It won't take you long to understand what I need. I'm a straight forward guy. I know what I like."

What he liked was to be obeyed, if what she'd heard of him so far was accurate.

"It's a lot of pressure," she said.

His brow descended as his chin rose. "You're scared?"

Sensing his hesitation, she exhaled a smile. "Me? No… I don't scare easily. It's a lot of pressure on us… on our relationship… while it's still so young."

"Don't worry about that, my sweet," he said,

touching her face. "We have all the time in the world to get acquainted… You just concern yourself with settling in."

Although she couldn't see it, Tulsi nodded in the direction of the third door, which was in the far corner behind him. "You didn't tell me what's behind the last door."

"I am," he said. "That corridor is your direct link to my office. We'll enjoy our meals together in the dining room behind you. That door will be locked at other times."

And he'd be able to come straight from his office into her bedroom. Somehow she knew without looking that the bathroom and closet doors wouldn't lock… not from the inside anyway.

"If I have to speak to you…"

"You can come to my office," he said. "If I'm conducting business, one of my associates will be on that door." On her side of it or his? "They'll let you know if it's an appropriate time to visit."

Let her know if he was busy threatening or murdering someone. What a boyfriend. Her mother had told her to find a partner who she could respect. Someone who enriched her life, not depleted her energy. Already Tulsi was exhausted being in Merchant's company.

"The men that I came with…" she said, figuring if Merchant was going to leave, she had a limited window to talk to him. Tulsi didn't want to make a point of going to his office when she had no idea what mood she'd find him in. "What will happen to them?"

"Do you care?"

The answer to the question was an important one. After spending so much time with them, it would be suspicious not to ask. But maybe Merchant preferred his women to be heartless. Tulsi might be able to feign disinterest for a while, but her curiosity would tear her apart. It would also be more than she could handle to witness her cohorts being teased or tortured. So she thought it was best to lean more toward honesty than callousness.

"I'm curious," she said. "We've been stuck together for weeks."

"Unavoidable," he said, squeezing her arms. "And for

the best. I found out what you were made of in that time."

"Yes," she said, smiling despite his biting grip. "I don't regret it. Not any of it."

That was a truth she could speak with confidence. Merchant could take the statement any way he chose. Tulsi thought only of Wreck. Everything that she had been through since her date with Kieran had brought her closer to the last man she'd chosen for herself. At the time she'd first asked Wreck to ruin her, Tulsi had no idea how much he would end up meaning to her.

"Good." He touched her face. "In time you will learn how things work, how I work. For the moment, enjoy your new home, settle in. I'll come for you soon."

Come for her soon? Merchant hadn't answered her question and hadn't given her any cause for hope. Her new home, her new life. Tulsi glanced around, this was a gilded cage if ever she'd seen one.

Merchant turned to head toward the door he'd said led to his office.

"Ilias," she said, struck by the need to hold onto his company. He turned back. "I won't do anything I don't want to."

It was slow, but after a long blink, his lips curved to a smile. "I wouldn't have you any other way, my sweet."

After opening the door, he left her alone. Even that didn't feel like truth. Wreck had said their rooms downstairs were likely bugged. He'd prepped her for her new home. Her cage was likely bugged too.

Still, there was nothing that she could do about that. Tulsi was on her own. She had to explore, learn everything that she could about this place and the man who was determined to seduce her. At any time, she could need information and she didn't plan to be unprepared.

THIRTY-ONE

FOR MOST OF THE night, Tulsi paced around, listening to sounds of movement beyond her bedroom walls. It didn't seem that she could hear anything specific from the office Merchant had spoken about. She considered tiptoeing along the private corridor from her room to the office doors. Except Merchant hadn't told her which side of the door his man would loiter on. Seeing Merchant again wasn't high on her wish list. It would happen eventually, but she wasn't going to court his attention.

The more she thought about their dinner conversation, the more uneasy she became. He'd managed to come across as reasonable, even charming. Tulsi had relaxed and begun to feel at ease with him. Yet, the signs of potential looming issues hadn't been buried deep. She'd been able to tell by his subtle reactions that there was a more severe man beneath the smiling exterior.

Men like that were the ones to really watch out for. The ones who could play it smart and calm were the ones who knew exactly how to manipulate others to their way of thinking.

Tulsi wasn't naïve to the seriousness of her predicament. This was where compliance had gotten her.

Hillam's death had changed everything.

With no other choice, she'd slipped under the covers of the sumptuous bed Merchant had dubbed hers and stared at the canopy above.

The idea of compliance had been to keep Merchant's men on her side. Maybe not on her side exactly, but she'd thought that the less trouble she gave them, the less trouble they'd want to cause her. Baines might be intrigued by her in a similar way to Merchant. Coombs wasn't. Tulsi hadn't learned much about the hierarchy or how much influence Coombs had. One thing she did know was that Baines was a higher-up. That might keep her safe… ish with Merchant.

Coombs was definitely middle management or below, somewhere closer to Teal's level. That meant they likely ate, slept, and hung out with the lower-downs. There were always more at the lower levels than the higher. They had greater numbers. Coombs would see to it that the greater numbers showed her no love. He'd make sure they wanted her blood almost as bad as he did.

Merchant said she had power. Tulsi fixated on that thought. Either she could cower and hope the minions showed her mercy or she could find out exactly what Merchant meant by power. He'd made it clear that strength was an aphrodisiac; Svana had told her the same. Maybe the trick would be not to break. What would happen if she never bowed down to him? Most likely, he'd kill her. Which was exactly what Coombs would want his posse to do.

Death.

One way or another, all she could do was fend it off for as long as possible.

To distract herself from the inevitable, probably gruesome, fate that awaited her, Tulsi thought about Wreck. Just two floors beneath her was the man she'd waited her whole life for.

Her mother used to say the universe balanced itself out eventually. She hadn't had to wait long for eventually. Just as she found her opposite, she was thrown into the path of another man.

Wreck hadn't wanted her, not long-term, but she was

convinced that he would've liked them to be together for more time than they'd had. Maybe it was the circumstances of their separation that stung him more.

Losing Sienna in the way he had affected the course of his life. That was obvious even without taking into consideration what he must have seen the night she died. Wreck wasn't a man who liked to be out of control.

The teenager Rowdy had spoken of already had issues. Yet, she got the impression he was more fun and laid-back in those days. Rowdy had said Wreck became darker; Tulsi couldn't imagine how someone could avoid that after witnessing such horror.

Thoughts of getting to know the man better, soothing her lover, creeping deeper into his heart, joined her as she slid into slumber. She only knew that because they were the last thing she remembered before waking up.

Her back ached. Funny that the nicest, softest bed she'd slept in for weeks turned out to be the one to give her pain. On a yawn, she sat up, and was instantly startled awake by the sight of a breakfast tray on the table by the window.

Someone had come in and put that there while she slept.

It made her feel violated. Who knew who it had been? Anyone could've come in and done anything to her and she had been lying there oblivious.

Clutching the sheet to her chest, she glanced around. The idea that she was being watched had been vivid in her mind the previous night. That was why she hadn't bothered changing out of the dress Merchant provided for her.

The only men in the building that she'd feel confident being near were Wreck or Rowdy. If it had been either of them, she'd like to think they'd wake her or leave a message somehow.

Throwing back the covers to leap out of the bed, Tulsi ran to the tray to search for a clue. The coffee was cold and the orange juice warm, she could tell that from just feeling the cup and glass. The croissant was probably stale. Even the fruit salad looked sad and unappetizing. The tray had been there a while.

Other than a paper napkin, she found nothing on the tray that could be written on or with. Nothing but the wood of the table lay beneath it. Her people hadn't been allowed in even under supervision.

As cover for her exuberance to get to the tray, Tulsi carried it to the bed and sat on the edge to consume what she could. The food didn't taste of anything, not while she felt so violated. Steeling herself wouldn't be easy in the face of Merchant's entitlement to her, but she'd have to build a tough exterior. On the journey to Merchant's, she'd been compliant. After meeting the man himself, she knew that letting a little of her fire show would keep her alive.

It wouldn't necessarily keep her safe.

Svana had spoken of beatings, of being beaten down. Tulsi had experienced being hurt at the hands of a male before, but she guessed her step-father's attempts would pale in comparison to Merchant's capabilities.

Whatever she faced, she had to do it with confidence. She would rather die with her head held high than give anyone the satisfaction of seeing her cower. Repeating these instructions to herself was supposed to strengthen her resolve. Except her focus stayed on the pounding of her heart in the deafening silence.

She was alone. Alone.

Fighting Hillam had been instinct. Except if Wreck hadn't been there to finish the job, she didn't rate her chances of being able to do it. There she was in a place with not only Merchant, but with dozens, possibly hundreds of other men. How would she be able to survive unscathed?

Her experience with Hillam ran through her head. Her damned imagination repeated it with the faces of Coombs, Delray and other strangers in his place. He'd almost had his way. Almost taken from her.

Wreck had got her through. Wreck…

Her chin rose as she found her strength. He was her strength. His scent on their bedsheets had provoked her into fighting Hillam.

Clarity changed her mood.

Tulsi didn't want Wreck there with her. She didn't

want him near her at all. Whatever feelings he might have for her would put him in jeopardy. Marrying that with the trauma he'd endured watching Sienna die, if he snapped there would be no stopping him and he'd die for sure.

Taking Hillam down had been easy. The idiot had been drunk and oblivious to Wreck joining them; he hadn't had the time to fight back. In a fair fight, one on one, even two on one, Tulsi didn't doubt Wreck's ability. But it wouldn't be a fair fight. She'd known that since watching Baines and Wreck stare each other down in Teal's apartment.

Inhaling her determination, she stood up. Leaving the tray on the bed, she headed for the bathroom. Worrying about whether Merchant was watching her was ridiculous. Avoiding the inevitable would make her look weak and scared. She was neither, not if it meant protecting Wreck.

Tulsi had to prove that she could handle herself, that she didn't need anyone to come in and save her. If she had to die, she would. She'd take that over watching Wreck hurt.

Stripping off, she got into the shower and began to wash her hair. Even if she wasn't really the tough badass the situation called for, she'd fake it. Holding on to her resolve, she vowed to do anything to protect the man she loved. Washing away her fear, Tulsi let tenacity take its place.

THIRTY-TWO

"I WANT TO SEE Svana," Tulsi said to the guy who brought in her dinner.

The breakfast tray had been replaced with a lunch one while she was in the shower. So, apparently, she had slept late. Tulsi hadn't been that hungry, so she hadn't touched it.

In the time since then, she'd explored every corner, crevice, and drawer in the bedroom, closet, and bathroom. As of yet, she hadn't ventured into the corridor to Merchant's office. Her interest level at seeing that particular guy was still at a zero.

"I, uh…"

She got the instant impression that this goon had been told he wouldn't have to talk. His mistake. The more she could do to make anyone uncomfortable, the better.

"What's the problem?" she asked, striding closer and raising her fists to her hips, which had the added bonus of thrusting her chest toward him.

Tulsi wasn't averse to using her sexuality in ordinary circumstances, and she hadn't really intended to use it against this guy. Playing with men who were violent for a living was never smart. But, in this situation, just the suggestion of her breasts being on display made the minion nervous.

That gave her a clue.

Yes, he noticed her chest, but immediately averted his eyes. He went so far as to actually turn his head, so there was no suggestion he was leering. In witnessing that action, Tulsi learned two things. One, she was being watched. There was no other reason for him to make such an exaggerated move. Two, Merchant's men had been told she was off-limits.

Excellent.

As much as she had no intention of testing the strength of the man's restraint, she could almost kiss this goon for his stupidity. Yeah, okay, so it wasn't stupid to let Merchant know that he had no intention of straying onto what was supposed to be the boss's property. But it was stupid to reveal to her that she was safe. Around everyone except Merchant anyway.

"What's the problem, sugar?" she asked, swaying her hips as she sashayed closer to draw a fingertip down the center of his chest. "You don't like the shape of a woman?"

"Yeah… Yeah, I do."

"Sure?" she asked, pushing her chest further out.

A flash of a frown toughened his brow. "I ain't no fag."

Nice to know Merchant's people were so tolerant of others. This guy had to be new. From what Svana had said, Merchant went whichever way his mood took him.

"I might ask you to prove that," she said and he immediately blanched, which made her smile. "You tell your boss I get lonely fast… and yes, that is me passing judgment on his hospitality."

"He… he won't want you upset."

"Then let me see Svana."

Demanding to see Svana was as much about testing these powers Merchant had mentioned as it was about concern. Some small part of her did probably resent the young blonde for making a move on Wreck. But, as he'd said, the fact that she did was odd given her ordeal.

Tulsi did believe what she'd said about trauma victims having varying reactions to what they'd been through. Still, she was confused and wanted a chance to get to know the youngster better.

"I can… ask the boss," the minion said, almost relieved that he'd come up with a response.

"You do that," she said, leaning back, giving the guy a well-deserved break. When he didn't move, she waved her hand at him. "Go on then, shoo."

Reversing, the guy stumbled as he fumbled for the door behind him and only just managed to get through it. Either the goons were afraid of Merchant or they were afraid of Hillam's killer. She'd taken a step to assert authority, now she'd just have to wait to find out what the consequences would be.

***

APPARENTLY, MERCHANT was not moved by her confidence.

The dinner tray sat there for hours, untouched. Tulsi sat on the edge of the bed watching the salad wilt and the steam thin and vanish above the rim of the coffee cup.

When her body got tired, she lay on her side, still staring at the food. Her eyes closed and she fell asleep.

In her dreams, she felt Wreck's touch, tasted his mouth, heard his voice in her ear. Tulsi surrendered to her lover without hesitation. Begging him to take her at his pleasure. Wreck needed no permission or encouragement.

Tearing her clothes from her body, he forced her onto her back and forced himself into her. Her vision began to blur and darken. The picture got fuzzy until all she could do was feel. His breath in her hair. His cock advancing and retreating. He needed her. He owned her. Tulsi experienced a sensation that was more than sex, more than a physical joining of bodies. His being consumed hers. Swallowing hers whole, she connected with his essence. It twined around hers, tangling and contorting their souls to fit two into the space of one.

The heat and pleasure of their joining changed in a snap. Her sight returned with a vision of Wreck above her as he'd been a dozen times. On the cusp of his release, his expression changed to horror. Blood began to seep from his chest. It dripped onto her at first, then began to gush. It flooded their sheets as he flopped to his back beside her.

Pressing her hands against the wound didn't stem the flow. Tulsi opened her mouth to beg him to stay. She tried to scream. Tried to tell him that she loved him. But the words wouldn't come. Her throat was closed, blocking her sentiment. No matter how she fought, she couldn't overcome her muteness. Wreck's eyes began to close as his hand rose toward her face.

But her lover didn't touch her. She didn't feel his fingertips on her skin. His arm loosened and fell to his side.

Wreck… Her lover was gone. Dead. Deceased. And she hadn't done a thing to help him.

Overcome by her grief, she gasped in a breath so deep that her lungs burned. Forcing the despair from her body, a scream that resonated from her, smashed every piece of glass around them. Windows shattered, lamps, glasses, everything. It didn't stop there. Furniture began to explode. In a shower of splintered wood and shards of glass, she fell against Wreck's lifeless body.

His heart no longer beat beneath hers. Pounding her fist against him, she begged him to return to her, apologized for how useless she was.

The terror of the moment became even more urgent when she began to feel his form fade from beneath hers. Rising to blink through her tears, she tried to figure out what was going on. But he continued to fade until his body disappeared to nothing beneath her.

Scared and confused, Tulsi curled her fingers in the now clean sheets she stared at. The blood was gone. Her love was gone. She was all alone.

A sinister laugh began to echo. Its volume grew until the walls shook. The vibration of it moved the bed beneath her. Tulsi flipped around onto her knees, pressing her hands to her ears, trying to block out the menacing sound.

In a snap, it stopped. She opened her eyes to see someone standing beyond the end of the bed. At first, it was nothing more than a silhouette. She squinted to try picking out more features as the image flickered like a mirage in the desert.

"My sweet, Pretty."

The whisper of Merchant's ominous words struck her hard. Just as the image of him cleared at the end of her bed, she woke with a start.

On a sharp inhale, she sat up. Looking around, she tried to remember where she was and what was going on. She was still in the room Merchant had put her in. In last night's clothes, she was lying the wrong way on the bed, right on the edge.

Squeezing her lips tight together, she sucked in a long breath through her nose and looked to the spot where Wreck had faded from the bed in her dream.

If she held onto her love for him, he would die. If Tulsi tried to assert any loyalty to him, or Rowdy, or Kieran, Merchant would make their lives hell.

All of a sudden, Tulsi understood Merchant's words.

She did have power. Maybe not in the way he'd meant, but she had power all the same. Power that she intended to wield.

Rising to her feet, she looked to the spot where the dinner tray had been the previous night. A lunch tray had taken its place. In the corner a small vase held a single red rose. Was that love? Was that what Merchant thought of her? That she would be won over by a flower on a tray.

Without thinking beyond the rage of losing her true lover, Tulsi snatched that damn vase and set her sights on Merchant's office. Her heart pumped her boiling blood to her tight muscles. Even in losing her mother, in being kept prisoner, in being attacked by Hillam, Tulsi couldn't remember ever being so fired up. Mad didn't begin to explain how she felt as the image of Wreck's bloody chest replayed in her mind over and over again.

No one would hold her back. Nothing would deter her.

Throwing open the dreaded door that she hadn't yet allowed herself to touch, she strode down the carpeted hallway toward the door at the end. No one stood in her way, which was lucky for them.

Grabbing the door handle, it didn't even occur to her that the door would be locked. It opened and she threw it out of her way to stride inside. Just over the threshold, she stopped, her sights set on the man standing behind the desk at the head of the room.

Fueled by her fury, she hurled the vase across the room in his direction. Merchant stepped back just in time. The porcelain hit the window frame behind him and shattered.

"You do not ignore me," she said, the thump of her heart almost overpowering her.

Keeping her narrowed eyes on him, she gritted her teeth hard. There were other men in the room, though she didn't take her focus from Merchant to identify them. She couldn't flinch. Not for a second. Either he'd kill her or she'd make progress. Either way, she wasn't endangering Wreck.

Merchant returned the intensity of her vehement stare. Neither would blink first. Inhaling and exhaling in short pants, Tulsi was a breath away from releasing a scream like the one from her dream when Merchant smiled.

His body relaxed and he blinked as he turned to the men who were in the center of the room. "You know my Tulsi, don't you?"

For the first time, she looked around. The vast room had to stretch the full width of the building. The thick carpet and heavy furniture would be more at home in an ancestral home than an apartment block in whichever city they were in.

Two shallow stairs led to the platform Merchant's desk stood on. Apparently, he liked to look down at his prey. It was made all the more intimidating by the dagger propped on a display stand at the head of the desk. She didn't dare think about why it was there or what it meant to him.

As for the men in the room, whether they knew her or not, Tulsi didn't know them. Not all of them. Baines spearheaded the group of five. Delray was in the background, but he was the only other man she recognized.

"Hello, Pretty," Baines said with some kind of amused pride. "I knew you were special."

"Push me, Baines," she snarled. "I dare you."

Merchant laughed. The sound was too similar to the one that she'd heard in her dream. Disgust crept up her spine making her squirm. She closed her eyes to try concealing her revulsion.

"My Sweet, please don't play with the underlings."

Play? Tulsi wasn't playing. There was a high chance if Baines came anywhere near her that she'd tear off whichever part of his body he touched her with. The letch might have had designs on her at Teal's. Now that Merchant had claimed her, she had more scope for fending off any man who tried to touch her.

Her attention snapped back to the man behind the desk. "I want to see Svana."

"I heard," he said, opening his arm toward her. "We can discuss that later. You're just in time for an important meeting."

Tulsi didn't want to appear unsure. It could diminish her effort to exude confidence. Holding her head up, she went toward the desk. "What meeting?"

"Come here," he said, pulling out the chair at his side of the desk.

When she got within reaching distance, he took her hand and guided her down into the chair while giving Baines the nod.

Baines in turn, nodded at one of his men. That guy went to the double doors at the other side of the room and another went to get a hard wooden chair from a corner.

Sinking into the leather of the vast chair Merchant had put her in, Tulsi pushed her shoulders back to straighten her spine. Whoever walked through that door, she couldn't react. Closing her eyes, she did her best to channel Wreck. He could do impassive. He could do confident. Indifferent. Unsympathetic. Every minute, Wreck didn't flinch in the face of any threat.

One goal.

That's what he'd said.

Whatever her goal was, she had to focus on that.

Toughen up.

He'd told her that too.

The words after replayed in her mind as well. *"If I'd stepped in, it could've been. Long as you're off their radar. They get to do what they like."*

That was… Her eyes popped open when clarity slammed into her. That's what he'd meant by one goal. She was his goal. Not for seduction or romance. Her safety was his goal. That was why he'd done what he had to with Putnam. Why he had let Delray and Coombs take Svana.

Whether he wanted to or not, Wreck felt responsible for her. Just like he'd felt responsible for Sienna. Setting her jaw, she garnered new resolve.

THIRTY-THREE

ONE GOAL.

Wreck.

Wreck was her goal. Whatever Tulsi had to do to ensure he wasn't harmed, she would do it. As soon as she could, she'd find a way to prove to him he wasn't responsible for her. She wouldn't let him go through that torture again. If something happened to her, it would break the man who was already broken enough. Tulsi wouldn't be responsible for him experiencing more pain.

Forget morals and boundaries. All that mattered was his safety. While she was on the inside, she had to follow his example. Showing him any favor would prompt Merchant into action. Action that she didn't want him to take.

If Merchant had warned his men against getting too close to her, that command would definitely extend to prisoners. Showing favor toward any prisoner would not go down well with Merchant. If Merchant did anything to Wreck, or gave him a distasteful order, her protests would sign Wreck's death warrant.

Wreck had said he was no one's hero. Tulsi couldn't claim to be either. But she'd made it clear to him in that first motel room that she would do whatever was necessary to keep him safe.

Her focus stayed on the door. Waiting for it to open again seemed to take an age. Anticipating Wreck, she did her best to stay calm. No matter his state or what Merchant threatened to do to him, Tulsi had to remain indifferent. Unmoved. Being apathetic could also be a step toward alleviating him of his sense of responsibility.

The door handle turned. In instant failure, her upper body edged forward in an involuntary show of anticipation. Just a tiny fraction, but enough that she wanted to curse at herself. Her only saving grace was that every man turned to the door as it began to open.

Merchant was just next to her with a hand on the back of the chair. She couldn't see his face and couldn't risk looking up at him to check if he'd noticed her reflex.

Someone was shoved through the door, he stumbled in and dropped to his knees before lurching forward and falling on his face. Pushing up a little higher, she looked down at the man as two other people came in behind him. The door was closed and the goons crowded around the figure on the floor. Whoever he was, it wasn't Wreck. Tulsi hadn't seen his face, but the build was wrong.

Two goons grabbed the victim under his arms and hauled him up. Another grabbed the back of the chair as the victim was dropped into the seat.

His head hung forward, his shoulders slumped. It seemed his will was broken; Tulsi couldn't blame him. His tee-shirt and jeans were dirtied and torn. His matted hair hung in chunks that were enmeshed with dirt and what looked to be crusted blood.

With nothing on his blackened feet, and his arms covered in bruises that were smeared with blood, she wondered who this stranger could be. His hands were bound in front of him. Not with zip-ties but with duct tape that kept his fingers linked.

"You're being rude," Merchant said, his firm voice almost taunted the man slumped in the uncomfortable chair.

Baines grabbed the man's hair to force his head back. It was difficult to tell if his eyes were closed or if he was actually looking their way. They were so swollen and bruised that she couldn't see anything beyond his injuries. Blood was smudged at his temple and at his hairline as well as across the beard on his chin. The unkempt look and obvious beatings led her to conclude that this man had been through an ordeal worse than hers.

"Look at the lady," Baines said.

With his fingers still clenched in the stranger's hair, Baines leaned around to slap both of his cheeks. The stranger didn't even try to pull away or object. Baines gave him a shake. The man gasped in a breath and coughed. He seemed so startled that she wondered if maybe he'd lost consciousness and the shake had brought him around.

"My sweet, do you know our guest?"

Even if she was supposed to, she wasn't sure she'd recognize a friend. His broken body and bruised face were not in their usual shape. They were not in any shape a person would choose.

"No," she said, scanning his clothes and hair. He wasn't the height of Wreck or Rowdy, and wasn't as muscular either. "Should I?"

"This is Styx," Baines said and shook him again. "Say hello to Pretty."

Styx. Kieran's friend. His cohort. Colleague.

Styx didn't do much of a job saying hello. He mumbled something, which was probably more than she'd manage in his state.

Her first thought was of Wreck. Not fear he'd end up in Styx's state or any carnal thoughts. No. Wreck got results. That was her first thought. She needed her man—her ex-man—to do what he did.

Keeping her focus on Styx, Tulsi pushed the chair back and rose to her feet. Inspecting the prisoner, she wondered if he was even aware of what was going on.

"What has he said?" she asked as she moved slowly around the desk. "Anything useful?"

Tulsi was surprised to discover that her own curiosity was awakened. After spending so long getting there and hearing about the missing money, she did want to know what had happened to it.

"Everything he told us implicates Rigby."

Kieran. Merchant's words were matter of fact. As she crouched in front of the semi-conscious man, she couldn't help but speculate. The smell of him was almost overwhelming. She closed her eyes to steel herself against it and chose to focus on what Merchant's tone implied.

"You don't believe him," she said, reaching up to flick Styx's hair away from his brow.

"I don't?"

"If you did, he wouldn't be in this state."

"I believe Rigby was involved."

A smile warmed her lips as she swiveled to look over her shoulder at Merchant. "But Kieran is no criminal mastermind."

Merchant returned the smile and nodded once.

She returned her focus to Styx whose head was lolling around on his neck.

"You have my sweet to thank, Scum," Merchant said. "If it wasn't for her, you would be dead already."

Tulsi wasn't sure what Merchant was hoping to achieve. She hadn't been at all involved in anything that happened to Styx. She'd only just learned that he was in the building. Until Merchant had identified him, she hadn't even thought to ask if they'd trapped Styx too. So many other things had transpired that he wasn't exactly high on her list.

Styx tried to say something else, but it came out as a groan.

"He needs water," she said, trying to dampen her sympathy for him.

It was easy to see someone in pain and feel bad for them. But for all she knew, this man was responsible for stealing Merchant's shipment. Not that she cared about Merchant's shipment. Except if it wasn't for the theft, she wouldn't be there. Wreck and Rowdy wouldn't be there either. They'd have repaid Teal and gone back to their lives.

Hillam would still be alive.

She and Wreck would never have had a chance to be together.

In a testament to her new attitude, she felt sad about the latter and indifferent to the former.

Noticing the blue of Styx's eye through his bruises, she could feel him trying to focus on her. Whoever he was, he was curious about her too. Though he seemed more suspicious in his intrigue. She couldn't blame him.

"He needs to tell the truth," Baines said, shaking Styx's head again. "What do you want us to do with him?"

Baines looked to his boss who was still standing behind the desk. From the stern expression on his face, she guessed he was expecting an order of further violence.

"Take him back to his cell," Merchant said. "And give him water."

Baines frown became confused. "Boss?"

"Just do it," Merchant snapped.

"Move it, asshole," Baines hissed, dragging Styx from the chair.

Styx fell to the floor. The others were quick to gather around to haul him up, getting in a few kicks as they did.

Standing up, Tulsi watched the men drag Styx out of the room and close the door behind him.

"You have sympathy for him?" Merchant asked from behind her.

Her focus was still on the door, though it didn't take her long to switch gears. "I have interest in what he can tell us," she said, bolstering herself and spinning around to face him. "Send Wreck in."

Merchant smiled. "You have faith in your former lover's abilities?" She didn't mean to react, but it seemed her silence was enough to betray her surprise. "Yes. I know about you and him." Moving from behind the desk, he walked around it to come in her direction. "You have an uncanny ability."

"What's that?" she asked, staying still when he touched her hair.

"To sense power," he said, his smile still on his face. "You ally yourself with it to keep yourself safe. You're used to keeping your options open." Tulsi wasn't exactly sure how he expected her to respond. "That's in your past now, my sweet.

He's in your past. Now that we're together, you will never need another man."

"That remains to be seen," she said.

His smile dropped. Anger flashed in his eyes, so she braced herself to receive a hit. Instead, he curled his fingers around her chin. "You need me to prove myself?"

She shook her head. "I don't need anything from you. But I am interested in whether you're all ego, no smarts."

He inhaled through his nose. "Am I more brawn than brain?"

"No," she said, not ignorant to the fact he didn't do the heavy lifting himself. Merchant was a delegator. "Use your assets to your advantage." That was what Wreck had said to Baines when he wanted to get at Putnam. "It's as much in Wreck's interest to find out what Styx knows. He gets results… Even if he doesn't, what have you got to lose?"

His gaze grew more intense as he probed her. "After seeing the state of him, you think Styx would still hold out?"

The evidence of the sustained abuse he'd suffered was written all over Styx. "It can't hurt to check."

With his grip on her chin, he tipped her head further back, giving himself more of her face to examine. "I've had men pounding on him for weeks," he said. "We don't need more of that."

Whatever Wreck did, it wasn't as simple as pounding on someone. Tulsi didn't know exactly what it was, but she had more belief in Wreck's ability than anyone on Merchant's crew. But in this proximity to a man she hadn't yet figured out, Tulsi chose to remain silent and just smiled instead.

"You are my secret weapon," he said, his smile curling his lips in a subtle yet much more sinister way than before.

"What would you like me to do for you?" she asked, forcing her hands to rise to his chest.

His attention dipped as she touched him of her own accord for the first time.

After a second, he crooked a brow and one side of his smile grew higher. "Did I hurt you?"

"Hurt?" she asked, not following his meaning.

"I have neglected you since our dinner, haven't I?"

Tulsi preferred to be in control of when they saw each other. But after the way she'd entered, she couldn't exactly deny what he'd inferred. "I don't enjoy sitting staring at the same four walls."

He nodded. "I understand. You're right. I should have made more of an effort."

Letting go of her chin, his fingers slithered through her hair to take hold of the back of her neck. "How are you going to get used to your new home if you're not allowed to learn how things work?"

Her new home. While Wreck and Rowdy were only required to stay there long enough to work off the debt, she was expected to remain indefinitely.

"This is an adjustment for all of us," she said, coming up with the vague statement in lieu of saying what she really wanted to. "Will you consider what I said about Wreck?"

Merchant shook his head. "He isn't our great strategy," he said. "You are."

"Me?"

"Yes. If you're so sure that Styx knows something he hasn't revealed, you should be the one to get it out of him."

Tulsi had no experience with coercion. Especially of the physical kind. But Merchant's smirk took her thoughts in a different direction.

"You want me to seduce it out of him?"

Merchant was quick to laugh. "With scum like that? Definitely not," he said. It wasn't reassuring that he didn't discount the idea entirely. "If I wanted you to use your wiles, I'd send you to Rigby. He's enamored with you. Isn't he?"

Without knowing what Kieran had said about their relationship to others, she couldn't risk denying their association. "Whatever he thinks we are, isn't what I think." Merchant considered her as she drew in a breath. "He took me to Teal's on our first date."

"Romantic."

"Not exactly what I'd call it."

The warmth of his laugh made her smile. Sometimes it was easy to forget for a second that her heartbeat was at this man's discretion. He could order anyone in the building to end her at any moment.

Tucking her hair from her face, he caressed her cheek. "Talk to Styx... Kill him with kindness."

So that was what he wanted. The soft, gentle woman to go in and put him at ease. That was obviously why Merchant had told Styx his life had been spared at her request.

"You want me to nurse him."

"It's no coincidence that you've mesmerized so many men," he said, tipping her chin up again. "You exude temptation."

Being flattered by his words was probably wrong. But there was a smidgen of her feminine core that appreciated the compliment. "Romance comes easy to you."

"With the right muse," he said, bowing lower. "Do a good job for me and we'll do romance later."

Still distracted by her instinctive response to his charm, Tulsi had no time to adjust her attitude before he was descending further. His lips met hers as she inhaled a quick breath. Wreck was the only man she wanted to kiss her. It had been easy to switch off when Baines violated her mouth with his. That man had no finesse.

Merchant did.

Damn, but he did.

As his tongue slid against hers, Tulsi's eyelids grew heavy. The gentle kiss didn't stay soft for long. The press of his mouth became more urgent. His need forced her head further back as his hands slid onto her waist. The grip of those sure fingers imprinted their possession on her. Merchant wouldn't give her up. That was the message she heard in his hold.

Wreck refused to own her. At every opportunity, he made it clear their relationship was a distraction. Whether she believed his indifference didn't matter. Wreck would never own her the way she wanted him to own her.

If excitement was what she was looking for, Merchant could deliver. His life was fast-paced, full of intrigue and scheming. He would own her. Possess her. Keep her.

But for how long?

Was surrendering to him worth the consequences? Once Merchant was finished with her, he wouldn't cast her aside or ghost her as other men might. He'd kill her or send her to a literal hell in one of his brothels.

She shouldn't be thinking about the strength in his hands or the slick massage of his skilled tongue. The man was a thug. A criminal. Potentially a violent sadist. Wreck was the first two, but he couldn't be accused of the last.

THIRTY-FOUR

JUST AS TULSI was about to push Merchant away and make some excuse about him distracting her from the mission he'd assigned her, one of the double doors opened. Merchant stopped kissing her to land his fury on whoever had interrupted them.

"What?" he snapped and she got a clear view of his short fuse.

"Sorry, boss," Baines said. Tulsi turned to get a better look at the man who she'd never heard sound contrite. "You want us to finish the scumbag now?"

"No," Merchant said, laying his hand on her shoulder. "Take Tulsi to him. Get her whatever she needs."

Baines' head twitched to the side. The request seemed to be unique. "You want Pretty alone with Styx? The thieving, lying asshole?"

"Yes," Merchant said without hesitation.

"What if he hurts her?"

"He can try," Tulsi said.

Merchant made a sound of approval. "Stay outside and if she orders it, kill him."

Baines eyes bulged, which gave her an odd feeling of satisfaction. Merchant had just given her powers of execution.

From Baines reaction, he hadn't expected that either. Wreck had killed for her, though she hadn't ordered him to. It was unlikely that she'd order Styx's death, but having that power did give her more confidence.

Turning to show Merchant a smile, she accepted his quick kiss.

"Get to work," Merchant said and nudged her forward.

She didn't need any encouragement to leave. Striding toward Baines with a sway in her hips that was more for the man behind her than the one in front, Tulsi didn't let anyone hold her up. She opened the door to the hallway and glanced at Baines.

"We have work to do."

Continuing out of the office, she left the door open, expecting Baines to follow her. When she heard the door close after a few steps, she got confirmation that he had. Delray and two others loitered at the end of the hallway. When they noticed her, they all snapped to attention.

"It's fine," Baines called. "We're taking her downstairs."

"Where?" Delray asked.

"To the asshole."

Tulsi kept going until she reached Delray and his buddies. A security lock on the door next to them stopped her from getting any farther. The handle wouldn't turn. Baines passed the others and ran a plastic card through the slot next to the number keypad. The door popped open.

"Oh, look at that, you get a fancy card," she said and was brazen enough to loop her arm through Delray's. "How come you don't have a fancy card, honey?"

Baines held up the card. "Upper management only."

She bobbed her brows in time with her concessionary nod. "Does someone want to show me the way?"

Tulsi glanced around at everyone waiting for someone to take the lead.

No surprise that Baines was the one to step up. "You stay behind me."

Maybe he didn't like her promotion from prisoner

to… whatever this was.

Still, she didn't know where Styx was located, so she had to follow someone. Going down two flights of stairs, she glanced at the door that led to where Wreck was being held. Wondering if he was still there or if he'd been given any news about her, she told herself not to slow.

It was possible that he hadn't asked about her. Maybe he didn't care. She was out of sight and off his plate. Wherever she was, Tulsi wasn't his responsibility anymore. Not that she really had been. If he believed that then her wish had been granted.

They went down another flight and Baines used his card again to get them through the hallway door. The one on this floor didn't look the same as the others. Nothing did. Made of metal with bolts at the top and bottom that had to be unfastened in addition to swiping the card, it became obvious that Styx wasn't in a comfortable suite.

Wreck hadn't told her about this floor. She'd worn a hood on their initial ascent, he hadn't. He'd have noticed the cell-like door. Nothing good could be behind a sturdy door like that. It didn't take much to figure out why he hadn't told her there was something worse than their first accommodations.

The gray concrete corridor that they entered was lit by pale almost sickly colored lights that didn't provide much illumination. There were six doors, three on either side. Up ahead a horizontal second hallway intersected the vertical one, which suggested there were more rooms—or cells—up ahead.

Baines went to the second door on the right and stopped. "He tries anything, we'll be right outside."

She nodded. "I'm not worried." He scanned his card and Delray pounced forward to undo the bolts. "I need food, clean water, soap, towels, and some clean clothes."

"Pretty—"

"Oh, and a knife," she said.

Delray finished and retreated from between them. Baines' brow moved. She didn't blame him for being hesitant, she could do a lot of harm with a blade. Instead of alleviating those concerns, she smiled. Baines nodded to one of the guys behind her while she kept her focus on him.

Delray came into her peripheral line of sight. "You're going to give her a weapon?"

"Boss says she gets whatever she needs," Baines said, assessing her.

Tulsi didn't flinch, but did lay a hand on Delray's. "If I wanted to hurt any of you, I'd ask for a gun, wouldn't I? Something automatic and fully loaded… Maybe if I feel the urge to cause someone pain after my tête-à-tête, I'll ask my new lover which one of you I should pick on."

These men knew she'd been in the suite next to Merchant's office. Unless he'd been explicit, his goons wouldn't know how far their intimacy had gone. It was fun to watch Baines absorb that semi-threat. The shoe was on the other foot now. It might not last… It definitely wouldn't if she got nothing from Styx she could share. That "she could share" was an important distinction she couldn't say out loud.

Baines smiled and shook his head. "Damn, Pretty. I knew there was something special about you."

As proud as he seemed, she couldn't help but think about the man who'd killed Alexis. The man who had come into the bedroom at Teal's and taunted her.

They stared each other down until the guy he'd sent away came back.

He hurried up at their side. "I got towels and clothes," he said, bundling the fabric into her arms. "I'll get food and water too."

"Just bring them in when you have them," she said, putting a hand on the final slide-bolt above the lock Baines had run his card through. "And the knife?"

The guy reached behind him and pulled a knife from his back pocket. He unsheathed it and handed it over. Tulsi pulled back the bolt.

Baines touched her shoulder. "Don't loiter in there."

If she'd ever received a command that she was likely to ignore, Baines' was it. The asshole was walking a dangerous line with her. Wondering if he realized it, she reminded herself that Baines was Merchant's closest lieutenant. It wouldn't be smart to go straight for the jugular. To drive a wedge between the men, she would have to be subtle.

In contrast, if Wreck happened to be the man in charge, she could get rid of Baines in a heartbeat. Sometimes life wasn't fair.

Pushing the door open, Tulsi slipped inside and was quick to close the door. It wasn't until she heard the clang behind her that she had a moment of doubt. If Baines wanted to lock the door and leave her locked up, there wouldn't be a damn thing that she could do about it.

Thoughts of her own safety ebbed when she saw the man in the center of the hollow gray room. In a chair, much like he had been upstairs, he sagged there. Unable to lift his head or move, he didn't even check who'd come in.

Walking toward him, she was distracted for a moment by the door to the right. It was open to show a bathroom. She saw the head of a bathtub and a toilet with a sink next to it. That had to be torture in itself. With his ankles strapped to the legs of the chair and a loop of duct tape around his torso pinning him to the back of the bolted-down chair, he couldn't use the bathroom even if he wanted to.

Even when she stopped in front of him, he still didn't attempt to look up. Either he got in trouble for looking his captors in the eye or he'd lost consciousness again.

Crouching down, she put her wares on the floor and reached for his face. His beard was unkempt; she doubted it was a deliberate style choice.

"Styx," she murmured, trying to encourage him to look up. "Can you hear me?"

His grumble wasn't anywhere close to a happy sound. As she began to worry that he could have a broken jaw, which would probably make it difficult for him to speak, he parted his lips to inhale.

Hazarding a smile, she gave him a few seconds to focus. Once again, Tulsi spotted the azure blue of his eyes shining from behind the swollen bruises impeding his vision.

"Hi," she whispered, stroking his face.

The smell coming from him was sickening, but she ignored it. It wasn't exactly easy, but to form a relationship with this man, she couldn't let him think she was repulsed by him. On a basic human level, after all he'd been through, it wouldn't be right to sneer. It wasn't his fault that his hygiene had been neglected.

The door opened, which startled Styx. He grunted and seemed to recoil; she laid a hand over his that were bound by the duct tape to offer reassurance. Glancing back, she saw the guy who'd been sent to get her supplies.

"It's okay," she said to Styx and stood up to retrieve the water bottle and plate with a couple of sandwiches on it. "Thank you. We'll need medical supplies. Painkillers, antibiotics, bandages." His surprise was palpable. Tulsi ignored it. "I'll need a razor too… and clippers or scissors… Oh, and a trash bag. Just put them inside and leave." He was glued to the spot. "Anything I need, remember? Chop! Chop!"

Tulsi stayed at the door, waiting for the guy to leave again. He stole more than a few looks at Styx before he slipped out.

Spinning around, Tulsi went back to Styx and sat on the floor. Putting the sandwiches by the towels and clothes, she uncapped the water bottle.

"My name is Tulsi," she said, figuring they should have a proper introduction. "They call you Styx, right?" Rising to her knees, she cupped his jaw and took the bottle to his lips. "Drink… It's fresh."

He made a good shot at opening his mouth as she tipped the bottle for him. Her progress was quickly halted when he coughed, sending water spraying out into the room and across both of them. After a stunned moment of silence, she laughed.

"Guess it's good I got these," she said, putting down the water to pick up one of the towels to dry them both off. "That was probably too fast… Let's just take this slow."

She retrieved the knife and he grunted again. Being attached to the chair, he couldn't go anywhere even though he tried to pull back.

"Don't worry," Tulsi said. "I'm not here to hurt you."

Probably figuring he didn't have any choice, or maybe just out of fight, Styx went limp when she touched his bound hands.

Showing him trust and compassion was the only way she could think of to get through. Picking at the edge of the duct tape, she used the knife to cut through it, being careful to avoid his skin. She could feel the tremble in his freezing hands. The tape was wrapped so tight, it had to be hindering his circulation.

Cutting just a little at a time, she winced whenever the glue stuck to his skin. With no other choice, she eased it loose while he hissed in pain. Blood under the duct tape proved his hands hadn't been exempt from the torture. The tips of some of his fingers were caked in dried blood too. Though it was difficult to tell without closer examination, she was sure he was missing more than a couple of his fingernails.

Speeding up as she got closer to his wrists, Tulsi settled into a rhythm and eventually put the knife on the floor to peel the tape away. Tossing it aside, she didn't pause and immediately got to work cutting through the tape on his ankles.

It was cleaner, fresher, though his skin beneath wasn't. The angry redness of his ankles suggested they'd been taped and un-taped more than once. After a few seconds of little movement, she noticed his hands rise from his lap. She was still cutting through the tape on his ankle, but glanced up to see him holding his hands in front of his face as he tried to curl and stretch his fingers.

His expression wasn't easy to decipher, but she got an impression of wonder from him. Maybe he'd given up hope of ever seeing his hands again. Either that or he was absorbing the depth of what he'd been through and learning what his injured extremities looked like.

"I don't know much about you," she said, stripping the tape from his first ankle. "I know you know Kieran Rigby... I know Kieran too."

Shuffling across to the second leg, Tulsi was more confident in sliding the knife beneath the tape now that she had some practice.

"Who are you?"

Those gruff, croaked words were the first thing she'd deciphered from him. Already it felt like she'd made progress.

"Tulsi Tern," she said, glancing up to flash a smile his way.

"Merchant's girl?"

Inhaling, she held the breath a few seconds and then let it out in a puff. "That's a more complicated question. Baines took me prisoner along with Kieran… We were brought here together. How long have you been here?"

"Kieran… Kieran is here?"

"Upstairs," she said, pulling off the tape and throwing it toward the strips she'd already removed.

"With… Merchant?"

His dry throat cut off his words and he went into another coughing fit.

"Hey," she said, grabbing the water bottle and holding it up to him. "Here." He snatched it off her and was quick to tip the liquid into his mouth. "Not too fast."

Tulsi tried to be both gentle and forceful in taking the bottle away from him. Just as she was about to offer him a sandwich, he seemed to get a surge of energy and began to pull at the duct tape that was holding him to the chair.

"I gotta get out of here," he said, trying in vain to pull the tape away.

Rising higher on her knees, she stilled his hand with hers and they made eye contact again. "Baines and his men are right outside the door," she murmured. He blinked up at the door. "I can't get you out of here."

All that energy vanished as he deflated. Tulsi cut the tape from his body and stood up. She left him alone to adjust to his new found freedom of movement and went into the bathroom to turn on the faucet over the bathtub. Letting it run long and hard for a while, she was pleased when the water began to warm. That was when she put in the plug to capture the liquid she hoped would rejuvenate the man in the next room.

"Good news," she called over her shoulder. "We might have caught a break!"

Her good mood took a sharp U-turn when a heavy arm shot around to yank her backwards. When her spine smacked against another form, the stench alone was enough to betray whose forearm was tightening around her throat.

"You're gonna get me out of here."

"I can't," she wheezed, clawing at his arm. "I can't let you go."

"If you're Merchant's girl, you can," he said, his words were joined by the spit that he hissed through his teeth. "I should kill you just for what he's done to me. You love that monster—"

"If he loves me, what do you think he'll do to you for hurting me?" she said, forcing out each syllable. "Think you're strong enough to take on all of them?"

"Maybe," he growled.

The sharp point of a blade poked beneath her ribs. Her eyes closed slowly. Rookie mistake. She'd left the knife just lying there among the other things she'd brought in. As much as Tulsi wanted to kick herself that wasn't the time to chastise herself. She had to be thinking straight if she wanted to make an alliance.

Opening her eyes, she let her anger rise though kept her voice low. "One shitty blade? That's your plan? Man, you're a fucking idiot," she said. "Baines is outside with a gang. Every door is security locked. You need a code to get out each one." Unless he stole Baines swipe card, but she wasn't going to give him ideas. "You want to get out of here, you have to get down another couple of floors. I don't even know where the damn exit is. They brought me into a garage or something and put a hood over my head before bringing me out. I know nothing about this damn place."

Releasing his arm, he grabbed hers and whirled her around to face him. "Who are you?"

"That's an interesting question," she said, not sure that she knew the answer anymore. "Let's start with what we can do for each other." Stepping aside, Tulsi showed the bathtub filling with water. "I'm offering friendship… which is probably more than you've got from anyone else here." She opened her arms. "Kill me, if that's what you want to do… You can, but then what? You rush Baines and die too? How does that help either of us?"

THIRTY-FIVE

THE PANT OF STYX'S breath moved his chest fast. As he considered her, his breathing slowed and his arm drooped.

"Merchant was going to kill me," he said. The knife fell from his fingers that were shaking much more than before. "Upstairs."

Maybe he had been going to kill Styx. Merchant had said that she was just in time for an important meeting. What transpired didn't seem that important. Merchant must have changed tack when she injected herself into the situation.

"You got a reprieve."

"Because of you," he said. "Why did you help me?"

She hadn't really. Letting him think that may be the quickest way to earn his trust, so Tulsi didn't correct him. "I want to know what happened."

His head seemed to grow heavy on his shoulders. "You want Merchant's shipment."

"I want to know what happened," she said again. "I don't like a mystery."

"I can't help you," he said, his words slowing. "I don't know where it is."

"No one does apparently. I don't believe it vanished into thin air."

"Ask Kieran."

"I did," she said, creeping a little closer when his muscles loosened further. He tried to bring his attention back up, but his head flopped again quickly. "We need to get you cleaned up. Come here."

The tee-shirt on his body was beyond saving. There was so much grime, sweat, and blood on it that she couldn't even tell what color it had started out. He seemed too weak to help her out; just standing up had taken a lot out of him.

Tulsi bent her knees to swoop down and pick up the knife from the floor.

"Hey," he mumbled when she stood up straight.

She caught his arm to prevent his retreat. "If I wanted to hurt you, I wouldn't have taken off the tape."

He seemed to accept that truth and gave a sort of nod. Using the knife, she cut the tee-shirt fabric and then tore it open. The bruises on his ribs were so angry that she almost recoiled. Instead of giving him anything more to worry about, she swallowed and went around him to help take his arms from the sleeves of the shirt.

"Do you know how long you've been here?" she asked. He gave a loose shake of his head as she moved in front of him again. "Have they beaten you every day?"

"What'd they do to Kieran?"

Not this. That was the first thought that came into her mind. Compared to what Styx had endured, Kieran had enjoyed a vacation.

"I'm going to take your pants off," she said, reaching for the button of his fly. "I swear I'm not making a move on you."

Her attempt at a joke just slid right off. But that was fine, Tulsi wasn't expecting a laugh, she just wanted to distract him from his question.

Unbuttoning his filthy jeans, she helped push them and his grubby underwear down, ignoring the unleashed smell. She'd never really thought about the strength of her stomach, but was grateful for it. During her mother's illness, she'd cleaned up plenty of soiled clothes and sheets. Some part of her was able to switch off and just deal with what needed to be dealt with.

Leaving him at the head of the tub, she turned off the hot faucet and tested the temperature. After putting in a little cold to ensure she didn't burn or shock him, she stood up to offer him a hand.

Styx didn't even object when she went to take his hand to guide him around the side of the tub.

"You have to step over."

It wasn't easy to negotiate his form into the tub. She helped to steady his leg while he leaned on her shoulders, but eventually, he got into the water after a few slips. Watching him sink into the water wearing such a grimace on his face was difficult. It was obviously hurting him. All she could hope was that it was a good kind of pain.

Rushing out of the room, Tulsi retrieved towels and the bottle of water and took them into the bathroom. He was lying back in the tub, his eyes closed, his head resting on the rim. With his eyes closed, he would probably look at peace if it wasn't for the color of the water and his face.

Putting the water on the floor, she raked through her supplies to find the smallest towel. Dipping it in the water, she skootched higher to begin cleaning the wounds on his chest and arms. His eyes didn't open, but he released his hold on the edges of the tub and slithered down until he was completely submerged.

His release made her smile. The guy probably felt the need to wash every inch of himself. The water was quickly changing color. It was a shame there was no shower. Sure, it would be harder to help him wash in the shower, without actually getting in with him, but they needed clean water.

Her smile began to fade the longer that he stayed under. There was no way she had the ability to pull him out herself. He was too big. Too heavy. If she had to call Baines in, Styx would no doubt feel the wrath of the man who seemed desperate to end him.

Rising higher on her knees, she grabbed for his arm under the water. Making the connection was enough. He shot up, out of the water, gasping for air as he did. She smiled again.

"You've been through so much," Tulsi said, pushing

his wet hair from his face.

He shook his head, sending arcs of water out in every direction. She yelped and ducked to hide behind the side of the tub. When the water stopped, she peeked up over the edge to see he was looking her way.

"There's no chance of me getting out of here alive," he said, which turned her happy mood on its head. "Me or Kieran."

She didn't like the implication or how certain he was of it. "I hope you're wrong," she said. "For all our sakes. Kieran and I weren't brought in alone."

"Who else—"

"It doesn't matter," she said. "His chance to get out of here lies with the innocent people who were dragged along with him."

"You?"

She shrugged. "I'm less interested in helping Kieran than the others will be."

Rowdy cared about his brother. Wreck cared about Rowdy. They were invested in getting the idiot out of the mess he'd stumbled into… or created, depending on how guilty he was. Tulsi cared about Wreck's safety, and maybe Rowdy's a little too. Without more information, she wouldn't waste any personal capital that she might have with Merchant saving Kieran. The guy hadn't exactly been declaring his innocence from the rooftops. He denied involvement, but Tulsi wasn't sure that she believed him.

"I don't get it."

She picked up the towel she'd used to start cleaning him and took it to the sink to rinse it out.

"I don't know what happened to Merchant's shipment. I don't know if you're to blame or Kieran is to blame or if both of you are innocent."

"You don't get it," he said on a sigh and sank lower into the water. Only this time, he leaned forward to pull the plug out. "It doesn't matter who is innocent. Soon as Merchant gets payback, he'll slaughter us all. He's not a forgiving guy."

Propping a hip on the sink, she let the water just run

through the towel. "That implies you need forgiveness. If you took the shipment—"

"What would I do with the shipment?" he asked. "I ran those drugs as a middleman. I got paid for driving, not for selling. I'm a cab driver for the underclasses. That's it…" His voice lowered to a mutter. "That's what I've been reduced to."

Wringing out the towel, she continued to clean it as the water drained from around him. "Maybe you wanted something more. Needed a little more dough for something."

He breathed out a laugh and used a hand to slosh the water so it took more of the grime to the drain. "You don't know why they call me Styx, do you?" He only glanced her way for long enough to see her shake her head. "If I needed money, I wouldn't turn to dealing drugs. I do what I do for Teal because it makes me accessible, keeps my network up to date."

She wasn't really sure what that meant and wasn't sure she wanted to ask. "Merchant said you implicated Kieran." He glanced her way again. "What did you tell him?"

"The truth."

Styx washed more of the filth from the side of the tub and then turned both faucets on to slop water onto his body.

"Here," she said, taking the towel with her when she went over to kneel at the side of the tub again. Wetting the towel, she retrieved the soap and was careful about cleaning the cuts on his back and arms. "The shipment didn't just vanish."

"No," he agreed, grabbing another towel from the floor. He was rougher in how he cleaned himself up. "But Kieran or me would be nuts to think about stealing from Merch… unless we had a serious powerbase behind us."

Wearing a frown, she thought about all she'd learned since Teal's. "Keaton," she said and his broad shoulders moved in a shrug. Tulsi shook her head. "No, Baines tried that avenue. It wasn't him."

Styx put the plug back in and let the tub begin to fill again. Shoving back, he paid no attention to the water that sloshed over the sides.

"Look, Tulsi… it's Tulsi, right?" She nodded. "I'm

sure Merch rocks your world and all…" He laid back to close his eyes again. "But if you think any lowlife would make a move like this without either his or Keaton's go ahead, you don't know what the hell you're talking about."

"Well, obviously it wasn't Merchant." His head rolled to the side and he cracked an eye… as well as he could. When he drew it off her to close it again, she found herself wearing another frown. "You think this is a setup? That the drugs aren't missing at all, that…"

Could Merchant be capable of that? Yes, he probably could. Tulsi couldn't figure out why the guy would "steal" his own merchandise and then make like it had been swiped. The only reason would be that he wanted to erase one of the accused… or start a war.

"Not so straight forward," he said on a long, almost pained exhale.

Noting how his flesh was pulled across his ribs reminded her of his food. Leaving the bathroom to retrieve it, she took the plate to him. Styx snatched it from her and began to gobble the sandwiches.

"You've got your appetite back."

"Never went anywhere," he said around the food he'd crammed into his mouth. "These bastards don't share well. They only fed me every few days."

She sighed and sat back on her heels. When she and her group got there, Merchant had ordered food to be laid out for them. Styx hadn't received the same hospitality. It made no sense why they would be treated so differently.

"Tell me about when they brought you here."

"Why?" he asked, thrusting the empty plate toward her.

His mood was all over the place. From weak and incapable, he'd had a surge of energy, brief though it was, seemed amiable, and now was barking again.

Tulsi tipped her head to the side. "I told you about how they brought me here."

"Why should I believe anything you say?"

"Why not?" she asked. "What have you really got to lose? If Merchant really did save you on my word, you owe me one."

"They shot me," he said, gulping and gulping like maybe the food was stuck in his throat. "Damn fools."

Tulsi hadn't seen anything that looked like a bullet wound or fresh stitches. "Shot you?"

Nudging his arm with the water bottle, she offered him the little amount of liquid that was left.

"With a tranq dart," he said, taking the bottle to finish off what was inside. Tulsi took it back and went to fill it with cold water at the sink. "Pussies."

The way he grumbled that word made her smile. Wreck would've used the same tone. "Do you have a family? A girlfriend?"

"Sure, come sit close while I list everything I love to you," he said and scoffed in disgust. "Merch thinks he can get to me that way, he deserves everything he gets."

She gave him the water bottle and then dipped her fingers in the bath water to find it wasn't so warm. Crawling to the other end of the tub, she turned off the cold.

"What about you?" he asked, more curious than before. "Before Merch, you have a fella?"

"Sort of," she said, moving her fingers in the stream of warm water.

"Who?"

She inhaled. "Not one interested in me," Tulsi said as she exhaled.

Retrieving the towel, she went back to the sink to wash it out again. "I don't believe that. You've got a set of balls to go with that fuck-me figure. You're a prize."

"My ex wouldn't say that."

Thinking about Wreck wasn't productive. He had a way of invading her thoughts and distracting her from the task at hand.

"Knowing who your current boyfriend is, I'd say you have shitty taste in men."

That was probably true. Giving him information was a way to earn his trust, but Tulsi didn't have all day. Heading out to the main cell again, she found the rest of the things she'd asked for. Gathering them up, she went back into the bathroom to see Styx using the soap to try washing his hair.

"Want me to cut it?"

She put everything on the floor by the towels and gave him painkillers and antibiotics from each of the separate sheets.

"How do I know what these are?" he asked, looking at the pills in his palm.

Tulsi filled the water bottle and thrust it his way. "If they wanted to kill you, they'd have done it upstairs."

Probably figuring he had nothing to lose, he swallowed them down. "Cut it short," he said, turning off the warm water and sliding to the back of the tub.

Tulsi opened out the trash bag on the floor to catch the hair she cut with the scissors. High on her knees, she wasn't in the most comfortable position.

"If Merch already knows what you know, why won't you tell me? I'll tell you what Kieran told me."

He sighed in frustration. "Day before the pick-up…" he said. "I was on a separate run, saw Rigby where he shouldn't have been, talking to someone he shouldn't be talking to."

"Who?" Tulsi asked, chopping chunks from his hair so it would be easier to shave.

He shrugged, sliding a little lower in the water, bracing his arms on the sides. "Don't know his name."

She frowned. "I don't understand. How do you know Kieran was talking to someone he shouldn't have been talking to if you don't know who it was?"

"I know what I saw, okay?" he snapped. "It was shady. I know shady when I see it."

"Okay," she said, figuring she shouldn't ask too many questions until she had the full story. "Did you ask him about it?"

"No," he said. "Never saw him after that. Next day, went to the meet with the courier, 'cept there was no one there. Whole thing smelled wrong. I split… I should've left town right then."

In one respect that gelled with what Kieran had told her. "So you never went to pick Kieran up?" Styx shook his head. "That's what he said. He told me he went to the place you were supposed to pick him up and you never showed."

"Merch is at least right that the whole thing stinks. Doesn't mean he isn't involved." In swiping his own merchandise? Tulsi kept cutting and thinking for a while. Styx's next question broke her concentration. "How'd you end up with Merch?"

"That's a long story," she said, reflecting on all she'd been through since Teal's. "Short version is, I killed a man."

Reaching around to put a hand over hers, he stilled her movement and twisted to meet her eye. "Who'd you kill?"

"A man who tried to take something I didn't want to give him."

"Wow," he exhaled. "No hesitation. No guilt. No remorse."

"Why would I have remorse?" she asked, pulling her hand from under his and pushing his face around, so she could keep cutting. "The guy was an asshole. The world's no worse off with one less guy like him in it."

"I believe that," he said. "Just not my experience that women can be so cold about it."

"Killing?"

Tulsi would never so much as hint to anyone that she hadn't been the one to murder Hillam. Since it had happened, she hadn't felt an ounce of regret or remorse. She'd taken such ownership of the crime that her psyche was almost coming to forget that she hadn't been the one to commit it.

"Like I said, balls to go with that figure," he said and tipped his chin toward his shoulder. "This asshole of an ex gonna come looking for you? If he tries to fight Merch for—"

"Merchant knows who I've been with." Both Bradley and Wreck. "He knows he has nothing to worry about."

"Sure he doesn't, 'cause he kills whoever gets in his way."

"I meant no one would be getting in his way."

"What else did Kieran say about the shipment?"

As much as Tulsi was sure that Kieran knew more than he was letting on, she wasn't quite ready to throw him under the bus. Anything she said in this room could be fed back to Merchant. For all she knew, Merchant intended to interrogate the prisoner again for any tidbit she might have revealed.

"Nothing," she said, omitting what Kieran had said in the motel bathroom. "He was cagey about it. I don't know if he knows more or if he was just trying to protect me."

"Protect you? Why would—wait, Kieran isn't the asshole ex, is he?"

"Not exactly," she said, gathering up the loose hair from the back of the tub and putting the scissors down to test the clippers had charge. "We went on one lousy date."

"You get around, don't you?"

Tulsi chose to take that as a joke. She moved around to sit on the edge of the tub and turned on the clippers.

While she finished with his hair and trimmed his facial hair, they didn't say much. As she cleaned up, Styx gave himself a more thorough wash.

Merchant had sent her down to the prisoner to get information. So far, she hadn't learned anything new. If she went back empty handed, Merchant may lose faith in her or restrict her movement again.

Once everything was cleaned up and piled by the cell door, she refilled the water bottle and handed over the clean clothes before leaving Styx alone to get dressed. Just a minute or two later, he came out, transformed from the man he'd been before.

"Sure you don't want to bust out of here with me?" he asked, glancing at the knife and scissors in her hands.

She smiled. "Don't think Merchant would appreciate you propositioning me."

"Guy's got to do what he can," he said, trying to stretch his muscles. "Like I said, I'm not making it out of here anyway."

She took a step toward him. "You could," she said. "Get out of here."

He stopped stretching to frown. "How?"

"The guy Kieran was talking to…" Styx began to shake his head. "Kieran has people with him, people on his side who can help buy his freedom… You're on your own."

"Merch already tried that," he said. "I don't work for free."

She wasn't exactly sure what that meant. "You'd be repaying the lost shipment."

The more of them who were working to pay down the debt, the quicker it would be paid off. That would get Wreck out of Merchant's circle faster.

"A shipment I didn't steal," he said and opened his arms. "They caught me in a place I'm always at, in the same shitheap car. If I took that shipment, I'd have had a plan, right? I mean, no dumbass would steal from one of the biggest guys in the city just to sit with his thumb up his ass. Unless the jerkoff was trying to make a point or asking for a bullet. I'm neither. 'Til this, I had no beef with Merch. I just did my thing and that was it."

He seemed vehement in a way Kieran hadn't. His lack of denial had always been curious to her. Styx was acting like she'd expect an innocent man to act.

"If you saw the guy again, the one Kieran was talking to, would you recognize him?" He shrugged. "If you can ID him, Merchant might let you go."

"Might," he said and scoffed again. "Don't hold your breath."

Going over to him, Tulsi took his hand and looked into his eyes. "Don't be useless," she murmured. "If you're useless to Merchant, he has no reason to keep you alive. Be open to IDing him."

"That means trouble for your one-time ex."

"Kieran got me into this. I don't think he deserves to die. But if he did something that caused all of us to go through what we've been through… Don't you think he should be the one to answer for his actions?" Styx just looked at her. "I'll try to have them send down more food. Anything else you need?"

"A weapon would be nice. A vehicle too."

She smiled and gave his hand a squeeze before backing off. "I'll see what I can do."

There was no chance that Merchant would authorize Styx having a weapon or a car, but maybe she could do something else for the prisoner. Her plan was still in its early stages, but as she gathered up everything that had been brought in and knocked to be let out, her strategy began to take shape.

THIRTY-SIX

"YOU ARE AN IMPRESSIVE woman," Merchant said as he poured wine into each of their glasses.

After leaving Styx's cell, Baines took Tulsi back to her suite. Merchant had sent down orders for her to change for dinner where she was supposed to update him.

It was as Tulsi showered and changed that she thought more about Merchant. Everyone seemed to believe that he was a suspicious person, untrusting and unforgiving. Yet, even after all she'd done, he had never shown that side of himself. Not to her anyway.

He put down the bottle and seated himself. Tonight was salmon. Only the best. It smelled amazing, but she was preoccupied.

Tulsi drank some wine while Merchant began to eat. As soon as she put the glass down, the words tumbled out of her.

"Why do you trust me?"

Merchant took his time about finishing his bite and then picked up his linen napkin to wipe the corner of his mouth. Maybe the whole point was to put her on edge, and it worked. Tulsi didn't like living with an axe swinging over her throat. With Wreck, even in the most terrible of situations, she was never afraid. Before he'd even uttered a word, she got a sense that he meant safety.

With Merchant, it was different. Despite his obvious wealth and command of his staff, she didn't feel safe or comfortable when he was around.

"I wondered how long it would take you to ask me that," Merchant said, laying his gaze on her. "The short of it is, Tulsi, I don't."

That answer didn't clear anything up. It just served to confuse her more. "But you sent me downstairs," she said, pressing her torso against the table. "You let me talk to Styx, and…"

He dipped his hand into the pocket of his jacket to produce something. A phone. Holding it up, he showed her the blank screen, then he turned it to himself to press a few buttons. When he turned it back, she couldn't help but be stunned by what she saw.

A vision of the cell with the bolted-down chair in the middle of the room and Styx, pacing the width of the space.

"Take it," he said, urging it closer. Transfixed by the image, she reached out to take the phone. "Swipe left."

Doing as told, she touched the screen to move to the next video. No one was in that room, it was the bathroom attached to Styx's cell, where she had helped him bathe.

"You were watching," she whispered. "You saw everything."

"Keep going," Styx said, a smile in his voice.

Swiping again, she gasped when she saw the living room of the apartment she had shared with Wreck, Rowdy, and Kieran on arrival.

It was empty until one of the bedroom doors opened. Kieran came storming out. Rowdy wasn't far behind him.

"It's not my call, Ki," Rowdy shouted after his brother who was storming toward the front door. "But it's not the wrong one."

Kieran whirled around, putting his back to the camera. "I've been stuck in this damn hole since we got here. We don't even know where Tulsi is… what he's doing to her."

"Tulsi can take care of herself," Rowdy said, putting

his hand in his pocket.

It was only then that she noticed he was wearing a jacket.

"She shouldn't have to. That's my job," Kieran spat. "She's my girl!"

Tulsi couldn't help her reaction, she breathed out her impatience. The guy still hadn't got the message.

"He doesn't know about you and Wreck," Merchant stated.

She shook her head. Merchant could tell him, she wouldn't make a big deal of it. Rowdy had been the one who was certain they shouldn't tell Kieran. To be honest, it was none of his business. Her life wasn't any of his business. Yet, he still seemed to think he had some right to it.

Rowdy crossed to his brother and took his upper arms. "We haven't forgotten about Tuls, okay? We've just gotta play nice for a while."

"For how long?" Kieran asked. "You don't give a damn about her. Wreck doesn't give a damn. I am the only one—"

"And what the hell do you think this gets you?" Rowdy asked, throwing up his arms. "For fuck sake, Kieran. There's nothing we can do from here."

"You're going out there," Kieran argued. "You're playing his damn game."

"Yeah and whose fucking fault is that? Who got us stuck here?"

"I told you, I had nothing to do with those damn drugs disappearing."

Wreck came striding out of the other bedroom, throwing his jacket around his shoulders. The sight of him tried to wring a gasp from her lungs. As Tulsi worked to subdue it, she noticed that what he'd put on wasn't a jacket. Not his usual one. He was putting on a hoodie, not his leather jacket.

Rowdy was wearing his regular jacket. Wreck had his in the apartment, or he had before. She couldn't think why he wouldn't be wearing it when it would be cold out.

"Let's do this," Wreck said, stalking across the room.

"We're talking," Kieran objected.

"You're a fucking pussy. Stay out of my face, Weasel," Wreck said, disappearing beneath the camera at the same time a banging sound suggested he was knocking on the outer door.

Sure enough it opened and Rowdy left his brother. Someone else beneath said something, but as she craned to hear what it was Merchant plucked the phone from her hand. Locking it up, he put it back in his pocket.

"You don't trust me," she said, her focus on her plate. "But I'm here with you… You were watching everything that happened with Styx… Everything that's happened since I've been here." Raising her attention, she narrowed her eyes on him. "Why? What is the game?"

"There's no game," he said. "I have done my research. I know that you have no long-standing alliance with Kieran, Rowdy, or Wreck. You met Kieran at the gym… it's the only thing that connects you. Am I wrong?" She shook her head, which made him smile. "Baines told me you were attractive. That was all I knew about you… He told me that you were Wreck's initially, something about the way he was with you at Teal's… But you didn't know him, did you?"

Again, she shook her head. "I don't know what—"

"Who you were was really inconsequential," he said. "We knew you weren't connected… No one had ever heard of you."

"So I was a nobody," she said. "What does that have to do with—"

"Until you murdered a man."

That was the pivotal moment, Tulsi wasn't surprised to hear that. Merchant had made it clear on the phone that her act of murder had turned his head.

"That got your attention?"

On a nod, he picked up his wine glass. "It did."

"So? What? You decided you wanted me because I was capable of murder?"

"I know people capable of murder. Plenty of them," he said. "But you were different. A woman from a normal upbringing who stood up for herself. Most of the women I meet are either too hard or are already damaged. Even those who are hardened by what they've endured are just putting up a tiresome front. They want to be broken or released from their pain."

Released from their pain seemed like an obvious metaphor for death.

"I've heard about what you do to women. Svana told me what to expect from you."

He smiled and swirled his wine in the glass. "Women talk. I know." He took the last mouthful of his wine and picked up the bottle to refill the glass. "I'm happy that you met my swan. She is an example of the type of woman I'm talking about. She's damaged... Not the kind of woman I could have a future with."

"A future?" she asked. "Don't tell me you're ready to settle down."

His laugh was reassuring. "No."

"Then why am I here?"

"You're different. I like different... You're naïve, yet you're smart. Ruthless, but innocent. You interest me."

Somehow, she felt that there was something he was holding back. "What else?"

The corner of his mouth curled and his eyes rose from the wine still in his hand. "What do you know about Wreck's reputation?"

This was about Wreck. At least in part. Concern for her own safety dwindled as alarm for her ex welled-up. "Having control of me does not mean having control of him."

"Perhaps not." His focus lasered in on her. "He saw something in you... You aroused him... No one has ever heard of a woman doing that."

"You think I'll do the same for you? That if you keep me here long enough, you'll see in me what he saw?"

"Oh, I see it," he said, adjusting himself to sit up straighter. "As Styx said, you have balls to go with that fuck-me figure."

"And you want a piece of that."

His amusement faded to be replaced by aroused determination. "I want a woman who will kill to protect what she loves."

Funny. Wreck would say he didn't want her to kill, that he'd do it for her. Tulsi smiled. "So all of this was just theater," she said, glancing around the room. "The suite, the clothes, the feigned trust?"

He shook his head. "No. You did what I told you to. You talked to Styx, you got through to him. That relationship will be invaluable to me… It already has been… You believed him, didn't you?"

"I think your men put him through hell. That no one would lie given that pressure."

"Styx is a killer. Known for killing up close. With his bare hands," he said. "But he didn't kill you. He could have."

"He didn't because I told him you would hurt him… and that there was no chance of escape."

"And he believed you," Merchant said. "If we work together, we can have what we both want."

"You don't know what I want."

"Excitement," he said, startling her. "A thrill… Danger…" Her surprise had to be written all over her face. Again, he smiled. "It arouses you… I've seen it. And I've seen how quickly you can adapt to any role. You want to be a part of a more exhilarating life. I can make that happen."

If Wreck had said that to her, Tulsi would've jumped in with both feet. "All I have to do is give myself to you."

"You're smart," he said. "You're not committed enough to any one faction… yet. Take the time to think about it… Think about who can provide what you want. Wreck might have offered that excitement first, but he lives a chaotic life. A nomadic one. No home. No roots. No stability… You can have a home here… And he can too."

So she was supposed to somehow lure Wreck to stay by choosing to stay herself. Tulsi considered it and what her options were in the situation. As long as she was locked up, under Merchant's guard, there was no chance of freedom.

"I'd be no good to you," she said. "After the chase was over and you had me… You'd get tired."

He shook his head. "No. You're a valuable asset. Not only in your ability to connect with people, or for your connection to Wreck, but because you're smart… and curious. Like you said to Styx, you don't like a mystery." She said nothing. "I know you've thought about it."

"Thought about what?"

"What you would do next. How you could figure out what happened to that shipment. After what Styx said, a part of you suspects me. You're smart not to push that doubt aside… But you have thought about how you'd learn more… haven't you?" Tulsi kept her mouth shut. It was disconcerting that he could read her. "Tell me… How would you do it?"

Though Tulsi hesitated for a moment, she knew she was going to tell him. In addition to wondering why he trusted her, she'd also speculated on how to discover who she herself could trust.

"Styx is doing nothing for you locked up. I would send him into the apartment with Kieran."

"And Rowdy and Wreck," Merchant said, shaking his head. "If they believe he's responsible, they'll kill him."

"I thought you said he was a killer too."

"Yes, but a bloodbath gets me nothing."

"Send me to Kieran first," she said. "Like you said, he's enamored, right? As long as I'm alone with him, I'll get more out of him."

"By sleeping with him? How would Wreck feel about that?"

"Wreck doesn't care about me, not in the way you think," she said. "But I wouldn't have to go all the way with Kieran… As you suggested, I can use my wiles." They shared a slow, yet amused smile that spoke to a developing kinship. "I have nothing invested in this other than my desire to know the truth. I don't know anything that can damage you. Even if I am lying, I know you see everything. I'd be dead before I left the floor."

His head tilted. "You could be… Except I do enjoy it when you misbehave."

Storming into his office had amused him more than it had angered him. "Then play with me. Use me. Put me in with Kieran. Even if I don't learn more facts, I guarantee we'll both get a better idea of how truthful he's being… Like when

Baines left Putnam to stew. Kieran is going stir crazy. He needs an outlet… Better me than someone else. He trusts me."

"And Styx?"

"Keep him where he is. After I'm through, send him in. You can utilize him, like with Wreck and Rowdy."

He shook his head. "We tried that. He refuses to work for me."

Pushing her shoulders back, she broadened her smile. "He did," she said. "Until he met me… I'm the leash you use with Wreck and Rowdy, right? Use that with him too."

Merchant smirked. "I don't think he fell in love with you after one meeting."

"No," she said. "Make sure you tell Rowdy and Wreck that they're not allowed to kill him. Wreck will do everything short of that if Styx doesn't fall in line… Wreck and Rowdy will get through to him. If you threaten to hurt Kieran or me, they'll force Styx to do whatever you want him to do… Wreck gets results. He prides himself on it. You know how valuable a man's pride is to him."

"My, you are the little plotter now, aren't you?" Leaning across the table, he picked up her hand to press his lips to her knuckles. "I'll consider it while we eat… Let's talk more about how you plan to work Kieran."

Merchant wanted her to plot. He wanted her to scheme. He couldn't know that giving Styx to the others was as much about their survival as hers. More so. If Styx was with Rowdy and Wreck, providing the men put their grievances aside, they'd have another member on their team. All of them wanted out, Styx could help them do that.

The guy also deserved a break. A night in a decent bed and a hot shower. He deserved to be fed and get back to his full strength. All of that could happen in the apartment. Also putting Styx and Kieran together would be their chance to exonerate themselves. If they were innocent, as both claimed to be, their questions to each other should prove that.

Whatever happened, Tulsi had to keep her focus on her one goal. Wreck. Whatever he needed to get out of Merchant's clutches, she was going to provide it… and she'd make sure Styx provided it too.

THIRTY-SEVEN

MERCHANT GRANTED HER WISH. Doing so had less meaning now that she knew he was monitoring her every move. He wasn't allowing her to see Kieran because he trusted her to get answers and return with them. No. He was allowing her to see Kieran because if the guy did slip up and reveal some big secret, Merchant would learn it right along with her.

Wreck would be careful if she was to get a minute alone with him. Kieran wasn't so aware of his surroundings. Perhaps that was why she felt nervous as Merchant accompanied her down stairs after they'd finished their meal.

The guy was no idiot. He hadn't been quick to grant her request, keeping her guessing. Tulsi had assumed he wouldn't acquiesce right away, so she hadn't hesitated when it came to necking the wine. It had been a helluva day after all.

"Call out if you need anything," Merchant said when they stopped outside the apartment.

"You'll be out here?" she asked, watching him unlock the door.

He smiled. "No need."

As he stepped back, he slid a hand into his pocket, reminding her that he had his phone to hand. Even if this was a ploy to attempt a great escape, they didn't have the security codes to get through the doors or a key that would allow them through any exit.

Instead of asking for rules or constraints, Tulsi set her sights on the door and went into the apartment.

Kieran was slumped in the middle of the couch, facing away from her, watching the TV. He had to have a remote control in his hand because the channel changed from sport, to a movie, and then went back to the football game.

"Finished cracking skulls and busting kneecaps?" Kieran grumbled without turning around.

"Not my usual method of persuasion." The sound of her voice startled him into leaping up. When he landed eyes on her, his jaw swung loose, which made her laugh. "Hi, Kieran."

"Tulsi," he gasped and threw the remote aside to dash around the couch.

She met him a few feet from the door and was surprised when he threw his arms around her and picked her up off the floor. "You're back."

"Temporarily at least," she said, patting his shoulders.

"Temporarily?" he said, putting her down, though he didn't take his arms from around her. "What do you mean?"

"We should talk."

It wasn't easy to extricate herself from his embrace. She managed it by taking his hand, so he didn't have to break contact completely. Leading him over to the couch, she sat down with him at her side.

"What has he done to you?" Kieran asked, his brow low. "You can tell me. Anything. I promise I'll—"

She put her fingertips to his lips. "You have to forget about me," Tulsi said. "I know you thought we might have a chance, but we don't."

His anger ramped up and he snatched her hand away from his mouth. "That's why he sent you here? He wants you to break up with me."

"Kieran, we had one date. We weren't in love. You've got to face the fact that we have no future."

"I don't want to do that."

Tulsi sighed. "We're in an unwinnable situation," she

said. "There's no way out of it. No chance for us."

He shook his head as he squeezed her hand tighter. "I don't believe that. We've been through this together for a reason."

The truth was, they hadn't been through anything together. Wreck had been with her from the beginning. He'd been concerned with her safety at Teal's and forced to accept her help throughout their journey to the hotel. There, they'd been able to explore their connection.

That was over now.

It occurred to Tulsi that Kieran wasn't the only one who had to accept the end. Wreck had been honest with her about his expectation of the relationship. Even though she said aloud that they were broken up, he was still the one she dreamed of. The one she craved.

Trying to hide her discomfort over the clarity that was making her nauseous, Tulsi forced a tight smile to her lips.

"Kieran," she said, keeping her tone level. "We are through."

Yanking her closer, he didn't lose any of his resolve. "He's making you say these things. Merchant wants you to—"

"He's not making me say this," she said. "I spoke to Styx."

That made not only his frown falter, but his grip as well. "You… What did the bastard say to you? If he hurt you—"

"He told me more than you did. I can't be with someone who won't be honest with me."

Kieran didn't seem to know how to respond. His eyes stayed on hers, but their expression changed. Pulling her hand to his chest, he bought some time before speaking.

"I want you to be safe."

"I am safe," she said and smiled. "Merchant is keeping me safe."

"No," he said, his head shake more adamant than before. "That's what he wants you to think. He wants you to think that you're safe. But he's crazy. He'll hurt you. That night with Svana—"

"He hasn't forced me to do anything that I don't want to do."

"That's what he wants you to think."

"He's not as awful as you think," she said, feigning a coy glance to the side. "He's… romantic."

Yanking her forearm against his chest, he squeezed hard again. "Oh my God, Tulsi, I thought you were smarter than this. Don't tell me you're falling for him… Have you… Have you…"

It wasn't difficult to guess that he wanted to know if they'd slept together. Tulsi didn't want to confirm or deny that, so she pretended she'd been too preoccupied with her swooning to have heard him.

"Kieran, if you know something…" she said, snapping out of her fake daze. "If you know something, you have to tell him. This is our life now, all of us. You have to accept that."

"No," he said, grabbing her head in both hands. "I won't lose you to him like this. Whatever he's doing to you… He's changed you."

"Tell Rowdy and Wreck to accept this life too. It's better than the one they were living. Merchant can offer them opportunities that they wouldn't get on their own."

"We have to get out of here," he said, out of breath. "We have to… You have to find a way to get all of us out of here."

Ever the gentleman, Kieran didn't think about staging a breakout, he asked for a way out.

"Merchant won't give up. Not until he finds his shipment. It's rightfully his. If you weren't involved in taking it, you have to tell him who did."

"I don't know! I don't know who took the damn drugs."

"Kieran," she said, stroking his face. "Don't get upset. All you have to do is tell him who you were talking to."

Kieran drew back. "Talking to?"

"The night before the shipment… Who were you talking to?"

"Oh my God," he breathed out and leaned away to

run a hand through his hair. "He knows about that?"

She smiled and slid her hand down his torso. "Merchant knows so much… He's incredible," she murmured, watching her hand move up and down his chest. "He accepts people for who they are… All of us."

"He's lying to you, Tulsi. You're in danger."

Rising over him, she pushed him against the back of the couch to climb onto his lap. The poor guy looked stunned again, but he got over it to cup her ass and pull her closer.

"Exciting, isn't it?" she whispered, arching closer until her lips were almost on his. "Come inside with me, Ki… Merchant will protect both of us."

His lips parted, she felt the draft of his inhale on her mouth and knew that she'd have to do the unthinkable. She'd have to kiss him.

Taking her time about closing her eyes, Tulsi vowed to make it quick.

"Helluva turn around."

The male voice made her sit up straight. Rowdy and Wreck were both just inside the apartment door. Neither appeared particularly amused.

"Shitty timing, bro," Kieran mumbled. Tulsi was having a tough time tearing her attention away from Wreck's. "We'll get privacy in the bedroom."

"No," Tulsi said, but had to quickly cover the abrupt exclamation. "Uh, Merch will want me back upstairs."

Climbing off Kieran's lap, she had a limited window to hurry across the room to the pair by the door.

"Tulsi," Kieran called after her.

"It's good to see you!" Tulsi said, approaching Rowdy. Throwing her arms around him, she did her best to drag him down to bring her mouth closer to his ear, so she could whisper. "Styx has been tortured here for weeks. Cover his ass and he'll cover yours."

She had no confirmation of that, but it was the only way she could think to tell him to play nice with the man who could help the men find their freedom. Knowing that the camera might just catch them, she kept her smile on her face and didn't even make eye contact with Rowdy as she uncoiled her arms from around his neck.

"Tulsi," Kieran said. "You have to stay."

Spinning around, she made a move to the side and stepped back, forcing Wreck to stay where he was unless he wanted to physically move her out of the way.

"Tell the truth about your conversation the night before the theft and I'll think about it."

"Conversation?" Rowdy asked. "What conversation?"

It was good that the brothers were focused on each other. It gave Tulsi the opportunity to turn to Wreck. As she expected, he was scowling down at her. Standing just behind Rowdy's shoulder, she knew that his position was the one in the apartment not covered by the camera above.

That didn't mean she was overt. Opening her arms, she kept her gaze locked on his and waited for him to hold her. Instead, he just glared. Grabbing his shoulders, she did her best to haul him down while keeping her tears at bay. After a few hesitant seconds, he relaxed to let her pull him into his arms.

"You will always be my ruin," she whispered against his ear, closing her eyes to breathe in. The next word she had to say was the hardest she'd ever uttered. "No." One of his arms clamped around her waist, pulling her closer. Turning her face against him, the tears were harder to subdue as she clutched the back of his head, digging her nails into his scalp. "You are not responsible for me. I choose my demise."

The brothers were still engaged in some kind of animated conversation, shouting at each other over the sound of the game on the television. Tulsi drew back and met Wreck's eye. It wasn't easy to let go; she had to force her arms to fall.

Wreck's arm loosened. His large hand slid to the small of her back and around to her hip. Once again his attention was intense. Gradually, his fingers began to curl until they were in a tight fist against her hip. He was squeezing the fabric of her dress so tight, she was forced to angle closer. There was no defeat in that hold, no sorrow in his focus. Wreck was, as always, solid and unchanging.

Taking her by surprise, his free hand shot up, around the back of her skull and he yanked her closer. Bowing to her level, he pressed his mouth against the top of her head. This was their final goodbye. Her lip wobbled at the same time she squeezed her eyes closed. A rebellious tear slipped from her lashes, she was quick to swipe it away before he let her go.

He'd told her that she was his whenever he wanted her until she told him no. After that, he would never touch her again. Never had never felt like such a long time.

Rather than stepping back or storming away, Wreck swerved around her to toss her toward the door. He'd been rough with her while they were having sex, she didn't expect that freeing him would make him violent.

"Get the hell out of here," he snarled, banging on the door, presumably to get the attention of whoever was outside.

Tulsi wanted to look at him, but couldn't let him see how their farewell was tearing her up. Movement outside the door signaled someone was about to free her, so she wiped her face and took a deep breath.

"Tulsi, please don't go!" Kieran called.

She couldn't turn around. Just sensing Wreck's form behind her was ripping at her insides. Her eyes were closed when the heat of his mouth touched the back of her ear.

"I only regret that it took me this long to find you," he murmured so quietly that she was lucky to recognize the words as hers. Her eyes opened. "Don't ever expect fair from me."

The door opened before she could think to turn or respond. The moment Baines came into view, Wreck thrust her forward. Baines caught her and leaned over to grab for the door. Tulsi managed to twist and catch one final look at Wreck before the door closed between them.

"You're everywhere, Pretty," Baines said, putting an arm around her. "I'm taking her upstairs, you bastards get them locked up."

Tulsi listened to Baines give his men orders while she reeled from what Wreck had said. The point of her words was to free him from any guilt or duty he might feel about whatever happened to her. As for his words… she had no idea what point he was trying to make.

THIRTY-EIGHT

WAS HE SPITTING her sentiment back at her? Reciting her words could be a cruel jibe. A way of telling her he'd known she was full of shit all along. The alternative was that he'd accepted the way he felt about her and wanted to let her know that he'd done a one-eighty.

Grabbing the pillow next to her head, Tulsi crushed it over her face and let out a long growling scream. The man was infuriating her and she hadn't even seen him for two weeks.

For two weeks, Tulsi had settled into the rhythm of her new life. She and Merchant ate dinner together every night. Most days, she would choose to go to his office. If she didn't, Merchant would summon her at some point. Most of the time, Merchant was just giving his men orders. She recognized most of the goons and knew a handful of names.

Baines took her for walks around the building, for exercise more than anything else. She still wasn't allowed to go outside. It had never occurred to her to be grateful for the polluted air of a city before. She'd taken it for granted and wouldn't ever again… if she ever got the chance to be out there again.

Merchant liked to hear her opinions on whatever was

going on. He ordered his men to go after anyone who owed him. That could be anything. Yes, he was in the loan sharking business too. So, in addition to drug or whore debt, he used his gangs to go after those who were late on payments. Sometimes he ordered violence even when a debt wasn't overdue. He liked to be regaled with the tales his guys came back with.

Without knowing who was on the receiving end of Merchant's warped amusement, Tulsi couldn't feel good or bad for the victims. Merchant tended to use implication and idioms to make his point. Rather than just coming right out and saying, "Beat the guy to a pulp" he'd find a way to be subtle. Everyone knew what he meant. Even she was becoming fluent in the subtleties of his language.

Although Tulsi had seen several of the same faces over and over again in the office, she hadn't faced any of the men she'd arrived with. They were still around. Merchant would give orders to take "them" on whatever mission he chose.

Every day since Merchant had told her he'd integrated Styx with Kieran and the others, she'd waited for the moment they wouldn't come back. Freeing Wreck from his responsibility to her wasn't enough it seemed. Kieran was still being held inside every night, which would be enough to bring Rowdy back. Her hope that Wreck and Rowdy would use Styx to aid their escape dwindled each time she saw Merchant wearing a smile.

The man was confident and had every right to be. Everyone was under his control and playing by his rules. Each night, in addition to their dinner, he was growing more expectant. A goodnight kiss had developed into a make-out session that Tulsi could do without.

It wasn't that he wasn't a good kisser, he was. Merchant was an amazing kisser… unfortunately. His hands knew what they wanted as well. What he wanted wasn't what she wanted. Every one of his men assumed they were intimate. When Merchant touched or kissed her in front of them, she never pushed him away or flinched. If he wanted everyone to believe that they were screwing, that was fine. As long as he didn't actually expect her to give it up any time soon.

The thoughts were fresh in her mind because they'd already eaten dinner that night. His kiss had become a dry-humping interlude on her bed. She'd never felt so pressured… or so unsure about what would happen when she had to push him away. Kissing her neck and even her breasts was okay. Tulsi could cope with that. Her mind tended to wander to the times Wreck had demanded her chest for his mouth in those moments. But hands up her skirt was not okay. That made her more than uncomfortable, it made her feel sick. Unfortunately, Merchant took her squirming as arousal.

Only a shrill tone from his phone granted her a reprieve. She'd never heard that sound from his phone before. From his quick reaction to it, she guessed it had a specific meaning. He'd leaped off the bed and strode through to his office while telling her to stay put.

It wasn't an angry order, though she could see his immediate tension. Merchant wasn't a man who panicked. He and Wreck had that in common.

Damn.

Hitting her face with the pillow, she tried to pound the man out of her head. Except all that did was remind her of his urgent rhythm.

"Damnit," she said out loud and sat up, tossing the pillow to her side.

That was it. Tulsi couldn't do it anymore. She couldn't wonder. The wondering was driving her nuts. Pouncing off the bed, she drove her fingers into her hair, giving it a little more volume as she strutted toward Merchant's office.

Demanding to see Wreck could only backfire on her. Except she couldn't ask to see anyone else because they wouldn't have the answers that she wanted.

Still trying to figure out how to broach the subject, Tulsi opened Merchant's office door and swung into the room with a flourish. "Teddy-Bear!" she proclaimed and then came up short.

Merchant was seated behind the desk, but he wasn't alone. At his side, perched against the desk next to him was the man she'd wanted to see.

"Wreck," she said, surprised not only to see him there, but that he seemed to be giving Merchant some kind of private counsel.

"My sweet," Merchant said with something of an apology in his voice though he managed to sound like he was scolding her at the same time. "I told you to stay in bed… Were you getting lonely?"

Although Wreck had turned away from her, she couldn't take her eyes away from him. "Hmm?"

"You didn't need to dress for Wreck," Merchant said, semi-amused. "He's seen all of you before."

Wreck's head snapped around in her direction; there was no mistaking the accusation in his glare. Her mouth opened a fraction, but what could she say? Coombs knew about them, so it wasn't a leap that Merchant knew. Except the way he'd said it implied she'd spilled their secrets. That's certainly what Wreck's scowl accused her of.

"I've got places to be," Wreck said, standing up from his perch.

"You're not squeamish, Wreck," Merchant said, enjoying a snicker as he stood up.

Wreck slowed and stopped at the front of the desk. He didn't turn around to face Merchant. His chin was down, but he did tip it her way. She felt the glare of his stare before she saw it.

"Ilias," Tulsi murmured, wishing she could do more to shut him up.

"My sweet," Merchant said, reverting to his typical condescension. "You were nothing to him. Isn't that what you said?"

Her throat dried, which made her word crack. "Yes."

"Many men don't like to face their mistakes from the past. You know how valuable a man's pride is to him."

The quick shift of his tone in that last sentence caught her interest. He was telling her something and when she looked at him, she got confirmation that it was nothing pleasant. Merchant was talking about his own pride. Not Wreck's.

A tremor in her lip as she curled them up was a symptom of her fear. Merchant wanted her to send a message and she didn't want to. Except if she didn't…

Wreck was vulnerable. Glancing his way, she saw he was waiting. For what? Did he want a signal from her that… what? She wanted him to end Merchant or a callous display that she was over him and onto the next guy?

Her ability to adjust to any role was one of the things Merchant liked about her. Doing it had never been more uncomfortable. Shifting her stance, she walked in a slow sashay toward Merchant, paying Wreck zero attention.

"I only wanted more wine," she said, pouting and linking her fingers as she hooked her hands over his shoulder. "I know better than to interrupt you while you're doing important work."

"We've had a situation, Pretty," Merchant said, snaking an arm around her to tug her body against his.

Keeping her smile wide, Tulsi tipped her head back and narrowed her eyes in a sultry blink. "Am I misbehaving?"

Merchant laughed and ran the back of his fingers down her cheek. "I love it when you misbehave…" He took his attention off her to look toward the man with his back to them. "Insatiable, isn't she, Wreck?"

The expectation was for Wreck to turn and engage them. He didn't. Tulsi wanted to be in his head. Just for that minute. To know that he wasn't planning on doing anything crazy. As much as she didn't want Wreck to see her in another man's arms, she wanted him to lash out even less.

All of them received a reprieve when the office door opened and Baines came in. When he saw the three of them, he paused and glanced around.

"We… gotta get going," Baines said. "Everyone else has hit the streets."

"We'll hold down the fort," Merchant said, giving her a slight shake. "I'm sure we'll find some way to entertain each other in an empty house. Won't we, my sweet?"

"We will."

What else could she say? Tulsi couldn't get away from Merchant while he held her so tight. If she tried to wriggle free, she'd show him up in front of Baines and Wreck. God only knew what he'd do to all of them if she embarrassed him.

"Get out of here," Merchant said. "Take your time. Do it right."

Wreck started across the room. Baines slipped out and waited until Wreck had departed past him to close the door.

After a few tense, silent seconds, Tulsi ventured to speak. "Did you find the shipment?"

Merchant swung her around to put her between him and the desk.

"No," he said, leaning forward, which forced her to lean back. "An old enemy is back in town... We told him never to come back. My people are going to take care of him."

"But they have to find him first," she said, rubbing the lapel of his jacket.

The angle of his body grew more acute, so he loomed further over her. Tulsi's back began to ache. What she really wanted to do was tell him to back off, but all she could do was add a little more pressure to his lapel.

"You're still attracted to him."

Focusing on her hand, she feared revealing too much of herself if she raised her attention. "Who?"

"Wreck," he said. "You still want him."

She widened her smile. "Don't be silly. You're all I need."

Tulsi clenched when he tipped his head to the side of hers and whispered in her ear. "Tell me about it."

"About what?"

Picking her up, he sat her on his desk and opened her legs to move between them. This was different, more intense than the times in her bedroom. Merchant was determined... His eyes lit with awakened interest when hers met them. Excitement. Desire. Merchant was turned on. By her? By Wreck? By the idea of her with Wreck? Svana's stories came rushing back. Tulsi hadn't seen Svana since the back of the van; she feared something grave had happened to the youngster.

"Sex," Merchant said, scooping his fingers through

her hair and coiling them in it to pull her head back. "I want to hear about it… Was he a good lover?" Merchant moved her head as he kissed her. "Did he satisfy you?"

"Merch, I—"

"I want every detail," he exhaled and pulled her head to the side to kiss her neck. "Everything."

His hand slid up the front of her thigh, under her dress. When it began to slither down the inside of her thigh, she grabbed it through the material. Her legs tried to close, but his were between them, in the way.

"We shouldn't do this here."

He kissed up the side of her neck and her ear before he spoke again. "We're going to do it everywhere."

She'd thought that she knew what it meant to be a man's trophy. Bradley had often treated her that way. The way Merchant liked to paw her while others were in the room suggested he thought of her as his prize too.

"You need to focus on your work," she said, fighting to push his hand out of her skirt. When her best wasn't good enough, she planted another hand on his chest to push harder. "Ilias—"

"I've waited long enough," he said, shoving her hands away.

Wrapping his fingers around her wrists, he pushed them down to the desk, looming even further over her.

"Stop," she said. The word wasn't as strong as she wanted it to be. "Stop!"

"Stop?" he said, grabbing her hips again. "Not until I'm satisfied."

Stepping back, he flipped her over to bend her over the desk. Tulsi kicked back and tried to straighten up. Merchant planted a hand on her spine to push her back down. Panic sped her heart as adrenaline poisoned her throat. His strength was nothing to Wreck's, but it was enough to subdue her.

Terror drew her gaze upward. Wreck had walked out that door not more than five minutes ago. He'd saved her from Hillam, but he wouldn't be rushing to her aid this time. Even if he tried, anything he did would lead to them losing their lives. Tulsi wouldn't be able to cover up Merchant's murder like she had Hillam's, not if Baines was with Wreck.

Her attempts to get out of Merchant's grip felt feeble and seemed to only increase his arousal.

"That's right, baby, you fight it," he said and laughed. "That's how I like it."

If her struggle really was arousing him further, she was in a no-win situation. Tulsi would not go limp and play dead. If she gave in this time, he'd expect her to give in every time.

Spitting her hair out of her mouth, she brought her head up again. Merchant was pushing up her dress, then she heard his fly open. She could not let him take from her. She wouldn't. The same thought kept repeating in her mind. She would not give up. She was a fighter.

Tulsi didn't think through what she was going to do when the glint of the dagger displayed on his desk caught her eye. Action overtook thinking. Her fingers were curling around the handle before she even processed moving. In the midst of Merchant's panting and taunting, she gritted her teeth and swung around, the dagger locked in her fist.

THIRTY-NINE

THE WEAPON SLICED through Merchant's flesh like it was warm butter. He staggered back a few steps, probably in shock. Looking down, he registered the dagger embedded in his abdomen.

The gravity of what she'd done hit her hard. Tulsi had just stabbed one of the most dangerous men in the country. Forget morals and boundaries. Wreck's words made sense. Tulsi had to be willing to go to any level to protect herself. Circumstance had forced her to prove her worth… to prove what she was capable of.

When it ascended to her, Merchant's gaze was as stunned as she felt.

Run.

If anyone found her there with the injured Merchant, they'd kill her for sure. The deep red of his blood spread over his crisp white shirt, saturating the fabric. If he got to a phone, he could call his reinforcements back. They wouldn't have gone far.

Touching her forehead with shaking fingers, she tried to process what she'd just done. Merchant took the handle of the blade and pulled it out of his gut. He was armed. Idiot. She was an idiot; she'd just armed him.

"Tulsi—"

"Do not come near me," she said, holding up both hands when he stepped her way.

Her hands caught her weight on the desk behind her when she recoiled. The edge of her finger touched something smooth. She glanced around and spied a heavy glass paperweight. Sliding her fingers up over the slick object, she gripped it, peeking around to Merchant who was pressing his hands to his wound that was bleeding faster without the blade stemming the flow. Blood seeped between his fingers and dripped down to the floor.

As his focus began to rise, she brought her arm up, using all of her body weight to give the paperweight in her hand more momentum. The moment the heavy object clashed with the side of his head, she let it go.

Merchant hit the floor just a fraction of a second after the paperweight made contact. He was out.

There was blood. So much blood. On his clothes, on the floor, and on his head now too. Pushing herself onto the desk, Tulsi slid her ass to the middle and spun around to climb off the other side. The door. She didn't even know if she could get out the room.

As far as she could see, there was no secure lock on this side and she had never seen anyone use one to exit. Shaking her head, she tried to clear her thoughts.

Whirling around, she went to the other side of the desk. Merchant was still passed out and bleeding. There was no time for shock. She needed to get out of there or she'd be dead for sure. Killing Merchant wasn't something Baines would forgive. Knowing how Merchant loved his camera network, she didn't doubt there would be footage of what she'd just done.

Crouching behind his head, away from the pool of blood, Tulsi held her breath. While being careful to avoid the crimson liquid, she raised his lapel and slid a hand into his inside pocket. That was where he kept his security key. Sure enough, her fingers touched hard plastic.

Grabbing it, she leaped up and ran to the office door.
Run.

Recalling Wreck's instructions, Tulsi began to make plans. Bus station. She had to get to a bus or train station. Although she didn't know where they were, she could grab a cab… But that cost money…

Money.

Using the keycard to get off Merchant's floor, Tulsi ran down to the apartment. Being as quiet as she could, she slipped the keycard into the lock and went into the hallway. She didn't know if empty house really meant empty house and she wasn't taking any chances.

If Kieran was there, they could get out. But that would leave Rowdy and Wreck at the mercy of Merchant's men. Tulsi didn't want them paying for her crime.

It turned out to be moot anyway. The apartment was empty. Either Kieran was out or he'd been moved.

Throwing open the bedroom closet, she was lucky to find her bag on the floor, still packed. Seizing it, Tulsi was about to flee when she caught sight of Wreck's leather jacket.

His instructions included that jacket. Reaching out to touch the leather, she wondered if that was why he didn't wear it. Did he leave the jacket in the building in case she needed it?

Slipping a hand between the open zipper, she sought the secret pocket and was shocked to find the money still inside. Taking the folded bills, she opened them out, intending to leave some for Wreck in case he needed them.

The slip of white paper in the center of the bills was unexpected. Unfolding it, she read one single word scrawled in black ink.

Run.

It was permission. Or an instruction. It was something and Tulsi knew it was for her.

Splitting the bills and stuffing some back in his jacket pocket, Tulsi threw her bag over her shoulder and started for the exit, keycard in hand.

Tulsi might not have been Hillam's killer, but she wasn't innocent of this latest crime. There was no way Merchant would make it. Tulsi was a murderer. For real… She didn't feel the least bit sorry. Merchant might be evil or he could be misunderstood, but if she hadn't fought back…

Wreck had prepared her for this. He'd tried to anyway. Life as she'd known it was over, just as she'd speculated it would be after walking into Teal's. *Change your name. Work cash in hand. Keep a low profile.* Those had been his orders.

After making her way downstairs, she found an exit onto the street. The keycard let her out into the darkness that would give her cover to get away clean.

But she wasn't clean. Tulsi was dirty. A murderer.

Striding down the street as fast as she could, the wind blew her hair from her shoulders. All the fresh air in the world couldn't blow away her sins. She had a feeling that living in hiding was going to lead to her breaking a lot more rules.

Her goal had been to ensure Wreck didn't feel responsible for her. Now she was abandoning him. In all the times they'd discussed it, she'd assumed that if anyone was going to be left stranded, it would be her.

But none of them had foreseen this. Tulsi was a wanted woman. Merchant's men would go to any lengths to get their revenge. She had to get far away fast. Saving her life meant giving up any chance of ever seeing Wreck again. The only solace was that this was what he'd wanted, a temporary distraction. Wreck didn't want to be obligated to her and her escape sent that message loud and clear.

Tulsi had never felt so hollow.

Killing a man didn't hurt as much as giving up the man she was desperate to be with. But that was a dream. Turned out her thoughts in Teal's stairwell were right. Nothing could come from their attraction. They were apart and would never see each other again.

TO BE CONTINUED...

Thank you for reading this tale!
If you can, please take the time to review.

~

**Ask your local library for more Scarlett Finn
novels!**
~

**For all things Scarlett Finn
check out:**

www.scarlettfinn.com

BOOK TWO

OUT NOW!

www.ingramcontent.com/pod-product-compliance
Lightning Source LLC
Chambersburg PA
CBHW011602210726

48287CB00012BC/2681